Childhood in Edwardian Fiction

Also by Adrienne E. Gavin

DARK HORSE: A Life of Anna Sewell

MYSTERY IN CHILDREN'S LITERATURE: From the Rational to the Supernatural
(*co-edited with Christopher Routledge*)

RE-EMBROIDERING THE ROBE: Faith, Myth and Literary Creation Since 1850
(*co-edited with Suzanne Bray and Peter Merchant*)

Childhood in Edwardian Fiction

Worlds Enough and Time

Edited by

Adrienne E. Gavin

and

Andrew F. Humphries

palgrave
macmillan

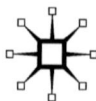

First published 2009 by
PALGRAVE MACMILLAN

Palgrave Macmillan in the UK is an imprint of Macmillan Publishers Limited,
registered in England, company number 785998, of Houndmills, Basingstoke,
Hampshire RG21 6XS.

Palgrave Macmillan in the US is a division of St Martin's Press LLC,
175 Fifth Avenue, New York, NY 10010.

Palgrave Macmillan is the global academic imprint of the above companies
and has companies and representatives throughout the world.

Palgrave® and Macmillan® are registered trademarks in the United States,
the United Kingdom, Europe and other countries.

ISBN-13: 978–0–230–22161–1 hardback
ISBN-10: 0–230–22161–0 hardback

This book is printed on paper suitable for recycling and made from fully
managed and sustained forest sources. Logging, pulping and manufacturing
processes are expected to conform to the environmental regulations of the
country of origin.

A catalogue record for this book is available from the British Library.

A catalog record for this book is available from the Library of Congress.

10 9 8 7 6 5 4 3 2 1
18 17 16 15 14 13 12 11 10 09

Printed and bound in Great Britain by
CPI Antony Rowe, Chippenham and Eastbourne

*To Dewayne and to Caroline, Gemma, and
Daniel for giving us the worlds enough and
time to tend to our Edwardian 'child.'*

*And
in memory of our Edwardian-born grandparents
Thomas Bevan Gavin (1904–1974)
Mary Gavin née Schwarz (1908–2001)
Margery Constance Humphries née Nudd (1905–1993)
Jessie Geneva French née Green (1910–1987)*

Contents

1   Worlds Enough and Time: The Cult of Childhood in
    Edwardian Fiction   1
    Adrienne E. Gavin and Andrew F. Humphries

Part I   The Child Lost

2   Pagan Papers: History, Mysticism, and Edwardian Childhood   23
    Paul March-Russell

3   Cult or Cull?: *Peter Pan* and Childhood in the
    Edwardian Age   37
    Karen L. McGavock

4   Intangible Children: Longing, Loss, and the Edwardian
    Dream Child in J. M. Barrie's *The Little White Bird* and
    Rudyard Kipling's '"They"'   53
    Adrienne E. Gavin

Part II   The Child at Play in Home and Garden

5   The Edwardian Child in the Garden: Childhood in the
    Fiction of Frances Hodgson Burnett   75
    Jane Darcy

6   Playing at House and Playing at Home: The Domestic
    Discourse of Games in Edwardian Fictions of Childhood   89
    Michelle Beissel Heath

7   Separated Lives and Discordant Homes: The Otherness of
    Childhood in D. H. Lawrence's Edwardian Fiction   103
    Andrew F. Humphries

Part III   Society's Child

8   Exhibiting Childhood: E. Nesbit and the Children's
    Welfare Exhibitions   125
    Jenny Bavidge

9   'Girls! Girls, Everywhere!': Angela Brazil's Edwardian
    School Stories   143
    Michelle Smith

10 Towards the Modern Man: Edwardian Boyhood in the
    Juvenile Periodical Press   159
    Stephanie Olsen

Part IV   Savagery and the Child

11 Primitive Minds: Anthropology, Children, and Savages in
    Andrew Lang and Rudyard Kipling   177
    Karen Sands-O'Connor

12 Truth and Claw: The Beastly Children and Childlike
    Beasts of Saki, Beatrix Potter, and Kenneth Grahame   191
    Elizabeth Hale

13 Murdering Adulthood: From Child Killers to Boy Soldiers
    in Saki's Fiction   208
    Brian Gibson

Notes on Contributors   224

Index   229

1
Worlds Enough and Time: The Cult of Childhood in Edwardian Fiction

Adrienne E. Gavin and Andrew F. Humphries

[I]n our own society the talk of benevolence and the cult of childhood are the very fashion of the hour. We, of this self-conscious, incredulous generation, sentimentalise our children, analyse our children, think we are endowed with a special capacity to sympathise and identify ourselves with children; we play at being children…. Know you what it is to be a child? It is to be something very different from the man of to-day.

(Francis Thompson, *Shelley: An Essay* [1908] 28)

Childhood in the Edwardian period was a subject of deep concern, fascination, and even obsession. Despite Romanticism's idealization of the child and Victorian advances in education, it was the Edwardians who truly made the child central to 'childhood' and childhood central to the Zeitgeist. Nowhere was this more evident than in fiction. Edwardian novels and short stories focused on children to an extent not before seen, nor continued in the same way after the outbreak of World War I. Literary children were no longer merely 'incipient adults' (Keating 221), but were beings in their own right: imaginative, free, and distinct from adults. In the Edwardian period for 'the first time it was widely recognized that children…have different needs, sensibilities, and habits of thinking; that they cannot be educated, worked, or punished like adults; that they have rights of their own independent of their parents' (Rose 178). Paternalistic 'seen and not heard,' 'spare the rod and spoil the child' notions of childhood were being swept away and children became protected, longed for, and recognized as having their own needs and desires.

1

The concept of childhood, too, became a symbolic counterweight to the urbanized, pressurized, anarchic stresses of modern life and a civilization felt to be in decline.

Gathering international expertise on childhood in fiction, this collection contains twelve original essays written by scholars in the United Kingdom, the United States, Canada, and Australia which assess the concept, role, and portrayal of childhood within British fiction of the Edwardian period. For the purposes of this volume the Edwardian period is defined as 1901–1914 and the major texts discussed are those published within this timeframe. Because the volume is interested in the literary marketplace of this time, works written earlier but first published in these years are included, while texts written during the period but not published until later are excluded. While the precise start and end dates of a movement in literature are in some measure necessarily arbitrary, this collection is presaged on the view that this time witnessed a new, intense, and distinctive fictional depiction of childhood. The volume seeks, too, to challenge assumptions often implicit in literary criticism that the Edwardian years were merely a continuation of the Victorian period or the start of the Modern. Certainly where fictional childhood is concerned, the Edwardian period had its own distinctive qualities and tastes.

Because the Edwardian obsession was for the pre-adolescent child, the volume's central focus is on childhood itself rather than puberty and the teenage years. Interweaving studies of single authors with analyses of trends in fictional childhood across several texts, the volume also aims to open up literary discussion between scholars of children's literature and scholars of adult literature, between those who work on canonical texts and those who research popular fiction, and between those interested in realism and those interested in fantasy. Analysis of fiction from all these areas is included as essential to understanding Edwardian fictional childhood. In particular the volume seeks to break down artificial boundaries between considerations of works written or marketed for children and examinations of adult texts. Such classifications obscure valuable symmetries, especially in a period when cross-writing for both readerships flourished.

Interested in historical and cultural positioning of British fiction in the period, the volume reads texts as distinctively of their time and place. This is not to suggest that Edwardian fiction mirrors exactly Edwardian childhood as it was lived. If it did one would expect a more eclectic picture of childhood and the wider presence of urban and working-class child characters. The predominant textual portrayal of childhood is of middle-class children living generally pleasant lives. Indeed, what Anna Davin suggests of the child in Edwardian art is equally true of the child in Edwardian fiction:

> [The] social diversity of children's experience [is] not well represented.... The homogeneous image of the Edwardian child reflects the contemporary preoccupation with universalizing a middle-class ideal, and obscures the existence of multiple Edwardian childhoods. (62)

Reflecting Edwardian ideals, the period's fictional children tend to exist in idyllic surroundings. Yet as Graham Hough observes:

> The concept of pre-1914 England as a long summer afternoon is quite false; it was filled with conflict, political, social, and ideological. But it is true that the fabric of high bourgeois culture was as yet unbroken, and it managed to hold all together in a precarious fusion until the war blew it away for ever. (476)

In addition to some very warm summers in a meteorological sense, an element in the sense of the 'long summer afternoon,' which was part of the period's own consciousness, was surely the prevalence of writing about or for children and childhood experience itself. Yet remembering growing up in a boarding school just before the outbreak of World War I, George Orwell reflects upon the unresolved tensions and inequalities of English life simmering beneath its apparently sumptuous surface:

> From the whole decade before 1914 there seems to breathe forth a smell of the more vulgar, un-grown up kinds of luxury, a smell of brilliantine and *crème-de-menthe* and soft-centred chocolates – an atmosphere, as it were, of eating everlasting strawberry ices on green lawns to the tune of the Eton Boating Song. (409)

J. B. Priestley notes that 'The Edwardian was never a golden age, but seen across the dark years afterwards it could easily be mistaken for one' (57). The tendency to idealize childhood, however, was widely evident during the period itself, with Edwardians feeling that there was something particularly special about the young of their time. Edward H. Cooper, for example, in his nonfictional *The Twentieth Century Child* (1905), states:

> Critics of the new cult of the child are heard occasionally to express a wish that their own sayings and doings had been treasured carefully by admiring friends, which sayings would be found, they allege, to be quite as clever as those quoted from the nurseries of the twentieth century. Regretfully and apologetically I doubt it. (7)

Childhood in fiction is of course an adult construct, often of 'whatever adults have lost and maybe never had' (Honeyman 4). The construct that predominates in Edwardian fiction is of childhood as a world (or worlds) apart from that of adults, both in time and imaginative possibility. As Dieter Petzold notes, 'Even where there is no physical separation, a profound mental separation is often assumed. Again and again it is suggested that adults and children are really worlds apart, separated by a gulf which few adults are able to bridge' (34). The child's separateness could become challenging: 'as childhood came to be seen as a state distinct from and potentially opposed to being "grown-up" ... it came to be figured as "other," with all the idealization, horror, and projection that such a status implies' (Briggs 168).

This collection's subtitle, *Worlds Enough and Time*, pluralizes the opening line from Andrew Marvell's 'To His Coy Mistress': 'Had we but world enough, and time' (1). Marvell's poem is one of seduction, but for Edwardian writers it was childhood that seduced, not (primarily at least) in a sexual sense, but in that childhood seemed to offer the 'worlds enough and time' lacking in adult lives. *Worlds* in the sense of places and states created by child-like imaginations where there is freedom to be light-hearted, playful, free from adult pressures, and uncorrupted in vision. *Time* in the sense that children experience it: expansively, slowly, in unlimited capacities. Unlike adulthood, childhood in the Edwardian ideal was not confined or defined by the industrialized, work-driven, time-constrained structures of grown-up 'civilization,' but instead was free to explore a multiplicity of worlds without pressure. For the Edwardians childhood became an escape, a solution, an ideal. Ellen Key's *The Century of the Child* (1900; English translation 1909), for instance, which became 'a world bestseller' (Cunningham, *Children* 171), presents the child as model for adults to follow and as the answer to the problems of the age.

Freedom from the strictures of time, in particular, was a signifier of childhood's separation from an adult world increasingly driven by timetables. By 1899 Standard Time had been established across the railways of Europe and life could be synchronized to the second. That fewer 'unreachable worlds' any longer existed in real life may also account for the period's fictional fascination with Arcadian childhood domains which are set apart from the industrialized urban. By '1901 three quarters of the [British population] were urban dwellers' (Walvin 18), and 'Edwardian Britain was the most urbanised country in the world' (Thea Thompson 37). Yet even the urban or industrial could become charged with the magic of children's imagination in Edwardian fiction through such vehicles as E. M. Forster's Celestial Omnibus ('The Celestial Omnibus' [1908]), or Algernon Blackwood's Starlight Express (*A Prisoner in Fairyland* [1913]) whose schedules run by the power of imagination alone.

The essays in this collection discuss texts which illustrate in different ways the heightened literary taste for childhood in the 1901–1914 period. Four recurring aspects of fictional Edwardian childhood emerge: a sense of adult loss or longing in connection with childhood, the centrality of the child at play in the home or garden, society's views of what children need or should be, and the child's connection with savagery and the pagan. These four aspects serve to group the essays into sections.

The essays in Part I reveal varying aspects of the 'The Child Lost': lost from adult life, lost from Victorian moralistic or religious conventions, or lost in the sense of being unknowable and unreachable. The child lost also includes children who are searching for a home or place of happiness like Mary Lennox in Frances Hodgson Burnett's *The Secret Garden* (1911), the children who return to an English country house in preference to a Christian heaven in Rudyard Kipling's '"They"' (1904), or Peter Pan who is shut out from home, adulthood, and life.

The Edwardian fictional child, as the essays in Part I show, is less sentimentalized than might be expected. Children are idealized but are not used for sentimental pathos, rhetorical flourish, or social moralism as they had been in Victorian novels by writers such as Charles Dickens. Edwardian fiction may set up an ideal vision of childhood but at the same time deconstructs and demythologizes it, moving towards a heightened realism in the portrayal of children. The Edwardians also commodified childhood, creating the child as an object of adult desire, 'a fetish,' an integral part of consumer society.

This consumerism is seen, for example, in the publishing for and about children which flourished in the period, creating a diamond age of gorgeously illustrated gift books and a merging of child and adult readerships for the same texts: 'With so many adult readers attempting to recapture their childhoods, the distinction between adult and juvenile fiction gradually dissolved' (Rose 183). As Jonathan Rose suggests, 'One extraordinary product of this childhood nostalgia was an unprecedented flowering of children's literature...no other generation in English history produced so many children's classics as the Edwardians' (181). Adult longing for childhood, and child characters who have no need of adults, became key literary themes, and there was a 'neo-Romantic attempt to convey the child's own point of view and way of life' (Keating 219).

As the discussions in Part I demonstrate, children's own feelings and experiences are expressed in Edwardian fiction and, in contrast to

Victorian depictions, the child is no longer used primarily for moralistic or religious ends. The Edwardian child is neither original sinner nor original innocent. Yet the period's child characters do elicit emotion; longed for or lost, they have an enormous emotional impact on adults. Lying beneath the surface joyousness of Edwardian depictions of childhood lies an acute sense of loss, even grief. That sense of loss in some cases is over *actual* children lost or longed for, but more widely is over what childhood variously symbolizes.

The lost child is often associated with mysticism, fantasy, and the supernatural. Writers also use fantasy to enhance a sense of children's otherness, to create a child-like perspective, or to invoke a magical, mythical sense of 'real' England. Edwardian fiction generally presents a particularly *English* rather than more widely British vision, even in the work of Scottish writers or British authors living outside England. As Anthea Trodd observes 'The England of Edwardian writing is a peculiar geographical entity...usually defined as the Home Counties. The myth is of England, not Britain' (24). The preciousness of childhood in the period's fiction is often linked to the preciousness of England; the longing for childhood is equally the yearning for an idealized unaltering, unfaltering England. 'Englishness' in itself becomes a moral concept: 'In *Terry, the Girl Guide* by Dorothea Moore, published...in 1912, "English" is insistently used by the girls as the ultimate word of moral approval' (Bratton 91). Cooper's 1905 view, too, is that English children were the world's best:

> at present the large majority of English children of all classes and all ages are the most charming companions in the world; from no point of view can the little folk of any other country with which I am acquainted bear comparison with them; and this state of affairs must not change for the worse. (136)

The essays in Part II, 'The Child at Play in Home and Garden,' examine a defining image of Edwardian writing: the child of garden and home. The symbolism of the garden or, in the case of J. M. Barrie and D. H. Lawrence, the island-as-garden, operates as a separate domain of childhood play, otherness, or escape from the adult home. By offering children adventure and freedom from the strictures of the adult world, the garden in Edwardian literature contains potential for regeneration. Part II's essays explore the ways in which domestic environments impact upon child characters either by implicating them in adult games and battles or by blurring Victorian-espoused family boundaries between adult and child. In texts such as Henry James's *What Maisie Knew* (1897 revised 1907) and Barrie's *Peter Pan* (1904) there develops a very Edwardian ambiguity between flirtation and play.

By focusing on territorial tensions, the discussions in Part II also highlight the precarious relationship between home and garden as, respectively, adult and child domains. Gardens offer freedom and adventure to children, who, for Edwardian writers, seem to represent the hope, natural resilience, and creative imagination society needed. Houses, by contrast, at times symbolize adult power and degeneration. These essays also reveal the importance of the child-in-the-garden in connecting the human and the natural worlds. Childhood is shown, too, to be part of a spiritual domain in a world becoming less spiritual. Writers like Lawrence, for example, connect childhood with primitivist celebration of unrestrained bodily instinct and naturalness, seeing a child-like uninhibitedness as an antidote to Victorian Puritanism.

The Edwardian period was a time when games, the spirit of play, and 'reversion to a childlike turn of mind' were lauded (Rose 178). Children's role within the domestic environment was acknowledged and the production of toys and merchandise for children increased exponentially as children's right to play was emphasized. Peter Pan's ' "I just want always to be a little boy and to have fun" ' (*Peter and Wendy* 170), reflects the Edwardian cultural desire for play that these essays examine and which Rose terms the 'Edwardian cult of childhood and fun' (xii) or 'Gospel of Fun' (as opposed to the Victorian 'Gospel of Work') (163–98). This spirit of play was evidenced by 'a reversion to a childlike turn of mind, often an outright refusal to grow up' which produced a 'list of eminent Edwardians who seem to have been stuck in childhood' (Rose 178). Some commentators have interpreted this quest for fun and 'desire to lavish more attention on children' as arising from the 'uncertainties of the adult public world – as an attempt to gain for and from children the sense of security that the outside world could not provide' (Kemp, Mitchell, and Trotter xiv).

The importance of play and games in the domestic environment accentuates tensions between adult domesticity and childhood freedom. Adults in Edwardian fiction are often reluctant to leave childhood behind and their attempts to retain childhood, or regain it in order to atone for adulthood behaviours, disrupts children's lives. While child characters in some texts such as Burnett's *The Secret Garden* (1911) and Lawrence's *Sons and Lovers* (1913) need rehabilitation as a result of neglect and damage suffered at the hands of adults, damaged adults themselves seek forms of childhood freedom as an escape from the dilemmas of maturity. The Edwardian home itself, as these essays show, can sometimes become a prison which forces children to assume adult domestic roles under the guise of play. This often means that 'real' play must take place outside the home and accounts in some measure for the fictional interest in alternative childhood worlds, such as gardens and islands, which are beyond adult jurisdiction.

During the Edwardian period parental and domestic powers over children diminished as the state increasingly assumed control over children's lives, according them rights independent of their parents. Part III, 'Society's Child,' provides an overview of the interaction between fiction and Edwardian society's attempts to provide for children's education, welfare, and health. The period saw a diminishing birthrate,[1] a declining infant mortality rate (at least among the upper and middle classes), and there was dramatic development in child welfare laws and practice. The Pyrrhic victory of the Anglo-Boer War (1899–1902) and the national shock that 'two out of five of those who volunteered to go to fight in South Africa were rejected because of poor physique' (Cunningham, *Invention* 184) led to panicked attention to children's health. Improving children's fitness was seen as integral to national security and Imperial survival. C. F. G. Masterman's *The Condition of England* (1909) expressed fears about modern city life producing physically degenerate children, and works such as those arising from the Royal Commission on Physical Deterioration (1904) and J. E. Gorst's *The Children of the Nation: How Their Health and Vigour Should Be Promoted by the State* (1906) urged that children should be seen as national assets which the state should protect and nurture into 'the coming race' (Gorst 204).

Established at Deptford in 1900, the first nursery school was hailed as signalling 'the dawn of "the children's century,"' and improvements in health and education were ushered in (Cecil 134). An unprecedented range of child and welfare legislation was passed in the period. Midwives were compulsorily registered from 1902, the Education Act of 1902 created a national education system with Local Education Authorities, the Education (Provision of Meals) Act 1906 mandated free meals for poor children, and in 1907 the Medical Inspection Act provided for medical inspections for school children. The Children's Act of 1908 introduced probation or 'borstal' rather than prison for child offenders, established separate juvenile courts, made child neglect a crime for the first time, and 'confirmed the growing practice of regarding a person as a child until the age of fourteen' (Walvin 167). 'By 1914 there were few areas of children's lives which were not regulated by statute and governed by judicial and administrative bodies' and 'it was clear beyond doubt that children had rights of their own, which were independent even of their own parents and which the state would try to safeguard for them' (Walvin 198).

Changes were not only state initiated. The period saw the Scout and Guide movements established in 1907 and 1910 respectively and Sigmund Freud's 'Essay on Infantile Sexuality' (1905) challenging the innocence of childhood.[2] To an extent never before seen children became the focus of legal, medical, literary, psychological, sexological, anthropological, political, sociological, anti-Victorian, and nationalistic interest. The Edwardian construction of childhood drew on Rousseauean and Romantic ideas about the benefits of the natural world but also integrally responded to matters at hand: Empire at its height but under evident threat, standardized education, legislative will towards the child, and child-like imagination as a palliative to the rushing mechanized city and a scientific age.

The essays in Part III demonstrate that literature participated in the debates about child welfare issues ranging from educational theory to eugenics, particularly in school stories, the juvenile periodical press, and fictions by Edith Nesbit. The school curriculum for girls, for example, became closely linked to broader concerns about motherhood and national degeneration. Periodicals aimed at boys, on the other hand, sought to inspire models of masculinity in young readers who were expected to become moral and physical leaders of nation and Empire. Fiction became increasingly involved in defining childhood in relation to welfare issues. Although less stringently expressed than in Victorian texts, Edwardian fiction, in a world less certain of its boundaries, saw itself as having a role in redressing declines in moral and physical health. Like those in Part II, the discussions in Part III emphasize the importance for children of play, games, and pastimes as an escape from the dangers and pressures of the modern world. Writers like Nesbit argued for more imaginative opportunity in children's play and education, while school stories and periodical fiction offered new combinations of adventure and excitement mixed with social and moral messages. Edwardian fiction expresses, too, contemporary expansion of children's education outside the domestic sphere and reflects the roles played by social and political movements in this process. Some authors, including Nesbit, were becoming active players in wider social discussions on child development even beyond their fiction.

Part IV, 'Savagery and the Child,' draws attention to the ways in which Edwardian writers often depict child characters in connection with savagery, the primitive, or the pagan. This is evident both in texts that, implicitly or explicitly, teach their intended readership of white British children how savagery might be assumed and regarded in other peoples, and in texts that impute a positive savagery, paganism, or beastliness to child characters themselves.

As Jenny Bourne Taylor notes, this was a time 'when a wide set of contemporary concerns about the nature of civilizations and empires and the subjects that they produce were embodied particularly acutely in the imaginary figure of the child' (91). At the height of Imperialism, discussion about the education of the child and of 'savage' nations at times coalesced and the literature of childhood often drew upon or reflected contemporary anthropological thinking about hierarchies of race, human development, and civilization. Some Edwardian writers grouped children together with primitive 'savages' as lesser beings who were perceived to be incapable of understanding certain things or who needed to be kept innocent of particular knowledge. According to this vision both child and savage required training into a 'civilized' state. Other writers include the white British child reader or character within 'civilization' as opposed to colonized or other 'savage' races. Such texts regard the white British child as a junior imperialist with responsibilities towards 'savages,' child or adult, according to a racial hierarchy.

Other Edwardian depictions of childhood reify the 'primitive,' delight in the instinctive or the beastly, and see childhood as the epitome of existence free from civilization. Savagery is here connected with the 'beastliness' of children who operate according to their animal instincts. Adult characters, by contrast, have socialized, constrained, and constricted habits of being. The child in such texts is a free natural being set against the civilized adult. These child characters are often shown breaking adult boundaries, behaving in an unsocialized way against adult dictates, and receiving (overt or covert) textual applause for their actions. Such characters are seen in the rural, pre-industrial settings of works by Kenneth Grahame, Beatrix Potter, and Saki. These fictions closely associate children with animals and often ally them with paganism, mysticism, magic, the gods, the supernatural, nature, instinct, ruthlessness and, to some extent, violence.

The four parts of this volume focus on prominent aspects of childhood in Edwardian fiction that have been highlighted by the contributors. The essays as a whole also identify qualities pervasive in fictional childhood of the period which serve to distinguish it from earlier constructions and make it distinctively Edwardian.

Romanticism's Wordsworthian idea of the child represents children raised in close connection to nature as the ideal. A symbolic figure representing innocence and untarnished human goodness, the Romantic child, unlike the Edwardian one, is usually a solitary figure. In Victorian fiction, childhood is often a time of powerlessness, trial, and emotional (and often physical) pain. By contrast to these earlier models Edwardian fiction sees the obsolescence of the lonely or solitary child, emphasizes the joys of childhood, and often neo-Romantically links children with nature – gardens, animals, woodlands, and islands. It also rejects the too-adult indulgences and experimentations of the 1890s. 'The Edwardian withdrawal into childhood was, in part,' as Rose observes, 'a reaction against the Decadent movement in literature. More generally, it was an attempt to rejuvenate – or escape from – a civilization that seemed old, dissolute, and sterile' (184).

Edwardian texts no longer focus so singularly on the solitary child figure of Romantic and Victorian literature and instead frequently centre on groups and siblings, reflecting, as Peter Keating has noted, the period's anthropological and sociological interests (221). The significance of religion in children's lives, too, plummets as more secular portrayals prevail. As childhood becomes its own world in Edwardian texts, the fictional child is also sometimes used 'as a means for establishing human values in an increasingly secular age' (Coveney 340).

Autonomy, integrity, and agency become the hallmarks of childhood in Edwardian fiction. Edwardian child characters are not controlled by adults nor do they long to grow up as an escape from childhood's vulnerability and victimization as they often do in Victorian fiction. Indeed, while in Victorian texts childhood is usually a comparatively brief, difficult step on the path to adulthood, in Edwardian literature children are rarely shown growing up. The Edwardian text seeks to 'fix' the child in a permanent childhood. In Romantic and Victorian writing, too, parents, teachers, employers, and religious figures have enormous control over children. Edwardian fiction sees this adult control dissipate. While Victorian literature depicted the power balance being weighted heavily in adults' favour, Edwardian fiction reveals the scales swinging triumphantly towards a child power base. There is a clear sense that it is not Father, but children, who know best. Fictional children are presented as independent, imaginative, troubling, mischievous, at one with nature and the supernatural, and, above all, as 'better' and more self-assured than adults.

Edwardian fictional children have no need of adults however much adults long desperately for children. Childhood in the period's fiction is ephemeral not only because it does not last, but also because it need not choose to engage with the adult world. The adult world appears to have little importance to or involvement in childhood. As Keating suggests:

> There is no single or simple explanation why so much independence was being granted at this time to fictional children. In addition to its links with anthropology and sociology, the change can be related to the greater independence being given to children by legislation, the pervasive mood of anti-Victorianism, the new demands for youthful heroes being made by Empire, and to a resurgence of interest in the education of young children. (226)

An emphasis on male connections to childhood also demarcates the Edwardian years as, in generalized terms – and in contrast to the more 'female' Victorian period – a 'masculine' period of literature. Certainly in its interest in the child as literary subject Edwardian writing echoed that earlier 'masculine' period: the Romantic era. It is often suggested that the first decade of the twentieth century marked a change from the Victorian cult of the little girl to Edwardian obsession with the boy. As Christine Roth argues, however, the change of spotlight from girls to boys was not absolute or overnight: there was overlap (51). As the essays in this volume verify, the cult of childhood in Edwardian fiction certainly encompassed children of both genders.

Childhood fully came into its own in Edwardian fiction, but from 1895 childhood had started to enter novels and short stories in new more intense ways, frequently from a child's-eye perspective. Kenneth Grahame's highly successful semi-autobiographical books *The Golden Age* (1895) and *Dream Days* (1898) captured a sense of real childhood, its views, delights, and adventures in stories about a group of orphaned siblings who live in a country house governed by 'Olympians': stultifying Aunts and Uncles who have all the authority but have no understanding of children's imaginations. Grahame's books clearly influenced Edith Nesbit's Bastable stories – *The Story of the Treasure Seekers* (1899), *The Wouldbegoods* (1901), and *New Treasure Seekers* (1904) – which, like Grahame's texts, are narrated by a child who tells of his life and adventures with his siblings and contains both scenes that are poignant without being Victorianly sentimental and elements that are comic. Indeed another marker that distinguishes Edwardian depictions of childhood from earlier ones is a general readiness to engage with the humorous qualities of children. Henry James, too, significantly advanced the child's perspective and questioned childhood innocence in *The Other House* (1896), *What Maisie Knew* (1897), and *The Turn of the Screw* (1898).

J. M. Barrie, whose *Peter Pan* would epitomize the Edwardian cult of childhood, also turned to the literary child in these final years of the nineteenth century in *Sentimental Tommy: The Story of His Boyhood* (1896), as did Rudyard Kipling with his *Jungle Books* (1894, 1895) and *Stalky & Co.* (1899). Elizabeth Von Arnim's *Elizabeth and Her German Garden* (1898) was timely in its recognition that sentimentalized and unrealistic methods of writing about children in fiction – '"you can't write effectively about children without"' mentioning '"a mother's knee,"' '"And pink toes,"' and being '"mildly pathetic"' (162–63) – needed freshening.

Some late Victorian views of childhood follow less delightful models. Arthur Morrison's *A Child of the Jago* (1896) focuses on a child of the London slums who turns to crime. Thomas Hardy's Little Father Time in *Jude the Obscure* (1895), who kills his siblings and then himself thinking it will help his parents, is the bleakest type of the child in late nineteenth-century fiction. Jude reports a doctor's view that:

> there are such boys springing up amongst us – boys of a sort unknown in the last generation – the outcome of new views of life. They seem to see all its terrors before they are old enough to have staying power to resist them. He says it is the beginning of the coming universal wish not to live. (355)

The Edwardians reclaim childhood from this pessimistic vision. Indeed, novels like Nesbit's *The Railway Children* (1906) and Burnett's *The Secret Garden* (1911) move actively towards optimism by emphasizing the regenerative capacities of children.

From 1895 the 'world apart' of childhood intensifies acutely in fiction, but adults still hold power and control the lives children lead. It is only in the Edwardian period itself – a new century with a new more playful king[3] – that fictional children achieve agency and autonomy and adults become less powerful. In Edwardian texts children become unreachable, self-contained, longed for: characters whose worlds run on their own grooves and who engage with adults only in ways and on terms that suit them. In the Edwardian period it is childhood – symbolized in the forever child Peter Pan – that has God-like wisdom and powers. Grown-up power is expunged from the world of children in Edwardian fiction. The Victorian governess's crushing of the young boy Miles at the end of *The Turn of the Screw* becomes, in Edwardian hands, the child

Conradin's contentedly buttering himself another piece of toast after contriving the death of his aunt in Saki's 'Sredni Vashtar' (1910).

If World War I marked the end of the Golden Age of children's literature, it also ended (assisted by wider dissemination of Freud's theories of childhood) the Edwardian golden age of childhood in fiction. Certain individual writers with a passion for childhood, like Algernon Blackwood, would continue to produce fictions in which childhood was central, but these were specific rivulets of storytelling. Fiction as a whole began flowing in more adult directions: breaking through barriers to sexual content, plunging into realist depictions of war, and rushing towards the cataracts of Modernism.

This volume encompasses discussions of texts by the Edwardian writers who most significantly contributed to childhood in the period's fiction: J. M. Barrie, Frances Hodgson Burnett, Angela Brazil, Kenneth Grahame, Henry James, Rudyard Kipling, Andrew Lang, D. H. Lawrence, Edith Nesbit, Beatrix Potter, Saki, and the juvenile periodical presses. Other writers who are not covered in depth because their contribution to the Edwardian fiction of childhood is not as central are nevertheless worth mentioning here.

Several leading Edwardian authors who might not be associated with literature of or about childhood nevertheless display clear traces in their work of the period's fictional fascination with children. Samuel Butler, for instance, demolishes the Victorian patriarchal family in *The Way of All Flesh* (1903), H. G. Wells depicts giant children challenging the adult social fabric in *The Food of the Gods* (1904) and in his short story 'The Door in the Wall' (1906) portrays the fragility of the childhood domain in a frenetic adult world. E. M. Forster in 'The Story of a Panic' (1904) and 'The Celestial Omnibus' (1908) creates children who are assisted by mythical or literary characters in their search for alternative authorities to the adult voice. Arnold Bennett, too, in *Anna of the Five Towns* (1902) and his *Clayhanger* trilogy (1910–1916) portrays childhood perspectives as being different from, and yet equal to, those of adults.

Childhood was also central to the bestseller of 1908, Henry de Vere Stacpoole's *The Blue Lagoon*, which ran through 16 editions before the outbreak of World War I (Cockburn 67). The story of two shipwrecked children who grow up in natural isolation on a deserted Pacific island, fall in love, and while still effectively children themselves, have a baby, the book sought to capture the 'wonderment' of children who must learn about the mysteries of life – death, love, sex, and birth – completely naturally. Unadulterated by society, religion, culture, and adults, child-hood on the island reflects the Edwardian ideal: non-urban existence separate from adults, glowing physical health, a sense of timelessness in an eternal summer, and instinctive closeness to nature.

The period was notable for the wide variety of subgenres or styles of fiction in which the cult of childhood was expressed. Algernon Blackwood, best known for his tales of the weird and supernatural, contributed significantly to the Edwardian fiction of childhood in *Jimbo: A Fantasy* (1909), *The Education of Uncle Paul* (1909), and *A Prisoner in Fairyland: (The Book That Uncle Paul Wrote)* (1913), which are intense, complex evocations of childhood and its importance to adult life and literary creation. George Douglas Brown's realist *The House with the Green Shutters* (1901) pits a sensitive son against a brutal father. Helen Bannerman's eight Edwardian books that followed her hugely popular *Little Black Sambo* (1899), although more recently controversial, were among the few then widely read in Britain that depicted black children at all. Urban working-class childhood was revealed in Arthur Morrison's *The Hole in the Wall* (1902). W. H. Hudson's unusual fantasy *A Little Boy Lost* (1905) tells of a boy whose wanderlust and passion for nature in a remote land takes him on a long overland adventure. Child characters and concerns in works such as Ford Madox Ford's *Christina's Fairy Book* (1906), John Masefield's historical novel *Jim Davis* (1911), and W. Heath Robinson's illustrated *Bill the Minder* (1912) also contribute to the period's fictional passion for childhood.

Forrest Reid and Katherine Mansfield both dipped their pens into the Edwardian ink of childhood but only fully established their reputations as writers of children outside the period. Although Reid's work as a whole shows an 'obsessive interest in children' (Coveney 269), his best-known Edwardian novel *The Garden God: A Tale of Two Boys* (1905) focuses on love and loss between two male adolescents rather than childhood itself. Similarly, apart from stories such as 'The Child-Who-Was-Tired' (1910) and 'How Pearl Button Was Kidnapped' (1912), Mansfield's most notable stories of childhood were published in post-Edwardian or posthumous collections.

Although expressed most acutely in fiction, the Edwardian cult of childhood also manifested itself in other literary genres. Significant texts which fall outside the parameters of this volume, but which should nevertheless also be borne in mind as part of the apotheosis of literary childhood include works such as Walter de la Mare's poetry, Hilaire Belloc's *Cautionary Tales for Children* (1907), and Edmund Gosse's (auto) biography *Father and Son* (1907). Arthur Mee's enormously popular *The Children's Encyclopedia* was published in fortnightly parts from March 1908 to February 1910 (and in volume form). Robert Baden-Powell's

Scouting for Boys: A Handbook for Instruction in Good Citizenship (1908) – the 'world-renowned "self-instructor" for boys, and all-time bestseller...possibly in fact the most influential youth manual ever published' (Boehmer xl) – was followed by Agnes Baden-Powell's *The Handbook for Girl Guides, or, How Girls Can Help Build the Empire* (1912). Plays for and about children were very successful on the Edwardian stage including Seymour Hicks's *Bluebell in Fairyland* (1901), Maurice Maeterlinck's *The Blue Bird* [*L'Oiseau Bleu*, 1908] first performed in England in 1909 and, above all others, Barrie's *Peter Pan* (1904) which best expressed, and entrenched, the Edwardian cult of childhood through Peter Pan himself who embodies the ultimate in child autonomy and agency by refusing to become an adult.

The volume opens with Paul March-Russell's 'Pagan Papers' which investigates fictions of childhood as microcosms of the mythologies surrounding Edwardian England as eternally sunny and leisurely before the onslaught of World War I. Discussing Saki's 'The Toys of Peace' (1914), May Sinclair's 'The Intercessor' (1911), Frances Hodgson Burnett's *The Secret Garden* (1911), and Rudyard Kipling's ' "They" ' (1904), *Puck of Pook's Hill* (1906), and *Rewards and Fairies* (1910), his essay explores portrayals of the home as a place of disturbance. It also considers childhood in relation to the concept of 'Deep England' as a place mystically sustained in fiction to fashion an English identity and establish an alternative to the period's preoccupation with efficiency and progress.

Examining J. M. Barrie's *Peter Pan* (1904) and *Peter and Wendy* (1911), Karen McGavock's 'Cult or Cull?' discusses the ways in which Barrie deconstructs notions of childhood. The Peter Pan texts, she argues, fetishize, demythologize, and desentimentalize childhood. Yet, as the essay argues, economic benefits accrued from the appearance of sentimentality in these texts, reflecting the Edwardian commodification of childhood which lucratively marketed texts at both adult and child markets.

Adrienne E. Gavin's essay, 'Intangible Children,' explores ways in which longing for children or grief over the loss of a child are manifested in the dream children of two early Edwardian texts: J. M. Barrie's novel *The Little White Bird* (1902) and Rudyard Kipling's short story ' "They" ' (1904). Her essay suggests that having such noted writers focus so intensely on yearning for children early in the period reflected and encouraged the obsession for childhood that Edwardian fiction so pervasively expresses. She also draws attention to the prevalence in Edwardian fiction of relationships between children and bachelor or bachelor-like characters.

In 'The Edwardian Child in the Garden' Jane Darcy discusses childhood in Frances Hodgson Burnett's Edwardian fiction. Examining Burnett's children's novels, particularly *The Secret Garden* (1911), and her adult texts *In the Closed Room* (1904) and *The Shuttle* (1907), Darcy demonstrates that the child in these works becomes a symbol of the possibilities of rebirth. Discussing the ways in which child characters and gardens intertwine or parallel each other, the essay illustrates that Burnett's fictional children have a much greater rapport than adults with nature, animals, and birds.

Michelle Beissel Heath's 'Playing at House and Playing at Home' explores the prominence of games and sports in Edwardian life. Discussing J. M. Barrie's *Peter and Wendy* (1911), Henry James's *What Maisie Knew* (1897, revised 1907), and Edith Nesbit's *The Story of the Amulet* (1906), she argues that Edwardian literature of childhood is filled with images of playful children whose role is to reveal tensions between play and domesticity.

In 'Separated Lives and Discordant Homes' Andrew F. Humphries examines D. H. Lawrence's ambivalence towards childhood as a stage which is both idyllic and disrupted. Discussing *The White Peacock* (1911), *The Trespasser* (1912), and *Sons and Lovers* (1913), Humphries explores children as separate from, or separated by, adult behaviours. He also discusses how interaction between adults and children in these novels indicates both a strong instinctive bond and an equal tendency to disrupt or destroy. The essay analyses, too, Lawrence's interest in the continuity between childhood and adulthood within individuals.

Examining Edith Nesbit, Jenny Bavidge's 'Exhibiting Childhood' reveals the role of the Children's Welfare Exhibitions held in London in 1912–1913 and 1914 in depicting Edwardian attitudes to childhood and child welfare. Contextualizing Nesbit through her involvement with the first exhibition, and discussing the ways in which Nesbit's fiction is central to our sense of Edwardian children's literature, Bavidge demonstrates the cultural and commercial influences surrounding childhood and its fictions in this period.

Michelle Smith's essay 'Girls! Girls, Everywhere!' discusses the ways in which Angela Brazil's Edwardian school stories provide interesting insights into the tensions surrounding the education of girls in secondary schools leading up to World War I. Smith examines the relationship between intellectual pursuit and moral responsibility and demonstrates that Edwardians increasingly linked the academic development of girls to the regeneration of the nation and Empire.

In 'Towards the Modern Man' Stephanie Olsen explores the ways in which periodicals helped construct concepts of Edwardian boyhood. She shows that periodicals instruct as they entertain by mixing reality, fantasy, and pastimes to inculcate the right sort of moral character expected of the Edwardian man. Through discussing periodical stories, she makes a connection between boys' conduct and the expectations and responsibilities of Empire and indicates how the moral conditioning of boys impacted upon the whole Edwardian family.

Discussing stories from Andrew Lang's *The Brown Fairy Book* (1904) and *The Orange Fairy Book* (1906) and from Rudyard Kipling's *Just So Stories* (1902), *Puck of Pook's Hill* (1906), and *Rewards and Fairies* (1910), Karen Sands-O'Connor in 'Primitive Minds' examines 'anthropological' children's literature, which presents children as 'primitives' who need civilizing. She demonstrates how Lang's work, influenced by social anthropology, links the concepts of 'child' and 'savage.' Kipling's texts, by contrast, influenced by physical anthropology, privilege white European children and teach the implied white British child reader about concepts of racial hierarchy and the fixity of the races.

In 'Truth and Claw' Elizabeth Hale discusses Kenneth Grahame's *The Wind in the Willows* (1908), Saki's 'The Penance' (1910) and 'Sredni Vashtar' (1910), and Beatrix Potter's *The Tale of Peter Rabbit* (1902), *The Tale of Tom Kitten* (1903), and *The Tale of Squirrel Nutkin* (1907). These texts, she shows, depict beastly children and childlike beasts who behave according to their own natural instincts and desires without regard to corrupt adult norms and concerns. Although portraying these child characters in natural settings draws on Romantic and Victorian models, Hale suggests that the association between children's unrepentant bad behaviour and animals is particularly Edwardian.

Exploring the amorality of youth in its resistance to an impotent adult Victorian conformity, Brian Gibson's 'Murdering Adulthood' examines a range of Saki's short stories including 'Sredni Vashtar' (1910), 'The Lumber Room' (1913), and 'The Story Teller' (1913). Children battle against adult pretension and convention in these stories, and Gibson also illustrates that Saki's attention turned by 1913 towards war and the usefulness of child rebellion to adult warfare.

Edwardian writers seem desperately to be capturing childhood within the pages of their fiction as if they sensed that their passion for expressing childhood had not long to live and so must be obsessively indulged. Framed between two disastrous wars, the Edwardian period made of childhood an idyllic haven or escape, yet also saw it as the focal point of future national security in a disintegrating moral world. This fact colours the fiction of these years, adding an undercurrent of menace and unease to childhood's apparent Arcadia. As Samuel Hynes reminds us, 'anxiety and the expectation of war were a part of the Edwardian consciousness' (53). Time was running out, quite literally, for the children of this generation, a factor that made the preservation of their fictional 'worlds enough and time' all the more compelling and childhood's values all the more precious.

Notes

1. '[T]he British birth rate fell sharply between 1900 and 1914 – a 10 per cent drop overall and considerably more among the affluent and educated classes. That decline was widely perceived as yet another sign of national decadence, and it aroused great public concern' (Rose 91).
2. Freud's ideas began to circulate in the Edwardian period, and seemed to have been instinctively understood by some writers, but 'were not influential in Britain until after the First World War' (Bland 88).
3. 'It was said in 1904, "there is scarcely a game or diversion dear to Englishmen which the King has not himself either enjoyed or else found pleasure in watching. He is, of all Englishmen, the complete sportsman"' (quoted in Dobbs 21).

Works cited

Barrie, J. M. *Peter and Wendy*. 1911. *Peter Pan in Kensington Gardens. Peter and Wendy*. Ed. Peter Hollindale. Oxford: Oxford University Press, 1991, 67–226.
Bland, Lucy. 'Sex and Morality: Sinning on a Tiger Skin or Keeping the Beast at Bay.' *The Edwardian Era*. Ed. Jane Beckett and Deborah Cherry. Oxford: Phaidon, 1987, 88–99.
Boehmer, Elleke. 'Note on the Text.' *Scouting for Boys: A Handbook for Instruction in Good Citizenship*. 1908. By Robert Baden-Powell. 2004. Oxford: Oxford University Press, 2005, xl–xliv.
Bourne Taylor, Jenny. 'Between Atavism and Altruism: The Child on the Threshold in Victorian Psychology and Edwardian Children's Fiction.' *Children in Culture: Approaches to Childhood*. Ed. Karín Lesnik-Oberstein. Basingstoke: Macmillan, 1998, 89–121.
Bratton, J. S. 'Of England, Home and Duty: The Image of England in Victorian and Edwardian Juvenile Fiction.' *Imperialism and Popular Culture*. Ed. John M. MacKenzie. Manchester: Manchester University Press, 1986, 73–93.
Briggs, Julia. 'Transitions (1890–1914).' *Children's Literature: An Illustrated History*. Ed. Peter Hunt. Oxford: Oxford University Press, 1995, 167–91.
Cecil, Robert. *Life in Edwardian England*. London: Batsford, 1969.
Cockburn, Claud. *Bestseller: The Books that Everyone Read, 1900–1939*. London: Sidgwick and Jackson, 1972.
Cooper, Edward H. *The Twentieth Century Child*. London: John Lane, The Bodley Head, 1905.

Coveney, Peter. *The Image of Childhood. The Individual and Society: A Study of the Theme in English Literature*. 1957. Revised edition with Introduction by F. R. Leavis. Harmondsworth: Penguin, 1967.

Cunningham, Hugh. *Children and Childhood in Western Society Since 1500*. 2nd ed. Harlow: Pearson, 2005.

——. *The Invention of Childhood*. London: BBC Books, 2006.

Davin, Anna. 'Edwardian Childhoods – Childhood and Children: Image and Diversity.' *The Edwardian Era*. Ed. Jane Beckett and Deborah Cherry. Oxford: Phaidon, 1987, 51–62.

Dobbs, Brian. *The Edwardians at Play: Sport 1890–1914*. London: Pelham Books, 1973.

Gorst, J. E. *The Children of the Nation: How Their Health and Vigour Should Be Promoted by the State*. 1906. London: Methuen and Co, 1907.

Hardy, Thomas. *Jude the Obscure*. 1895. Ed. Patricia Ingham. Oxford: Oxford University Press, 1996.

Honeyman, Susan. *Elusive Childhood: Impossible Representations in Modern Fiction*. Columbus, OH: Ohio State University Press, 2005.

Hough, Graham. 'English Criticism.' *The Twentieth-Century Mind: History, Ideas and Literature in Britain*. Vol. 1 *1900–1918*. Ed. C. B. Cox and A. E. Dyson. Oxford: Oxford University Press, 1972. 475–84.

Hynes, Samuel. *The Edwardian Turn of Mind*. London: Pimlico, 1968.

Keating, Peter. *The Haunted Study: A Social History of the English Novel 1875–1914*. 1989. London: Fontana, 1991.

Kemp, Sandra, Charlotte Mitchell and David Trotter. Introduction. *The Oxford Companion to Edwardian Fiction*. 1997. Oxford: Oxford University Press, 2002. ix–xviii.

Marvell, Andrew. 'To His Coy Mistress.' 1681. *The Complete Poems*. Ed. Elizabeth Story Donno. Harmondsworth: Penguin, 1972. 50–1.

Orwell, George. 'Such, Such Were the Joys.' 1947. *The Collected Essays, Journalism and Letters of George Orwell*. Vol. 4. Ed. Sonia Orwell and Ian Angus. 1968. Harmondsworth: Penguin, 1970. 379–422.

Petzold, Dieter. 'A Race Apart: Children in Late Victorian and Edwardian Children's Books.' *Children's Literature Association Quarterly* 17:3 (Fall 1992): 33–6.

Priestley, J. B. *The Edwardians*. London: Heinemann, 1970.

Rose, Jonathan. *The Edwardian Temperament, 1895–1919*. Athens, OH: Ohio University Press, 1986.

Roth, Christine. 'Babes in Boy-Land: J. M. Barrie and the Edwardian Girl.' *J. M. Barrie's* Peter Pan *In and Out of Time: A Children's Classic at 100*. Ed. Donna R. White and C. Anita Tarr. Lanham, MD: Scarecrow, 2006. 47–67.

Thompson, Francis. *Shelley* [*: An Essay*]. 1908. London: Burns Oates & Washbourne, 1925.

Thompson, Thea. *Edwardian Childhoods*. London: Routledge & Kegan Paul, 1981.

Trodd, Anthea. *A Reader's Guide to Edwardian Literature*. Hemel Hempstead: Harvester Wheatsheaf, 1991.

Von Arnim, Elizabeth. *Elizabeth and Her German Garden*. 1898. Intro. Elizabeth Jane Howard. 1985. London: Virago, 1998.

Walvin, James. *Child's World: A Social History of English Childhood 1800–1914*. Harmondsworth: Penguin, 1982.

Part I
The Child Lost

2
Pagan Papers: History, Mysticism, and Edwardian Childhood

Paul March-Russell

One of the most frequently cited studies of modern children's fiction and its relationship to the making of Edwardian society is Humphrey Carpenter's *Secret Gardens: A Study of the Golden Age of Children's Literature* (1985). The title, however, is double-edged. It is not only an account of a canonical set of writers, including J. M. Barrie, Kenneth Grahame, and E. Nesbit, but it is also an analysis of how these writers posited a 'Golden Age,' a 'secret garden,' in their works. Carpenter plausibly argues that these writers constructed an Arcadian facsimile of childhood, a fantasy world into which they could project their own personal, spiritual and psychological anxieties, an emotional haven into which they could retreat. Following Carpenter's lead, historians of the period, such as Hugh Cunningham (152–8), have shown how the efforts of educational and social reformers became interlinked with the sentimentalized childhood of children's literature. At the root of both child welfare and children's novels, such as Grahame's *The Wind in the Willows* (1908), lay a vision of England as Albion that has been re-explored in recent years, most notably by Peter Ackroyd.

Yet, while childhood is certainly idealized by writers such as Barrie and Grahame, Carpenter's psycho-biographical approach focuses almost exclusively upon the author-figure. He diminishes the effects of cultural and historical contexts to argue for a very Romantic conception of both childhood and the role of the author, in which the fictionalized portrait of the child is the sole property of the author's inspiration, the direct result of conscious and unconscious motivations. Consequently, despite the plausibility of his argument, Carpenter's approach cannot explain the cultural construction of Edwardian childhood, since it tends to deny more historical and less author-centred readings. Furthermore, in characterizing the fictions of childhood as a vessel for their authors' fears and desires, Carpenter tends to consolidate an image of Edwardian England as a kind of 'Neverland,' a fragile and ultimately precarious shelter from, to paraphrase James Joyce, 'the nightmare of history' (*Ulysses* 34). While, on the one hand, Carpenter does show this myth to be a product of the writers themselves, on the other hand, by concentrating so much upon the psychological as opposed to the ideological lives of the writers, Carpenter's analysis effectively bolsters the myth without taking it apart. The aim of this essay is to suggest one way in which childhood fictions can be demystified as a microcosm of the mythologies that, as in Juliet Nicolson's *The Perfect Summer* (2006), continue to surround Edwardian England as an eternally sunny and leisurely realm before the onslaught of World War I.

Peter Keating, in particular, has shown that the literary representation of childhood changed dramatically and unpredictably during the era from 1880 to 1914 (219–27). Whereas, at the start of this period, Frances Hodgson Burnett presents the angelic Cedric Erroll in *Little Lord Fauntleroy* (1886), by the end of this phase, she creates the awkward and contrary Mary Lennox in *The Secret Garden* (1911). Carpenter puts this transformation down to the decline in organized religious belief. Cedric, whose characterization echoes the saintly protagonists of Elizabeth Prentiss's *Stepping Heavenwards* (1869) and Susan Warner's *The Wide, Wide World* (1850), is simply anachronistic in the years after 1900. Yet, Gillian Avery has suggested a further set of reasons, including a widespread revolt against the moral reticence of the nineteenth century (185). If so, then however mediated, the evolution of children's fiction shares with adult literature a need for greater candour and realism in a negotiation of Victorian literary conventions as in, for example, Arnold Bennett's denial of the reader's expectation for a happy outcome to his novel, *Anna of the Five Towns* (1902).

At the same time, however, children's literature cannot be absorbed within other literary changes due to its own particular mode of development. During the late Victorian and Edwardian periods, the distinctive generic qualities of children's literature were being shaped, on the one hand, by the responses of child readers to new fiction that, in turn, encouraged further innovation. On the other hand, the emerging dialogue between writers and their child readers was framed by the moral and social influence of parents, guardians, teachers and libraries. E. Nesbit's writing offers a case in point. While her attempt to see the world from the child's perspective, most notably in *The Story of the Treasure Seekers* (1899), accords with the general tendency for greater realism and ambiguity, Nesbit remains resolute in her emphasis upon moral and social order, especially at the end of *The Railway Children* (1906). In other words, while there is a valid observation to be made about the greater licence in children's and adult literature from this period, it is necessary to regard these tendencies, at best, as parallel movements. One does not necessarily inform the other while the evolving practice of children's fiction, as distinct from the adult novel, also has to be taken into account. As Keating states:

> There is no single or simple explanation why so much independence was being granted at this time to fictional children. In addition to its links with anthropology and sociology, the change can be related to the greater independence being given to children by legislation, the pervasive mood of anti-Victorianism, the new demands for youthful heroes being made by Empire, and to a resurgence of interest in the education of young children, whether inspired by Education Acts or the educational value of *Kindergarten* play being advocated by the English followers of Froebel. (226)

In short, it is impossible to encapsulate the nature of the changes involved within children's literary representation, although it is also clear that these changes were integral to the dynamic of the Edwardian period. Far from being a hangover from the Victorian era, Edwardian culture was vital and distinctive as historians such as Paul Thompson have suggested. Consequently, this account does not seek to encompass the many-sided construction of Edwardian childhood, but concentrates instead upon an important element that distinguishes it from earlier conceptions, and which also isolates the Edwardian moment from its historical predecessor: the identification of childhood with the mystical as opposed to the metaphysical, the pagan in contrast with the angelic. Instead of being seen as a retreat into the reassuring world of Arcadia, this movement can be more clearly understood in terms of an emerging dialectic between on the one hand a rational, urban and commercial society, and on the other hand, magical and folkloric beliefs that were galvanized by what Alun Howkins called the Edwardian 'discovery of rural England.'

Three contrasting adult stories, Saki's 'The Toys of Peace' (1914), Rudyard Kipling's '"They"' (1904), and May Sinclair's 'The Intercessor' (1911), can be used as a set of coordinates to map out this discourse. Saki's comic tale satirizes the earnest and naïve aspirations of liberal, middle-class parents. Eleanor Bope is inspired by 'an exhibition of "peace toys,"' 'not miniature soldiers but miniature civilians,' in the hope of civilizing children's 'primitive instincts' ('Toys' 441). She persuades her brother, Harvey, to buy a set of suitable presents for her children, Eric and Bertie, rather than the toy soldiers and cavalry that they are expecting. Harvey purchases models of 'a municipal dust-bin,' 'the Manchester branch of the Young Women's Christian Association,' 'tools of industry,' public buildings, civil servants and cultural figures, such as Sir John Herschel and John Stuart Mill ('Toys' 443). He tries to encourage the children to hold an election using the toys, but they already have a clear idea of what elections are: ' "noses all bleeding and everybody drunk as can be," echoed Bertie, who had carefully studied one of Hogarth's pictures' ('Toys' 444). The boys' scepticism is not only derived from an innate love of violence but also from their reading of cultural sources: popular tales of Empire, Roman, and European history, figurative art. As Harvey himself ponders, would it 'be possible to compile a history, for use in elementary schools, in which there should be no prominent mention of battles, massacres, murderous intrigues, and violent deaths?' ('Toys' 445). As if to answer Harvey's question, the children adapt the toys so that they can re-enact the French Revolution. Yet, despite the story's opening premise that violence stems from natural instinct, the satire does not merely play nature off against culture. Rather, it argues that violence is part of human history, so that the children's destruction of their toys is redeemed as an ironic critique of the adults' attempt to go against the lessons of history. Misbehaviour is justified not on the terms expressed in Kipling's *Stalky & Co* (1899), 'A trifle immoral, but then – boys will be boys' (245), but in terms of what it means to be human. It is in regarding the child as human, and not as divine or primitive, that Saki sets the child against the liberalizing and moralizing constraints of civilization.

Kipling, too, was concerned by the passage of English history, literally making it come alive in *Puck of Pook's Hill* (1906) and *Rewards and Fairies* (1910). Yet, he had already presented a car journey through the Sussex countryside at the start of ' "They" ' as a type of time travel:

> I found hidden villages where bees ... boomed in eighty-foot lindens that overhung grey Norman churches; miraculous brooks diving under stone bridges built for heavier traffic than would ever vex them again; tithe-barns larger than their churches, and an old smithy that cried out aloud how it had once been a hall of the Knights of the Temple. Gipsies I found on a common where the gorse, bracken, and heath fought it out together up a mile of Roman road. (' "They" ' 243)

In exploring the landscape, the narrator discovers a beautiful Elizabethan house occupied by a blind woman and a host of mysterious, fleet-footed children. Returning repeatedly to the site, as if by his car's 'own volition' ('"They"' 249), he gradually learns the house's secret. The children are ghosts drawn to the woman who, through a form of second sight, can see the colours of 'the naked soul' ('"They"' 253), which outline the Orphic Egg, an ancient symbol for eternity. In particular, the narrator realizes that one of these children is his own for whom he silently grieves:

> The little brushing kiss fell in the centre of my palm – as a gift on which the fingers were, once, expected to close: as the all-faithful half-reproachful signal of a waiting child not used to neglect even when grown-ups were busiest – a fragment of the mute code devised very long ago.
>
> Then I knew. And it was as though I had known from the first day when I looked across the lawn at the high window. ('"They"' 263)

The narrator's temporal and spatial journey is also an emotional quest, an unconscious exploration of his own submerged feelings and repressed memories. The children are depicted as mischievous woodland sprites, constantly teasing and evading the narrator until he recognizes the purpose of his search, so that the landscape not only draws upon folkloric beliefs but also acts as a metaphor for the narrator's unconscious self. The ramble through English history that opens the story not only gives way to mythological happenings, and the recovery of hidden, personal histories, but is also justified by the narrator's psychological fulfilment: his recognition of his lost child. In '"They,"' the spectre of the child is not just a phantasm of the mind but the reminder of a physical object associated with human love, whose loss determines the lives of those who remain. Throughout the story, the narrator is constantly mindful of his own behaviour. The remembrance of the child and, with it, the beginnings of a successful mourning, reveals the protagonist's civilized conduct to be dependent upon his emotional repression.

Like '"They,"' 'The Intercessor' is also concerned with a lost child, but whereas Kipling's tale is deeply affecting, Sinclair's narrative is nightmarish. The story opens with Garvin, an estate agent, who dreams of 'wild open stretches, everlastingly unbuilt-on, for moors and fells, for all places that have kept the secret and the memory of the ancient earth' ('Intercessor' 177–8). Garvin's desire leads him to lodge at Falshaw's, a 'gaunt and naked' house on the Yorkshire moors 'of terrible and unforgetting and unforgotten age' ('Intercessor' 178). Mrs Falshaw is pregnant but is convinced that she will lose the child. Though there are no other children present, Garvin is repeatedly disturbed by something resembling a 'child's cry, except [for] the carnal dissonances and violences':

> The grief it uttered was too profound and too persistent, and, as it were, too pure; it knew none of the hot-blooded throes, the strangulated pauses, the lacerating resurgences of passion. At times it was shrill, unbroken, irremediable; at times it was no more than a sad sobbing and whimpering ... as of a creature malignly re-created, born again to its mysterious, immitigable suffering. ('Intercessor' 186)

The child then appears before Garvin, tracing out its route around the house when it was alive. He eventually learns that the child is Effy, Mrs Falshaw's daughter who had died three years earlier. Following the birth of Effy, Mr Falshaw had had an affair, claiming that 'He'd given [his wife] the child; and it ought to be enough for her' ('Intercessor' 206). Both parents had mistreated and abused Effy until her early death. Now Garvin realizes that 'He had been made the vehicle of [her] spirit':

> What really possessed him and remained with him was Effy's passion. Effy's passion (for the mother who had not loved her) was *the* supernatural thing, the possessing, pursuing, unappeasably crying thing that haunted the Falshaws' house. ('Intercessor' 209–10)

Unlike Kipling's 'mute code,' Effy's innocent and overwhelming desire for restoration is ultimately destructive:

> He saw the child approach again fearlessly ... Urged by the persistence of its passion, the child hovered for a moment, divinely coercing, divinely caressing; its touch fell now on its mother's hair, now on her cheek, now on her lips, and lingered there.
> And then the woman writhed and flung herself backwards in her chair away from it. Her face was convulsed with a hideous agony of fear. ('Intercessor' 213)

Sinclair's story draws upon her admiration of the Brontës and, in particular, the pre-Freudian emphasis within Gothic literature upon the home and the family as sites of taboo and transgressive desire. It contrasts with Kipling's tale because its keynote is melancholic rather than a slow release of traumatic emotion. Yet, it shares with both Kipling and Saki a view of the domestic realm as a place of disturbance, especially where the power relationship between the adult and the child has shifted. In all three examples, the child is regarded as human with human feelings even where, as in Effy's case, her innocent passions verge upon the demonic. None of these writers attempt to hide these emotions. Rather, they all argue that the disguising or distortion of feeling, often in the name of social conduct, is to be opposed through what their child-figures represent.

Underlining this use of the child is a discontent on the part of the writers with the current organization of society, in particular, the overhang of late Victorian moralism. Both Garvin and Kipling's narrator are outsiders in their fictional worlds; H. H. Munro's hiding behind the pseudonym of Saki indicates his own social and (possibly) sexual estrangement from the world he describes. Yet, Kipling's expression of delight to Charles Eliot Norton in November 1902 on moving to the Sussex countryside – 'the most marvellous of all foreign countries that I have ever been in' (*Letters* 113) – captures the sense felt by many Edwardians of rediscovering rural England. New technologies, such as the motor car, the bicycle (most famously depicted in H. G. Wells' *The History of Mr Polly* [1910]) and cinema (the films of Sagar Mitchell and James Kenyon), reopened the countryside for urban dwellers. At the same time, as Alun Howkins (63–9) has explored, the countryside came to be regarded by political figures on both Right and Left as a panacea for the ills of the city, in particular, by reconnecting with traditional modes of living: an inspiration for the folklorist Cecil Sharp and a source of satire for D. H. Lawrence in 'England, My England' (1915, revised in 1921–22). Yet, as G. R. Searle has shown, political responses were also mediated by the dissemination of eugenic thought embodied by the mantra of 'national efficiency' following the South African War. At the heart of these political and cultural reactions exists the emergence of what Patrick Wright has termed 'Deep England': a vague yet resonant cluster of images that envisage a myth of the English countryside as essential and timeless (the real England, as it were, in contrast with the towns and cities), thereby reifying the cause and effect of history.

A sentimentalized version of Deep England has often underpinned the rhetoric of right-wing politicians from Stanley Baldwin and Winston Churchill to Margaret Thatcher and John Major. Yet, as Krishan Kumar has suggested (175–225), the search for an English identity necessarily involves the search for an historical origin: a moment when Englishness becomes recognizable. Kumar himself proposes the late nineteenth century; yet, it is apparent that late Victorians and Edwardians were themselves on a quest for origination. The formulation of a Deep England not only reifies history, as Wright contends, but in its transition into myth also transgresses these more sentimental accounts. As George Orwell implies in his essay, *The Lion and the Unicorn* (1941), the cosy images of warm beer, village cricket and old maids dissolve into a more complex history. Similarly, the route into Deep England results in more mystical and disturbing content than these versions can accommodate.

In *Minima Moralia* (1955), Theodor Adorno dismissed mysticism as 'a metaphysic of dunces' (241). Yet, such a criticism elides the historical basis for mysticism's popular appeal as well as the role it has played in fashioning part of English national identity. Sometimes running alongside, sometimes intertwining with the development of Modernism in the work of, for example, T. S. Eliot, E. M. Forster and D. H. Lawrence, mysticism supplied a set of ideas with which to oppose the hegemonic values of efficiency, routine and hierarchy. In her book, *The Reform of Time* (2001), Maureen Perkins has shown that the establishment of clock-time and the reform of the calendar during the second half of the nineteenth century mediated the growth of progress as both an intellectual and social concept. As an optimistic belief in the idea of progress became dominant in British society, so more pessimistic beliefs enshrined in traditional practices such as prophecy, fortune-telling and the reading of dreams were discounted as superstition. Prediction became less of an art and more of a technique, a mechanical component within a rational and ordered society. Mysticism therefore appealed to Edwardian writers, not necessarily because they were devout believers, but because it proposed a different mode of living to contemporary society, an alternative way of thinking about the origins and meaning of English identity.

In this respect, Kenneth Grahame emerges as an exemplary figure. His *Pagan Papers*, although published in 1893, establishes many of the preoccupations of the Edwardian period. Grahame's Paganism, as his biographer Peter Green notes, takes a milder form than the Decadent accounts of Aubrey Beardsley or Arthur Machen (Green 137–43). As embodied by the figure of Pan, it assumes a non-utilitarian approach to life in which work is abhorred and 'loafing' or reclining are valued: 'His is now an astral body, and through golden spaces of imagination his soul is winging her untrammelled flight' (*Pagan Papers* 50). In escaping the regimen of work, Grahame's loafer imagines himself into those rural retreats where 'Pan and his following may hide their heads for yet a little longer, until the growing tyranny has invaded the last common, spinney, and sheep-down' (*Pagan Papers* 71). Whereas historical time is 'dotted with date and number and sign,' the loafer notes his 'relief in turning to the dear days outside history': 'For then the Fairy Wicket stood everywhere ajar – everywhere and to each and all' (157). If history, like work, has been colonized by routine, then Fairyland offers not only an Arcadian refuge but also an imaginary site in which democratic society can be rethought. It is the same Utopian space that underwrites the tension of country and city in Forster's *Howards End* (1910) or when Ford Madox Hueffer speculates in *The Soul of London* (1905) on whether the capital has a spirit that goes beyond mere economic force.

Jonathan Rose, in his intellectual history of the Edwardians, has labelled their cult of childhood, and in particular their attraction to mysticism, as a 'gospel of fun,' a refusal to grow up that produced 'unhealthy softness' and 'rank silliness' (196, 197). Far from it. Whereas Rose discounts Edwardian mysticism as a retreat from historical reality into an idealized infancy, thereby reinforcing the cultural stereotype of the Edwardians as drifting into the nightmare of global warfare, the mystical response can instead be seen as a counter-reaction to a history that has been divested of its charm by becoming a tool of instrumental reason. In *Puck of Pook's Hill*, Kipling (an author diametrically opposed to Grahame's loafer yet one who still draws upon myths of Pan and other related figures) presents his child protagonists, Dan and Una, with a cavalcade of historical episodes that reinvest that history with magic, action, drama and the exotic. Both *Puck of Pook's Hill* and its successor, *Rewards and Fairies*, evoke the sense of wonder and foreignness that Kipling himself found in the Sussex Downs. Instead of factual accuracy, Kipling constructs a historical montage, whose mythic quality compensates for the commercially and politically devalued imperial heartland satirized in stories such as 'The Village that Voted the Earth Was Flat' (1913). To this end, Kipling effectively deploys a pair of devices. First, he estranges the reader's preconception of historical narrative through the use of magic and, in particular, the figure of Puck himself. Second, the reader is encouraged to view the events through the eyes of Dan and Una. Their curiosity and delight not only draw the reader in but also enthuse. History becomes a form of child's play, an enthusiastic response that runs counter to popular late Victorian guides, such as Eleanor Bulley's *Great Britain for Little Britons* (1882), where the child inquisitor acts as no more than a cipher. Contrary to Rose's account, sequences such as *Puck of Pook's Hill* are not simply fun for fun's sake. Instead, their use of magic reinvests historical narrative, and beyond that an English identity, with passion and imagination mediated through history as a form of story-telling. Not history as *le grand récit* but as dialogic, an open-ended conversation that extends the principle of nursery games involving both adult and child.

Yet, it is a dialogue that is ultimately conducted with the reader since Puck has it in his power to erase the children's conscious minds of what they have witnessed. In other words, knowledge of Deep England remains occluded as part of magic rather than memorialized as part of official history. While this suggests a mystifying and essentialist response, insofar as the source of Englishness is not only veiled in mystery but also rendered occult, reading becomes a key with which to enter its hidden meanings. Reading, by extension, is conjoined with a sense of the magical and the imaginative. Like the 'mute code' in ' "They," ' *Puck of Pook's Hill* is immersed in secret languages, the forgotten words for places and objects. While Dan and Una are enchanted, so that they consciously forget what they have seen, the reader is in a position to see this magical process in operation. In other words, the reader witnesses Puck's magic both as a child (through Dan and Una) and as an adult (we gain a knowledge of which Dan and Una, at least at the conscious level, remain innocent). The act of reading becomes not only bound with the function of magic, but in their intersection, offers also a vantage-point from which the work of enchantment can be seen and understood. In other words, while on the one hand, Puck shrouds the mystery of Deep England by casting his spell upon the children, on the other hand, the reader is placed in a privileged position by seeing how the magic of Deep England is woven. Far from essentializing the notion of Englishness, the mysticism associated with *Puck of Pook's Hill* works to reveal the charm of national identity as a material process, a cultural and historical activity to which Kipling's writing contributes.

At the root, then, of Kipling's reconstructed history lies the transformative power of magic whether as art or belief. In Burnett's *The Secret Garden*, Colin pronounces:

> Magic is always pushing and drawing and making things out of nothing. Everything is made out of Magic, leaves and trees, flowers and birds, badgers and foxes and squirrels and people. So it must be all around us. In this garden – in all the places. (205)

As Colin explains, magic is simply a name for something that he senses but which he cannot define. Perhaps this essence, as Burnett is compelled to suggest in the final chapter when the novel restores the patriarchal order (see Foster and Simons 188–90), is a form of positive thinking: 'To let a sad thought or a bad one get into your mind is as dangerous as letting a scarlet fever germ get into your body' (241). Yet, it is a nominal 'sad thought,' Mr Craven's concealment of the garden following the death of his wife, which provides Mary with the incentive of pursuing its whereabouts. Despite what the omniscient narrator suggests, it is the melancholy of Misselthwaite Manor that inspires Mary to seek out the garden and, in so doing, to begin the process of drawing herself out from her own melancholy following the death of her parents and her rude arrival from India. Since the novel, like Sinclair's 'The Intercessor,' predates the dissemination in England of psychoanalytic concepts, including the process of grief-work in Freud's 'Mourning and Melancholia' (1917), *The Secret Garden* adapts the imagery of Romantic Gothic in order to describe Mary's transformation. Like Jane Eyre, Mary uncovers the secrets of the manor house and, as a consequence, restores the garden to its former beauty and reconciles Archibald Craven with his son, Colin. The melancholic spell, which begins first in the novel with Mary's unloving upbringing and the nightmare horror of the plague, initially freezes time. Misselthwaite Manor, abandoned by Mr Craven to his servants while his bed-ridden son is confined to a mewling infancy, is a place outside of time, outside of history. The enchantment starts to unfold once Mary has been attracted to the melancholy of the place to uncover its mysteries. In unlocking the garden, and gradually restoring it to life, so Mary dispels the magic by moving time forwards. Eventually, the manor house is restored to the historical time of successive generations through the reconciliation of father and son. In the process, the catalyst, Mary, is displaced from the centre of these changes. Instead, she is moved to the periphery, to a position outside of history that is occupied also by her aide, Dickon. While on the one hand, this switch suggests Burnett's own conformity with dominant gender relations, on the other hand, Mary and Dickon embody a similar position to that of Kipling's Puck. They are associated with a life-giving notion of Deep England: a mystical vision that must remain outside the official historical account but which nevertheless underwrites its existence. Again, the reader is placed in a privileged role because he or she can see this process in operation. Instead of Misselthwaite Manor being restored to the eternal timelessness of father-son inheritance, its history is dependent upon the natural mysticism represented by Mary and Dickon.

Dickon is the most ambiguous figure in the novel since he is portrayed as both a rustic innocent and an incarnation of Pan:

A boy was sitting under a tree, with his back against it, playing on a rough wooden pipe ... And on the trunk of the tree he leaned against, a brown squirrel was clinging and watching him, and from behind a bush nearby a cock pheasant was delicately stretching his neck to peep out, and quite near him were two rabbits sitting up and sniffing with tremulous noses – and actually it appeared as if they were all drawing near to watch him and listen to the strange low little call his pipe seemed to make. (*The Secret Garden* 83)

Whereas in the figures of Mary and Colin there is a depth of psychological realism, even if mediated through the vocabulary of Gothic romance, Dickon is other-worldly. He is closer instead to the characterization of Pan in *The Wind in the Willows*. His representation exposes the limitations within the narrator's closing sentiment of positive thinking. As ' "the most Magic boy in the world" ' (*The Secret Garden* 220), Dickon indicates that magic, or whatever it is that underlines the story's power, defies definition. It passes from the world of observable fact to another dimension of potent mysticism.

By comparison, the early fantasies of E. Nesbit appear less ambitious. Magic, in the form of a Psammead or a Phoenix, intrudes into the real world rather than embedding historical time as in Burnett or Kipling. Unlike a character such as Dickon, Nesbit is keen to stress the ordinariness of her protagonists: they 'were not particularly handsome, nor were they extra clever, nor extraordinarily good. But they were not bad sorts on the whole; in fact, they were rather like you' (*The Phoenix and the Carpet* 21). In seeking to identify the child reader with her characters, Nesbit emphasizes above all else familiarity and mimesis, so that when the magical element enters the narrative, it is realistically explained: the Psammead is found in a gravel-pit, the Phoenix's egg arrives bound in a carpet from a junk shop. Yet, as Nesbit suggests to the child reader, if 'you believe all that ... you will find it quite easy to believe that before Anthea and Cyril and the others had been a week in the country they had found a fairy' (*Five Children and It* 14). In other words, magic becomes a secret to be shared between the author and her child readers, whereas in Kipling, the reader is placed in a knowing position as both an adult and as a child. For Nesbit, magic is a child's prerogative not to be entrusted to adults who, in her novels, remain ignorant. While this association with childhood seems to essentialize magic, Nesbit's deflation of her protagonists casts magic in less idealistic terms than in Burnett or Kipling. Instead of being nurturing and life-giving, Nesbit's magic is unpredictable and often disastrous. This impression is not only created by the children's misuse of magic but also by the magical figures themselves, such as the Phoenix and the Psammead, who are frequently grumpy and cantankerous unlike Grahame's Pan or Kipling's Puck.

The mystique of Deep England is not only being played with here but with it also the socialization of children that forms a fundamental element. Whereas Burnett and Kipling offer an image of the nation-state bolstered by a mythic sense of cultural identity, Nesbit's use of magic throws this vision into doubt. Unlike Dan and Una or Mary and Colin, Nesbit's children are aware of the civilizing process, as for example, in the inconclusive discussion from *Five Children and It* after their baby brother has temporarily been transformed into an adult. Cyril argues that, when old enough, the child should be bullied so that he grows up properly, Jane suggests kindness, Robert thinks he can be corrected ' "as he goes along" ' while Anthea does not see the need for moral improvement (*Five Children* 178). Not only is socialization left as an open question, but the children do not necessarily see how or why it should apply to them. For if they did, if they were genuinely reformed by their experiences, there would be no further adventures, but like Kipling's Mowgli in *The Jungle Books* (1894–95) or Burnett's Mary and Colin, they would have to take their places within the social order of historical time. While on the one hand, Nesbit seems to be one of the more sceptical writers of the mysticism that underlines both Edwardian childhood and attitudes towards the nation, on the other hand, she is one of its most forceful advocates by insisting upon the child's point of view. By seeing the world from the child's perspective, in which fairies and phoenixes become part of everyday life, Nesbit critiques the process of socialization even where that extends to (adult) conceptions of cultural identity. In the period after World War I when, as Paul Fussell has argued in *The Great War and Modern Memory* (1975), the certainties of historical time were shattered, Edwardian children such as W. H. Auden and George Orwell would continue to unpick the nature of their society.

Works cited

Ackroyd, Peter. *Albion: The Origins of the English Imagination*. London: Chatto and Windus, 2002.

Adorno, Theodor W. *Minima Moralia*. Trans. E. F. N. Jephcott. 1955. London: New Left Books, 1974.

Avery, Gillian. *Nineteenth Century Children: Heroes and Heroines in English Children's Stories 1780–1900*. London: Hodder and Stoughton, 1965.

Bulley, Eleanor. *Great Britain for Little Britons*. London: Gardner and Darton, 1882.

Burnett, Frances Hodgson. *The Secret Garden*. 1911. Ed. Alison Lurie. London: Penguin, 1999.

Carpenter, Humphrey. *Secret Gardens: A Study of the Golden Age of Children's Literature*. London: George Allen and Unwin, 1985.

Cunningham, Hugh. *The Children of the Poor: Representations of Childhood Since the Seventeenth Century*. Oxford: Basil Blackwell, 1991.

Foster, Shirley and Judy Simons. *What Katy Read: Feminist Re-Readings of 'Classic' Stories for Girls*. Basingstoke: Macmillan, 1995.

Fussell, Paul. *The Great War and Modern Memory*. New York and Oxford: Oxford University Press, 1975.

Grahame, Kenneth. *Pagan Papers*. 1893. 4th ed. London: The Bodley Head, 1904.

Green, Peter. *Kenneth Grahame 1859–1932*. London: John Murray, 1959.

Howkins, Alun. 'The Discovery of Rural England.' *Englishness: Politics and Culture 1880–1920*. Ed. Robert Colls and Philip Dodd. London: Croom Helm, 1987. 62–88.

Joyce, James. *Ulysses*. 1922. Ed. Jeri Johnson. Oxford: Oxford World's Classics, 1989.

Keating, Peter. *The Haunted Study: A Social History of the English Novel, 1875–1914*. London: Secker and Warburg, 1989.

Kipling, Rudyard. *The Letters of Rudyard Kipling, vol. 3: 1900–10*. Ed. Thomas Pinney. London: Macmillan, 1996.

——. *Puck of Pook's Hill*. 1906. Ed. Sarah Wintle. London: Penguin, 1987.

——. *Rewards and Fairies*. 1910. Ed. Roger Lewis. London: Penguin, 1987.

——. *Stalky & Co.* 1899. London: Macmillan, 1982.

——. ' "They." ' 1904. *Traffics and Discoveries*. 1904. Ed. Hermione Lee. London: Penguin, 1987. 243–65.

Kumar, Krishnan. *The Making of English National Identity*. Cambridge: Cambridge University Press, 2003.

Nesbit, E. *Five Children and It*. 1902. Harmondsworth: Puffin, 1959.

—— *The Phoenix and the Carpet*. 1904. Harmondsworth: Puffin, 1959.

Nicolson, Juliet. *The Perfect Summer: Dancing into Shadow in 1911*. London: John Murray, 2006.

Orwell, George. *The Lion and the Unicorn: Socialism and the English Genius*. London: Secker and Warburg, 1941.

Perkins, Maureen. *The Reform of Time: Magic and Modernity*. London: Pluto Press, 2001.

Rose, Jonathan. *The Edwardian Temperament 1895–1919*. Athens, Ohio: Ohio University Press, 1986.

Saki, 'The Toys of Peace.' 1914. *The Short Stories of Saki*. London: The Bodley Head, 1930. 441–6.

Searle, G. R. *The Quest for National Efficiency: A Study in British Politics and Political Thought 1899–1914*. Oxford: Basil Blackwell, 1970.

Sinclair, May. 'The Intercessor.' 1911. *Uncanny Stories*. 1923. Ed. Paul March-Russell. Ware: Wordsworth Editions, 2006. 177–216.

Thompson, Paul. *The Edwardians: The Remaking of British Society*. 2nd edn. London: Weidenfeld and Nicolson, 1984.

Wright, Patrick. *On Living in an Old Country: The National Past in Contemporary Britain*. London: Verso, 1985.

3
Cult or Cull?: *Peter Pan* and Childhood in the Edwardian Age

Karen L. McGavock

Peter Pan is regarded as being at the forefront of the Edwardian cult of childhood (White and Tarr 51), having 'initiated or played a larger part than any other work in initiating a fashion for "fairy" literature and illustration in the Edwardian nursery' (Carpenter 170), and Peter Pan does symbolize the youth and vitality of the age. Yet this essay will reveal the deep irony of this statement through exploring the ways in which James Matthew Barrie deconstructs or 'culls' childhood, challenging the conventional representation of children in the Edwardian era and undermining the sentimental construction of childhood promulgated in merchandise of the day. Although Barrie is often deemed to have created the epitome of childhood in Peter Pan, consideration will be made of ways in which *Peter Pan* can be regarded as a catalyst for change in the representation of childhood. The extent to which Peter Pan, therefore, 'force[s] us to challenge the most prevalent ideology of turn-of-the-century child-adult relations' will be explored (Coats 4).

There were many contradictions in Edwardian society surrounding childhood and its representation. The old construction of childhood which represented children as original sinners was juxtaposed against, yet inherent to, the modern construction of childhood which represented children sentimentally. This presents a 'double image' of the child (Mavor 3).

While legislation was being brought in to protect children against exploitation in the workplace in the form of The Children's Act of 1908, children were, at the same time, being fetishized and exploited for adult gain as childhood was commodified. They were being industrialized by the very society that sought to protect them from 'the excesses of industrial societies' (Jenks 100). As a raw material, the child is malleable, 'benefiting' from being knocked or moulded into shape, often physically, by adults. Childhood is defined and refined in them by this process. They are *informed, reformed,* and sometimes *deformed* through the construction of childhood that represents them. Fixing the child as object implies that there is a 'purpose of "childhood"' (Jenks 120) suggesting that childhood has an extrinsic purpose, a utility. This is a far cry from the sentimental construction of childhood that came to be valued not as a means to an end (of adulthood), but rather as an end in itself. As modernity and progress result in the degeneration of civilization, the role of the child as pure saviour has been subverted. Children become assimilated into mechanisms for change. Regarding children's fiction as a mechanism for social change seems to be a logical extension of the construction of the child as utility. To a certain extent Barrie can be seen to be instrumental to this process since he implicitly uses *Peter Pan* to change the construction of childhood in Edwardian culture.

In Edwardian society, children were converted into desirable objects and childhood was exploited. Childhood was conceived of as part of consumer society, as a luxury afforded by a prosperous consumer culture comprising a growing middle class with greater levels of disposable income and more leisure time. The orchestrated gap between childhood and adulthood was exploited by twentieth-century consumer society. The child was constructed as a fetish, an object of desire, for adult gratification. As Marina Warner suggests, 'the cult of the child often reflects adults' dreams rather than children's interests' (158).

It is lucrative to engineer a gap between childhood and adulthood. In order to create a niche to be exploited in the marketplace, childhood and adulthood had to be separated and children's literature, though satisfying principally the needs and desires of adults, was packaged for children. There are considerable financial benefits to commercially categorizing and sentimentalizing childhood. Attempts were therefore made by adults to preserve their longing for the child by 'fixing' childhood, defining it, framing it and preserving it in print through the mediums of literature and photography.

Adults may even be accused of plundering the cache of childhood by investing in children. This movement is wonderfully captured in Barrie's depiction of the mercenary Mr Darling as a man not only prepared to sell his own soul for personal gain, but something even worse – he is prepared to sell the shadow of another. On finding Peter Pan's shadow, Mr Darling is quick to exclaim to his wife that 'There is money in this, my love. I shall take it to the British Museum to-morrow and have it priced' (*Peter Pan* 1.1.184–5). In a further exchange between

Mr Darling and Mrs Darling at the end of the story, he delights in the attention he has received in being captured on a picture postcard going to work in his kennel: ' "Ah, Mary, we should not be such celebrities if the children hadn't flown away" ' to which Mrs Darling replies, ' "George ... you are sure you are not enjoying it?" ' (*Peter and Wendy* 211).

Before considering ways in which Barrie culled childhood it may be helpful to outline the chronology of *Peter Pan* versions and to summarize Barrie's position as an Edwardian writer. In this essay, reference will mainly be made to the prose version of *Peter Pan* – published as *Peter and Wendy* (1911), but on occasions the term 'fiction' will be applied in a broader sense to refer to the play version of *Peter Pan* first performed in 1904.[1]

Arguably the first incarnation of Peter Pan occurred in *Sentimental Tommy* (1896) in which Tommy imagines a little boy lost in the woods and is consoled by the thought that he would remain a boy forever. 1902 heralded the second incarnation of Peter Pan in *The Little White Bird*, a prose work marketed for adults which includes a substantial section about a character called Peter Pan who lives in Kensington Gardens. It is interesting that, certainly at this stage, *Peter Pan* was not marketed at a child audience. In 1906, Barrie freed Peter Pan from the constraints of an adult novel, reprinting sections of *The Little White Bird* under the title of *Peter Pan in Kensington Gardens* with illustrations by Arthur Rackham. Barrie transposed the story into dramatic form as *Peter Pan or The Boy Who Would Not Grow Up* which was staged for the first time on 27 December 1904 at the Duke of York's Theatre in London. On 22 February 1908, an extra scene, 'When Wendy Grew Up' made its first and last stage appearance in Barrie's lifetime (Hollindale vii). *Peter Pan* made a further transition, from play to prose, with the publication in 1911 of *Peter and Wendy*.[2]

Sources which may have inspired Peter Pan include Barrie's five child companions, the Llewelyn Davies boys, Barrie's elder brother David who died young and so never grew up, the son Barrie never had, Barrie himself, and the mythic Pan. Barrie's most candid revelation about Peter Pan comes from a programme note for the 1908 Paris production of *Peter Pan*:

> of Peter you must make what you will–perhaps he was a boy who died young and this is how the author perceives his subsequent adventures. Or perhaps he was a boy who was never born at all; a boy whom some people longed for but who never came–it may be that these people hear Peter more clearly at the window than children do. (quoted in Ferguson 11)

Unlike Barrie's character, Tommy, who is described in *Sentimental Tommy* as a 'boy who *could* not grow up,' Peter Pan *chooses* not to grow up. The difference between the two is subtle but significant. Tommy's description is passive and submissive whereas Peter Pan's is active and dismissive. This corresponds to the changing construction of childhood at the time Barrie was writing. *Peter Pan* oscillates between categories. Although Edwardians may have fetishized childhood in print, the child was not passive in this process. Barrie rather unconventionally rendered the child active as an agent of reform rather than passive amidst the process of change. Far from sentimentally constructing the child, *Peter Pan* deconstructs the relation synonymous in post-Romantic literary tradition between children and innocence and demythologizes childhood.

As economic and market forces were promoting childhood Barrie's contemporary, Sigmund Freud, was also deconstructing associations between childhood and innocence, particularly in his discussion of the child as a sexual being. Just after the reputed 'birth' of childhood in the early part of the twentieth-century, with the publication of Ellen Key's *Barnets århundrade*, translated as *The Century of the Child* (1909), Sigmund Freud mapped its death when he reconnected childhood to adulthood. In 'Three Essays on the Theory of Sexuality' (1905) Freud challenged the status quo by regarding children as sexual rather than pre-sexual beings. By closing the gap between the two, he gave children once more the status of miniature adults. Barrie and Freud shared a desire to explore contradictory forces between childhood and adulthood and challenged the sentimental construction or 'cult' of childhood. As Jenks explains: 'Freud's discussion of childhood sexuality led to a contemporary furore and two decades of abuse for re-invoking 'original sin' in a libidinal form' (124).

Edwardian society fetishized childhood and Peter Pan epitomized this process. As Jacqueline Rose explains, *Peter Pan* is a 'vehicle for what is most unsettling and uncertain about the relationship between adult and child. It shows innocence not as a property of childhood but as a portion of adult desire' (Rose xii). Vadim Linetski agrees with Rose but indicates that

> only the child can ensure the convergence and resonance between heterogeneous discourses of (conflicting) adult desires. The child is welcome not as an object of gaze, but as a mouth-piece/mediator. (8)

It seems that the child's nineteenth-century status as mute image (being 'seen and not heard') prevailed in the twentieth century. The child is regarded as a passive receptacle, 'an object of ardent desire' (Linetski 6). As an 'object of desire' Peter Pan is rendered fixed. To suggest that children's fiction has an object implies that there is an end-point, a 'telos' which Peter Pan does not have because, as Linetski states, 'the essence of desire is to have no object' (6–7). In this respect, Barrie fetishizes childhood in Peter Pan.

In recent years, Rose has made a significant contribution to discussions on Barrie, exploring the 'cult' of Peter Pan and adult obsessions with the text. Rose's boldest claim is that Peter Pan neither is, nor ever has been, a text for children. Peter Pan first featured in an adult novel and 'when Peter Pan was first performed as a play in 1904... the audience was made up of London's theatre-going elite, and there was hardly a child among them' (Mackail 366). Peter Pan attracted 'a hard-core following of matinée fanatics who occupied the front row of the stalls to hurl thimbles at Peter and abuse at Hook' (Birkin, *J. M. Barrie* 118). This culminated in George Bernard Shaw claiming that Peter Pan was '"foisted on children by the grown-ups"' (quoted in Green 89).

The Edwardian rise of interest in childhood probably occurred because of increasing commercialization. There were contingent commercial benefits for Barrie in appearing to sentimentalize childhood. As Jackie Wullschläger comments: 'sentimental, whimsical, yet with a hard nose for commercial success, Barrie fitted his preoccupations to the times' (120). As childhood was commodified, sentimentality was manufactured:

> *Peter Pan*...ushered in a greater commercialization of children's literature. *Peter Pan in Kensington Garden*, published in 1906 and illustrated by Arthur Rackham, was the Christmas gift of choice for children swept up in the Neverland of the fairy story. After *Peter Pan*, the book industry began to produce not only more elaborate editions of children's books, like Rackham's, but also better and cheaper editions. The Edwardians' idealized children also became an ideal market. (PBS 2002)

Peter and Wendy responded to the consumer 'demand for a "classic"' (Rose 85) – the popular reception of *Peter Pan* resulting in the public demanding publication. *Peter Pan* became a phenomenon, propelling the work into cult status. Humphrey Carpenter explains:

> The effect of *Peter Pan* was...more immediate than that of any earlier work of children's literature...We are dealing here not just with a piece of imaginative creation by one man, but with a public phenomenon. (Carpenter 170)

From its outset, *Peter Pan* was 'converted into almost every conceivable (and some inconceivable) material forms' (Rose 103). An example of a cheaper colour illustrated book for children was 'The *Peter Pan Picture Book* published at five shillings by Bell in 1908' (Rose 109). Rose indicates that, 'after 1911, there were four versions of *Peter Pan* circulating simultaneously' (White and Tarr 220).

The proliferation of published versions of *Peter Pan* also symbolized wider change in the market which came to be divided:

> between the child recipient of the Christmas gift and the child reader, the former the object of a new and increasing commercial attention (aesthetic luxury and value), the latter the displaced focus of anxieties about the commercial and literary effects on the book trade of the changing educational policy of the state (overproduction, devaluation). (Rose 108)

Adults were buying *Peter Pan* both for themselves and for children, blurring the boundaries between sentiment and instrument – between the idealized child and the actual child.

Although not originally marketed for children, the play was adapted for child audiences. R. D. S. Jack claims that the play only became sentimental, 'when the drama's attraction for children became evident' and some of the darker elements in the original version were deleted ('From Drama' 9). The shift of women from sexualized wives to mothers was similarly 'a necessary adjustment to make *Peter Pan* more evidently a play for children' (Hollindale xii). *Peter Pan* thus evolved to become a play predominantly targeted at child audiences.

Hodder and Stoughton published exclusively for adults until J. M. Barrie produced works suitable for children (Rose 106). They then exploited his works through mass marketing, flooding the marketplace and capitalizing on the collectability of the books through producing differentiated versions. Differentiation, defined by Jack Zipes as a process that conditions, constructs, commodifies, controls, and consumes readers through carefully orchestrated marketing, is a more lucrative marketing strategy than homogenization. Separating children from adults by sentimentalizing and fetishizing them creates two potential consumer groups instead of one, offering double the profit.

Peter Pan is generally lauded as being central to the genre of children's fiction but close inspection of the text reveals and reflects the contradictory representations of childhood at this time. Rose complains that

> a glorification of the child ... not only ... refuses to acknowledge difficulties and contradictions in relation to childhood; it implies that we *use* the image of the child to deny those same difficulties in relation to ourselves. (Rose 8, emphasis added)

So, the mythology of the child conceals tension in relation to childhood. It should therefore follow that if one demythologizes the child, as Barrie does, tensions are revealed in relation to both childhood and adulthood.

In Peter Pan, Barrie's lack of sentimentality towards childhood is clearly revealed. Barrie was not pleased with the Peter Pan statue he commissioned for Kensington Gardens, complaining ' "it doesn't show the Devil in Peter" ' (quoted in Ormond 101). Barrie once commented that he hated 'sentimentality like a slave hates his master' (*The Greenwood Hat* 9). This intriguing comment suggests that he is bound to sentimentality by association but despises being restricted by its constraints. There is here a clear indication that Barrie effectively dons the façade of sentimentality to deconstruct it and so 'culls' this saccharine representation of childhood dominant in the Edwardian period.

At the same time as he subverts the association of children with divine grace, Barrie also subverts the association of children with original sin. Barrie's belief that children are not entirely innocent is revealed in his reference to children in his short anthology piece 'The Blot on Peter Pan' (1926). One of the children Barrie addresses in this work asks a question with 'cheerful brutality' (97) – a phrase which denotes the oxymoronic sadomasochism of childhood and depicts children as innocent sinners. This linguistic tension bears out the fact that Barrie fights on two fronts. In his dedication to *Peter Pan*, Barrie indicates that the Llewelyn Davies boys 'reached for the tree of knowledge' (*Peter Pan* 76). In growing up, they enacted a Lapse or Fall. Barrie sustains this image of children as original sinners when he has Michael comment:

> MICHAEL (reeling) Wendy, I've killed a pirate!
> WENDY   It's awful, awful.
> MICHAEL No, it isn't, I like it, I like it.
> (*Peter Pan* 5.1.184–6)

Michael's repetition of 'I like it, I like it' serves to mimic the association between the idyllic representation of a child as a cherub and the perverse and sinful enjoyment of killing. This scenario demonstrates

Barrie's keenness to expose conflict and to blur boundaries. He favours neither categorization of childhood.

Barrie's enthusiasm for exploring ambiguities of character is borne out in the character of Hook, who is described as 'not wholly evil' (*Peter Pan* 4.1, stage direction preceding line 259), and Tinker Bell, who is 'not wholly heartless' (*Peter Pan* 2.1, stage direction preceding line 252). Yet Barrie also periodically reaffirms the stereotype of children as innocent and happy, as is borne out in Peter Pan's comment, ' "I just want always to be a little boy and to have fun" ' (*Peter and Wendy* 170). He is only too aware, however, that not all little boys have fun. This is to misrepresent children naively and sentimentally. Barrie reinforces constructions and then undermines them to be deliberately provocative. Barrie refers to Peter Pan as 'beatific' (*Peter Pan* 4.1, stage direction preceding line 259) and as the devilish 'one aboard' Captain Hook's ship (*Peter and Wendy* 199). Cookson, the pirate, explains that ' "they do say the surest sign a ship's accurst is when there's one on board more than can be accounted for" ' (*Peter and Wendy* 199). Indeed Hook refers to Peter Pan's presence as the ' "spirit that haunts this dark lagoon" ' (*Peter and Wendy* 147).

Barrie deconstructs sentimental constructions of childhood in his description of Peter Pan as 'heartless.' He uses this word at least twice in reference to children: 'off we skip like the most *heartless* things in the world, which is what children are, but so attractive; and we have an entirely *selfish* time' (*Peter and Wendy* 166, emphasis added). 'Heartless' is also the final word he uses in the story: 'so long as children are gay and innocent and *heartless*' (*Peter and Wendy* 226). The word choice is curious, exposing a cynical agenda conventionally attributed to adults. Barrie juxtaposes both sentimental and sinister constructions of childhood in this phrase. Barrie also flouts sentimental conventions by choosing to create a story which does not clearly end happily. Although restored to Neverland, Peter Pan remains unsafe and insecure – on constant alert for pirates and abandoned by the Lost Boys, condemned to exist in repeated and perpetual limbo.

Since childhood and adulthood are inextricably implicated in one another, it is perhaps not surprising that analysis of childhood in *Peter Pan* also yields interesting insights into the construction of adulthood. Through employing the 'Darling' name, Barrie mocks the convention of the 'ideal family,' for it soon becomes apparent that the family is dysfunctional. Mr Darling seems to suffer from a form of neurosis and needs medicine in order to cope with reality. By subverting the conventions associated with adulthood, Barrie presents Mr Darling in childish mode. He comments ' "it isn't fair" ' that he is obliged to take his medicine when his children refuse to take theirs (*Peter and Wendy* 84). His refusal to take a dose of his own medicine literalizes metaphor since Mr Darling has one rule for his children and another for himself, so pours his medicine into Nana's bowl. At the end of the tale, he also literally ends up in the doghouse (*Peter and Wendy* 209). Barrie purposely has the same actor play Mr Darling and Captain Hook, encouraging consideration of the two characters as divided parts of the same whole. They resemble each other in their insecurities and in their flaws. In this way Barrie depicts adults as incompetent and irresponsible. They require medicine to help them to cope with difficulties so that children must take control of situations where adults fail. Conventional constructions of adulthood are therefore disrupted. Indeed Rose suggests that 'J. M. Barrie's 1911 version of *Peter Pan* undermines the certainty which should properly distinguish the narrating adult from the child' (Rose 68).

Barrie explores the reflexivity between childhood and adulthood, showing that the interface between childhood and adulthood is not impenetrable. It is a permeable membrane, which allows elements from each state to cross over freely. Barrie's interest in reflexivity perhaps began when his elder brother David was killed in a skating accident on 29 January 1867 and Barrie virtually became David in order to maintain his mother's affection. In *Margaret Ogilvy* (1896), Barrie notes, 'when I became a man, he was still a boy of thirteen' (15).

Reflexivity of age and youth is also played out on the Edwardian stage. After the Children's Act (1908), which stated that children under the age of 14 were not allowed to perform on stage after 9 pm (Aller 86), adults often played the parts of children. Barrie explores the reflexivity between childhood and adulthood in his representations of the 'adult-in-child' and the 'child-in-adult' (Hollindale xxii). The tensions between constructions of childhood and adulthood are now distributed and co-exist within the child and adult. Barrie blurs distinctions between childhood and adulthood, rendering *Peter Pan* fraught with tensions and instabilities of character and language. Indeed, it could be said that Peter Pan is the unstable text *par excellence*. In *Peter and Wendy* Barrie changes position at least three times in one passage, 'in a crescendo of insistence and anxiety: "grow up," "will grow up," "must grow up"' (Rose 68) until there is no clear distinction between the adult narrator and the children he is describing:

All children, except one, *grow up*. They soon know that they *will grow up*, and the way Wendy knew was this. One day when she was two years old she was playing in a garden, and she plucked another flower and ran with it to her mother. I suppose she must have looked rather delightful, for Mrs Darling put her hand to her heart and cried, 'Oh, why can't you remain like this for ever!' This was all that passed between them on the subject, but henceforth Wendy knew that she *must grow up*. You always know after you are two. Two is the beginning of the end. (*Peter and Wendy* 69, emphasis added)

By doubling the adult and child, Barrie exposes fragments of the child-in-adult and the adult-in-child. This can be seen in the doubling between Peter Pan and Captain Hook. Hook was never originally intended for inclusion in the play. He was added because Barrie needed an additional act for a scene change to be made and so he bridged a gap. In 'Good Ideas of the Twentieth Century,' Andrew Birkin reveals that

from his later revision notes it's clear that he completed his first draft without any mention of Hook at all. He didn't need a villain for the simple reason that he already had one: Peter Pan. Captain Hook's inclusion only came about as a result of a technical necessity. The stagehands needed a front cloth scene to give them time to change the scenery. (Birkin, 'Good Ideas')

Hook and Pan double each other in words and action. Indeed sometimes the voice of the one mimics the other. Peter can imitate Captain Hook's voice perfectly In his imitation of Hook, it is possible to regard Hook as the doppelgänger of Pan and vice versa. Peter Pan doubles as both antagonist and protagonist, but there appears to be some debate about Peter Pan's claim as hero of the play. Although Andrew Birkin asserts that 'Peter Pan was the first of the pre-teen heroes' ('J. M. Barrie' 118), counter-claims that he is an anti-hero or antagonist are perhaps more cogent. As Nicol observes, 'the heroic qualities of Barrie's protagonist are ambiguous' (1). Barrie himself refers to Hook and Pan not as complement and supplement but as two parts of the same whole. This is reaffirmed in Barrie's description of Peter Pan as 'the avenger' (*Peter and Wendy* 201). Peter Pan appears to be an anti-hero, an antagonist like Hook. Ironically Peter Pan, whilst symbolizing youth, refuses life. The retorts that each character make to the other are also paralleled. Hook describes Pan as ' "proud and insolent youth" ' and Pan describes Hook as 'dark and sinister man' (*Peter and Wendy* 202). The doubling between Pan and Hook serves to illustrate the ways in which Barrie explores tensions between childhood and adulthood.

Interestingly, the original title Barrie gave to the play of *Peter Pan* was *The Great White Father* (Birkin, *J. M. Barrie* 106) so it seems that Barrie envisaged Peter Pan as more than a symbol of youth or as a son (the Young Pretender to Hook's Old Pretender). However, Barrie also represents Peter Pan as a paternal figure. By having Peter Pan challenge his role as father to the Lost Boys – ' "It is only make-believe, isn't it, that I am their father?" ' (*Peter and Wendy* 161) – Barrie ably connects the two diverse depictions of Peter Pan intended from the outset. There is an interchange of pretences between child and adult and adult and child throughout *Peter Pan*. Ultimately neither the eternal child nor the mature adult gain through existing in their isolated states – they both lose in the end. Barrie's vision is therefore dystopian. The tragedy is that growing old and not growing old both result in losses. At the end of the play, instead of rejoicing in the fact that Peter Pan remains forever young, we lament it.

Through the ineptitude of adults, Peter Pan cries alone. He is sensitive to adults letting him down, exclaiming, 'don't cheat me mother Wendy, – I'm only a little boy' (*Peter Pan* 1.1.200). Here Barrie confers maternal responsibilities on Wendy, evoking Roland Barthes' depiction of 'the mother-as-child.' Carol Mavor suggests that, 'Wendy was a little mother who flew back to Neverland ... (despite her efforts not to grow) and grew too much for Peter's liking' (Mavor 5). The argument Mavor proposes is that Barrie was regressive, desiring to restrict the growth of children in order to preserve them as forever young.

Indeed Barrie parodies this in *Peter and Wendy* with the explanation that, when new lost children arrive at his underground home, Peter finds new trees for them to go up and down by, and instead of fitting the tree to them he makes them fit the tree (*Peter and Wendy* 133). In Peter Pan's efforts to fit each of the boys to trees, they remain fixed in size. In his desire to avoid categorization it seems Barrie rather hypocritically categorizes others. Wendy's longing for fixity is contrasted against the mermaids' elusiveness, when she exclaims, 'I did so want to catch a mermaid' (*Peter Pan* 3.1.20). Her closeness to adulthood is revealed in this impulsive remark since Barrie aligns fixity with adulthood. Fixity and adulthood are also aligned in Peter Pan's instruction to the grown up Wendy to ' "keep back, lady, no one is going to catch me and make me a man" ' (*Peter and Wendy* 217). The suggestion is that adults are not only fixed, but fix others. Adulthood for Barrie is typified by irreversibility and stagnation. This representation of adulthood is exemplified in Hook's desire to categorize Peter Pan. He enquires, ' "Vegetable? Mineral? Animal? Boy?" ' (*Peter and Wendy* 148) in his pursuit to identify Peter

Pan by type. Barrie realizes that the choice is to fix or be fixed which is significant because it reveals the negativity conventionally associated with adulthood, set in contrast to the freedom associated with childhood.

Barrie also subverts conventional associations with adulthood, representing them antithetically so that adults are regarded with suspicion and mistrust. Indeed Fiona McCulloch indicates that children's writers themselves may be regarded as performatively duplicitous by virtue of the fact that as adults they double and masquerade as children. She argues that children's writers authorize 'a fiction for children whose fundamental crux pivots upon the adult/child literary imbalance, necessitating a narrative deception of "playing double," a power game of distrust and disillusion' (McCulloch 66). When Hook appears nice, he is actually nasty. Barrie indicates, 'he was never more sinister than when he was most polite' (*Peter and Wendy* 115). Yet Barrie undermines complete categorization since he states that Hook is 'not wholly evil; he loved flowers (I have been told) and sweet music (he was himself no mean performer on the harpsichord)' (*Peter and Wendy* 181). In the play, this line reads, Hook is 'not wholly evil: he has a thesaurus in his cabin, and is no mean performer on the flute' (*Peter Pan* 4.1, stage direction preceding line 259). Surely, however, this does not compensate for his malicious behaviour. He is also depicted as being vulnerable: 'what really warps him is a presentiment that he is about to fail' (*Peter Pan* 4.1, stage direction preceding line 259) and this undermines the Edwardian era's representation of adults as being in control. Similarities between Captain Hook and Mr Darling are acknowledged by Barrie in his decision to have the same actor perform both roles and is revealed in their shared weaknesses.

Childhood was constructed in opposition to adulthood. If childhood is maintained in a form where children are represented as innocent and sentimental, then adults are represented as manipulators, corrupters, and exploiters of childhood and vice versa. Barrie was writing at a time when there had been a change in society's regard for childhood. Edwardians, unlike their predecessors, did not regard children as original sinners instead they regarded them as innocent. However this change in the construction of childhood also resulted in adults being regarded as corrupt and controlling. An important aspect of Barrie's contribution as a writer, and an important aspect of his representation of characters, is that he challenged boundaries and subverted convention in areas which he felt were misrepresented or misrepresentative. Barrie subverted categorizations by appearing to sympathize with them, thereby upholding the 'cult' of childhood and then, simultaneously, deconstructing them, thereby 'culling' childhood. It could be said that Barrie strove to 're-right,' to correct the construction that children are innocent, by destabilizing this concept. While appearing to reinforce categorizations between the adult and child, Barrie undermines them and covers his tracks by blending characteristics of the two. On other occasions, he explicitly subverts the social roles conventionally attributed to children and adults so that children are empowered and protect adults and adults are weakened. Peter Pan expresses frustration in being let down by adults. He:

> was so full of wrath against grown-ups who, as usual, were spoiling everything, that as soon as he got inside his tree he breathed intentionally quick short breaths at the rate of about five to the second. He did this because there was a saying in the Neverland that every time you breathe, a grown-up dies; and Peter was killing them off vindictively as fast as possible. (*Peter and Wendy* 168)

This serves to underline the fact that Barrie does not depict childhood sentimentally. Barrie has been regarded as a creator of sentimental, whimsical, and melodramatic novels and plays but this is a misconception. Lady Cynthia Asquith (Barrie's secretary and confidante) fervently believed that, far from being a sentimentalist, guilty of escapism, to her mind 'Barrie is not sentimental. The real sentimentalist refuses to face hard facts. Barrie does not. For all his reputed "softness" he is no escapist' (218). As Hollindale suggests, Barrie provides 'nostalgia armour-plated' (xxi).

The deconstruction of childhood seems ironic in *Peter Pan* – a work deemed to be seminal to children's literature and produced at a time when commercial companies were celebrating and commodifying childhood, packaging it in sentimental ways. As Rose explains:

> Hodder and Stoughton, who published *Peter Pan*, were not children's publishers, but Barrie was one of their most successful and heavily promoted writers, and they had their own publicity journal, *The Bookman*, which was started in 1891 ... *The Bookman* produced no less than seven portfolios and supplements on *Peter Pan*. The 1905 Christmas number, for example, with a Barrie photograph on the cover and a supplement of photographs from the play, had reached a 200 per cent premium on its original price by November 1906

(*Peter Pan* already a 'collector's item'). It was on the back of this that *Peter Pan in Kensington Gardens* was issued in the following year. (Rose 106–7)

It seems that

the heavy commercial promotion of *Peter Pan* becomes more than an incidental factor of its history. It reveals both how marketable the child was for the book trade, and the gap which could in fact hold between this reality and something which might finally reach its destination as literature for children. (Rose 106)

For the Edwardians, therefore, *Peter Pan* 'had very little to do with a child reader. Rather it illustrates just how far the child had become one of the chief fantasies – object of desire and investment – of the turn of the century publishing trade' (Rose 107).

Although there was a rising cult of childhood in the Edwardian era, the same consumer culture initiated a cull. Barrie was clearly aware that childhood was evolving at the time he was writing. He remarked, 'Children who were certainties in the old times have now become riddles' ('The Blot on Peter Pan' 88). In the Edwardian period, contradictory constructions of childhood and representations of children prevailed, some of which continue to this day. By exploring the liminal space between childhood and adulthood in *Peter Pan*, Barrie contributes to our awareness of the evolving nature of childhood and adulthood.

Barrie's contribution goes beyond this, however, in his creation of a character that symbolizes 'process.' Peter Pan can be regarded as a catalyst, as one who generates change but who remains in himself unchanged. The idea that Peter Pan symbolizes 'process' is borne out in the way that he is suspended between states. Barrie describes him as a 'betwixt and between' (*The Little White Bird* 186). Owing to his atemporality, Peter Pan is suspended. The death of childhood can be regarded figuratively as a mode of development and this is symbolized to great effect in Peter Pan. Peter Pan symbolizes death in a number of ways and indeed Susan Mansfield even goes so far as to suggest that Peter Pan 'is Death, who empties the nurseries like a plague' (2).

Childhood 'died' (or began to deconstruct) in the Edwardian era, not long after it was 'born' (or was constructed). Furthermore, the Edwardian society that invented the uniquely modern, Western construction of childhood is also responsible for its deconstruction through the implosion of hitherto inviolate categories. Instead of reaffirming and re-inscribing childhood, *Peter Pan* actively and inescapably undermined and deconstructed the concept of childhood to which it was heir.

Notes

1. The most authoritative version of Barrie's play, *Peter Pan or The Boy Who Would Not Grow Up*, was published for the first time in 1928. Barrie perpetually revised the play from the first performance staged in 1904 until this date.
2. In 1920, the final addition was made to *Peter Pan* when Barrie wrote his dedication to the play in readiness for the definitive version of the play published in 1928.

Works cited

Aller, Susan. *J. M. Barrie: The Magic Behind Peter Pan*. Minneapolis: Lerner, 1994.
Asquith, Cynthia. *Portrait of Barrie*. Edinburgh: James Barrie Publishers, 1954.
Barrie, J. M. *Margaret Ogilvy*. London: Hodder and Stoughton, 1896.
——. *Sentimental Tommy: The Story of His Boyhood*. London: Cassell, 1896.
——. *The Little White Bird*. London: Hodder and Stoughton, 1902.
——. 'The Blot on Peter Pan.' *The Treasure Ship: A Book of Prose and Verse*. Ed. Cynthia Asquith, London: S. W. Partridge, 1926. 82–100.
——. *The Greenwood Hat: A Memoir of James Anon 1885–1887*. London: Peter Davies, 1937.
——. *Peter and Wendy*. 1911. *Peter Pan in Kensington Gardens. Peter and Wendy*. Ed. Peter Hollindale. Oxford: Oxford University Press, 1991. 67–226.
——. *Peter Pan or The Boy Who Would Not Grow Up*. 1928. *Peter Pan and Other Plays*. Ed. Peter Hollindale. Oxford: Oxford University Press, 1995. 73–154.
Birkin, Andrew. *J. M. Barrie and the Lost Boys*. London: Constable, 1979.
——. 'Good Ideas of the Twentieth Century: Peter Pan and Sir James Matthew Barrie.' *Without Walls*, Channel 4, 15 June 1995.
Carpenter, Humphrey. *Secret Gardens: A Study of the Golden Age of Children's Literature*. London: Unwin, 1987, 170–87.
Coats, Karen. 'Child-Hating: Peter Pan in the Context of Victorian Hatred.' *A Children's Classic at 100: Peter Pan In and Out of Time*. Eds. Donna R. White and Anita Tarr. Oxford: The Scarecrow Press, 2006. 3–22.
Ferguson, Gillian. 'On the Never Never.' *The Scotsman* 27 December 1994: 11.
Freud, Sigmund. *Three Essays on the Theory of Sexuality*, 1905. Authorized translation by James Strachey. London: Imago, 1949.
Green, Roger Lancelyn. *Fifty Years of Peter Pan*. London: Peter Davies, 1954.
Hollindale, Peter. Introduction. *J. M. Barrie: Peter Pan and Other Plays*. Ed. Peter Hollindale. Oxford: Oxford University Press, 1995. vii–xxv.
Jack, Ronald Dyce Sadler. 'From Drama to Silent Film: The Case of Sir James Barrie.' *International Journal of Scottish Theatre*. 2:2 (December 2001). Accessed 5 September 2007, http://www.arts.gla.ac.uk/ScotLit/ASLS/ijost/Volume2_no2/2_jack_rds.htm.
Jenks, Chris. *Childhood*. London: Routledge, 1996.
Key, Ellen. *The Century of the Child*. [*Barnets århundrade*] Trans. Ellen Key. New York: Knickerbocker Press, 1909.

Linetski, Vadim. 'The Promise of Expression to the "Inexpressible child": Deleuze, Derrida and the Impossibility of Adult's Literature.' *Other Voices*. 1:3 (January 1999): 1–17. Accessed 5 September 2007, <http://www.english.upenn.edu/~ov/1.3/vlinetski/child.html>.

Mackail, Denis. *The Story of J. M. B.* (Sir James Barrie, Bart. O. M.). London: Peter Davies, 1941.

Mansfield, Susan. 'Haunted by the Lost Boys.' *The Scotsman*. 21 December 2001. Accessed 5 September 2007, <www.arts.scotsman.com/home/text_only.cfm?id=4801&type=news>.

Mavor, Carol. *Pleasures Taken: Performances of Sexuality and Loss in Victorian Photographs*. North Carolina: Duke University Press, 1996.

McCulloch, Fiona. ' "Playing Double": Performing Childhood in Treasure Island.' *Association of Scottish Literary Studies: Scottish Studies Review*. 4:2 (Autumn 2003): 66–81.

Nicol, Patricia. 'Barrie's Boys.' *The Sunday Times* (Scottish Supplement). 5 March 2000: 1–2.

Ormond, Leonee. *J. M. Barrie*. Edinburgh: Scottish Academic Press, 1987.

PBS. 'The First Golden Age: Short Bio: Sir James Barrie 1860–1937.' 2002. Accessed 5 September 2007, <http://www.pbs.org/wgbh/masterpiece/railway/age/barrie_bio.html>.

Rose, Jacqueline. *The Case of Peter Pan: or, The Impossibility of Children's Fiction*. Basingstoke: Macmillan, 1992.

Warner, Marina. *No Go the Bogeyman: Scaring, Lulling and Making Mock*. London: Chatto and Windus, 1998.

White, Donna R. and Tarr, Anita. *Children's Classic at 100: Peter Pan In and Out of Time*. Oxford: The Scarecrow Press, 2006.

Wullschläger, Jackie. *Inventing Wonderland: The Lives and Fantasies of Lewis Carroll, Edward Lear, J. M. Barrie, Kenneth Grahame and A. A. Milne*. London: Methuen, 1995.

Zipes, Jack. *Sticks and Stones: The Troublesome Success of Children's Literature from Slovenly Peter to Harry Potter*. London: Routledge, 2001.

4
Intangible Children: Longing, Loss, and the Edwardian Dream Child in J. M. Barrie's *The Little White Bird* and Rudyard Kipling's ' "They" '

Adrienne E. Gavin

> Nothing can be more splendid, he thought, than to have a little boy of your own.
>
> (J. M. Barrie, *The Little White Bird* 124)

It is often assumed that J. M. Barrie's *Peter Pan* (1904) was the founding fiction of the Edwardian literary cult of childhood, but Barrie's own novel *The Little White Bird* (1902) and Rudyard Kipling's short story ' "They" ' (1904) are among earlier Edwardian texts that reveal that the 'cult' was already thriving before Peter Pan landed on the stage to became its most enduring symbol. Dappled with longing for children lost or never born, who manifest fictionally as intangible dream children, *The Little White Bird* and ' "They" ' give early and intense impulse to the very Edwardian desire to capture children on the page. They also reflect the period's fictional foregrounding of relationships between child characters and bachelors or bachelor-like men.

Born in the 1860s, Barrie and Kipling by 1901 had each experienced the longing for or loss of children that permeates *The Little White Bird* and ' "They." ' Both were also noted writers whose fame would escalate further in the Edwardian years. Barrie had already published *Sentimental Tommy: The Story of His Boyhood* (1896) – 'one of the most inspired [novels] on childhood yet written' – and by '1902, his name was such a draw that more than one of his plays was often on in London at the same time' (Chaney 1, 1). He would soon achieve vicarious immortality through the phenomenal success of his play *Peter Pan* and its later novelization *Peter and Wendy* (1911). Kipling had achieved even greater prominence through works including several for or about children: the two *Jungle Books* (1894, 1895), *Stalky & Co.* (1899), *Kim* (1901), and *Just So Stories* (1902). In the ensuing Edwardian years he would write his most 'English' works of childhood, *Puck of Pook's Hill* (1906) and *Rewards and Fairies* (1910), and be awarded the 1907 Nobel Prize for literature.

Autobiographically inspired and using seemingly revelatory first-person narrators, *The Little White Bird* and ' "They" ' nevertheless avoid factualism in favour of supernatural realism. Ostensibly realist, these fictions are infused with supernatural or fantasy elements, in particular vividly imagined or ghostly dream children. Objects of intense emotional desire on the part of their percipients, these children have either never existed or are the ghosts of children who have died. That these intangible children are revealed supernaturally or through dream visions operates as a distancing mechanism by making the narrator's and writer's grief more expressible and more readable. It also serves a consolatory function in that the supernatural, like capturing a child in words, allows life to extend before birth and beyond death.

That two authors as prominent as Barrie and Kipling, early in the period, could write so intensely about longing for and losing children surely added impetus to, and even gave literary permission for, the obsession with childhood that Edwardian fiction so pervasively expresses. Certainly the period's literature granted particular licence to male expressions (characters' and authors') of longing for children, and was still portraying such masculine yearning in texts as late as Algernon Blackwood's *The Education of Uncle Paul* (1909) and *A Prisoner in Fairyland: (The Book That Uncle Paul Wrote)* (1913). The period's fiction, too, displays an abundant avuncularity: bachelor uncles or uncle-like characters repeatedly develop close relationships with children in works ranging in kind from Edith Nesbit's Bastable books to Henry de Vere Stacpoole's bestseller *The Blue Lagoon* (1908). Even non-fiction texts, such as Robert Baden-Powell's *Scouting for Boys* (1908), imply the centrality of relationships between children and bachelor/uncle type men. In his book of observations and advice on children, *The Twentieth Century Child* (1905), Edward H. Cooper claims the specialness of such territory:

> I have understood, from a proverb to that effect, that 'bachelors' wives and old maids' children' are objects of much scorn to the experienced married person and parent; but no one has ever said a word in condemnation of bachelors' children. (v)

The Little White Bird and ' "They" ' both focus on the specialness of 'bachelor's children.' Barrie's narrator is a confirmed bachelor, and, while Kipling's narrator is ultimately revealed to be a grieving parent (and therefore may not in fact be a bachelor), he is presented in a very bachelor-like way in that he makes no mention of wife or family, comes and goes as he chooses, and is 'to all appearances a bachelor' (Mason 204). Both narrators like, seek out, and have an excellent understanding of children and both know the games and toys that children enjoy and are attracted by. For each narrator, however, his longing for children and his special relationship with an 'intangible' child, from whom he realizes he must part, results in a rending of the heart that is like 'the very parting of spirit and flesh' (' "They" ' 264).

First serialized in *Scribner's Magazine* from August to November 1902, Barrie's *The Little White Bird* is in some ways one of the strangest works of fiction ever published. '[I]f there was ever a "queer" story written,' one contemporary reader observed, 'this is certainly entitled to first place' (I. W. V. BR12). Yet the novel's rich emphasis on childhood fantasy and play, its portrayal of a special bachelor–child friendship, and its eviscerating expression of a man's longing for his dream child, make it almost the normative text of its times. Early in the period it clearly expressed, and surely helped swell, the Edwardian craving for childhood. A 'colossal best-seller' (Birkin 95), it sold 20,000 copies in Britain alone within a week of its book publication ('Among the English Authors' BR10). Because Peter Pan makes his first appearance in the novel, too, it is a direct precursor of the epitome of the Edwardian cult of childhood: Barrie's *Peter Pan*.

While Peter Pan is not the central focus here, his centrality to the period's depiction of childhood mandates some comment about his role in *The Little White Bird* where he is a more tragic figure than the stage Peter. The subsequent popularity of Barrie's play meant, too, that the six-chapter Peter Pan section of *The Little White Bird* – an interpolated narrative of about one-third of the novel's length – was extracted and published in 1906 as a stand-alone text. Titled *Peter Pan in Kensington Gardens* and illustrated by Arthur Rackham, this was one of the lavish gift books produced for or about children in the Edwardian period.

The Peter Pan section of *The Little White Bird* reveals how Peter came to live with the birds and fairies in Kensington Gardens. '[A]ll the children in our part of London were once birds in the Kensington Gardens,' the narrator relates, and

> the reason there are bars on nursery windows and a tall fender by the fire
> is because very little people sometimes forget that they have no longer
> wings, and try to fly away through the window or up the chimney. (20)

Seven-day-old Peter Pan does forget and flies back to the Gardens where he lives on the birds' island in the Serpentine, becoming a never-aging, flightless 'Betwixt-and-Between': part human, part bird (104). Having procrastinated over returning to his grieving mother, he discovers when he tries to do so that it is too late; his mother is sleeping peacefully in his nursery 'with her arm round another little boy' (127). After 'beat[ing] his little limbs against the iron bars' of the window and crying out for his mother he flies sobbing back to Kensington Gardens (127). There he remains forever, every night sailing from the island to the Gardens where 'he plays exactly as real children play. At least he thinks so, and it is one of the pathetic things about him that he often plays quite wrongly' (114).

The Peter Pan section of the novel echoes in a more fantastic way the loss of and longing for children seen in the main narrative. Glimpsed in Peter's mother's mourning after his disappearance, it is seen more starkly in Peter's self-defined role in the Gardens. Vaguely remembering that he was once human, he is 'especially kind to the house-swallows when they visit the island, for house-swallows are the spirits of little children who have died' (151). He also digs graves and erects tombstones for children who die after being locked in the park or 'fall[ing] unnoticed from their perambulators' (152). 'But how strange for parents,' the narrator comments, 'when they hurry into the Gardens at the opening of the gates looking for their lost one, to find the sweetest little tombstone instead. I do hope that Peter is not too ready with his spade. It is all rather sad' (153).

The narrative interruption created by the Peter Pan section was not to all contemporary tastes, as a reviewer commented during the novel's serialization[1]:

> It is perhaps a comparatively small blemish … that the long digression … which relates to Peter Pan … should seem maundering and call a halt to one's hitherto unbroken rhapsody of praise … [It] is full of delicate fancy, but as surely it tires the reader a little and makes him hope, when he has finished this installment, that Peter Pan has fled from the scene of the story forever. ('Mr. Barrie's Fancies' BR16)

Peter Pan did anything but flee forever; as protagonist of an eponymous culture text he became the most enduring character of Edwardian fiction. He did, however, disappear from Barrie's novel although his status as an intangible 'forever child' and his connection with the loss of children mirrors the thematic concerns of the main narrative.[2]

Peter Pan's story may be 'all rather sad' but so is the longing for a child expressed by the narrator of the novel as a whole, Captain W—, an ex-military bachelor in his forties who regularly spends time in his Pall Mall club and knows that he is regarded as 'among the whimsical fellows' (64). Overtly, *The Little White Bird* is the story of Captain W—'s relationship with David A—, the child of a young ex-governess/artist couple. Covertly, the novel is about Captain W—'s longing for his own imagined son and dream child, Timothy. Timothy is the little white bird of the title, a dream child who can never be born: for 'the little white birds are the birds that never have a mother' (50).[3]

Barrie's own biographical longings and losses have been widely rehearsed: the death of his mother's favourite son David aged 13, Barrie's desperate attempts to replace his lost elder brother in his mother's affection, his own longing for children and childless marriage which ended in divorce, his close friendship with the five Llewelyn-Davies boys, his guardianship of them from 1910 following their parents' deaths, and his own child-like, not-wishing-to-grow-up qualities. As Jacqueline Rose writes, *The Little White Bird* is 'a biographical landmine in relation to Barrie himself' (23). In its primary narrative the novel is regarded generally as a fictionalization of Barrie's relationship with the young George Llewelyn Davies (Birkin 42; Chaney 160).

In its complex unstable narrative and fluid mixing of fantasy and realism the novel is almost a premodernist example of postmodernism. The narrator's voice varies from whimsical embitterment to poignant longing for a child; from spiteful jealousy of David's mother to gruff kindness towards both his parents. The narrative flickers between fantasy stories as told to children, a history for David of his relationship with Captain W—, an account of what the narrator and David do together, and invective directed at David's mother, Mary. Proud that he has 'never in [his] life addressed one word' to Mary (2), Captain W— nevertheless, with her knowledge, develops a close friendship with David and, in ways variously humorous and vindictive, battles with her for the allegiance of her son.

Through his voyeuristic intervention in the relationship of David's parents-to-be, Captain W— almost breeds David at a distance as his surrogate son. He yearns both for an absolute 'right' to David and for a child who is his own in a way the already-parented David never can be. When David is born Captain W— invents his own imaginary baby, Timothy, but his jealousy of real fatherhood and fears that he does not sound authentically paternal are provoked when David's father asks after Timothy: 'I...listened coldly while he told me what David did when you said his toes were pigs going to market or returning from it... [He] knew so much more about babies than is fitting for men to know, that I paled before him' (41). Desperate to maintain the fiction that he has his own child, he answers David's father's inquiries about 'how Timothy slept, how he woke up, how he fell off again, what we put in his bath' (44) by describing the habits of his St Bernard (named like Barrie's own) Porthos for whom he buys children's toys. Like Timothy and David, Porthos serves as a surrogate child for Captain W— and functions also as a useful attractant to real children on daily walks in Kensington Gardens.

Realizing that the difficulties of keeping up the fiction of Timothy may prevent him from developing a real relationship with David, Captain W— decides that Timothy must die so that he can send David the baby things his parents cannot afford with the excuse that he no longer needs them. Mary, however, is not fooled and writes to him showing 'she knew all... and that there never had been a Timothy' (62).

The killing off of his dream child makes Timothy very real to Captain W— and he experiences profound loss: 'I was loth to see him go. I seem to remember carrying him that evening to the window with uncommon tenderness... and telling him with not unnatural bitterness that he had got to leave me because another child was in need of all his pretty things' (50). He grieves over not sharing Timothy's childhood:

> I wished (so had the phantasy of Timothy taken possession of me) that before he went he could have played once in the Kensington Gardens, and have ridden on the fallen trees, calling gloriously to me to look; that he could have sailed one paper galleon on the Round Pond; fain would I have had him chase one hoop a little way down the laughing avenues of childhood... I think he knew my longings, and said with a boy-like flush that the reason he never did these things was not that he was afraid, for he would have loved to do them all, but because he was not quite like other boys; and, so saying, he let go my finger and faded from before my eyes into another and golden ether; but I shall ever hold that had he been quite like other boys there would have been none braver than my Timothy. (50)

With the intangible Timothy lost, Captain W— concentrates on his relationship with the tangible David, and by the time David is three is 'seeing [him] once at least every week, his mother, who remained culpably obtuse to my sinister design, having instructed Irene [David's nurse] that I was to be allowed to share him with her' (82–3). Captain W—'s 'sinister design' is to supplant Mary in her son's affections: 'to burrow under [her] influence with the boy, expose her to him in all her vagaries, take him utterly from her and make him mine' (81).

His relationship with David brings Captain W— many joys. He plays games with David, tells him stories, and experiences 'peculiar pleasure' (12) when David accidentally calls him father or when shopkeepers assume David is his son: 'I am always in two minds then, to linger that we may have more of it, and to snatch him away before he volunteers the information, "He is not really my father"' (12). The relationship, however, also causes him pain by reminding him of the longing at the core of his life.

One of the most profound, and from modern perspectives problematic, chapters of the novel involves the anticipated '"tremendous adventure"' of David spending the night at Captain W—'s (154). When David arrives, Captain W— tries to conceal both his inexperience of day-to-day parenting and his thrill at having a tangible child to tend to. When it is time for bed he takes David to his bedroom, which has 'an extra bed in it tonight, very near my own' and a 'new mantelshelf ornament: a tumbler of milk, with a biscuit on top of it, and a chocolate riding on the biscuit' (155). He takes off David's boots ready for his bath:

> with all the coolness of an old hand, and then I placed him on my knee and removed his blouse. This was a delightful experience, but I think I remained wonderfully calm until I came somewhat too suddenly to his little braces, which agitated me profoundly.
> I cannot proceed in public with the disrobing of David. (155)

What agitates Captain W— so profoundly about David's braces might readily be assumed to be paedophiliac impulse, but this risks overlooking that the *little* braces may instead trigger a moment when the grief of longing for his own child threatens to overcome him. Yet the chapter raises further questions. Reassuring David who has woken frightened in the night, Captain W— asks '"And there is nothing else you want?"' and when David tells him '"I don't take up very much room"' (157), responds:

> 'Why, David…do you want to come into my bed?'
> 'Mother said I wasn't to want it unless you wanted it first,' he
>   squeaked.
> 'It is what I have been wanting all the time,' said I. (157)

David flings himself into bed with Captain W— who reports:

> For the rest of the night he lay on me and across me, and sometimes
> his feet were at the bottom of the bed and sometime on the pillow,
> but he always retained possession of my finger, and occasionally he
> woke me to say that he was sleeping with me. I had not a good night.
> I lay thinking.
>
> Of this little boy, who, in the midst of his play while I undressed
> him, had suddenly buried his head on my knees ... Of David's dripping
> little form in the bath, and how when I essayed to catch him he had
> slipped from my arms like a trout.
>
> Of how I had stood by the open door listening to his sweet breath-
> ing, had stood so long that I forgot his name and called him
> Timothy. (157)

Critics including James Kincaid and Jacqueline Rose have discussed
the conscious or subconscious paedophiliac impulses in adult-child
'friendships' and the eroticising or voyeuristic qualities more generally
of writing or reading the child. Such readings on one level become
inescapable after Freud and in light of current cultural alarms over child
safety. Today's default assumption suspects a single man who desires to
be very close to a child of being sexually rather than paternally inclined:
a paedophiliac predator rather than a father *manqué*. Yet this was not
the general Edwardian view, nor does it reflect the novel's expression of
profound longing for a child of one's own. Similarly, David's clutching
of Captain W—'s 'finger' might be read as symbolically phallic, but this
risks ignoring that Captain W—'s finger was the last touchpoint he had
with his own child Timothy as he 'died': '[Timothy] let go my finger and
faded from before my eyes into another and golden ether' (50).
As Andrew Nash points out, 'the suggestion in this chapter of a
paedophiliac desire seems not to have been confronted until Grahame
Greene [in 1969] published a mock-satirical article in the *Spectator*
entitled "Regina v Sir James Barrie"' (213 n. 157). By contrast, it was the
purity of the novel that contemporary reviewers highlighted: 'There
is something so youthful about [*The Little White Bird*], so fresh and
unsullied ... One feels that the heart of Mr. Barrie must be pure, indeed,
to fathom the depth of purity in a baby's soul' ('Holiday Books' BR6). 'If
a book exists which contains more knowledge and more love of children,
we do not know it' stated the *Times Literary Supplement*, terming the
novel: 'whimsical, sentimental, profound, ridiculous Barrie-ness; utterly
impossible, yet absolutely real ... one of the most charming books ever

written... To analyse its merits and defects... would be to vivisect a fairy' ([Child] 339).

Painfully aware that David is not his own, Captain W—'s sleep is not calm. His night brings the tangible closeness to a child for which he yearns, but also stirs his aching longing for fatherhood. Some of this pain he soon expresses in rancorous spite towards David's mother: 'When Mary does anything that specially annoys me I send her an insulting letter. I once had a photograph taken of David being hanged on a tree. I sent her that. You can't think of all the subtle ways of grieving her I have' (158).

He longs for his dream child Timothy, but knows that as David grows up he, too, may disappear: ' "I work very hard to retain that little boy's love; but I shall lose him soon; even now I am not what I was to him; in a year or two at longest... David will grow out of me" ' (171). Captain W— here expresses an aspect of the pervasive Edwardian sense of the loss of childhood. While Victorian fictions portray child characters as beings who must and should grow up and generally show them doing so (except for the numerous child deaths used for pathos), Edwardian texts are interested in depicting the child *as* child. More overtly and more metafictionally than most works of the period (although Blackwood's *The Education of Uncle Paul* and *A Prisoner in Fairyland* come close), *The Little White Bird* demonstrates the omnipresent Edwardian attempt to capture 'forever children' in fiction.

Captain W— himself increasingly uses fiction in his attempts to capture David from his mother and from time. His schemes fail because both tasks are impossible, just as fiction cannot ultimately compete with the real and real children cannot truly be captured in fiction. However full of joy children themselves are in Edwardian fiction, there is almost always, as *The Little White Bird* particularly evidences, an inherent textual awareness that fictional children can only ever be lesser simulacra of living ones. This awareness, like the knowledge that children cannot 'forever' be, is integral to the sense of loss and longing that drifts though Edwardian fictions of childhood.

Captain W— feels 'distressed and lonely, and rather bitter' (183) when David, aged five, becomes friends with seven-year-old Oliver Bailey. Oliver is a further threat to his goal of emotional centrality in David's life: 'For years I had been fighting Mary for David, and had not wholly failed... was I now to be knocked out so easily by a seven-year-old? I reconsidered my weapons, and I fought Oliver and beat him' (183).

The weapon he uses is fiction. Telling the boys stories about what they would do on a desert island makes them 'as faithful to [him] as

[his] coat-tails' (183). When David reveals one day that, like Oliver, he is to start at Pilkington's school when he is eight and will then no longer play in Kensington Gardens Captain W—, pained, turns his weapon on David by finishing the desert island story 'abruptly in a very cruel way' (188). Describing the boys ten years later revisiting 'the wrecked island of their childhood' (189), he casts David as a young man who cannot remember him more than as ' "a man with a dog. I think he used to tell me stories in the Kensington Gardens, but I forget all about him; I don't remember even his name" ' (189). Stung by the ending David cries ' "It's not true…it's a lie!…I shan't never forget you, father" ' (189). This assurance gives Captain W— pleasure, but he tells David:

> 'You will forget, David, but there was once a boy who would have remembered.'
>
> 'Timothy?' said he at once. He thinks Timothy was a real boy, and he is very jealous of him. He turned his back to me, and stood alone and wept passionately…You may be sure I begged his pardon, and made it all right with him, and had him laughing and happy again before I let him go. But nevertheless what I said was true. David is not my boy, and he will forget. But Timothy would have remembered. (189)

Captain W—'s longing for a child of his own lies at the heart of the novel and at the base of his attempts 'to be even with' Mary over her powers of motherhood (193). When David tells him that his sister Barbara is coming, Captain W— 'conceive[s]' his 'final triumph over Mary' (193). Knowing that Mary has thought of writing a book called 'The Little White Bird,' he is convinced 'that the white bird was the little daughter Mary would fain have had…and so long as she had the modesty to see that she could not have one, I sympathised with her deeply' (194). ' "She will never be able to write it," ' he tells David. ' "She has not the ability. Tell her I said that" ' (195).

Himself the author of 'a little volume on Military tactics' (193), Captain W— believes he has found the ultimate 'means of exulting over' Mary by writing the book that she has indeed put aside (195). His plan is that 'when, in the fulness of time, she held her baby on high, implying that she had done a big thing, I was to hold up the book. I venture to think that such a devilish revenge was never before planned and carried out' (195). Three weeks after Barbara's birth, he exultantly writes a dedication to Mary in his completed 'The Little White Bird' claiming that in abandoning her book and instead having a baby: 'you chose the lower road, and contended yourself with obtaining the Bird.

May I point out ... that in the meantime I am become the parent of the Book? To you the shadow, to me the substance' (201).

Captain W— and Mary now meet for the first time and Captain W— tells her that in producing her baby daughter she has ' "not got the great thing," ' the book that she ' "craved for most of all" ' (206). He is wrong, she tells him: ' "it is I who have the substance and you who have the shadow, as you know very well" ' (206). He is also mistaken about her book, she reveals: ' "It was never of my little white bird I wanted to write ... It was of your little white bird ... it was of a little boy whose name was Timothy" ' (207). After reading his book – which is metafictionally Barrie's *The Little White Bird* – Mary rightly observes ' "How wrong you are in thinking this book is about me and mine, it is really all about Timothy" ' (207).

As Nash suggests, inventing Timothy gives the narrator 'the sublimated emotion of paternity he so desires in real life' (Nash xiv), yet the presence of David 'continually reminds [him] of the superior claims of reality' over fantasy (Nash xiv). Neither constructing nor 'killing' his intangible 'forever child' Timothy quells Captain W—'s desire for his own child. He can also neither supercede Mary in David's life nor prevent David from growing up except by capturing him in his book.

'[A]s *The Little White Bird* so clearly demonstrates, there are only two ways of [having a child who could last for ever] – having the child die early or, alternatively, writing the child down' (Rose 25). In *The Little White Bird* Barrie and Captain W— attempt to write the child down: to keep it preserved, connected to the adult, and child-like. Although not in such a metafictional way, Kipling in his story also attempts to write the child down, but for both Kipling and his narrator ' "They" ' also crucially revolves around a child who 'dies early.'

Like *The Little White Bird*, Kipling's ' "They" ' was published initially in *Scribner's Magazine*, appearing in August 1904, four months before *Peter Pan* was first performed. 1904 was a year ripe with literary awareness of childhood: a *New York Times* reviewer as early as July terming 'the present "the children's hour" in literature' ('Topics' BR477). Reviewing Frances Hodgson Burnett's novel *In the Closed Room* (1904) – in which a girl spends time with a ghost child before she dies herself – the *Times Literary Supplement* commented: 'We trust that a fashion for supernatural stories of children is not setting in; but it is, of course, always dangerous when a man of genius writes anything as original as "They" ' ([Lucas] 413). Henry James's *The Turn of the Screw* (1898) was fresh in memory, but the Edwardian period saw a 'remarkable eruption of ghostly tales' together with the 'intensively subjectivist tendency' in fiction seen in both Barrie and Kipling's texts (Sullivan 2, 114).

Usually read as reflecting his grief over the 1899 death of his six-year-old daughter Josephine, '"They"' is one of Kipling's most 'laceratingly personal' stories (Mallett 137). The 'They' of the story's title are children: the spirits of dead children who, as the story's prefatory poem 'The Return of the Children' implies, have begged to leave a Christian heaven of 'harps' and 'crowns' and 'dove-winged' cherubs to return merrily home (242). The home to which these intangible children return is 'the House Beautiful' (254), a perfect country house set in an idyllic garden of fountains, hedges, and topiaried horsemen and peacocks. Approached through ancient woods, the house is in a hidden part of the county, which the bachelor-like male narrator, seemingly drawn there by fate, discovers while out exploring in his motor car.

The story recounts the narrator's three visits to this place with which he is enraptured. It is a place '"out of the world"' (245) in terms of geographical remoteness, chronological lack of modernity, and super-natural otherworldliness. On each visit he glimpses the children and spends time with the house's presiding presence, Miss Florence, a blind woman who loves and longs for children but has '"neither borne nor lost"' children of her own (263). In the gardens, the woods, and the house itself, the blind woman hears the children and calls them to her but she cannot see them and does not always get the response she seeks. The narrator also hears the children and has fleeting visions of them. Like Miss Florence he wants to coax these seemingly shy children to come to him. It is only near the very end of the story, when his mind is briefly distracted from thinking about the children that he feels one of them kiss his palm, just as his dead daughter used to do. Only then does he understand what Miss Florence and the local people who walk in the woods with the children know: the children are ghosts of sons and daughters lost.

Like *The Little White Bird*'s childhood of stories and adventures in Kensington Gardens, the childhood of '"They"' is idyllic and character-istically Edwardian. It is a summer-country-house childhood of freedom, companions, a beautiful garden to play in, ancient woods to explore, and a rambling house of toys and hiding nooks which '"must have been made for children"' (248). Utterly English, utterly safe, utterly upper-middle-class, it is a world of 'the utterly happy chuckle of a child absorbed in some light mischief' (245), of children '"off together on their own affairs"' (251) or 'frolicking like squirrels' (253). The story's consolatory vision is that children from any class may spend their afterlife in this English heaven on earth.

Typically of Edwardian fiction (*The Little White Bird* is an exception here) the general focus is not on an individual child but, as the title emphasizes, on plural children: 'They.' Also typically, these children display autonomy and agency and exist in a world apart from adults. The word 'they' emphasizes their otherness in that they are not living, but also in that they are not adults. Highly elusive and only fleetingly seen or heard, these intangible children engage with adults only as and when they choose and usually keep themselves '"at a distance"' (245). The narrator only glimpses the children or 'see[s] them with the tail of [his] eye' (253). Apart from Miss Florence, whose blindness is accompanied by a kind of extra-sensory perception, it is only those who have lost a child who can see or hear – and not fear – the children. Almost every adult in the story is a bereaved parent: some have accepted their loss; others like the narrator are facing it; for one it is freshly raw; and Miss Florence grieves over not loss of, but not having, children.

When Miss Florence asks the narrator during their first conversation if he has seen and heard the children, he reveals himself as someone who understands childhood ways by saying '"if I know anything of children, one of them's having a beautiful time by the fountain yonder. Escaped, I should imagine"' (245). When she asks if he is '"fond of children?"' (245), he 'g[ives] her one or two reasons why [he] did not altogether hate them' (245). The first person he sees at the house is 'A child [who] appeared at an upper window,' who he thinks 'wave[s] a friendly hand. But it was to call a companion, for presently another bright head showed' (244). Repeatedly, fleetingly, he notices this girl as he discusses with Miss Florence whether the faces of the dead can be seen in dreams. Throughout the story he glimpses children as the bereaved do, seeing the loved one in flashes and glances everywhere. This echoes what Kipling's father wrote of Kipling's visions of his own lost daughter:

> The house and garden are full of the lost child and poor Rud told his mother how he saw her when a door opened, when a space was vacant at table, coming out of every green dark corner of the garden, radiant – and heart breaking. (quoted in Carrington 437)

'"Remember…if you are fond of them you will come again"' (248), Miss Florence tells the narrator as he departs after his first visit, and it is the children, not Miss Florence, that he returns to see. Needing to repair his car near the woods on his second visit, he tries to tempt the children to him:

> I made a mighty serious business of my repairs and a glittering shop of my repair kit, spanners, pump, and the like, which I spread out orderly upon a rug. It was a trap to catch all childhood, for on such a day, I argued, the children would not be far off. (250)

Listening to the woods, he thinks he can hear 'the tread of small cautious feet' (250), but the children do not usher forth. Like Captain W— with his toys and stories, he tries to attract the children to him: 'I rang my bell in an alluring manner, but the feet fled, and I repented, for to a child a sudden noise is very real terror' (250).

Miss Florence, too, as she frequently does, tries to call the children to her and recognizes that the narrator has arranged his tools '"like a playing shop!"' (250). When he expresses hope that the children might on his next visit know him well enough '"to let [him] play with them – as a favour"' (254), she tells him '"It isn't a matter of favour but of right"' (254). It is unclear to him at this stage that 'right' means the right of a parent to reconnect with a dead child, but the issue of 'rights' in connection with children concerns Miss Florence deeply, just as it has Barrie's narrator.

Like Captain W— Miss Florence has longed desperately for children and knows that some people regard her as peculiar. As she shows the narrator on his third visit, her house has been made ready for children with toys and infant furniture, but to him it seems like a house not waiting for children to arrive but one that children have just left. This reflects their inverse sense of childhood: his that children can disappear suddenly through death and hers that one day her children may come. Both are about to make a connection with the children that is described using the term 'triumphant.' Miss Florence cries *'triumphantly'* when, like the narrator, she hears the 'rustle of a frock and the patter of feet' (260, emphasis added). Crying out '"Children, oh, children! Where are you?"' (260), she embarks with the narrator on a game of hide-and-seek with the children, but they are 'always mocked by [their] quarry' (260).

When the narrator and Miss Florence go into the Hall for tea, he at last sees the children hiding behind a screen and decides 'to force them to come forward later by the simple trick, which children detest, of pretending not to notice them' (260). When a tenant farmer comes to speak with Miss Florence the narrator asks whether he should leave and she tells him '"Certainly not. You have the right. He hasn't any children"' (261). '"Ah, the children!" I said, and slid my low chair back till it nearly touched the screen that hid them. "I wonder whether they'll come out for me"' (261). When his mind drifts away from the children for a moment, he feels his hand taken by a child's hands: 'So at last I had *triumphed*' he states (263, emphasis added):

> The little brushing kiss fell in the centre of my palm – as a gift on which the fingers were, once, expected to close: as the all-faithful half-reproachful signal of a waiting child not used to neglect even when grown-ups were busiest – a fragment of the mute code devised very long ago. (263)

'Then I knew,' he writes. His dead daughter is here. 'And it was as though I had known from the first day when I looked across the lawn at the high window' (263).

As with Miss Florence and Captain W— (who describes his plan to write 'The Little White Bird' as 'conceiv[ing] my final *triumph* over Mary' [193, emphasis added]), Kipling's narrator's triumph is Pyrrhic and draped in sorrow. Like Captain W— lying awake at night with David or realizing his book is merely 'the shadow,' Kipling's narrator and Miss Florence experience moments when the magnitude of their loss and longing is brought home to them. The narrator's comes when, after sitting in silence following the kiss, he listens to Miss Florence's expression of her longing for children. 'I looked at the broad brick hearth,' he states 'saw, through tears I believe, that there was no unpassable iron on or near it, and bowed my head' (264). This 'unpassable iron' is usually taken to refer to the folk belief that cold iron prevents the passage of ghosts and spirits, thus the lack of iron in the hearth reveals to the narrator that these children are indeed ghosts who have been welcomed into the house. Yet it might also be read as reflecting the narrator's realization that there are no real children here who need to be kept safe from flames, or that children who had been here have had no unpassable iron to prevent them from flying away like Peter Pan. Whichever meaning brings profoundly home to the narrator that there are no living children here.[4] He knows at heart that the child who kissed him is not his real daughter just as Captain W— knows that Timothy is not his real son; they are idealized visions of what is most longed for.

Miss Florence's need to believe is acute. She tells the narrator that the toys in the house had initially been part of her make believe about having children, but that then the children had actually come and she has heard them. Her initial elation turns to envy, however, when the Butler's wife, Mrs Madden, tells her that she has seen her dead daughter, and Miss Florence realizes that these children are not hers by right and can never really be hers at all. She cannot see them not only because she is blind, but because, unlike dead children who can be glimpsed in memory or dream, her children have never existed. ' "I have no right, you know – no other right. I have neither borne nor lost – neither borne nor lost!" ' she tells the bereft narrator (263).

The notion of 'neither bearing nor losing' is expressed earlier in the story by a local woman whose grandchild has died and who reports that her grieving daughter is walking in the woods (with her ghost child) which opens the heart: ' "Dat's where losin' and bearin' comes so alike in de long run, we do say" ' (258). Losing and bearing children opens the heart she claims, but Miss Florence's heart already seems open. She tells the narrator that the children have come

> because I loved them so ... *That* was why it was, even from the first – even before I knew that they – they were all I should ever have. And I loved them so! ... They came because I loved them – because I needed them. I – I must have made them come. (263)

Her love has drawn the children to her, but what she really longs for is to be loved *by* a child. Like Captain W— with his longing visions of Timothy, she realizes this will never be because the only way to be loved in that blind way by a child is to be that child's parent: to bear a child or lose a child who longs to return to you. ' "Oh, you *must* bear or lose," she sa[ys] piteously' to the narrator. ' "There is no other way – and yet they love me. They must! Don't they?" ' (264). Throughout the story she projects her desire onto the children. When she asks the narrator on his first visit to drive his car around so that the children can see it she asks if she can ride in it because ' "They'll like it better if they see me" ' (246). Getting into the car she calls ' "Children, oh, children! Look and see what's going to happen" ' (246) in a voice the narrator states 'would have drawn lost souls from the Pit, for the yearning that underlay its sweetness' (246). She asks him to listen with her for the children but hearing nothing says ' "Oh, unkind!" ... weariedly' (246). Later she corrects herself: ' "It was wrong of me to say that. They are really fond of me. It's the only thing that makes life worth living – when they're fond of you, isn't it? I daren't think what the place would be without them" ' (246).

Like Captain W— she knows that she has no 'right' to the children of others, yet she yearns for the children to claim her, to love her as they would love a mother. At root, like the return of the dead, it is an impossible dream but one which extreme longing makes virtually incarnate in the intangible children – the Timothys and 'Theys' – of Edwardian fiction.

Kipling's narrator and Miss Florence handle the overwhelming emotion provoked by their sense of the children's presence in different ways. The narrator resolves that 'though [it] was like the very parting of spirit and flesh,' he will never return to the house to seek his child again (264). Miss Florence dwells in her love for the children and keeps her hunger alive that one day she will receive a sign that her love for them is requited. The same procreative cruelty that forces Captain W— to recognize his book as the shadow and Mary's new baby as the prize and which keeps him sleepless the night David stays, means that it is Kipling's narrator, not Miss Florence, who receives the tangible kiss that would have given her in her blindness all she yearned to 'see.' Kipling's narrator, who has fathered and lost a tangible child, has the 'right' to dwell in visions but chooses to move away from that pain. For Captain W— and Miss Florence the intangible is all there is and their longing remains. Vicarious parenting, by sharing the children of others or by writing the child down, serves to give them some solace, but at core their sorrow is permanent; they know at heart that their children are only visions and shadows.

It is worth noting as an aside that although '"They"' does express, through the inclusion of Miss Florence, female longing for children, the story is essentially that of the bachelor-like male narrator's attempts to connect with the ghost children and his emotionally profound experience with one of those children. Like *The Little White Bird*, Kipling's story privileges the bachelor–child relationship and in doing so also reflects a common corollary of that emphasis in Edwardian fiction: the expunging (or attempted expunging) of mother figures.

Mothers in Edwardian fiction are notable for their absence. Made absent variously through death, through narrative elisions that remove them from the story, through glib statements of idealization that explain them away in any real sense, they are also often marginalized by the narrative dominance given to relationships between children and uncle/bachelor-like characters. Edwardian texts such as *The Little White Bird*, '"They,"' or W. H. Hudson's *A Little Boy Lost* (1905), seem able to accept and present female characters who long for children but once women become mothers the texts start to retaliate. Such 'retaliation' may be subtle; the narrator of '"They,"' for example, simply makes no mention at all of the presumably also grieving mother of his child.

Or such retaliation may be overt: in *The Little White Bird* and works such as D. H. Lawrence's *Sons and Lovers* (1913) the attack on the mother becomes a central aspect of the narrative. The subtle approach gives more success to the uncle-bachelor character in that his relationship to children remains dominant in the story. Overt attacks on mothers generally fail because, as in *The Little White Bird* and the various incarnations of *Peter Pan*, attempts to expunge the mother actually accord her a narrative attention which confirms rather than denies her maternal power. Even on the cusp of seeming, gleeful victory over the mother comes the heartbreaking realization that it cannot be won. For bachelors like Captain W— (who has thought on the night of David's birth ' "Why should it all fall on her? What is the man that he should be flung out into the street in this terrible hour? You have not been fair to the man" ' [32]) realize that they can neither create their own child nor replace the mothers of others.

In their treatment of childhood, *The Little White Bird* and ' "They" ' chronicle some of the deepest emotions humans can experience: longing for or grief over a child. Two of the earliest and most famous Edwardians to write of childhood in this way, Barrie and Kipling created some of the period's most haunting fiction. A sense of childhood's intangibility, however, also pervades Edwardian fiction more widely. Collectively, Edwardian authors reveal childhood as a world apart: untouchable, unreachable, unattainable, something with which it is a 'triumph' to connect. Like Barrie and Kipling's narrators, writers of Edwardian fiction also endeavour, in some cases desperately, to capture childhood and 'forever children' within their pages.

Intangible children could be kept forever within the pages of fiction, but tangible children could be lost. For post-Edwardians part of the poignancy of reading these two texts is knowing that for their writers loss, longing, and children would again fuse. Barrie's own longing for children was eased by his guardianship of the Llewelyn Davies boys from 1910, but this came only through the tragic deaths of the boys' parents. Tragedy would strike further; on 8 April 1915, the *New York Times* reported that 'The original David of The Little White Bird,' Barrie's 'adopted son' George Llewellyn Davies, had been killed in action in Flanders, aged 21 ('War Takes Barrie's David' 1). On 19 May 1921 Barrie would lose a second son when 20-year old Michael Llewelyn Davies drowned with a friend at Oxford – a possible suicide (Birkin 291). Five months after Barrie lost George, Kipling lost his only son, 18-year old John, who was reported missing at the Battle of Loos on 27 September 1915.

Notes

1. In its serialization only four of the Peter chapters (chapters 13–16) were included, making the focus on Peter shorter and darker (Nash 3). The serial version left him flying sobbing back to Kensington Gardens.
2. The serialization suggests, more than the book version does, 'that Timothy and Peter Pan are one and the same' (Nash xv).
3. W. H. Hudson's *A Little Boy Lost* (1905) also makes use of the image of a bird with white colouring in connection with an unborn child who is later lost to his mother.
4. A connection between intangible ghost children and hearths is also seen in E. F. Benson's story 'How Fear Departed the Long Gallery' (1911) in which twin toddlers who have been murdered and burnt in a fireplace return to haunt the long gallery of a house. Initially causing death and other injury to their percipients, they become friendly ghosts when one woman welcomes them with pity for their plight. Other welcome ghost children are seen in Algernon Blackwood's stories 'Clairvoyance' (1911), which contains longed-for infant ghosts who give solace to a childless male narrator and 'The Attic' (1912), which offers a consolatory vision of a child ghost to a mother and uncle.

Works cited

'Among the English Authors and Publishers – Latest Announcements.' *New York Times* 15 November 1902: BR10.
Barrie, J. M. *The Little White Bird.* 1902. *Farewell Miss Julie Logan: A Barrie Omnibus.* Ed. Andrew Nash. Edinburgh: Canongate, 2000. 1–215.
Birkin, Andrew. *J. M. Barrie and the Lost Boys.* 2003. New Haven and London: Yale University Press, 2005.
Carrington, Charles. *Rudyard Kipling: His Life and Work.* Rev ed. London: Macmillan, 1978.
Chaney, Lisa. *Hide-And-Seek With Angels: A Life of J. M. Barrie.* 2005. London: Arrow Books, 2006.
[Child, Harold Hannyngton] 'The Little White Bird.' *Times Literary Supplement* 14 November 1902: 339.
Cooper, Edward H. *The Twentieth Century Child.* London: John Lane, The Bodley Head, 1905.
'Holiday Books.' *New York Times* 6 December 1902: BR6.
I. W. V. 'He Cannot Understand It.' *New York Times* 15 November 1902: BR12.
Kincaid, James R. *Child-Loving: The Erotic Child and Victorian Culture.* London: Routledge, 1992.
Kipling, Rudyard. '"They."' 1904. *Traffics and Discoveries.* 1904. Ed. Hermione Lee. Harmondsworth: Penguin, 1987. 242–65.
[Lucas, E. V.] 'Christmas Books, VIII.' *Times Literary Supplement* 23 December 1904: 413.
Mallett, Phillip. *Rudyard Kipling: A Literary Life.* Basingstoke: Palgrave Macmillan, 2003.
Mason, Philip. *Kipling: The Glass, the Shadow and the Fire.* London: Jonathan Cape, 1975.

'Mr. Barrie's Fancies.' *New York Times* 4 October 1902: BR16.

Nash, Andrew. Introduction, A Note on the Text, and Explanatory Notes. *The Little White Bird*. 1902. *Farewell Miss Julie Logan: A Barrie Omnibus*. By J. M. Barrie. Edinburgh: Canongate, 2000. vii–xix, 3–4, 210–15.

Rose, Jacqueline. *The Case of Peter Pan or The Impossibility of Children's Fiction*. 1984. Philadelphia: University of Philadelphia Press, 1993.

Sullivan, Jack. *Elegant Nightmares: The English Ghost Story from Le Fanu to Blackwood*. Athens, OH: Ohio University Press, 1978.

'Topics of the Week.' *New York Times* 16 July 1904: BR477.

'War Takes Barrie's David.' *New York Times* 8 April 1915: 1.

Part II

The Child at Play in Home and Garden

5
The Edwardian Child in the Garden: Childhood in the Fiction of Frances Hodgson Burnett

Jane Darcy

The English spring of 1901 was exceptionally cold; Frances Hodgson Burnett spent it at her much-loved country home, 'Maytham' in Kent, which she rented from 1898 to 1908 and which contained the garden she loved most. In 1901, at the start of the Edwardian period, she was 52 years old and already a highly successful writer, having published over 50 novels and plays in the preceding 20 years. Although in her own lifetime and beyond, her most famous work was *Little Lord Fauntleroy* (1886), today Burnett is best known for her classic Edwardian children's novels, *A Little Princess* (1905) and *The Secret Garden* (1911). Since *The Secret Garden* is such a rich text for what it reveals about her attitudes to childhood it will be addressed in some detail here. However, although Burnett's most enduring books have been for and about children, like other children's writers of her day, she also wrote for adults. Thus this essay will consider some of her adult fiction in the context of its representation of the child, in particular *In the Closed Room* (1904) and *The Shuttle* (1907).

By far the most significant event in Burnett's life – one which affected the way she saw childhood and which influenced her development as thinker and artist in the Edwardian period was the 1890 death from tuberculosis of her 15-year old son, Lionel. She was devastated by his death, wanting to believe almost to the end, that he would get well and that she could make him well. Once he had died she wanted to believe he was still 'living.' The rather romantic, idealized view of childhood she had previously exhibited in her writing, typified by *Little Lord*

Fauntleroy (1886) became hard to sustain in the face of such loss. After Lionel's death Burnett was, according to her most recent biographer Gretchen Gerzina, 'never again the same' (142). She thought constantly of her son and frequently wrote letters to him; she could not bear to think of his body in the earth and had his grave in Paris walled and lined with flowers and boughs to prevent the soil touching the casket. From then on she became even more preoccupied with childhood as a time of joy and hope and the garden with its flowers and birds became her most potent symbol of its potential for regeneration. For her, Lionel was now fixed in a perpetual childhood which she sought to explore in her fiction as a way of giving life to him. In her work just prior to and during the Edwardian period Burnett thus combines a sense of nostalgia for a lost childhood, very typical of the time, with an intense personal engagement that manifests itself particularly in the narrative voice. More broadly, her work contributes to what Kimberley Reynolds has called the 'Great Tradition' of children's literature, which 'has always been characterised by its elevation of childhood and its questioning of adult wisdom and orthodoxy' (72).

The freedom and adventure offered to children by the rambling but securely walled Edwardian garden is central to Burnett's vision of child-hood; it recurs in almost all her fiction and very much marks her out as a writer of her time. Her own earliest memories of the joy of a garden were when she was a child and came across her first 'secret' garden in Salford. Her memories resurfaced as she developed the Maytham garden in the early 1900s and found expression also in the garden she created late in life at her newly built home, Plandome, Long Island. It was here in her last and most American home that all Burnett's feelings and thoughts about Edwardian gardens and what they represented came together and she wrote *The Secret Garden*. But the garden for Burnett was never merely an idea or symbol; she had a good knowledge of gardening as an art and a practical activity and a great love of flowers, particularly roses. The constant regeneration and renewal involved in working with a garden connects with her spiritual belief, taken from the New Thought and Christian Science, that nothing that ever lives will die, but is constantly remade. The child is the symbol for the possibility of her own re-birth and that of her dead son.

Nowhere is this more explicit than in *The Secret Garden*. Although always intended as a children's story, it was published first in America in 1910 in an adult publication, *The American Magazine*, under the title of 'Mistress Mary.' It was not highly thought of when it was published or during Burnett's lifetime although it received some critical attention.

One reviewer dismissed it as being a ' "new-thought" ' story and claimed it was over-sentimental (quoted in Gerzina 263); the *Bookman*, however, considered it to be ' "more than a mere story of children" ' and noted its ' "deep vein of symbolism" ' (quoted in Gerzina 263). As Gerzina notes, 'no-one spotted it as the enduring classic it would become, and certainly no one set it above her other books such as *Fauntleroy*' (263). Yet *The Secret Garden* has continued to grow in popularity with adults and children and is now undoubtedly one of the most highly acclaimed and best loved of all children's books.

Burnett's paralleling of the garden and the child is very clear in *The Secret Garden*. The narrative brings together a neglected garden and two neglected children and shows how their growth is interdependent. The garden needs the children to love and care for it and they need the garden for the sense of purpose it gives them and for its walled security and beauty. On one of Mary's first visits to the garden she clears some space for the plants to grow and comments out loud, ' "Now they look as if they could breathe" ' (81). This establishes early on a connection between the human and the natural worlds. Even before this, when she was in India, we are told that Mary has tried to make things grow by creating little gardens but she fails because the climate is too humid and the soil poor. The secret garden, where she does establish herself and grows well again, is very English and very Edwardian in its structure and ambience, being one of a series of interconnected gardens in a grand country house. In the real life story of such gardens we see how the charmed life that existed in this halcyon period for the upper classes came to an abrupt end during and after World War I when many gardens fell into disrepair and decay. Many of the dedicated gardeners like Ben Weatherstaff in *The Secret Garden* and his equivalent in *The Shuttle* were either dead or no longer as willing to undertake the labour-intensive and painstaking work that such magnificent gardens required.

Burnett's 'philosophy' is very similar in both her adult and children's fiction. It is not an especially complex philosophy but it is a timely, positive and life-affirming one which both sustained her as a person and provided a framework for her writing. At the turn of the century in the United States and also to some extent in Britain, religious movements such as Christian Science and the New Thought were becoming increasingly popular. Christian Science, founded by Mary Baker Eddy, emphasizes the positive power of spiritual faith as an agent in physical healing and growth. The New Thought has had various manifestations in its 250-year history but its practitioners all share core beliefs in 'the centrality of mind, the focus upon the immanence of God and the divine within' (Mosley 70). It is an evolutionary model stressing the possibility for constant growth and improvement in the human race and which strives to bring together Eastern and Western philosophical and religious traditions. Burnett never actually joined or affiliated herself very closely to any one church or movement, though her surviving son, Vivian, became a Christian Scientist. She did, however, draw a great deal on the various teachings of such movements to confirm and develop her own instinctive sense of the world and to fulfil her needs as mother and artist. In a memoir of his mother, *The Romantick Lady* (1927), Vivian Burnett confirms that his mother: 'was not able to accept [Christian Science] wholly, and, though from time to time she turned to it for help, she never absolutely enrolled herself as a Scientist' (371). From this brief description of the central ideas of both Christian Science and The New Thought it is possible to see how they connect with her emphasis on the potential of the child. Children are often represented as providing hope for humanity because of their openness to new ideas, their natural resilience and their natural urge towards growth and happiness.

Children are a presence in Burnett's fiction in many guises from strong young girls like Mary Lennox, Sarah Crewe, or Bettina in *The Shuttle*, who are outspoken and full of life, to more typically Edwardian sick children who have a ghostly other-worldly quality and who sometimes, but not always, are brought back to health through belief in their own capacity to be well. A character like Mary fits in well with what Peter Keating has said about children in Edwardian fiction: that they ceased to be so 'pious, industrious and well-mannered: instead the admired child was likely to be seen as imaginative, inventive, self-reliant and constantly in trouble' (220). He adds that 'children were suddenly allowed to be themselves in literature' (220). But other of Burnett's child characters are more typically sickly, though they may recover like Colin in *The Secret Garden* who has been read by Shirley Foster as a fictional resurrection of Lionel: 'The portrait of Colin Craven, lying pathetically on a sickbed, suggests consumptive symptoms, while his ultimate recovery can be read as a projection of [Burnett's] wish-fulfilment' (Foster and Simons 173).

The novel does have a sense of loss and a typically Edwardian nostalgia for an earlier happier time when Mary and Colin had mothers who were still alive but, whereas in some other classic Edwardian children's books like *Peter and Wendy* (1911) and *The Wind in the Willows* (1908) loss and nostalgia remain the keynote, in *The Secret Garden* this is turned around. When Colin begins to believe that there is 'Magic' in the garden and that he may be able to walk, this thought then overrides any physical weakness he has. We are told quite explicitly in the chapter 'In the Garden' that Colin's recovery is a result of his own physical efforts and 'new beautiful thoughts' (289) which have come about as a result of his meeting Mary and being told about the secret garden. The narrator makes this connection clear:

> One of the new things people began to find out in the last century was that thoughts – just mere thoughts – are as powerful as electric batteries – as good for one as sunlight is, or as bad for one as poison. To let a sad thought or a bad one get into your mind is as dangerous as letting a scarlet fever germ get into your body. (288)

This seems to be an absolutely central part of Burnett's philosophy and is closely related to the representation of childhood in her fiction insofar as children are shown to be more open to growth and change than adults and are often in need of rehabilitation because of the neglect and damage that adults have inflicted on them.

At first the idea of the garden appeals to Colin only on an imaginative level when Mary tells him about it. But this is a start: 'Shut in and morbid as his life had been, Colin had more imagination than she had and at least he had spent a good deal of time looking at wonderful books and pictures' (212). The power of imagination is then a sustaining force; mere thoughts of the secret garden are positive and healthy before Colin even experiences the garden itself. Life begins to return to him through the power of positive thinking: 'When new beautiful thoughts began to push out the old hideous ones, life began to come back to him, his blood ran healthily through his veins and strength poured into him like a flood' (289). So the garden and the children grow together. The 'beautiful thoughts' must be supplemented by fresh air, good food and outdoor exercise but given the right conditions life can return to both plants and children.

The children in *The Secret Garden* believe they are made powerful because of 'the magic' and are able to communicate telepathically with Mr Craven, even though he is so far away. In contemplation and in a dream Mr Craven perceives that something is going on in the garden and feels compelled to return to Misselthwaite Manor. He learns later that his dream and the voice of his dead wife talking to him correspond exactly with the moment at which Colin declares that he will live for ever and ever. It is a spiritual moment and confirms Burnett's belief in the power of the human mind. Typically, however, the plot does not strain credibility too much; she backs up the mystical moment with the arrival of a letter from Susan Sowerby asking Mr Craven to return to the manor. However, what is also significant and effective about the expression of this whole incident in *The Secret Garden* is the role of the narrator and her relationship with the child reader. Burnett has the ability to create the scene in such a way as to make it comprehensible and concrete enough for an older child reader, whom she never patronizes, but also engaging and relevant for an adult. The narrative persona is a deliberately constructed one. Here we see how she draws the child – and even adult – reader into an intimate sharing of her joy in gardens through the punctuation, rhythm of the prose and choice of phrasing, moving deftly from the particular to the general:

> They always called it Magic and indeed it seemed like it in the months that followed – the wonderful months – the radiant months – the amazing ones. Oh! The Things which happened in that garden! If you have never had a garden, you cannot understand, and if you have had a garden you will know that it would take a whole book to describe all that came to pass there. (239)

Burnett apparently loved children's company and seems always to have wanted to give them treats and make them happy. However, not every child in Burnett's fiction is either inherently strong or susceptible to new life and growth. She also creates children who are other-worldly and drawn to death. Where Colin recovers from a deathly existence, Rosalie's son Ughtred in *The Shuttle* is weak and deformed as a result of his father striking his mother during her pregnancy and remains so. He is a strangely knowing unearthly boy, rather in the vein of some of Thomas Hardy's child characters such as Little Father Time in *Jude the Obscure* (1895). He tries to act as his mother's protector and confidant, much as young Jude does, and tells his aunt Bettina about how he once tried to intervene in his father's abuse of his mother only to be beaten with a riding whip: ' "of course he said it was because I was impudent, and needed punishment...He said she had encouraged me in American impudence" ' (84).

Here we can see that Burnett is critical of the harshness of English parenting. Ughtred is a victim of his father's physical brutality and of a view that children should be seen and not heard. By contrast the relationship between the American parent and child is shown to be open, frank and equal. Right from early childhood, Bettina and her father in the same novel are close and have mutual respect for each other, so much so that when she is little more than a girl he entrusts her to travel to England to save her sister Rosalie from her cruel husband.

Many of Burnett's children are neglected by their parents, either through lack of affection, selfishness or simply doing what was considered normal for children at the time. Mary Lennox is ignored by her selfish party-loving parents in India and left to the care of an ayah; Colin Craven is also abandoned to the care of servants on account of his father's grief after his wife's death. Sarah Crewe in *A Little Princess* is sent by her widower father to a boarding school in England where, after his untimely death, she is harshly treated by those who should be caring for her. Unhappy and neglected children, isolated in large Edwardian houses, are set in contrast to the healthy, happy and well balanced children like Bettina or Dickon in *The Secret Garden* who live a full family life.

It is one of the defining features of Burnett's life and writing that she was a transatlantic figure; she crossed the Atlantic many times and was equally at home in England and America, eventually becoming an American citizen in 1905. As with a writer like Henry James, whom she admired and knew, it places her in a position where she knows and understands the restrictions and conventions of middle-class English society but can also see them from the outside, as one who has in a sense been freed from them. Her most enduring child characters are 'outsiders' in respectable upper-middle-class English society, either in terms of their gender, nationality, culture or class – or a combination of these. Mary Lennox in *The Secret Garden* and Sarah Crewe in *A Little Princess*, for example, have spent their young years in India, and Bettina in *The Shuttle* comes from America.

The Shuttle makes much use in both plot and characterization of the cultural differences between Europe and America. In an introduction to a 1967 reissue of the book Marghanita Laski referred to it rather disparagingly as ' "poor man's James" ' (quoted in Thwaite, 198) but it is much more than this. In the heroine, Bettina, Burnett presents the reader with a young woman who could conceivably be Mary Lennox as an adult. The picture we are given early in the novel of Bettina as a child of eight years old is similar to that of Mary. She is outspoken and does not behave in the deferential way expected of a young English girl. In the novel she is contrasted with her feeble older sister, Rosalie, and is described as having 'a stronger and less susceptible nature' and as having 'a straight young stare which seemed to accuse if not to condemn' (8). She instinctively recognizes her sister's suitor, Sir Nigel, as the fraud that he is, 'and being an American child, did not hesitate to express herself with force' (8). The narrator explains that:

> Sir Nigel had known only English children, little girls who lived in that discreet corner of their parents' country houses known as 'the schoolroom,' apparently emerging only for daily walks with governesses; girls with long hair and boys in little high hats and with faces which seemed curiously made to match them. Both boys and girls were decently kept out of the way and not in the least dwelt on except when brought out for inspection during the holidays and taken to the pantomime.
>
> Sir Nigel had not realised that an American child was an absolute factor to be counted with, and a 'youngster' who entered the drawing-room when she chose and joined fearlessly in adult conversation was an element he considered annoying. (8)

Sir Nigel tells Bettina she is ' "too cheeky" ' and informs her sister that ' "They wouldn't stand that sort of thing in England" ' (9). Later in the novel, when Sir Nigel has married Rosalie, bullied and abused her, reducing her to a nervous wreck and has spent all her money on drink and high living, Bettina comes to her sister's rescue.

In her criticism of the passivity of children Burnett's thinking accords with educational theory of the time, especially that of the American John Dewey. Dewey was writing in the early twentieth century but his ideas derive broadly from a tradition that starts with Jean-Jacques Rousseau's writings and takes in Friedrich Froebel on the way. He supports the idea that children should not be passive recipients of adult instruction but should be encouraged to ask questions and learn for themselves through experiment and experience. Like the ideas emanating from Christian Science and the New Thought, it is a positive evolutionary model, based upon a belief that individual education and actions can contribute to the final overall goal of human perfectibility.

Like Ughtred, Judith, an American child character in one of Burnett's shorter fictions, *In the Closed Room* (1904), is also a very strange creature and is drawn irresistibly to other worlds so that she eventually disappears altogether. Ann Thwaite describes *In the Closed Room* as 'a work which looks like a children's book but is not' (136). Judith's family are poor and her parents have to work so hard they do not have a great deal of time for the child. They are down-to-earth, practical people but she is not like them in looks or personality, being dreamy and thoughtful. They do not understand her:

> Judith's relation to her father and mother was not a very intimate one. They were too hard worked to have time for domestic intimacies, and a feature of their acquaintance was that though neither of them was sufficiently articulate to have found expression for the fact-the young man and woman found the child vaguely remote. (3)

She is described as being like her Aunt Hester who had the same sort of strange unearthly quality and who died suddenly while apparently talking to someone no-one else could see. Judith feels an affinity with her dead aunt and we are told that, 'Her mental attitude was that of a child who, knowing a certain language, does not speak it to those who have never heard and are wholly ignorant of it' (4). There is an implication in the text that the parents do not take enough time and trouble with Judith and that, although they are content and uncomplicated, they are limited in their perceptions. Often in Burnett's work adults are not only neglectful of children but also less insightful and sensitive than children. This sense that the child is privileged with an inner eye that the educated adult lacks, harks back to Romantic thinking about the child being father to the man.

Judith sometimes has mystical dreams of her aunt:

> The places where she came upon Aunt Hester were strange and lovely places where the air one breathed smelled like flowers and every-thing was lovely in a new way, and when one moved one felt so light that movement was delightful, and when one wakened one had not got over the lightness and for a few moments felt as if one would float out of bed. (4)

She herself believes she is not 'quite real' and that she does not 'belong to the life she had been born into' (5). A change comes for her when she moves with her parents to an old house where they are to be caretakers and encounters there, in a supposedly 'closed room,' at the top of the house a little girl who, like Aunt Hester, has already appeared to her in a dream. The room is always open for Judith. Just outside the room is a roof garden with flowers which seem dead but come back to life at the girl's touch. While she is playing with the girl one day Judith sees that the garden does not end at the street but stretches out 'in a broad green pathway – green with thick, soft grass and moss covered with trembling white and blue bell-like flowers' (19). It seems the strange little girl who Judith has encountered comes and goes between death and life, but this is never quite clear.

Here we see the child and the garden intertwined once again. As well as representing the possibility of rebirth and new life beyond, the garden is a metaphor for the creative potential of the imagination. For Judith, the world beyond the closed room may be entirely one of her own imagination (we are never really told), but it is more real than the mundane everyday world of her parents. In the end the parents find Judith 'asleep' in the room and also discover that the little girl who has appeared to Judith had died in the same room. Judith's mother recognizes that she is dead rather than asleep and says it was just the same with her Aunt Hester. It is a sad, even macabre story suggesting that death is never far away or necessarily 'unreal' for an imaginative child. The land beyond the roof garden is an after-life but is very clearly connected to this life and is even indistinguishable from it. *In the Closed Room* is another dramatization of Burnett's belief that life always goes on and that somewhere the child Lionel is waiting for her. Ann Thwaite supports this view, writing that Burnett was convinced, even 15 years after his death, that 'Lionel was still Lionel, real, himself, able to look over her shoulder and help her,' adding that, 'This feeling was conveyed most strongly in *In the Closed Room*' (Thwaite 136).

Certain 'special' adults share children's second sight and instinctive knowledge in Burnett's fiction and empathise with them. Rather like Wordsworth's peasants, they tend to be of a lower social class and live in harmony with nature or may follow mystic, Eastern philosophies. Like the child characters they are often outsiders, cut off from the upper-middle-class adult norm by social position but able to communicate with the children because children have fewer preconceived ideas about who it is appropriate to talk to or simply because, being servants, they come across the children more often. In *The Secret Garden*, Ben Weatherstaff and Susan Sowerby fall into this category, as do the servant Ram Dass in *A Little Princess* and the gardener in *The Shuttle*. In contrast, many of the allegedly respectable and responsible adults are shown to be emotionally dysfunctional. Judith's parents in *In the Closed Room* are too concerned with the practicalities of daily life to see beyond the mundane. The Misses Minchin in *A Little Princess* and Mrs Medlock in *The Secret Garden* are portrayed as insensitive and even bullying towards the children in their care and respectable upper-middle-class men like Mr Craven in *The Secret Garden*, and Mr Carrisford in *A Little Princess* have become emotionally sterile and self-absorbed through grief and loneliness. Burnett seems to have seen herself, in both her life and her art as one of the special adults. Both Thwaite and Gerzina record the fact that she sought out children's company when, as she often was, she was separated from her sons (Thwaite 130; Gerzina 137); it was as if by spending time with other children she could make up for her absences from home, which were often frequent and long. Burnett has a child-friendly narrative voice in her fiction for children too and quickly establishes an equal relationship between narrator and narratee. It was evidently important to her to be in a child's world and to see from a child's point of view. This tells us much about both Burnett's outlook and about the way adults at this time saw the child and childhood as having a special status. The child often envisioned in Edwardian fiction is one of adult construction, about which Jacqueline Rose has written: 'If children's fiction builds an image of the child inside the book, it does so in order to secure the child who is outside the book, the one who does not come so easily within its grasp' (2).

When Lionel was dying it became the chief purpose of his mother to keep from him the knowledge that this was the case, so she distracted him with a barrage of toys and games and treated him like a child half his age. After his death she wanted to believe she had loved him above all else, done all that was best for him – although she had spent long periods of time away from him – and that he still somehow lived on. In her created fictional worlds only her ideal vision prevailed. In this context Rose's comments seem particularly apt but they are also equally appropriate to describe the tragic undercurrent in some of the best Edwardian fiction for children, particularly fantasies such as Barrie's *Peter Pan* and Grahame's *The Wind in the Willows* which are permeated by a sense of pain and loss. This is not to diminish the achievement of these works but the fragility of their seemingly idyllic worlds may be viewed as emblematic of the Edwardian age. By comparison *The Secret Garden* and *A Little Princess* are quite robust and positive, which is in no small part owing to the psychological realism of the central child characters, Mary Lennox and Sarah Crewe. The opening of *The Secret Garden* demonstrates this: 'When Mary Lennox was sent to Misselthwaite Manor to live with her uncle everybody said she was the most disagreeable-looking child ever seen. It was true too' (2). How could Mary be anything other than cross and unpleasant given the way she has been brought up? This realism marks a shift from the mid-Victorian tendency to represent ill-treated children as angelic and attractive in spite of their poverty and the abuse they have received. Oliver in Charles Dickens's *Oliver Twist* (1837–38) and Jessica in Hesba Stretton's *Jessica's First Prayer* (1867) are two examples of this.

Rapport with birds and animals is also almost exclusively the preserve of children and 'special' adults in Burnett; Dickon with his crow and Ram Dass with his monkey fall into this category. In this respect Burnett again draws very much on a Romantic tradition of childhood in which the uneducated or unconventional person has a closer affinity with the kind of intuitive sense demonstrated by animals. It is not uncommon in Edwardian children's books to see celebration of instinctive knowledge and insight over the rational, the adult and the educated. In *The Wind in the Willows*, where the animals are more like children than real animals, there is an incident in which Mole and Rat are walking through the countryside when Mole suddenly feels something 'like an electric shock' (48), an instinctive 'pull' towards home. The narrator comments on the absence of the intuitive sense in humans: 'We others, who have long lost the more subtle of the physical senses, have not even proper terms to express an animal's intercommunications with his surroundings, living or otherwise' (48).

There is a key passage in *A Little Princess* which illustrates a similar point. Once her father has died and she is penniless, Sarah Crewe is banished to a bare attic at Miss Minchin's seminary where she is very lonely and befriends a rat who she talks to and feeds scraps. The rat seems to 'know' that Sarah is not to be feared. The narrator here interjects:

> How it is that animals understand things I do not know, but it is certain that they do understand. Perhaps there is a language that is not made of words and everything in the world understands it. Perhaps there is a soul hidden in everything and it can always speak, without even making a sound to another soul. But whatsoever was the reason, the rat knew from that moment he was safe-even though he was a rat. (131)

Burnett again aligns herself with those who are able to communicate instinctively with the birds and beasts. In her memoir, *My Robin* (1912) recounting her befriending of the robin in the garden at Maytham which inspired the robin in *The Secret Garden*, she expresses perhaps more clearly than anywhere else her sense of the 'knowingness' of birds and animals and her belief in an equal relationship between living things. In order to understand the robin's point of view she describes how she acted: 'I hold myself very still and feel like a robin' (6). The narrator of *My Robin* seems to be addressing a child audience, even though this is not specifically a child's text. The positioning and tone of voice of both narrator and narratee seem to blur the boundaries between an adult's and a child's level of perception and understanding.

There is an implied correlation between the instinctive knowledge that animals have and that of children, and a child who lives close to nature, like Dickon, is especially knowledgeable – even privileged – in this way. Whereas Colin is very imaginative and has read many books, which opens him to the possibility of change, Dickon's knowledge of the moors and his 'way' with animals – playing to them on his pipe like Pan – is presented within the narrative as equally valuable. This is evident when Mary describes Dickon to Colin: 'He is not like anyone else in the world. He can charm foxes and squirrels and birds just as the natives in India charm snakes. He plays a very soft tune on a pipe and they come and listen' (147).

Knowledge comes not just from books but from lived experience and sensitivity to the natural world. It is a notion that harks back to Wordsworth and the Romantic child but it also looks forward across the twentieth century, as John Rowe Townsend recognises in his assessment of Burnett's work in *Written for Children* which encapsulates what this essay also argues. He remarks on the growth in complexity of Burnett's work from 'the one-dimensional' *Fauntleroy* through 'the more subtle *A Little Princess*' to 'the rich texture of *The Secret Garden*,' and adds that 'there is a corresponding increase in the depth of the central child characters' (65). In *The Secret Garden* he notes the emphasis upon the children's longing for adult level achievement, describing them as inner-directed, self-reliant, constructive and co-operative. 'These are not Victorian virtues. The Victorian ideal was that children should be good and do as they were told' (66). Burnett's 'doctrine' is for Townsend, 'new, significant and potentially subversive' (66). As this essay has shown it is also distinctively Edwardian.

Works cited

Burnett, Frances Hodgson. *In the Closed Room*. 1904. Project Gutenberg eBook. 1 July 2004. Accessed on 23 April 2007 <www.gutenberg.org/dirs/etext04>.

——. *A Little Princess*. 1905. London: Puffin Classics, 2003.

——. *The Shuttle*. 1907. Project Gutenberg eBook. 18 March 2006. Accessed on 23 April 2007 <www.gutenberg.org/files/506/506-h/506-h.htm>.

——. *The Secret Garden*. 1911. Ed. Dennis Butts. Oxford: The World's Classics, 1987.

——. *My Robin*. New York: F. A. Stokes, 1912.

Burnett, Vivian. *The Romantick Lady*. New York: C. Scribner's Sons, 1927.

Foster, Shirley and Judy Simons. *What Katy Read. Feminist Re-readings of Classic Stories for Girls, 1850–1920*. London: Macmillan, 1995.

Gerzina, Gretchen. *Frances Hodgson Burnett: The Unpredictable Life of the Author of "The Secret Garden."* 2004. London: Pimlico 2005.

Grahame, Kenneth. *The Wind in the Willows.* 1908. Ed. Peter Green. Oxford: Oxford University Press, 1999.

Keating, Peter. *The Haunted Study: A Social History of the English Novel 1875–1914.* London: Secker and Warburg, 1987.

Mosley, Glenn R. *New Thought, Ancient Wisdom: The History and Future of the New Thought Movement.* Philadelphia: Templeton Foundation Press, 2006.

Reynolds, Kimberley. *Children's Literature in the 1890s and the 1990s.* London: Northcote House, 1994.

Rose, Jacqueline. *The Case of Peter Pan or The Impossibility of Children's Fiction.* Rev. ed. London: Macmillan, 1992.

Thwaite, Ann. *Waiting for the Party: The Life of Frances Hodgson Burnett, Author of "The Secret Garden."* London: Faber and Faber, 1974.

Townsend, John Rowe. *Written for Children: An Outline of English-language Children's Literature.* 5th ed. London: The Bodley Head 1990.

6
Playing at House and Playing at Home: The Domestic Discourse of Games in Edwardian Fictions of Childhood

Michelle Beissel Heath

As early as 1868 Anthony Trollope warned that sports

> have a most serious influence on the lives of a vast proportion of Englishmen of the upper and middle classes. It is almost rare to find a man under forty who is not a votary of one of them; – and among most men over forty the passion for them does not easily die out. (5)

It would be a fallacy, then, to suggest that sports, games, and play were primarily Edwardian occupations. Certainly games and sports have been played for centuries, and historians such as Neil Tranter, Mike Huggins, and Richard Holt rightly point to the growth of sports throughout the Victorian era. Yet while Victorians presided over a tremendous growth in sports and games, it was Edwardians who saw their apotheosis. As Andrew Horrall observes about the sport of cycling alone, 'though the first amateur cycling club was founded in 1869, it was three decades before the sport boiled over in sensation' (54).

Ultimately, it was Edwardians, not Victorians, who witnessed the increased acceptance of sports, games, and play both on an international and domestic level. To realize this, one perhaps needs only to remember that the Olympic Games were revived in 1896 and brought to English soil in 1908. Moreover, the Victorian view of sports as manly public schoolboy pursuits shifted significantly by the turn of the twentieth century with the advent of the figure Sally Mitchell calls the 'New Girl,' an adolescent female who carved out a space of her own, a space which included sports. Edwardians, more than their Victorian predecessors, increasingly grappled with and accepted the roles that sports and games could have in the lives of women and children. Victorians' unease over the gendered nature of croquet culminated in Edwardians' embrace of lawn tennis and cycling, and the emergence of popular children's leisure movements such as Robert Baden-Powell's Boy Scouts and eventual Girl Guides.

Unsurprisingly, then, Edwardian literature of childhood is filled with images of playful children, and particularly of female children exploring and experiencing the possible gendered dimensions of play. Nowhere is this more the case than in moments of domesticity. In Frances Hodgson Burnett's *The Secret Garden* (1911), Mary Lennox may play happily outside in the garden, and happily in the little Indian room, but once she meets her cousin Colin in the house, it is all his, and her playful tendencies must succumb to performing ayah-nursing acts and serving as native guide for his explorations of the garden, house, and Indian-room. As critics such as Elizabeth Lennox Keyser and others have long noted, the book shifts in focus from girl-child to boy-child, and by its end seems to forget Mary altogether in its restoration of the lords of the great manor. By the end of the text, Colin Craven has house, garden, and even story. But Mary's actions and the plural 'lords' (one an adult, one a child) suggest another preoccupation affiliated with domesticity in Edwardian texts of childhood: the play of adulthood and domesticity itself.

In texts as varied as Henry James' *What Maisie Knew* (1897; revised 1907), J. M. Barrie's *Peter and Wendy* (1911), and Edith Nesbit's *The Story of the Amulet* (1906), children are depicted as playing at being grown-ups, often in the form of playing house or maintaining domestic order, but in so doing they show how much adults play at it, too. Adulthood is threatened by these texts, which at every turn promise to give adults the lie, to expose their deepest secrets, and reveal the intersections between reality (often dark) and play (often equally as dark). More to the point, these texts consistently suggest that home and play cannot co-exist. When they try to dwell together, they only do so uncomfortably: home is an interference to true play in these texts. It is as if in trying to play together play realizes it is in competition with itself: one can play at home – at 'playing house' – in these texts, but doing so reveals that domesticity itself is a game, a system of order, acts, and imagined space imposed on individual players often, though not always, by choice. Domestic play has its own rules, some even necessary for survival, but many inventive embellishments. Through their attempts to separate play and home, adult writers often try desperately to keep play-worlds and real-worlds separate, but just as often reveal the deception, the lack of actual separation. A real fear in depicting playing-at-home is its ability to dispel the deception of who is doing the playing and even what the game really is. Who the adult is, and who the child is, blurs in the process as well, and the ensuing confusion threatens to destroy domesticity, society, and sometimes even world.

It is in fact adults,' and not children's, play that is the preoccupation of James's *What Maisie Knew*. The danger of this play by adults becomes clear in a proclamation issued early on by Maisie's governess, Mrs Wix. Suggesting that play belongs to Maisie's mother, she tells the child, ' "Well, my dear, it's her ladyship's game, and we must just hold on like grim death" ' (69). In *What Maisie Knew*, adults' strategic games-playing marks, if not outright causes, the disintegration of the family, the house, and domesticity itself. Other casualties include the lower classes and childhood. Every turn of James's novel reveals someone playing a game, but that someone is rarely if ever a child or even a lower-class adult. The child Maisie and the working-class governess Mrs Wix are swept up in the whims of others at their games, but are unable to play their own. Maisie's stepfather, Sir Claude, gives her 'ever so many games in boxes, with printed directions...The games were, as he said, to while away the evening hour; and the evening hour indeed often passed in futile attempts on Mrs. Wix's part to master what "it said" on the papers' (55). They never do make out 'the puzzle of cards and counters and little bewildering pamphlets' (56), a fact which may confirm Maisie's belief 'from her earliest childhood...that the grown-up time was the time of real amusement' (43–4).

Maisie's belief in the joys of adulthood also reflects James's impression of childhood as limited in power and perception. In his later preface to the novel, James expounded on his child character's famed perception, insisting that he realistically restricted it to what his 'wondering witness materially and inevitably *saw*; a great deal of which quantity she either wouldn't understand at all or would quite misunderstand' (Preface xxviii). This perception, however, is implicitly linked to gender, as James also readily admitted:

> All this would be to say, I at once recognized, that my light vessel of consciousness, swaying in such a draught [as the corrupt environment of Maisie's adulterous parents and step-parents], couldn't be with verisimilitude a rude little boy; since, beyond the fact that little boys are never so 'present,' the sensibility of the female young is indubitably, for early youth, the greater, and my plan would call, on the part of my protagonist, for 'no end' of sensibility. (Preface xxvi)

In other words, for James' own game involving adult characters and readers to succeed, Maisie, he believes, must be a girl.

So, an Edwardian girl becomes the centre of a novel of events she only witnesses in fragments, but experiences in full; she becomes the centre of a world of Edwardian play that excludes her even as it allows in adult females in seemingly unprecedented ways and numbers. In this novel, women are prime games-players. When Mrs Wix comes to announce Maisie's mother's impending marriage to Sir Claude, her stepmother Mrs. Beale maintains that it is 'a game like another, and Mrs. Wix's visit was clearly the first move in it' (37) . After one of her mother's adulterous suitors, Mr Perriam, visits the schoolroom, Maisie can only liken the event, and the realization of her mother's changing affections, to the child's game of 'puss-in-the-corner, and she could only wonder if the distribution of parties would lead to a rushing to and fro and a changing of places' (72), a shifting with which Maisie, tossed about in the novel from house to house, parent to parent, is already quite familiar, even though she is not a willing participant, and never quite manages to get her own corner, her own secure familial home. Indeed, Maisie quickly realizes that even 'with two fathers, two mothers, and two homes, six protections in all, she shouldn't know "wherever" to go' (75). Adults' games quite literally destroy her family and home environment, in part by multiplying them to the point of irrelevance and essential non-existence.

What Maisie Knew, then, is ultimately a critique of play as a destruction of family life, but it is above all a critique of female games-playing, promoting a view that such play destroys both motherhood and child-hood. The character who bears the brunt of James's wrath is Ida Farange, Maisie's mother and a renowned billiards-player. In his preface, James pointedly observes that Maisie 'makes her mother above all...concrete, immense and awful' (Preface xxx). Ida's worst offence is failing to be a mother, a failure which creates a child incapable of play, and that is almost directly attributable to billiards, and to the games-playing, and therefore coquetry, it encourages. Although women were continually called to play billiards by the sport's manual writers throughout the nineteenth century, and despite attempts to attract women to the sport through such means as 'the Miniature Billiard-tables' that were 'admirably adapted for ladies' (Pardon 2), women continued to be a rarity in the sport, so much so that in 1915 a billiards manual suggested that 'it will be a splendid thing for billiards when the ladies make up their minds to enjoy to the full their handsome heritage in the "game beautiful"' (Reece and Clifford 2).

James's Ida, then, as a female billiards player, is already an anomaly at the beginning of the novel. More problematic, however, she is apparently a *good* billiards player. William Broadfoot in his 1896 manual perhaps phrases the problem most bluntly: 'one is warranted on meeting a youngster whose knowledge of the game and handling of the balls have reached professional form in concluding that his skill is evidence of a misspent youth' (446). It is surely this idea of time misspent that James wants his readers to associate with Ida Farange. What billiards also associates her with is the 'science' of billiards, a science that its adherents referred to again and again by praising its mathematical properties, and suggesting that 'it is not the individual shot that tells at billiards, but rather the artful leaving of the balls in a position that tends to further scoring' (Gordon 148). This 'science' pervades the text, populating it with adult characters who are always, to put it in terms employed frequently in the novel, trying to figure out who will be squared and how to square everyone else. The end result is that no one is squared, but also that everyone is, particularly in the culmination scene of the square – of Mrs Beale, Mrs Wix, Sir Claude, and Maisie – that ends the text. This squaring has prompted numerous critical discussions, including Barbara Eckstein's notable essay that takes as its aim 'Unsquaring the Route of *What Maisie Knew*,' but Sheila Teahan's comment on Maisie being left over as a ' "residuum" or remainder that must be erased' is of particular note (223).

In *What Maisie Knew*, it is Maisie's childhood, her child status, that is the odd remainder, and that the adults around her actively erase in order to engage in their own playful pursuits. When they are not trying to forget or eliminate Maisie's childhood, they are using it in their own strategy-games, and it is this use of Maisie at which Ida in particular excels. In fact, in his first interview with Maisie, Ida's second husband, Sir Claude, reveals how much Ida has used the little girl as a billiards ball targeted at an object in her games. He comments that he 'knew her ever so well by her mother, but had come to see her now so that he might know her for himself' (45).

Ida's behaviour is repeated in the circumstances which lead to the eventful visit of 'the immensely rich' Mr Perriam to the schoolroom (70). When Maisie and Mr Perriam meet, his eyes are compared to 'polished little globes' that roll 'round the room as if they had been billiard-balls impelled by Ida's celebrated stroke,' as indeed they are; as Ida shortly admits to Maisie, he has been brought there because ' "I bored him with you, darling – I bore every one" ' (70). Ida continues this use of Maisie with lover after lover: the Captain, during his scene with Maisie, also admits that Ida 'has told [him] ever so much about [her]' which makes him 'awfully glad to know [her]' (111). The Captain lets slip – much to Maisie's surprise – the other notions Ida has deluded him with, mainly that Ida is 'tremendously' fond of her daughter, and that the child's and mother's separation is merely due to Ida's belief that Maisie does not like her (113).

Leaving the home to play billiards or pursue other entertainment, and doing so at the expense of the family, is lambasted in billiards manuals, but is precisely the activity for which Ida is notable. An 1895 American account of the history of billiards highlights the sport's benefit to families, but criticizes the British by claiming that

> in households where billiard tables are to be found, and other means of amusement exist, there is not that tendency to 'run out for an hour' after dinner, which means an evening at the club or elsewhere, and the absolute destruction of home life, which has not thus far attained that footing in this country which it enjoys in England, and should be ours by right of inheritance. (Cady 3)

Billiards does not keep Ida at home, and does lead to the 'absolute destruction of home life' for her family. In addition to her billiards prowess, a trait of Ida's that readers are immediately made to understand is that 'she was a person who…was always out' (6). Spending time within the comforts of the family circle is not Ida's forte, but using billiards as an excuse to cover over her amorous behaviours is: when Maisie recognizes her mother with the Captain in Kensington Gardens, Sir Claude has his doubts, telling her that her mother is at Brussels, having 'gone to play a match.' It is Maisie who supplies 'at billiards?' (105). Ida has gone to play a match – just a different type of match than her husband expects.

What Maisie Knew, then, is deeply suspicious of play, particularly when that play finds its way into adults' hands. In such a situation, James's text suggests, play becomes a destructive force, where children, using James' phrase for Maisie, find themselves 'rebounding from racquet to racquet like a tennis-ball or a shuttle-cock' (Preface xxiii). Play here razes all it comes across, child and adult alike, in its disintegration of domesticity. Play in *What Maisie Knew* threatens the home, promises to show up its pretences, show domesticity itself as a grand game played by adults. In the process, childhood is rendered a bereft state of being. Left with childhood's limitations, susceptible to adults' impositions and control, Maisie finds that her childhood is not only threatened, but claimed as an adult prerogative, so much so that the fun of childhood becomes adulthood, with children reduced to mere objects in adult sport. Having been turned into complete adult preoccupations, games, sports, and play are reduced to mere elements of control, while the potentially stabilizing features of domesticity are forgotten, as is childhood and its games and play, its promises and its critiques. In the end, mothers become unmaternal, fathers unpaternal, and children more than lost. In the end, one suspects, even Neverland cannot find Maisie, the true Lost Child.

If Maisie is a Lost Child, so is Barrie's Wendy, who is more lost as a child than the Lost Boys could ever fear to be. Wendy is an Edwardian adult's perfect child, if that adult be represented by the likes of Ida Farange and Lois Bates. A cursory glance at games listed in children's games manuals of the late nineteenth and early twentieth centuries reveals many adult influences: 'Trades,' 'I Apprenticed my Son,' 'Lodgings to Let,' 'Coach and Four,' 'Schoolmaster,' and 'Judge and Jury.' None of these, however, compare to the games presented in Bates's *Games Without Music for Children* (1897). Its riveting games include 'Laying the Breakfast-Table,' 'Knitting Game,' 'Taking Father's Tea,' 'Getting Ready for Bed,' and 'Washing One's Self.' As the titles alone imply, the point of these 'games' is to train children to take on everyday domestic chores with pleasure. The games mimic chores and adult manners, and part of the 'play' is to create an imaginary house in which these chores and behaviours can be undertaken. Borrowing from children's own desires to mimic adult behaviours and things, these games represent adult complicity, adult attempts *á la* Foucault to render children's bodies docile, well-behaved, and ordered in the ways adults want them to be.

Yet children and their games are wonderfully resistant, as Ida Farange learns through her own daughter's stubborn silences. Children take adult impositions and hurl them back. No matter how hard they try, adults cannot quite take over or control childhood play, or break children's games and playing habits. Lois Bates's games did not transform children's play and replace perennial favourites, and children still do not always say 'thank you' after receiving a gift, go to bed without protest when told, or set a table properly. It is this dual nature of complicity and resistance that marks the games of domesticity, flirtation, and adventure offered in *Peter and Wendy*.

Overall, home and the domesticity it supplies is threatening in *Peter and Wendy*; in fact, homes are little better than prisons which force children (mostly girls) to work under the guise of play. Even before she sets foot in Neverland, Wendy's desires are to play house and mother, desires that render her Bates's and Ida's perfect adult-child, but these desires also consistently betray the very play involved in domesticity and housekeeping. Disparaged early in the text as 'a stay-at-home' (27), Wendy is tempted to go to Neverland by Peter's promise of being allowed to ' "darn our clothes, and make pockets for us" ' (31). More than that, she positively gloats and revels in such chores: her 'face beam[s]' whenever 'she s[its] down to a basketful of [the Lost Boys'] stockings, every heel with a hole in it' (69). She even makes a game of mimicking adult women's complaints over such a situation; with that beaming face, she 'would fling up her arms and exclaim, "Oh dear, I am sure I sometimes think spinsters are to be envied!" ' (69). The book insists on the truth, that the activities are more chores than play – 'those rampagious boys of hers gave her so much to do. Really there were whole weeks when, except perhaps with a stocking in the evening, she was never above ground' – but at first glance Wendy, it seems, only sees the allures of the play (69).

Despite their and her joyful play-acting, however, all of the children, even Wendy, do share a sense of danger surrounding the house. The Lost Boys' first act of play when Wendy lands in Neverland is literally to encase her in a house, and they realize it is a trap from the beginning; they visit Wendy inside the little house they build, but do not sleep there. Wendy also seems aware of the trap and is not quite 'at home' in the house. Despite the cosy evening she spends in it guarded by Peter from the outside, she only spends one night there, and as soon as she is politely able to do so, moves into the children's underground home. The house as trap is ultimately confirmed by the pirates' use of it to convey the kidnapped children to the *Jolly Roger* in the text's culminating scenes (109). The house may put up a little stream of chimney smoke in sympathy with the children's plight, but it still serves its prison function.

The image of the house as a prison that betrays adults' own playing at domesticity is perhaps best encapsulated in the abode of Tinker Bell. Described early on as being the size of a 'bird-cage,' and 'shut off from the rest of the home by a tiny curtain,' Tink's wall recess home is literally her gilded cage (68). It is not as 'homely' as the little house built for Wendy, but its effect is the same. Once inside her house, Tink is trapped in it, trapped by the adult behaviours she models. Being 'most fastidious' and making certain that the curtain is 'always kept drawn when dressing or undressing,' Tink opens herself up to the control, exposure, and ridicule of others (68). Such behaviour allows Peter to threaten her into doing exactly as he wants; if she does not, he says, he will ' "open the curtains, and then we shall all see you in your *negligée*" ' (100). Yet this threat of exposure is a reminder of the ways in which flirtation and sexuality are themselves play. This play is present when Wendy, while Peter converses with her in his night-time visit to her bedroom, 'indicated in the charming drawing-room manner, by a touch on her nightgown, that he could sit nearer to her' (27). It is also present in Peter's ignorant realization that there is something Wendy, Tiger Lily, and Tinker Bell want to be to him that is not ' "mother" ' (92).

Flirtation, too, is present throughout children's games of the period through (non-thimble) kissing forfeits offered as prizes or punishments for certain games-playing behaviours or results, and through games such as 'Hissing and Clapping.' In this game, described in several manuals including *The Games Book for Boys and Girls* (1906) and J. K. Benson's *The Book of Indoor Games for Young People of All Ages* (1904), all male players leave the room while each female player chooses one of them. When each male player is allowed to re-enter the room, he must (depending on the version) sit, kneel, or stand near the female player he believes has chosen him. If he guesses correctly, he is applauded and perhaps kissed; if he guesses wrongly, he is hissed out of the room and made to try again. Sometimes the female players are also made to leave the room and try their luck at guessing. In both children's texts and games, then, adult drawing-room flirtatious behaviours are on display and played at, with a result being that those same drawing-room behaviours are shown as mere games and acts, cunning feats of fun and strategy. Where and when the flirtation is real, and where and when it is 'just' a game is not always clear.

Beyond its hints of flirtatious sexuality, however, Tink's home is both antithetical to play and a game itself. 'Beautiful,' but 'rather conceited, having the appearance of a nose permanently turned up,' Tink's house is described as an 'exquisite boudoir and bed-chamber combined':

> The couch, as she always called it, was a genuine Queen Mab, with club legs; and she varied the bedspreads according to what fruit-blossom was in season. Her mirror was a Puss-in-boots, of which there are now only three, unchipped, known to the fairy-dealers; the wash-stand was Pie-crust and reversible, the chest of drawers an authentic Charming the Sixth, and the carpet and rugs of the best (the early) period of Margery and Robin. There was a chandelier from Tiddlywinks for the look of the thing, but of course she lit the residence herself. (68–9)

Filled with furniture – and not just any furniture, but antique, not-to-be-broken, played on, or, as with the chandelier, even used furniture – Tink's house is not a house for children and their often furniture-destroying play. At the same time, Tink's furniture is the furniture of fairyland, of the land of fairy tales and of play and games, as well as the furniture of collecting, which is itself a sport.

Threats of sexual impropriety and condescension may mark Tinker Bell's house, but the blurring of play and supposed domestic reality become even darker as the story proceeds. By its end, houses and domesticity imply not only playing at adult behaviours and imprison-ment, but death. Onboard the *Jolly Roger*, the children almost succumb to the allures and adventures of a pirate lifestyle. It is Wendy, the text's stand-in symbol of domesticity, who prevents the games and fun from proceeding, and who increasingly sets the children onto the path of returning to domesticity and the Darlings' house. Just as she earlier attempted to thwart the fun by inserting school into the play-world, she insists upon humdrum reality rather than adventure or play upon the pirate ship. Appalled by the ship's bad housekeeping, and so disdainful of Captain Hook's dirty ruff that she nearly causes him to faint from her contempt, Wendy imposes domesticity upon play, and extends that domesticity to include death under the supposed cover of a real mother's expectations that her ' "sons will die like English gentlemen" ' (120–1).

Mothers, houses, and domesticity here mean real death, which even Hook realizes. With his adherence to the 'good form' of the public school world, and his shame at Wendy's domestic contempt, Hook cannot quite leave the world outside the play-space of Neverland behind. Hook knows Wendy's true power and danger; as James Kincaid points out, her 'smothering motherdom' 'skew[s]...erotics,' and assists her in being 'a disturber of the peace and play' (Kincaid 285–6). Wendy's danger is her domesticity, her power to eradicate play itself in part by competing with it and for its attention. Both Wendy and the crocodile- and Time-chased Hook know that the distinction between play and reality in Neverland is not so clear as Peter may wish, and that domesticity and other adult real world games, notions, and acts find their way in. The children must eat real food in addition to make-believe food, and death is possible. Peter Pan's famous line that 'to die will be an awfully big adventure' (84) is ultimately a betraying incursion of reality, a feature of adult interest, complicity, and conspiracy; it is adults who truly want to believe that death will be an adventure, as children, so adults believe, do not yet understand the concept of death. A boy who plays 'Follow my Leader' by touching sharks' tails and who engages regularly with adult pirates can hardly be considered as having thought seriously about the ramifications of his actions (honest-to-goodness possible death), and if he has, then he is not merely a cocky, childish, and seemingly invincible child, but a suicidal one.

Neverland, in its domesticity and play, then, is both an imagined dream-world of games and a part of the real world, as its very name – Neverland, a non-existent place, a colonial name for an actual uninhabited region in Australia – reveals. Domesticity not only intrudes upon the pirates' ship, it surfaces and encroaches upon play in the Neverland realm most conducive to play: the children's house underground. In that quaint home:

> a Never tree tried hard to grow in the centre of the room, but every morning they sawed the trunk through, level with the floor. By tea-time it was always about two feet high, and then they put a door on top of it, the whole thus becoming a table; as soon as they cleared away, they sawed off the trunk again, and thus there was more room to play. (68–9)

In *Peter and Wendy*, domestic elements such as meal-tables just get in the way of play, and must be made the best of, transformed or destroyed to allow play to continue. In Neverland, unlike in Maisie's world, this is possible, but like Peter's resistance to being father to the Lost Boys even as he acts as authority-figure, to ensure its very survival play needs to keep up a noble resistance to domesticity, and make the best of unfavourable circumstances. The house underground, 'rough and simple, and not unlike what baby bears would have made of an underground house in the same circumstances,' epitomizes this attempt (68). Fit for animals, it is hardly a house. This is bad for domesticity, perhaps, but good for play.

What Maisie Knew and *Peter and Wendy* represent well the tensions between play and domesticity in Edwardian texts of childhood, but nowhere is that tension clearer than in Nesbit's *The Story of the Amulet*. A single example from Chapter 6 succinctly symbolizes the incompatibility of play and domesticity in these texts. The chapter opens with a stanza from the game-song 'How Many Miles to Babylon,' and then proceeds:

> Jane was singing to her doll, rocking it to and fro in the house which she had made for herself and it. The roof of the house was the dining-table, and the walls were tablecloths and antimacassars hanging all round, and kept in their places by books laid on their top ends at the table edge.
> The others were tasting the fearful joys of domestic tobogganing. (90)

The chapter begins with a nursery rhyme song sung to a doll, but the song is more than a song, just as the doll is more than a doll, and the nursery is not quite a nursery. The song is a remnant of a child's game of chase and running, of asking how far one may run, and then defying that prescription. The doll here is a substitute for an actual human baby, a child for the child Jane who has created her own nursery under the easily-usurped dining-room table. Neither baby nor nursery are 'real,' but the game is. Jane attempts to disconnect the game-song from the game itself, but the very chanting of its famed verse connects the game with Jane's attempt to create a safe, games-free, little haven for herself, and hints at how futile the effort is. Jane has created the house to exclude herself from her siblings, who are engaged in play that is dangerous enough that their nurse, 'though a brick in many respects, was quite enough of a standard grown-up to put her foot down on ... long before any of the performers had had half enough of it' (90). Rather than slide down a staircase on a tea-tray, Jane chooses to hide inside the house, but a real house alone is not good enough. Dangerous games such as 'domestic tobogganing' intrude even there, so she retreats even further – into a play house-within-the-house.

But there is still no escape from games; not only do games frame the house-that-Jane-built (the narrative begins with Babylon, turns to a house, and then offers stair sledding), they make their way into both real and play houses and point out that a house itself is merely a game. Play, in other words, threatens to be more real than houses in this text, and Jane's play-house ultimately implodes under its pressures. As the text continues, Jane's house-within-the-house is forced to give way to games as the other children come in from their disrupted sledding and, through their very presence and gaming spirit, boot Jane out of her house and onto the stairs, the very site of the tobogganing game. Propelled by her outspoken resistance to beginning a new 'real' game, once on the stairs she loses the play-house's powers of protection and her own powers of games-resistance. Sitting on the stairs, crying and upset at the others, she defiantly continues singing her game-song of Babylon, and in the process attracts the attention of the 'learned gentleman' and sets herself onto the path of a 'real' Babylon game. The learned gentleman's talk of ancient Babylon lures Jane into volunteering that she would not mind visiting it, an admission immediately picked up on by the other children, who cry out '"Done!"' (96), and thereby trap Jane, through game ethics, into participating in the 'real' game. Once she sets foot on those stairs, it is all over for her: play the game she must.

The point of this excursion into Nesbit's text, and into James's and Barrie's as well, is simply this: when games appear in Edwardian fiction of childhood, houses crumble. Reality and play blur, and children's games offer critiques of the supposed powers of domesticity to hold together the fragments of society. When Nesbit's children go to ancient Babylon in pursuit of their real game, they leave the learned gentleman convinced that it is all a 'jolly game' which he can no longer believe in or play (96). Despite all the adult's beliefs, however, the game will not stay a game. Not only do the children leave the house to go to Babylon, but Babylon also comes to the house. The adventure results in the Queen of Babylon visiting the children's home, and highlights class tensions and hierarchy in Edwardian Britain. To the Queen of Babylon, Britain's working-class people are no different than slaves, and the children are forced to admit that no one is allowed to visit their king and queen (137–41). The 'game' both critiques and betrays reality, suggesting that early twentieth-century Britain is little better in its class relations and views than ancient Babylon with its slaves and dungeons. Ultimately, these Edwardian texts of childhood suggest, the British home offers no protection against such truths, child's play refuses to remain outside the bounds of reality, and the very notion of fictions of childhood may be taken to mean that childhood itself is a fiction of adults at play, selfishly refusing to leave their own Neverlands.

Works cited

Barrie, J. M. *Peter and Wendy*. 1911. *Peter Pan: Peter and Wendy and Peter Pan in Kensington Gardens*. Ed. Jack Zipes. New York: Penguin Books, 2004. 5–153.

Bates, Lois. *Games Without Music for Children*. London: Longmans, Green, and Co., 1897.

Benson, J. K. *The Book of Indoor Games for Young People of All Ages*. London: C. Arthur Pearson, 1904.

Broadfoot, William, ed. *Billiards*. London: Longmans, Green and Co., 1896.

Burnett, Frances Hodgson. *The Secret Garden*. 1911. Ed. Alison Lurie. New York: Penguin Books, 1999.

Cady, A. Howard. 'Billiards.' *Spalding's Home Library*. 1.7 (January 1895). 3–38.

Eckstein, Barbara. 'Unsquaring the Route of *What Maisie Knew*.' *The Turn of the Screw and What Maisie Knew*. Ed. Neil Cornwell and Maggie Malone. New York: St. Martin's Press, 1998. 179–93.

The Games Book for Boys and Girls: A Volume of Old and New Pastimes. London: Ernest Nister, 1906.

Gordon, Lord Granville. *Sporting Reminiscences*. Ed. F. A. Aflalo. London: Grant Richards, 1902.

Holt, Richard. *Sport and the British: A Modern History*. Oxford: Clarendon Press, 1989.

Horrall, Andrew. *Popular Culture in London c. 1890–1918*. Manchester: Manchester University Press, 2001.

Huggins, Mike. *The Victorians and Sport*. Hambledon: Cambridge University Press, 2004.

James, Henry. Preface. *What Maisie Knew, In the Cage*, and *The Pupil*. 1908. New York: The Modern Library, 2002. xxiii–xxxii.

——. *What Maisie Knew*. 1897. New York: Charles Scribner's Sons, 1908. New York: The Modern Library, 2002.

Keyser, Elizabeth Lennox. ' "Quite Contrary": Frances Hodgson Burnett's *The Secret Garden*.' *Children's Literature*. 11 (1983): 1–13.

Kincaid, James. *Child-Loving: The Erotic Child and Victorian Culture*. New York: Routledge, 1992.

Mitchell, Sally. *The New Girl: Girls' Culture in England, 1880–1915*. New York: Columbia University Press, 1995.

Nesbit, E. *The Story of the Amulet*. 1906. New York: Penguin Books, 1981.

Pardon, George Frederick [pseudonym Captain Crawley]. *The Billiard Book*. London: Longmans, Green, and Co., 1866.

Reece, Tom, and W. G. Clifford. *Billiards*. London: A & C Black, 1915.

Teahan, Sheila. '*What Maisie Knew* and the Improper Third Person.' *The Turn of the Screw and What Maisie Knew*. Ed. Neil Cornwell and Maggie Malone. New York: St. Martin's Press, 1998. 220–36.

Tranter, Neil. *Sport, Economy and Society in Britain, 1750–1914*. Cambridge: Cambridge University Press, 1998.

Trollope, Anthony. *British Sports and Pastimes*. London: Virtue & Co., 1868.

7
Separated Lives and Discordant Homes: The Otherness of Childhood in D. H. Lawrence's Edwardian Fiction

Andrew F. Humphries

D. H. Lawrence's Edwardian novels, *The White Peacock* (1911), *The Trespasser* (1912), and *Sons and Lovers* (1913) reveal childhood as both idyllic and disrupted. Children are presented as separate from or separated by adult behaviours, and interaction between adults and children in these novels indicates, along with a strong instinctive familial bond, an equal tendency to disrupt or destroy. The 'otherness' of childhood in Lawrence is seen in the ways in which adult and child characters perceive each other as somehow alien while also familiar.

Peter Coveney suggests Lawrence's fictional children represent a movement away from the 'escapist, nostalgic attitudes' of late nineteenth-century representations of childhood. Children in Lawrence are not 'regretful symbols wriggling on the pin of their author's own escape' (Coveney 283). In the juxtaposition of child-adult perspectives in his narrative, Lawrence, Coveney notes, is not seeking to use the child as a hiding place from the responsibilities of the adult world. Neither are readers, as they might be in Saki, presented with an alien adult world against which the child's consciousness is mischievously justified. Neither does Lawrence idealize a mythic childhood state in the manner of J. M. Barrie against which adulthood is mourned as a death of the child.

Andreas Suter in *Child and Childhood in the Novels of D. H. Lawrence* (1987) focuses on the continuity of childhood and adulthood in Lawrence's vision: 'everybody remains a child...as long as he has not attained his equilibrium, or at least his full individuality. People who are still on their way to their own true selves are as yet incomplete, and therefore child-like' (37). This study interestingly sees Lawrentian childhood as adulthood not attained. Suter focuses on the ways Lawrence interchanges concepts of child and adult to indicate levels of maturity and equilibrium. He terms adults like Gerald Crich in *Women in Love* (1920) or Clifford Chatterley in *Lady Chatterley's Lover* (1928), who have not developed their adult equilibrium and still seek maternal dependency, 'false babies' (Suter 135). Carol Sklenicka's *D. H. Lawrence and the Child* (1991) emphasizes Lawrence's idealizing of the childhood consciousness. Analysing his psychological writings she argues that Lawrence portrays childhood as a pristine state against which adult experience may be judged:

> Lawrence sees childhood as a source of direct renewal, a realm in which a healthful spiritual balance may be *re*covered, rather than as a locale where repressed complexes may be *un*covered and disentangled. The vitality and pristine quality of the child are ideals for the soul in Lawrence, a state of being to be reclaimed and cherished by adults. (4)

Sklenicka claims that Lawrence's novels reveal his 'lifelong fascination with the origins of character in childhood and a conviction that child consciousness is worth recovering' (55).

While these studies seek to give the Lawrentian child a symbolism which fits neatly into the aesthetic and ontological claims Lawrence made (largely in his psychological writings during the 1920s), such a view should not distract us from the direct child-adult opposition in his Edwardian novels. Lawrence shares, with other Edwardian writers, a sense of the trauma and separateness which adults inflict on children. The separateness of the child is created by conflicts between adults and children and conflicts between adults and their childhood selves. While making the child the central witness to adult conflict and allowing his fictional adults to engage with their childhood selves, Lawrence reveals adult and child selves as parts of the same organism. His Edwardian fiction investigates the challenging interaction between these two modes of being. Thus the child and the adult are to each other both alien and familiar. Lawrence establishes a starkly antagonistic perspective between adults and children while also seeking to extend a sense of their kinship.

Mark Kinkead-Weekes cites Lawrence's ability in life to connect with children despite remaining childless himself: 'he never talked down from a grown-up height, nor tried to lower himself to a child's level, but inclined courteously as to a smaller equal – and then, when properly acquainted, became great fun' (234). Lawrence 'clearly respected the "otherness" of the child' (Kinkead-Weekes 234).

Lawrence remarked to Lady Cynthia Asquith about her son John in a letter on 3 June 1918 that children were powerfully connected to adult crises: 'like barometers to their parent's feelings. There is some sort of queer, magnetic psychic connection – something a bit fatal, I believe' (*Letters III* 247). This connection, for Lawrence, linked both child and adult in a shared neurosis which potentially bound each to the other's destruction. The psychological damage done to Paul Morel by his parents is not avenged at a stroke like Conradin's elimination of his persecuting aunt in Saki's 'Sredni Vashtar' (1910) where closure is celebrated by the indulgence of another piece of toast. Instead the child Paul must exorcize his 'sickness' as the maturing Paul by growing beyond his mother who delays his adulthood by holding onto him even in death.

Echoing wider Edwardian concerns, Lawrence attacks parental inadequacy and calls for a greater psychological interest in childhood development in his essay 'Education of the People' (1918). Ellen Key, similarly, in *The Century of the Child* (1909) urged what Juliet Dusinberre has summarized as a requirement that 'parents should educate themselves not in the myth but in the living realities of childhood' (15). The Froebel-influenced journal *Child Life* as early as 1901 included an article entitled 'The Child as the Director of the Parent's Education' focusing on the ' "disqualifications of the average parent" ' and society's ' "sheer inability to answer truthfully and rationally the natural questions of an intelligent child" ' (quoted in Dusinberre 16). Lawrence's adults and parents evade childhood's 'living realities' while seeking their own childish escape from adult responsibilities. The gamekeeper Annable's children in *The White Peacock*, for example, are realistically grounded while the adults, Lettie and Cyril Beardsall and George and Emily Saxton, seek childhood nostalgia as an escape from their own adulthood. Likewise in *The Trespasser*, Siegmund McNair and Helena Verden usurp a childhood domain denied to the *actual* children of the novel.

Unsettlingly poised between child and adult domains, Lawrence's novels explore a growing awareness between 1900 and 1914 of a crisis emerging on the threshold between child and adult understanding. This was a result of a breakdown of Victorian parental confidence, as historian Robert Cecil reveals:

The attitude of parents towards their children born towards the end of the nineteenth century was not, on the whole, a healthy one: it tended to vacillate between an undiscerning faith in childish innocence and an equally misguided determination to treat disobedient children as sons of Belial. Both extremes were based on ignorance of the child's nature; it is as if the great majority of Victorian parents forgot what it was like to be a child. (132)

In Lawrence's novels the crisis is most evident in the way the otherness of childhood haunts adult reality so that elements of mythic nostalgia are allowed to inform adult neurosis. These early novels deal with attempts to 'forget' as well as regain what it is 'like to be a child.' Lawrence highlights the implications of a childhood distorted by controlling or intrusive adult agendas but also exposes adulthood as unnerved by its simultaneous closeness to and separation from the childhood domain.

In 'Education of the People' Lawrence argues, paradoxically, that the child should be educated by being left alone (121). He sees childhood as a period of innocent savagery, protected in its 'primal consciousness' from the damaging 'mental consciousness' of the adult world (128). Like many Edwardians influenced by their readings of James Frazer, Siegmund Freud, or Edward Carpenter, Lawrence turns to concepts of the primitive to idealize child nature and freedom in terms of uninhibited bodily instinct.

In art, public reactions to Roger Fry's first Post-Impressionist Exhibition of November 1910 exposed this conflict between adult 'civilization' and childhood 'primitivism.' Critics like Wilfrid Scawen Blunt attacked drawings resembling those of an ' "untaught child of seven or eight years old" ' as being ' "not works of art at all, unless throwing a handful of mud against a wall may be called one" ' (quoted in Hynes 329). Desmond McCarthy defended these primitivist paintings in the preface to the exhibition catalogue claiming that they invited viewers to look at the world anew: ' "Primitive art, like the art of children, consists not so much in an attempt to represent what the eye perceives, as to put a line round the mental conception of the object" ' (quoted in Butler 215). Lawrence's early novels also begin to promote childish consciousness as a new way of *adult* seeing in an attempt to challenge what he perceived as damagingly rigid and stifling moral attitudes.

The White Peacock reveals this challenging of adult structures through childhood ways of seeing. Lawrence's interest in the rejection of adult convention in favour of the primitive naturalism of childhood is boldly asserted by the 'educated' gamekeeper Annable to justify the cheerful lawlessness of his offspring. His anarchic rejection of convention confirms in his children a naturalist primitive code in opposition to the Nethermere society of the novel. After Annable's sudden mysterious death, the children run wild, disappearing for days into the woods, stealing and poaching. Annable may talk a good philosophy of childhood freedom against society but it is a freedom which indulges his own prejudices yet hardly 'frees' his children in any material sense. There is no provision for the social reintegration of the children after his death. The 'freedoms' he offers his children encourage them to resist conformity to existing adult codes rather than enable them to establish their own autonomous childhood domain.

By contrast, the more middle-class child, 12-year old Mollie Saxton who is taught by her teacher-sister Emily in Standard Six, is already mimicking adult sophistication. She is described ambivalently as 'clever' by her brother George who is not sure whether to approve or reject such cleverness (4). Lawrence's ambivalence about what natural children should be is immediately implied. By contrast, Annable's children are lawless, unstructured, and untutored in adult expectation. The products of wild and 'tutored' childhood are brought together by Lawrence when Emily Saxton and Cyril Beardsall visit Annable's family just after Emily has been attacked by a wild dog while out walking in woods near Annable's house. Annable lives in one of the broken down cottages called 'The Kennels,' a name giving added metaphorical weight to the attacking dog whose bite has led them there. It also hints at the darker side of animal primitivism exemplified in Annable's vision of childhood.

Moments before the attack, Emily has been gathering beechnuts in the woods which make her '"long for [her] childhood again till [she] could almost cry out"' and make her declare '"there are no more unmixed joys after you have grown up"' (69). Lawrence does not dwell upon Emily's self-conscious nostalgia at this point: instead he presents in opposition a picture of childhood that dispels such rosy myths.

The cottage they enter is a scene of domestic mayhem, which although amusing in part is disturbing in its evidence of neglect. Annable is notably absent. His eldest daughter Sarah Ann is 12, the same age as 'sharp' and 'clever' Mollie Saxton, but while Mollie is nurtured and educated at the heart of a warm family, Sarah Ann stands apart 'holding her bare arms to warm them' wearing only 'a skirt with grey bodice and red flannel skirt, very much torn' (70). There is a wild naturalness beneath this poverty suggested by 'her black hair' hanging 'in wild tails onto her shoulders' (70). There is nothing restrained about these children, for all the mother's threats to govern as she makes 'a rush for the urchin' Sam who is tipping tea into the milk basin (71). The anti-social but

instinctive child Sam is primitive and raw, untouched by adult social
niceties or the disguises that Annable terms ' "smirking devilry" '
practiced by ' "human rot" ' (132). Lawrence endorses Annable's rejection
of adult dishonesty and presents the animal 'honesty' of the children
as both naturally uninhibited and (for his middle-class readership)
alarming. We can see this when Sam aggressively refuses the coin Cyril
offers him, then chases Cyril and Emily 'howling scorn and derision' at
them because they had given his brother a 'rickety knife' meant for
him (73). In Annable's children Lawrence seems both to lament
parental neglect yet celebrate the naturalness in children that it allows.
In the adult Saxton and Beardsall characters, as well as potentially
in the child Mollie Saxton, Lawrence cautions against the potential
repression of naturalness that too early sophistication encourages. The
novel recognizes the paradox that loss of naturalness may be a result of
having a supportive and 'civilized' family.

It is difficult to decide whether Lawrence is appalled or delighted by
the affront to middle-class decorum that Annable's family represents.
One senses a strong hint of the latter when Annable defends his unruly
children as a ' "lovely little litter," ' a ' "pretty bag of ferrets" ' and as
' "natural as weasels" ' that are ' "bred up like a bunch o' young foxes, to
run as they would" ' (131). Annable celebrates the fact they are ' "natural" '
and can ' "fend for themselves like wild beasts do" ' fulfilling his amoral
code that a human should ' "be a good animal" ' (132). Annable's seems
a view close to Lawrence's own celebration of primitive amorality yet
its triumphalism is undermined by the family at The Kennels whose
dysfunctionality will lead to starvation, juvenile delinquency, and
violent death.

The second part of the novel, narrated by middle-class Cyril Beardsall,
focuses on his sister Lettie's romantic choice between farmer and childhood sweetheart George Saxton and wealthy mine owner Leslie Tempest.
The wistfulness about childhood lost in the face of adult responsibility,
evident in part one of the story, becomes more acute. The novel's main
focus here is not so much on actual children, but on young adults whose
childhood longings are never fully abandoned but are sacrificed in the
final chapters to the insistent demands of adult convention. Lettie, for
example, chooses materialism and social position over the romance of
a marriage to her childhood sweetheart.

She has a sense of loss about this decision which she feels irrevocably
separates her from her childhood. This is expressed as a loss of naturalness as if adulthood separates her from nature. For example, Lawrence
describes her out on one of her final walks with Emily, George, and

Cyril before her marriage to Leslie as both free and childlike but bound by her future. She is 'on in front, flitting darkly across the field, bending over the flowers, stooping to the earth like a sable Persephone come into freedom' (207–8). This Persephone is no longer a child but an adult: her freedom is fleeting. As George shows them a lark's nest her comments about nature reveal her awareness of her loss of childhood. She envies the larks she sees leaving eggs in a nest then bounding off 'gladly.' She wishes she could be ' "free" ' to have ' "a good time as well as the larks" ' (208). She wishes she and George could be ' "wild" ' like the birds but realizes that they must ' "consider things" ' (208).

At almost the same time, on the eve of the Saxtons' eviction from their childhood farm, George's last mowing of the fields has a nostalgic tinge. When Cyril recalls the moment it seems like a departure from their idyllic childhood world rather than from a place of work and function. It reminds Cyril of their boyish days and he recalls George's mother saying that ' "George is so glad when you're [both] in the field – he doesn't care how long the day is" ' (224). Their impending separation from the idyllic timeless field of their boyhood marks their childhood as a lost domain.

Lawrence's characteristic shift between realism and idyll in the novel is also seen at the end of Part Two, when on the eve of Lettie's wedding, Cyril tells a group of friends a fairy tale about a ' "pale and fragile" ' (232) young woman who is accidentally shot and killed by her lover as she comes to greet him disguised as a fairy. She has played a fantasy role and been punished for it. Lettie shocks the other women in the company by seeing the ending as ' "beautiful" ' (232). Her literariness has distanced her from real feeling and identification with the human message of the tale while the younger Marie Tempest, still described as a ' "girl," ' is moved by the sadness of the tragedy and the man's loss. George later has a more literal response to the tale: ' "[Lettie] said it ended well – but what's the good of death – what's the good of that?" ' (233). George marries another woman but remains caught emotionally in his past love for Lettie. Her choice of Leslie triggers the death of her imaginative or 'fairy tale' self in a way that resembles Wendy's rupture from Neverland in J. M. Barrie's *Peter and Wendy* (1911) when the boy Peter returns in the final chapter to find her married and 'only a woman now' who has ' "forgotten how to fly" ' (*Peter and Wendy* 151). This very Barrie-like wistfulness about lost childhood in adults returns in Lawrence's next novel *The Trespasser* (1912).

In *The Trespasser*, musician Siegmund McNair's escapist adulterous holiday in the Isle of Wight with his violin pupil, 28-year old Helena

Verden, is in itself a withdrawal from adult responsibility into child-like indulgence. *The Trespasser* was adapted by Lawrence from the real life diaries of his Croydon schoolteacher friend Helen Corke. The diaries describe Corke's doomed affair with married music teacher Herbert Baldwin Macartney which led to his suicide in August 1909. Lawrence transforms Corke's personal loss into a telling coverage of Siegmund's breakdown and the deterioration of his parental role. With this creative shift Lawrence immediately makes children and childhood the haunting motif of adult indiscretion.

When Siegmund enters his Wimbledon home the night before departing to meet Helena, the scene captures both his affection and his disgust for family life, signalling the conflict within him which will haunt his attempted infidelity. He moves 'stealthily, for fear of disturbing the children' (50), which is ironic considering his intended wider disturbance of their security. The kitchen is full of the signs of careless parenting and structureless upbringing. Lawrence combines the drabness and dreariness of the room, which reflects Siegmund's mood, with the otherwise healthy examples of childhood normality (50). 'Boots and shoes of various sizes' are 'scattered over the floor' and the sofa is 'littered with children's clothing' with 'crusts of bread-and-jam' and 'newspapers' on the range (50). Siegmund in evening dress, groping under the sofa for his slippers steps on 'two sweets underfoot' (50). In a different fiction this picture would be the prelude to an affectionate family saga but *The Trespasser* must balance Siegmund's love of his children with the fulfilling of his own childish need: the gaining of Helena.

Lawrence's touch is subtle and not over-sentimental. Siegmund's amusement at leaning back in his chair to find a 'small teddy-bear, and half of a strong white comb' and seeing this as 'the summary of his domestic life' (51), demonstrates Lawrence's gift for isolated moments of simple realism which create what Helen Corke describes as Lawrence's 'truth in symbols' (8). Siegmund wonders 'why Gwen had gone to bed without her' teddy bear and a 'strong feeling of affection for his children' comes over him, 'battling with something else' (51). As he takes the teddy bear up with him to leave between the two sleeping girls, 'Gwen and Marjory, aged nine and eleven' (51), Siegmund sees himself in the mirror, 'like a ghost' (51). He sees a youthfulness which rivals his children's. Significantly not seeing the 'grey at the temples,' Siegmund is aware of a mouth 'full with youth' so that when he looks at the children before retiring to his room, we sense that their childhood is an obstacle to his own continued play. Moments later he chastises himself for being 'Thirty eight years old...and disconsolate as a child!' (52). His childish need for Helena is, he acknowledges, on a level with and in opposition to, his daughter's need of her teddy-bear.

Lawrence's psychological perceptiveness in seeing adult betrayal in terms of childhood compulsion and irrationality allows us to indulge Siegmund's affair as we might a child's passion against adult censure. How often does Lawrence in these novels set up 'play' against adult (and often female) censure. Siegmund's wife is the humourless unimaginative adult against which Siegmund must assert his childlike freedom. Sigmund Freud's work in his *Three Essays on the Theory of Sexuality* (1905) deals with adult recourse to childhood memories and dreams to answer adult neuroses and Siegmund's attempt to redefine his adult self through play is closely linked to Freud's analysis, if not consciously so on Lawrence's part. Freud said in his 1908 essay 'Creative Writers and Day-Dreaming' that

> as people grow up, they cease to play, and they seem to give up the yield of pleasure which they gained from playing. But whoever understands the human mind knows that hardly anything is harder for a man than to give up a pleasure which he has once experienced. What appears to be a renunciation is really the formation of a substitute or surrogate. In the same way, the growing child, when he stops playing, gives up nothing but the link with real objects; instead of *playing*, he now fantasises. (37)

Siegmund's affair with Helena is like a wish-fulfilment or fantasy where he can retreat to a childlike state to fulfil the play that his conscience would not otherwise allow. Like a fiction writer, in Freudian terms, Siegmund attempts to become the creative child to live out his fantasy without scruple or shame. His attempt to see adult transgression as child's play and somehow forgivable, however, is his most dangerous rationalization.

Lawrence has a sneaking regard for the child who undermines an adult even while seeming to be defeated and in this he resembles many writers of the period, notably Saki, Frances Hodgson Burnett, and J. M. Barrie. Dusinberre notes Lawrence's debt to children's fiction in that he 'annexes into the adult novel emotions first explored in books about children' (32). The pattern of *The Secret Garden* (1911) or *Peter and Wendy* (1911), in which children remove themselves from adult reality into their own imaginative worlds, is inverted in Siegmund's escape from his own adult conscience to fulfil his childish imaginative desires.

The Trespasser epitomises the 'adult wish to return to the uninhibited sensuality of the child' (Dusinberre 22).

Like children's fiction of the time, Lawrence's early novels are continually shifting between mythological expectations and challenging realities. In *The Trespasser* the Isle of Wight becomes a forbidden land of pleasure where adults can be like children and sexuality mimics a chaste Wagnerian innocence. The island fantasy which suspends adult conscience and taboo in order to explore childhood play had already become a popular influence on the Edwardian consciousness through Peter Pan's adventures in Neverland as well as novels like Henry de Vere Stacpoole's *The Blue Lagoon* (1908). After meeting Helena on the island, Siegmund uses an analogy with fantasy to describe his feelings:

> Siegmund woke with wonder in the morning. 'It is like the magic tales,' he thought, as he realised where he was, 'and I am transported to a new life, to realise my dream. Fairy tales are true after all.' (72)

Siegmund evades his children to become a child again. He pursues this Peter Pan-like freedom with an early swim which Lawrence repeatedly describes as 'play' (73). He dives under the water 'laughing' then stoops again 'to resume his game with the sea,' feeling it 'splendid to play, even at middle age,' with the sea as 'a fine partner' (73). Siegmund delights 'in himself' (73), achieving a primitive identification with the innocence of natural savagery and a childlike wish to share his discovery of the 'little pool' of clear water with Helena (73). Siegmund's recognition of his own shadow 'very faintly' (73) in the water of the pool reminds us of the mirror in his house earlier. It leads him to move beyond his simple delight in himself to a more adult awareness of his flesh and physique and his desire for sexual fulfilment with Helena. (There is something of the Freudian infant in Siegmund's awareness of his sexual body as if newly discovered here.) The reflection, however, brings him back to face the consequence of his adult choice: he is there not as an innocent child but as an adulterer (73). Attempts to adopt the amorality of the primitive child are subtly undercut in Lawrence by adult moral consciousness.

Later in the story, as Siegmund 'wander[s] hand in hand' along the beach with Helena, they come across a *real* child leaning over a pool who reminds Siegmund of his youngest daughter and he is unable to 'look back' at Helena when she mentions the child's 'beautiful eyes' (85). This encounter shatters his illusion of the innocence of his liaison. In attempting to escape his home (and consequently his children),

Siegmund enters a world where childhood and adult needs become increasingly confused.

This confusion is clearly shown when Siegmund and Helena watch sea anemones and run over rock-pools. Siegmund's heart is 'leaping like a child's with excitement' and Helena later sits on a stone dabbling her 'pink toes' in the sea feeling 'absurdly, childishly happy' (94). Siegmund sees her 'child-like indifference to consequences' (94) as something that separates them in moral awareness. He evades adulthood; she is incapable of achieving it. Siegmund becomes the 'father' to Helena's 'child' in a bizarre role-play. He tells her she is 'only six years old today' and carries her while she nestles up to him 'smiling in a brilliant, child-like fashion.' He kisses her 'with all the father in him sadly alive' (95). The cross-over between adult and child perspective here is both uncomfortable and yet symbolic of Siegmund's impossible dilemma. He can only have the child in Helena, not 'capture' the woman fully and sexually. He cannot have both Helena and his family yet wants to secure both. In carrying the 'child' Helena he synthesizes the woman he desires sexually with the children he would sacrifice to achieve this. This sexual confusion becomes acute when Siegmund plays the parent telling the child Helena to put her 'stockings on' and dries her wet feet while she runs her fingers through his hair (95).

On the final day of their holiday, Siegmund decides he must revisit his favourite 'little bay' but this time the sea is not so reassuring and Lawrence suggests the fragility of Siegmund's grip on reality as he sees 'sea-women with dark locks, and young sea-girls with soft hair vividly green, striving to climb up out of the darkness into the morning, their hair swirling in abandon' (135). Fairy tales are no longer an escape but a reminder of the world's cruelty and indifference as Siegmund is frightened by the 'frantic efforts' of these phantoms beneath the surface where the submerged terraces seem 'cold and dangerous' (135).

The real cruel indifference, however, is reserved for his return home to Wimbledon. Siegmund is ignored in his own sitting room by his wife and the two eldest children, Vera and Frank, in a strained unpleasant episode (172–3). Siegmund's later encounter with his five year-old favourite daughter Gwen in the bathroom is the most disturbing (178). The rebuff the father receives from a child too young to be so knowing is evidence of how the McNair children have been systematically turned against him in his absence. We are left as readers torn between sympathy and sanctimony. Siegmund deserves rejection, perhaps, and yet the real victims are the children caught between the mother's understandable but explicit contempt and their own sense of betrayal by the father's absence.

Lawrence's description of Gwen as both small child and questioning adult is poignantly economical. In a novel which has used childhood and childish fantasy to fulfil adult dreams, Lawrence shows here finally what a real child can be. Like Miles and Flora in Henry James's *The Turn of the Screw* (1898) a child's actions and questions at this age can be quite direct, deliberate, and unsentimental: it is the adult eye that invests children with sentimentality not the children themselves. The dialogue between Gwen and Siegmund reinforces this deliberation and calculation. Gwen is the stronger of the two. Siegmund admits the power of her gaze which makes him feel himself 'shrinking' under her 'child's look' which is 'steady, calm, inscrutable' (177). Flora's testing innocence in James's novella is unnervingly recalled here. Gwen probes him with questions in her 'condemning tone' and finally rejects his gentle enquiries about her lost tooth and his offer of embrace and chocolate (179). Later Siegmund is made to feel like 'a family criminal' (174) while Gwen, caught in the silence between father and family, stands 'regarding her mother in the greatest distress and perplexity' (180), unable to fathom the complexity of the marital situation. When she approaches her father to announce dinner Gwen is told to ' "[g]o away" ' and she returns to her mother 'crestfallen' (182).

Gwen is the only family member who continues to ask questions of her father, caught as she is in the crossfire between Siegmund and the combined forces of her mother and older siblings. She is the one most damaged, and her eyes still 'res[t] a moment or two on the bent head of her father' (188) while the others continue to ostracize him.

Later that evening, unable to 'return to a degrading life at home' but also unable to 'leave his children and go to Helena,' a fevered Siegmund commits suicide alone in his bedroom (202).

Dusinberre's claim that 'the growth of social anthropology at the turn of the century contributed to a new awareness of family power structures' (19) is evidenced here. Lawrence's presentations of adult–child encounters imply a meeting of equals where psychological realism rather than a Victorian moral framework is the guide to characterization, something he later exploits to even greater effect in *The Rainbow* (1915).

Isolated in his own family home, Siegmund's suicide symbolizes his escape from an adult crisis that his childlike excursions with Helena could not repair. It is his children, and Gwen in particular, whose alienation causes his sense of degradation. It is also his love for the children that could save him but which prevents his escape to a happier if delusory childhood world of his own making with Helena. Suicide, he convinces himself, is the only solution. Gwen's last infantile attempts to break family ranks and re-establish a relationship with her father are what makes his death more poignant. Forgetting Helena, the reader remembers the little figure of Gwen. In *Sons and Lovers*, Lawrence intensifies this portrayal of childhood sacrificed to adult strife but examines in more depth the far-reaching consequences of this.

In the first part of *Sons and Lovers* (1913) the intimacy of the Morel family home is both painfully inclusive and brutally divisive in that the children's entanglement in the adult agenda separates them from their own growth and development. Coveney claims that 'the intensity and vitality of [Lawrence's] children represent important qualities he intended to express through them' (269) and that 'the sensitivity of childhood in Lawrence is not something cultivated for itself, but for what it might sensitively become' (276). Lawrence presents childhood as an indicator of the health of society as a whole, and in *Sons and Lovers* the sense of the damaged child in the emerging adult is exemplified in William and Paul Morel as well as in Miriam Leivers. Their struggle to integrate into the adult world is explored by Lawrence in that elements of the child re-emerge in maturity to justify adult crises. For example, when Paul breaks up with Miriam after having sex with her she tells him he is a ' "child of four" ' (340) and sees him at that moment as ' "an unreasonable child … like an infant which, when it has drunk its fill, throws away and smashes the cup" ' (340). This both condemns and excuses his immaturity. Miriam also uses childish fantasy to justify her aloofness from the world as well as her sense of latent and miscast potential: 'She herself was something of a princess turned into a swine girl, in her own imagination' (172).

Lawrence's portrayal of early childhood in *Sons and Lovers* is vivid and realistic and begins to establish an organic continuity between child and adult self which is extended in his next novel *The Rainbow*. The novel opens with seven-year-old William Morel's excitement at the arrival of the Wakes. Margaret Drabble reminds us that for the Edwardian working-classes 'the one thing they would not relinquish were the Wakes' despite the efforts of employers and ministers to stop these holidays. They represented, writes Drabble, a 'huge orgy of festivity in the drab lives of the people' (13–14). Lawrence loved fairgrounds and had already used them in *The White Peacock* and would do so again in *The Rainbow*. In William's excitement and Mrs Morel's resistance Lawrence captures not only the social ambivalence to the Wakes Drabble refers to but also quite simply the sort of daily mother–child negotiations in mining homes like his own.

Gertrude Morel's resistance also establishes something particular about her relationship with her children which will impact on their maturity. Lawrence makes us feel the excitable lightness of the child against the irritated heaviness of the adult as Mrs Morel tries to structure and channel William's impetuousness. She resists his 'play.' Paul Thompson interestingly cites a study of Edwardian childhood in Edinburgh where only two out of 87 adults surveyed remember their mothers 'as ever taking part in their imaginative play' (277).

William is a robust and playful 'boy of seven' (11), always running, competing and challenging. He is described as 'a very active lad' who establishes an urgency his mother struggles to keep up with (11). Mrs Morel attempts to be more measured but William's compulsive focus is irresistible:

> The lad began hastily to lay the table, and directly the three sat down. They were eating batter pudding and jam, when the boy jumped off his chair and stood perfectly still. Some distance away could be heard the first small braying of a merry-go-round, and the tooting of a horn. His face quivered as he looked at his mother.
>
> 'I told you!' he said, running to the dresser for his cap.
>
> 'Take your pudding in your hand – and it's only five past one, so you were wrong – you haven't got your twopence,' cried the mother in a breath. (11)

Lawrence's observation here is instinctively aware of the rhythms of parent–child negotiation. Mrs Morel is caught up in his urgency despite herself. The measured control deteriorates into a stammering 'in a breath' as she struggles to match his desperation. William's mesmeric obsession with the noises of the Wakes is typical of a boy his age yet it also signals a feature of the adult William which is never resolved and contributes to his untimely death: he is drawn to the fast merry-go-round of the wider world but is unable to engage with this in separation from his mother.

When Mrs Morel trudges up to the Wakes later on we sense her resistance to it: 'She did not like the Wakes' with their 'grinding' organs and 'odd cracks of pistol shots, fearful screeching of the cocoa-nut man's rattle, shouts of the Aunt Sally man, screams from the Peep-show lady' (12). This is the world of the childhood grotesque. Its lurid atmosphere of misrule, drawing William to a wider world of adventure where a lion is 'famous' for killing a negro and maiming two white men (12), disturbs the mother. The whirl of noise and danger Lawrence revels in here makes William 'wildly excited' (12) but alienates Mrs Morel. William's motivation, however, is for his mother's approval. He has won 'two egg-cups with pink moss-roses on them' (12) for his mother and he is 'tip-ful of excitement' because she is there sharing the experience (12).

William is disappointed when his mother has to go home. A child's reluctance to let a good thing end is keenly expressed by Lawrence here and yet the lines following place this simple emotion into a more telling context regarding William and his mother's relationship in the novel as a whole:

'What are you goin'a'ready for?' he lamented.
'You needn't come if you don't want,' she said.
    And she went slowly away with her little girl, whilst her son stood watching her, cut to the heart to let her go, and yet unable to leave the wakes. (12)

William is unable to fulfil his childish impulse here because his mother will not indulge it and, despite his instinctive and very individual appreciation of things, he is already looking to his mother to give these events and feelings meaning and purpose. He is drawn towards the otherness of the Wakes yet restrained by his sense of obligation to an adult perspective. This conflict between a manic desire to engage with the world and a reluctance to do so at the expense of his mother is a feature of William's development and ultimate fate. His mother sees his interest in the world beyond her sphere as a compensation for her own disappointed ambitions as a miner's wife. She is the 'motor-force' (44) behind her children's aspirations, yet she retains the right to remain detached from their excitement as if this were the proper adult response to childish impulse.

William is the focus for rupture between his mother and father in two memorable episodes. In the first Mrs Morel flies at her husband for cutting the one-year-old William's hair. She has been proud of his prettiness with the 'twining wisps of hair clustering round his head' (23). At this point we are told William was 'fond of his father, who was very affectionate, indulgent and full of ingenuity to amuse the child.' The two 'played together, and Mrs Morel used to wonder which was the truer baby' (23). This criticism of her husband's immaturity could equally serve as a tribute to the naturalness of Morel's affinity with the child's consciousness. The 'child-father' Gertrude can indulge soon becomes the violating male adult she must oppose when he presents her with the toddler William 'cropped like a sheep, with such an odd round poll' (23). The cropped child becomes the catalyst for a much broader division. Mrs Morel goes 'very white, and...unable to speak' and her response to Morel's faltering justifications is almost violent. Suddenly the reader feels Lawrence's fear for the child-father in Morel:

> She gripped he two fists, lifted them, and came forward. Morel shrank back.
>
> 'I could kill you, I could!' she said. She choked with rage, her two fists uplifted.
>
> 'Yer not want ter make a wench on 'im,' Morel said, in a frightened tone, bending his head to shield his eyes from hers. His attempt at laughter had vanished.
>
> The mother looked down at the jagged, close clipped head of her child. She put her hands on his hair, and stroked and fondled his head.
>
> 'Oh – my boy! –' she faltered. (24)

This is the first of many parental battles the children witness. What this sudden shift from familial intimacy and security to hatred and division reveals is how childhood becomes sacrificed to marital strife in a way which implicates the child in warring adult perspectives. Morel knows after this that 'something final' has happened (24), and Mrs Morel remembers the scene 'all her life, as one in which she had suffered the most intensely' (24).

In a later episode Morel storms in from work threatening to beat the 11-year old William after complaints from Mrs Anthony that he has torn her son's shirt collar (67). Gertrude reduces her husband to a child himself in these arguments, mainly through her superior articulation but this time also cleverly slipping into the boy's language: ' "He was running after that Alfy, who'd taken his cobbler" ' to disarm the husband and show her momentary sharing of the child's anarchic freedom (67).

Lawrence uses humour against seriousness in another key episode when Morel leaves home after his wife accuses him, correctly, of stealing money from her purse to buy drinks. In a grand but flawed gesture, Morel walks out with a 'bundle in a blue-checked enormous handkerchief' like something in a pantomime (58). Mrs Morel's bravery is momentarily checked when she considers what will become of her family if 'he went to some other pit, obtained work, and got in with another woman' (58). The children coming in from school are distraught at his disappearance. He is a symbol of their economic security even if he might be a 'scotch in the smooth, happy machinery of the home' (87). Gertrude's instinct that he is incapable of really going proves true when she finds his 'bundle' in the coal-place at the end of the garden. Her laughter is as much from relief as amusement. Her sharing of the joke with the children, however, inviting them to 'go down to the coalplace and look behind the door, and then you will see how far he's gone' (59) is wilfully destructive in its compromising of what little dignity the father has left in his children's eyes.

For Gertrude the children's grief at the thought of their father leaving is comic. She calls them a ' "silly pair of babies" ' and watches William slink out and Annie trot after him 'sniffing up her tears' then reappear in 'great excitement, hugging the bundle' (59). Lawrence tells us the children go to bed after this 'relieved but not yet at ease' (59) and we feel this phrase encapsulates their precarious childhood security. William's 'hugging' of the bundle is a small almost unnoticeable touch but it reveals that his father's presence at this point is more than a 'scotch' and that Morel's relationship with his children is, at least, rescuable. Gertrude's own bitterness and contempt because she is 'tired of him, tired to death' (60), cuts across her children's independent relationships with their father. Her opposition to him contributes to her children's loss.

The children's shifting and contradictory perceptions of their father add to the sense of their insecurity. There are many harmonious scenes when Morel is working on something and involving his children but we are also told of their fear of him so that 'the children felt secure when their father was in bed' (90) as if he can be both ogre and protector at the same time. Lawrence takes this ambivalence into an evocative moment when he describes the children in bed listening to the miners tramping to the night shift:

> They listened to the voices of the men, imagined them dipping down into the dark valley. Sometimes they went to the window and watched the three or four lamps growing tinier and tinier, swaying down the fields in the darkness. Then it was a joy to rush back to bed and cuddle closely in the warmth. (90)

The children are made secure by their familiarity with the otherness of the miner's routine. It is both known to them and unknown, drawing out their imaginations yet making the 'cuddle' and separateness from the miners' darkness all the more satisfying. Their part-fear part-identification with the mysterious passing miners puts the relationship with their father into a cultural perspective.

One further scene indicates Lawrence's sense of the power and evocation of childhood imagination. His description of the lamp-post surrounded by darkness which the children play around on winter evenings combines anxiety with adventure, human warmth and community with isolating cold and obscurity in a way which resembles the childhood pictures of Alain Fournier's novel *Le Grand Meaulnes*, also published in 1913.

> There was only this one lamp-post. Behind, was the great scoop of darkness, as if all the night were there. In front, another wide, dark way opened over the hill brow. Occasionally somebody came out of this way and went into the field down the path. In a dozen yards, the night had swallowed them. The children played on. (*Sons and Lovers* 101)

The children: the Morels, the Pillins, Emmie Limb, and Eddie Dakin, are paradoxically 'brought exceedingly close together, owing to their isolation' (101). They alternately fight and 'flee home in terror' or sing songs which Mrs Morel hears from her parlour and their voices coming out of the night have 'the feel of wild creatures singing' (102). Lawrence, like James Joyce in the early part of *A Portrait of the Artist as a Young Man* (1916) is able to shift seamlessly between the mythic or epic and the mundanely real, capturing a sense of childhood imagination and logic. One such moment is Paul Morel's recollection of a fight:

> Paul never forgot, after one of these fierce internecine fights, seeing a big red moon lift itself up, slowly, between the waste road over the hill-top; steadily, like a great bird. And he thought of the bible, that the moon should be turned to blood. And the next day he made haste to be friends with Billy Pillins. (101)

Paul's boyhood imagination is alive suddenly to larger possibilities in his familiar world. Thompson claims that 'on the streets, as in the school playgrounds, a remarkably independent children's culture flourished, with its own secret pacts and passwords, ancient games and adaptations from Edwardian music halls' where the 'borderline between rough and respectable behaviour was much less clear in the children's street culture than in the adult world' (55). Part One of *Sons and Lovers* captures this coexistence of the restrained adult home culture and the more 'savage, competitive and hierarchical' child's culture beyond the threshold (Thompson 55). This epitomizes Lawrence's awareness of the shifts in power in Edwardian family life that E. M. Forster was also exploring and which had been the preoccupation of H. G. Wells, Samuel Butler, and Arnold Bennett since the early 1890s.

F. R. Leavis claims that 'in the rendering of children Lawrence...has no rival' (193). Certainly in Lawrence's awareness of the power of childhood consciousness he deserves this credit. In representing how adult–child relationships lead to separateness, his Edwardian novels acknowledge ambivalence about what it is to be either child or adult in an era when these distinctions were shifting ground. The otherness of childhood in Lawrence, then, lies as much in the separating of the child from its natural self inflicted by adult strife as it does in Lawrence's concern to show the separateness and distinctiveness of the child's consciousness. What offers to connect the child and the adult regeneratively is Lawrence's exploration of the child within. Where his Edwardian novels explore the consequences of childhood separateness, *The Rainbow*, Lawrence's first post-Edwardian novel, will reap the benefits of this exploration to reveal the regenerative child as a new and challenging voice.

Works cited

Barrie, J. M. *Peter and Wendy*. 1911. *Peter and Wendy and Peter Pan in Kensington Gardens*. Ed. Jack Zipes. London: Penguin, 2004. 5–153.

Butler, Christopher. *Early Modernism: Literature, Music and Painting in Europe 1900–1916*. Oxford: Oxford University Press, 1994.

Cecil, Robert. *Life in Edwardian England*. London: Batsford, 1969.

Corke, Helen. *D. H. Lawrence: The Croydon Years*. Austin: Texas University Press, 1965.

Coveney, Peter. *Poor Monkey: The Child in Literature*. London: Rockliff, 1957.

Drabble, Margaret. *Arnold Bennett*. London: Weidenfeld, 1974.

Dusinberre, Juliet. *Alice to the Lighthouse: Children's Books and Radical Experiments in Art*. 1987. Basingstoke: Macmillan, 1999.

Freud, Sigmund. 'Creative Writers and Day-Dreaming.' 1908. *Twentieth-Century Literary Criticism*. Ed. David Lodge. London: Longman, 1972. 36–42.

Hynes, Samuel. *The Edwardian Turn of Mind*. London: Pimlico, 1968.

Kinkead-Weekes, Mark. *D. H. Lawrence: Triumph to Exile, 1912–1922*. Cambridge: Cambridge University Press, 1996.

Lawrence, D. H. *The White Peacock*. 1911. Ed. Andrew Robertson. Cambridge: Cambridge University Press, 1983.

——. *The Trespasser*. 1912. Ed. Elizabeth Mansfield. Cambridge: Cambridge University Press, 1981.

Lawrence, D. H. *Sons and Lovers*. 1913. Ed. Helen Baron and Carl Baron. Cambridge: Cambridge University Press, 1992.

——. 'Education of the People.' 1918. *Reflections on the Death of A Porcupine and Other Essays*. 1925. Ed. Michael Herbert. Cambridge: Cambridge University Press, 1988. 86–166.

——. *The Letters of D. H. Lawrence Volume III*. Ed. James T. Boulton. Cambridge: Cambridge University Press, 1984–85.

Leavis, F. D. R. *D. H. Lawrence: Novelist*. London: Chatto and Windus, 1955.

Sklenicka, Carol. *D. H. Lawrence and the Child*. Columbia, MO: Missouri University Press, 1991.

Suter, Andreas. *Child and Childhood in the Novels of D. H. Lawrence*. Zurich: Juris, 1987.

Thompson, Paul. *The Edwardians: The Remaking of British Society*. 1975. London: Routledge, 1992.

Part III
Society's Child

8
Exhibiting Childhood: E. Nesbit and the Children's Welfare Exhibitions

Jenny Bavidge

Edith Nesbit's reputation as a quintessential Edwardian children's author is due as much to her involvement in the social context of her times as to the nature of her work, which is often hailed as marking the beginning of modern children's fiction. This essay seeks to place Nesbit in a very particular context – her involvement with the Children's Welfare Exhibition held at London's Olympia from 31 December 1912 to 11 January 1913 – but also seeks to show how that context cannot be seen as an inert backdrop to the development of Nesbit's writing, or to the kind of fiction it produced. Rather, a reading of the Exhibition's own rhetoric suggests that literature was co-opted by those concerned with the lives of Edwardian children, and helped to define categories of childhood around welfare issues.

The Children's Welfare Exhibition, supported by the *Daily News and Leader*, had two incarnations. The first ran for three weeks in 1912–13 and the event was then repeated on a larger scale in April of 1914. The two Exhibitions encouraged debate around the nature of childhood and child welfare, ranging from educational systems to eugenics. Although the Exhibitions were very much celebrations and discussions of British childhood, the directors may have been influenced by similar events previously held in the United States. Several screens illustrating children's welfare in America were on loan from the 1911 Children's Welfare Exhibition which had been held in Chicago, inspired by the belief that 'the city which cares most for its children will be the greatest city' (*Children's Welfare Exhibition Catalogue* 1912–13, 34). Nesbit attended the first Exhibition to publicize her novel *The Magic City* (1910). She read fairy tales in a session chaired by G. K. Chesterton and erected a demonstration 'magic city' model following the method of *The Magic City*'s hero, using books, household objects, scraps, and waste paper as building materials.

The Exhibitions cannot be claimed to have been landmark events. The theme was not revived at Olympia after 1914 and is not mentioned by the historical surveys of welfare and reform in the period. However, they can be said to have been distinctively Edwardian events that focused on childhood in a uniquely co-ordinated and unprecedented way. They drew together commercial enterprise with the new movements in health, women's rights and family life in a manner which reflected the newly national debate about the nature, potential, and dangers of childhood. In particular, the Exhibitions' rhetoric and agenda can be aligned with the discursive developments in child welfare which Carolyn Steedman has so extensively described. Steedman documents

> the way childhood came to be understood and described within various disciplines and bodies of thought (developmental linguistics, pediatrics, medicine, education, social welfare work and so on), but also the way in which childhood in a much more general sense, was reformulated to mean something new – something abstract yet explanatory, something 'true' – for a large number of people seeking explanation of human subjectivity and the meaning of life. (Steedman, 'Bodies, Figures and Physiology' 20)

The Exhibitions featured discussions of children's literature (primarily fairy tales), alongside debates and lectures on the aspects of child development, psychology and health, Steedman discusses. Although it would be tempting to treat the Exhibitions as a 'snapshot' of Edwardian attitudes to childhood, the commercial and somewhat eclectic nature of much of the Exhibitions' content precludes such a project. A more interesting approach is to read the Exhibitions' construction of its ostensible object and to ask what the place of children's literature was in that debate and how Nesbit's work, including her treatise on child psychology *Wings and the Child* (1913) and the subtextual models of child-rearing represented in Nesbit's novels, appear in the light of her involvement in this public venture.

Following Jenny Bourne Taylor's argument around the influence of Margaret McMillan on the work of both Nesbit and Frances Hodgson Burnett, it is at this moment that we see the development of the children's author as an alternative 'authority' on childhood, and the semi-acknowledgement of the children's book as an examination of the psychology of children and the state of childhood itself. The author of children's literature emerges in this era as an actor and public participant in the new sciences of childhood, rather than remaining a remote moralist or simply an entertainer. Nesbit's involvement shows how children's literature was co-opted into the diffuse debates about children's welfare in this period, especially in the promotion of imaginative play to counter anxieties about the nature of contemporary childhoods. Rather than demonstrating that her novels can simply be 'explained' by this context however, a reading of the rhetoric and competing languages of the Exhibitions show text and context to be mutually constitutive. Instead of operating in separate spheres of fact and fancy, they overlap, reproduce, influence and imitate in a process which, in fact, produces the 'children' who were addressed by both novels and public discussion.

The 1912–13 Children's Welfare Exhibition had solid institutional and Establishment support. It was opened by Clementine Churchill, the wife of Winston Churchill, and included Prime Minister Herbert Asquith and the Duchess of Westminster, as well as heads of higher education institutions, the heads of the major public schools, and church dignitaries, among its patrons. The directors had a broad remit: to 'illustrate the wonderful progress of recent years in providing for the mental, physical and social welfare of the younger generation' (*Catalogue* 1912–13, 9). Anticipating the 1914 event and looking back on the first Exhibition, the *Daily News* noted that it had 'to some extent the character of an experiment, breaking new ground.' The newspaper's feature article suggested that readers were confronting

> in this Exhibition, perhaps for the first time so far as the general public is concerned, a great and challenging fact, a sign of the times. I mean the fact of the softness of our age towards its children... At some points the Exhibition stands for the final and absolute revolt of thinking people against the doctrine of 'spare the rod and spoil the child.' At others for a less violent but equally and perhaps more swiftly growing revolt against the spiritual materialism generally linked with that physical doctrine. (Perham, 'Grown Ups,' 5)

Certainly, the 1912 Exhibition, at which Nesbit was present to publicize her novel *The Magic City*, was a cheerful and eclectic mix of the reformatory, the entertaining and the commercial, where one could hear a lecture on eugenics, attend a Fairy Pageant, indulge in some basket-making or browse stalls representing Heal's Furniture Store or

Cadbury's chocolate. The NSPCC shared an exhibition stand with Horlicks and a Miss Maud Venables presenting 'Stencilling for Amateurs'; the Simplified Speling Sosieti (sic) was adjacent to the Women's Imperial Health Association, while the Band of Hope distributed its tracts next to Waldes & Co., makers of Press Studs and Dress Fasteners. The best represented area of child welfare was, in fact, footwear, with no less than five stalls devoted to shoes, boots, or polish.

As Julia Briggs recounts, Nesbit provides a sense of this jolly mix of people and pursuits in her 'affectionate' description of the event in *Wings and the Child* (*A Woman of Passion* 351), a description which rather belies the fact that Nesbit was annoyed by the lack of help she felt received from the Exhibition's organizers:

> Let me remember how many good friends I found among the keepers of stalls...how the Boy Scouts 'put themselves in four' to get me some cocoa-nuts for roofs of cottages, how their Scout Master gave me silver paper ponds, how the basket makers on one side were to me as brothers, how the Cherry Blossom Boot Polish lady gave me hairpins and the wardens of Messrs. W. H. Smith's bookstall gave me friendship...how the Queen of Portugal came and talked to me for half an hour in the most flattering French, while the Deity from the *Daily News* looked on benign. (*Wings* vii)

Much of the Exhibition was given over to hobbies, crafts, and the demonstration of outdoor pursuits. The Boy Scouts and the recently formed Girl Guides both presented model encampments. There was much emphasis on modern approaches to health and well-being, with daily demonstrations of Swedish Gymnastics, but there was an equally strong lobby for more traditionally British pastimes, with country dancing on the 'Dancing Lawn' and a garden railway. A good deal of the Exhibition time and space was given over to pastimes which were very clearly offering a view of the child under pressure from modernity and the Edwardian version of 'toxic childhood.' The daily 'Pageant of Faerie' for example, told the following story:

> In an age of electricity and aeroplanes Fairyland is apt to seem a very long way off. It has even been reported that Puck is dead and that there never was a Peter Pan...Mr Strahan, therefore, has written a play showing how three children who didn't believe in Fairies found Fairyland again and how the Spirit of Learning was vanquished when he tried to mislead them, and how they saw many strange and

marvellous things ... how, in short, they discovered that the universe is far more wonderful than some wiseacres would have us think. (*Catalogue* 1912–13, 37)

Elsewhere in the Exhibition, however, the Spirit of Learning still held sway and the lecture series which provided the Exhibition's claim to be most interested in education was as varied as the trade stalls. The lecture programme covered educational systems and theories including home-teaching, Montessori and open air schools as well as promotions of pastimes associated with children – folk dancing, Punch and Judy, and of course Nesbit, Chesterton, and Greville MacDonald (the son of George Macdonald) on fairy tales. The influence of Friedrich Froebel and the new sciences of childcare can be felt in titles such as 'The Effect of Beauty on the Training of Children' and 'Demonstration Lesson in "Citizenship" to a Class of Children.' This focus on education and children's culture shifts, however, by the time of the second Exhibition when many more of the speakers are recognizable names from the suffrage movement.

Indeed, there is a distinct difference in the understanding of 'welfare' in the agendas and rhetoric of the two Exhibitions. The influence of the suffrage movement was particularly apparent in the second Exhibition and this invoked a differing idea of childhood and child welfare between the two events.

The liberal and socially-concerned *Daily News and Leader* (founded, of course, by Charles Dickens in 1846) sponsored and supported the two Exhibitions under the aegis of social reformers of the day, including Charles Cadbury, and as part of wider support for welfare legislation. On 1 January 1913, the *Daily News* printed a report of the opening of the Exhibition under the headline 'A Fairyland in London.' Neville Foster addressed the visitors to the Exhibition's first day by explaining (according to the *Daily News*) that its aim was to 'present the subject of children's welfare in a comprehensible yet attractive way.' 'By children,' the newspaper explains, 'he meant boys and girls of all ages, "from the time they come into the world to the time they go out into the world" ' (*Daily News*, 1 January 1913, 1). The Exhibition would have three main 'positions': that children should be fed wholesome food, that they should be trained 'thoroughly and systematically' and that the same system and thoroughness should be brought to bear on their recreation. The subsequent reporting of the Exhibition by the *Daily News* is overwhelmingly focused on the charm of the whole occasion, down to the detail of Mrs Winston Churchill's ostrich feather hat and the 'gay fairy' and 'jolliest of brownies' who dutifully handed over her bouquet.

Despite this editorial certainty, however, the flexibility of the category of childhood, particularly around debates about child labour, becomes apparent when reports of the Exhibition's many charms are printed alongside news reports of criminal activity and dramatic incidents involving children who presumably would be included in Mr Foster's classification of a 'child.' In the same issue of the paper, there are stories about a 14-year old maid accused of stealing from her employers and escaping to Portsmouth dressed as a boy; a 'young Jewish lad, a true son of the Ghetto' who returning from his work as a furrier's apprentice had fallen asleep while putting his younger siblings to bed and then awoken in time to save them from a house fire; and the arrest of two 13-year old 'Artful Dodgers,' fully kitted out in coats with extra-large pockets (*Daily News*, 1 January 1913, 5).

A further example of this flexibility occurs when Nesbit's article 'A Magic World,' a plea for imaginative freedom in children's play and development, which is discussed in more detail below, appears in the same edition as a report from the North of England Education Conference, where the subject of education for child workers was discussed. The article notes that the conference had acknowledged that 'under present conditions in many industries, child labour was indispensable, partly owing to its low cost and partly to the fine sense of touch and agility of young fingers' (*Daily News*, 6 January 1913, 7). At the other end of the social and economic scale, the newspaper's reports of the Exhibitions also reflect the somewhat conflicting attitude of the organizers towards the categories both of 'children' and of 'welfare.' This is, in part, due to the commercial nature of many of the contributors, and the *Daily News* carried daily full page articles offering 'advice to parents' from the major sponsors which were little more than advertisements with a childcare 'spin,' for example:

> There is no happier moment, to the giver and receiver alike, than when the child, on the tiptoe of expectation, receives from one who is kindly disposed, a pocket of delicious sweetmeat. In such a case the happiness of anticipation is often equal to the joy of realisation. We would, however, not go so far as to say this is describing a gift of Mackintosh's Toffee-de-Luxe. (*Daily News*, 11 April 1914, 5)

While this sort of negotiation between commerce, sensationalist journalism, and serious discussion of welfare issues was revived for the second Exhibition, the most striking difference between the two events is the domination of the 1914 Exhibition by the National Union of Women's Suffrage Societies (NUWSS). Announced in the *Daily News* under the headline 'Young England at Olympia: An Exhibition About Children and For Children,' the second event was very much more political, socially radical, and feminist. Whimsy maintained a foothold, primarily in the daily show which featured no less than 400 child performers taking roles in a pageant entitled 'Springtime.' Again, the storyline of the pageant was primarily concerned with re-enchantment and follows a very similar plot to the 1912–13 entertainment; two children who have ceased to believe in fairies are transported into a magical kingdom and shown the error of their ways.

Despite the tenacity of Fairyland, the suffragist and women's 'issues' focus of the 1914 Exhibition suggest that the welfare of the child is dependent less on the maintaining of a separate and precious child identity, and more on the child as a player in a social network of oppression and struggle. Indeed, the second Exhibition programme suggests that the debates of the 1913 Exhibition have already moved on:

> The guiding principle remains unchanged – namely, to illustrate with all possible completeness the progress that is being made in those matters which concern the real welfare of boys and girls – hygiene, education, amusement – and at the same time to provide a delightful holiday haunt for the children themselves. (*Children's Welfare Exhibition Catalogue*, 1914, 9)

The influence of the Suffragette involvement structures and organizes the narrative of the 1914 Exhibition. The floorspace was divided into four sections: a Children's Playhouse, The Cornish Riviera (complete with beach), trade exhibits and stalls, and the Woman's Kingdom section, designed to reflect 'the fact that the two main inspirations of the suffrage movement have been the sanctity of the home and the welfare of children' (*Catalogue*, 1914, 9). The fuller guide to and explanation of the Woman's Kingdom found in the section devoted to it, however, rather reverses the equation. Women's interests are represented not because children's welfare inspired female suffrage, but because woman's suffrage was essential to any developments in children's welfare:

> future national welfare depends almost entirely on women. It is because women realise this fact that they demand to be given the full rights and responsibilities of citizens, a demand which the promoters of the Children's Welfare Exhibition have always supported heartily. (*Catalogue*, 1914, 43)

We cannot know Nesbit's reaction to this new incarnation of the 'loving-kindness' and emphasis on magical experience of the 1913 Exhibition. By the time of the second Exhibition, Nesbit's influence and popularity were waning. Her husband Hubert Bland had been steadily losing his sight (and died, in fact, during the second Exhibition's run, on 14 April), and her own health was poor. Sales of both *The Magic City* and *Wet Magic* (1913) had been disappointing and as she had no book to publicize it is not at all surprising that she did not plan to attend the Exhibition.[1] Indeed, there is less involvement overall from mainstream literary names in the 1914 Exhibition. Greville McDonald returned, lecturing again on the subject of 'The Need of the Fairy Tale in Education' and Elizabeth Clark was present on several days throughout the Exhibition to hold a Story Hour for child visitors,[2] but the entertainments and sets (the Riviera and Playhouse) were of a more practical and experiential bent than the emphasis on the imagination of the first Exhibition.

The second Exhibition was certainly more explicitly reformist and radical in tone. Lectures concentrated less on different educational models and more on gender politics, with most centring on women's suffrage, economic and legal rights.[3] In the later Exhibition, the zeal for conversion and Panesque rhetoric of believers and non-believers is primarily at work in its promotion of women's emancipation. The description of the Woman's Kingdom section pits its certainties against the scepticism of the unconverted:

> Where the Suffragist, the genuine Socialist, the true Liberal and the whole-hearted Democrat all disagree with the reactionary of any party is in the matter of woman's concern with anything outside the welfare of the child, the family, the home, and the matter of the home. The present Woman's Exhibition at Olympia is nothing else but a big object lesson for the doubters, a concrete proof that women's work and women's interests, if they centre in the home are not limited to it. ('Women's Work for the Nation' 5)

So, children's welfare was cast in many different lights at the varying stages of the Exhibitions' lives. We can see it as a category in motion, constructed by different interest groups. Nesbit's own relationship to suffragism was complex too, as Briggs has explained (Briggs, *A Woman of Passion* 333–5). The villain of *The Magic City* is the 'Pretenderette,' a lady who wants to take over the City and who mirrors the nasty nurse who destroys the children's model city in the real world. As Briggs suggests, the implication of the character is that 'suffragettes were a threat to social order – aggressive, unfeminine women who had sacrificed love to self-seeking demands for power' (Briggs, *A Woman of Passion* 333). How, then, do Nesbit's literary and philosophical reflections on childhood and children's welfare sit in the context of the Exhibitions' 'experiments' and changes in focus?

During the run of the 1912 Exhibition, Nesbit contributed a short article to the *Daily News* entitled 'A Magic World.' It covered the same ground as would *Wings and the Child* later that year, asserting the importance of play and the imagination and squaring up to the 'Gradgrinds' with assertions such as, 'If I had my way, children would be taught no facts unless they asked for them' ('A Magic World' 5). Published alongside a large photograph of the Magic City, the article appealed to the power of story-telling, play and 'belief.' A child may be told, she suggests, about the wonders of the natural world alongside other appeals to its imagination and sense of empathy drawn from fairy tales and creative religious instruction:

> Then you tell [the child] of other things no more miraculous and no less, of fairies and dragons, and enchantments, of spells and magic, of flying carpets and invisible swords. The child believes in these wonders...why not? ('A Magic World' 5)

Nesbit's Froebel-influenced philosophy of children's literature and child development was at home in the atmosphere of the Exhibition, which for all its interest in modern systems, often speaks in a language of magic, beauty, and retreat from the modern world. Greville MacDonald lectured on 'The Educational Value of the Fairy Tale' at both Exhibitions, presumably following the idea of 'fairy sense' espoused in his 'The Fairy Tale in Education' (1913). MacDonald's argument for fairy-tale reading is allied to a Christian education, in that fairy tales introduce children to ways of thinking and understanding which are necessary for the appropriate understanding of Biblical stories. 'Fairy sense' is to be encouraged, it is as 'innate as the religious sense itself' (Macdonald 25). This is very close to the argument Nesbit makes in her article, where she argues that without an education in imagination, fancy, and 'belief' via secular works, the child cannot be expected to develop a proper religious sense:

> hard-fingered materialists crush the beautiful butterfly wings of imagination, insisting that park and pews and public houses are more real than poetry; that a looking-glass is more real than love, a viper than valour. ('A Magic World' 5)

That a similar party-line promoted by the Exhibition was absorbed by its child visitors is evidenced in the stories told by these visitors themselves. The *Daily News* offered daily prizes for Under-16s who produced the best short essays describing their visits. One winner describes visiting the Magic City and spins a little fantasy about shrinking to be able to enter it, written very much in the style of the novel itself. The *Daily News* remarks on 15-year old Andrew Rothstein's 'rather ambitious' style in his prize-winning essay:

> when the soft voice of Mrs Bland [Nesbit] told me that the marble columns of the temple were lengths of broomstick, white-washed and sewn up, even when she explained how she had made the graceful palms out of matchwood and green paper...the charm still rested on me, and when at length, I was reluctantly obliged to go, I felt that I was still under the spell of the beautiful city. (*Daily News*, 7 January 1913, 7)

Another winner, Mabel Wigham, writes about the Fairy Pageant:

> The aim of the play is evidently to increase belief in fairies, for the story shows three non-believing children, who watch fairies performing the sprightly antics, and before long are converted, so to speak, and swear never to doubt or disbelieve again. (*Daily News*, 3 January 1913, 7)

Mabel, in her account of the 'aim of the play,' seems aware of what is being required of the child audience of the Pageant, and the 'magic' elements of the wider Exhibition. The requirement that they should not *doubt* and that non-believers should be 'converted' is at the heart of the impulse Jacqueline Rose identifies in *Peter Pan* (and all adult-child inter-actions) as all that adults 'want or demand of the child' (137). In its promotion of the Magic City, the *Daily News* emphasizes the 'appropriate' reaction to the wonders therein:

> The keys to the Magic City are held by Mrs 'E. Nesbit' whom you will find waiting to escort you through the portals, if you are lucky; and as Mrs Nesbit herself has told us, the magic begins to work as soon as you feel yourself growing small enough to roam about the hills and winding ways of the Magic City just as the boy and girl did in the charming story she wrote some time ago. You must be a most unusual child if you go away unthrilled by the magic realism of Mrs Nesbit's story-telling. (Perham 'Little People' 5)

For all the insistence on the spontaneous magic of the City and its context in the Exhibition, Briggs quotes a letter from Nesbit to her brother which rather betrays the less enchanting side of the project as an early example of tie-in merchandizing:

> I had no idea when I undertook this Magic City building what a bother it would be, or I should never have undertaken it – but they say it will be a good advertisement. I am also to read fairy tales at Olympia. (quoted in Briggs, *A Woman of Passion* 350)

The City was a 'good advertisement' for the book, but as well as dramatizing the action of the novel, it also reflected and illustrated the aims and contradictions of the Exhibition itself. Nesbit creates a city – as Briggs notes, one which in its literary manifestation is literally made out of other books (*A Woman of Passion* 331) – which encourages a narrative of children escaping into a fantastic construction made out of the bits and pieces of the adult world. It is a rich metaphor, suggesting children's entrance into language, or as Bourne Taylor suggests, the self-reflexive moves of Nesbit's narrative strategy which weaves children's literature from existing adult genres and 'recapitulations' of existing stories. Bourne Taylor also discusses the creation of miniature worlds (in Nesbit) or stories based around 'social animism' (in Frances Hodgson Burnett) as dramatizations of a theory of mind which sees childhood as a state that can only be retrospectively reconstructed. Nesbit's fiction dramatizes 'the ways in which childhood was configured as a liminal space in Edwardian children's fiction...the child...stands on the threshold of the boundaries between different fields of knowledge at the turn of the twentieth century' (Bourne Taylor 107). The Magic City can be seen therefore, as less a space of total fantasy as this kind of liminal space. Moreover, in the context of the rhetoric of the Exhibition, it becomes a site, like literature itself, where children's reactions could be tested out, and judged.

Further, Nesbit's City becomes a kind of microcosm of the Exhibition itself: made from bits and pieces which assert a philosophy of child development and child identity whilst simultaneously denying that it is involved in anything so miserable as an educational philosophy or system. Both City and Exhibition express the difficulty of trying to establish a view of child development which cannot allow itself to abandon the assertion of the unsayable magical mystery of childhood, and particularly of doing so within a commercial setting. This appears to be what the Exhibition wants to take from Nesbit's work. There is no mention or reference to her (gentle) addressing of welfare questions in novels such as *Harding's Luck* (1909), for example.

Hints of critical readings of the Exhibitions' narrowness occasionally appear in the *Daily News* itself. Writing during the 1914 Exhibition, James Douglas appears to satirize the whimsical tone of the Exhibition by reporting on the 'Grim games of London urchins in the Park,' a description of the use made by children of a pile of sand that appeared in St James' Park:

> Sand castles were popular, magic palaces had their architectural adherents, there was a certain run on ramparts and caves, but undoubtedly the great game here was 'Funerals.' (Douglas 2)

This is far from the image of the Exhibition's own Cornish Riviera, but the Exhibitions, in their different ways, both reflect and feed into the development of a new language of welfare, developing throughout the Edwardian era, as noted by Steedman, Harry Hendrick, and Christine Piper. Hendrick suggests that welfare developments in the late nineteenth and early twentieth centuries moved away from 'a concern with the rescue, reclamation and reform of children' to the 'involvement of children in a consciously designed pursuit of the national interest, which included all-round efficiency, public health, education, racial hygiene, responsible parenthood and social purity' (Hendrick 41). This, of course, is also Steedman's argument and both recognize the importance of the discursive practices which produce the categories by which this new body of subjects is to be identified and 'made visible to the professions' (Hendrick 41). The Exhibition produces its own ideal visitor before the event, the sixpence-paid-awe-inspired admirer of spectacle and progress. It presents itself very much as part of the 'march of civilisation tale' that Rex and Wendy Stainton Rogers identify as one account of the 'history of child concern,' the contrasting account being 'the conspiracy theory tale' which suspects the values, rhetoric and aims of the agencies involved in child welfare (72–3).

While not quite a 'conspiracy theory tale' we can look to a short story by Saki (H. H. Munro), for a rather more jaundiced account of the Exhibition. In Saki's story, 'The Toys of Peace' (1913), a Fabianesque brother and sister, Harvey and Eleanor, are inspired by a display of 'peace toys' to be mounted at the forthcoming Exhibition of 1913. They purchase a complete set of the toys for Eleanor's two sons, including models of municipal buildings, such as the Manchester branch of the Young Women's Christian Association, accessorized with dustbins and sanitary inspectors, and J. S. Mill and Felicia Hemans action figures.

'Are we to play with these civilian figures?' asked Eric.
'Of course,' said Harvey, 'these are toys; they are meant to be played with.'
'But how?'
It was rather a poser. 'You might make two of them contest a seat in Parliament,' said Harvey, 'and have an election –'
'With rotten eggs, and free fights, and ever so many broken heads!' exclaimed Eric. 'And noses all bleeding and everybody drunk as can be,' echoed Bertie, who had carefully studied one of Hogarth's pictures.
'Nothing of the kind,' said Harvey, 'nothing in the least like that. Votes will be put in the ballot-box, and the Mayor will count them – and he will say which has received the most votes, and then the two candidates will thank him for presiding, and each will say that the contest has been conducted throughout in the pleasantest and most straightforward fashion, and they part with expressions of mutual esteem. There's a jolly game for you boys to play. I never had such toys when I was young.'
'I don't think we'll play with them just now,' said Eric. (391)

Harvey checks on his nephews after repairing to his study to consider the merits of a history book, 'for use in elementary schools, in which there should be no prominent mention of battles, massacres, murderous intrigues, and violent deaths' (392). The children, naturally (Saki would say), have immediately set the figures to work enacting a battle with liberal use of red ink and a bloody narrative. Saki satirizes both the well-meaning, self-congratulatory tone of the Exhibition's organizers, while rejoicing in a version of childhood which is pragmatic, unsentimental and bloodthirsty.

Peeping in through the doorway Harvey observed that the municipal dustbin had been pierced with holes to accommodate the muzzles of imaginary cannon, and now represented the principal fortified position in Manchester; John Stuart Mill had been dipped in red ink, and apparently stood for Marshal Saxe.

Louis orders his troops to surround the Young Women's Christian Association and seize the lot of them. 'Once back at the Louvre and the girls are mine,' he exclaims. We must use Mrs. Hemans again for one of the girls; she says 'Never,' and stabs Marshal Saxe to the heart. (392)

Saki's unsentimental view of childhood here (in the same vein as other stories in the 1914 *Beasts and Super Beasts* collection such as 'The Storyteller' and 'The Schartz-Metterklume Method') argues against everything the Exhibition stood for and aimed at. Saki's targets are of course, often women (particularly aunts) and his arguments in these stories seem to be particularly aimed at a view of childcare as feminized and controlling. This tone is rather closer to Nesbit's own subtle undermining of the sentimental image of the child in her work, which centres round the (sympathetic) puncturing of her child characters' romantic or heroic illusions by the intrusion of real life into fantasy, or the inevitable return home from a fantastic realm. Nesbit, however, remains a Fabian optimist in comparison to Saki, and her works clearly align themselves with the 'softer' version of childhood of the Exhibitions and the various strands of welfare reform that they 'showcased.'

In fact, the Bastables, or the family of *The Railway Children* (1906) would have been the target audience of the Exhibitions, but they would certainly not view themselves as beings in need of 'welfare.' Despite their (romantic) financial difficulties, the children in both stories maintain a strong sense of themselves as middle class even when in straightened circumstances. The address of the novels is obviously to the middle-class child, as in *Harding's Luck* where the reader is told, 'Dickie knew all about pawntickets. You, of course, don't.' (*Harding's Luck* 14). Her working-class children in *The Story of the Amulet* (1906) or in *Harding's Luck* have to escape out of time to free themselves of the miseries of contemporary society and poverty. Nesbit's hopes for children's lives belongs more to the 'march of progress' version of children's welfare, as demonstrated in the episode in *The Story of the Amulet* set in a Fabian Utopia , with lessons on citizenship, plenty of fresh air and freedom of movement.

The Exhibition can be seen, then, to define the child and childhood as an object of study and also, in related ways as a consumer. Literature sits comfortably within this process. 'What better present can you get a child,' asked the advertising for W. H. Smith's at the 1912 Exhibition, 'than a book?'

As Jenny Bourne Taylor suggests, in this period, a 'new market niche' of the 'children's author' was coming into being. (Bourne Taylor 105), particularly for women writers. This was a role that could combine an interest in children's welfare and also maintained an idea of the children's author themselves as a kind of liminal figure, just as the *Daily News* described Nesbit hovering at the entrance to the Magic City, holding the 'key' to magical and transformative experience. Nesbit's involvement as both 'exhibit' and speaker at the Exhibition demonstrates how in the twentieth century authors of imaginative literature for children have come to be featured in public debates such as those entered into by the Children's Welfare Exhibitions. They are presumed to have a (childlike) insight into children's lives and feelings, to be possessed of a unique ability to remember back into their own childhoods, or even to have retained some vestige of the child they were. Indeed, as Sue Walsh describes it, the public perception of children's literature as well as children's literature criticism frequently appeals to the idea of the children's author as being in a state of 'arrested development' (Walsh 28–9). Conversely, authors may also be spoken of as experts, presumably dispassionate and objective, in the way that children think and behave. Throughout her fiction, Nesbit depicts writers as heroes with an intuitive understanding of children and an ability to speak 'their' language. Her author-heroes tend to be from the same character mould: they share an instinctive understanding of and empathy with the child characters' dilemmas and scrapes, and often speak in a mode recognizable as that of the rhetoric of popular children's fiction of the day. Albert-next-door's Uncle in *The Story of the Treasure Seekers* (1898) and *The New Treasure Seekers* (1904) is such a writer, as is Mrs Leslie, a famous writer and poet whom two of the children meet on a train. She is interested in Oswald and Noel because they use lines from Kipling's *The Jungle Book* (1894) and she has all the author's approval: 'she didn't talk a bit like a real lady, but more like a jolly sort of grown-up boy in a dress and hat' (*Treasure Seekers* 57). The name 'Leslie' is similar enough to 'Nesbit' and the poem she gives the boys is so in keeping with Nesbit's style that the fictional character appears as an idealized self-portrait. Oswald approves of her poem 'for it shows that some grown-up ladies are not so silly as others' (*Treasure Seekers* 55). Mother in *The Railway Children*, the most idealized of all Nesbit's adults, is, of course, an author, and an author who writes, unashamedly, for money after her husband's ruin, in a similar 'jolly' vein to Mrs Leslie and Nesbit herself.

Nesbit's narrative is itself an homage to the literature of the day, incorporating, or 'thieving' as Marah Gubar describes it, as well as gently lampooning the style and rhetoric of boys' adventure stories. The metafictional place of writers within Nesbit's work – including the use of the different rhetorics borrowed from other authors – is a crucial feature of the double-voicedness which has become perhaps the most commented upon aspect of Nesbit's work. The discussion of the nature of childhood and adult-child relationships in the 'cross-talk' of the novels is, indeed, the mark of her supposed new 'realism' as Rose describes it (82).

The novels' address to adult readers, which implicitly offer a model as to how children should be treated and educated, certainly chimes with the 'soft attitude' that the Children's Welfare Exhibitions promoted, but also refutes the image of the child from earlier children's fiction. In an issue of *Children's Literature* devoted to cross-writing for adults and children, Erika Rothwell describes the Bastables, for example, as overturning Romantic and Victorian images of the child as redemptive, innately morally superior, and preternaturally good. Briggs agrees, noting that a new code for children's 'natural' behaviour was emerging, one which tolerated and rather encouraged certain kinds of naughtiness and celebrated high spirits, a code that 'Nesbit's books seek to instil in her readers' ('E. Nesbit' 83).

What is advocated in Nesbit's novels then, is a version of the experiments and developments in the wider world of children's welfare. As the headline for the Exhibition quoted earlier had it, these are works 'for children and about children,' which, like the events at Olympia, hold two ideas about childhood in tension. Both tell a story about an enlightened age which knew children better than they had been known before, and eschewed the redemptive or reformative impulse of earlier attitudes, but which maintained at its heart a belief in the category of the child and an idea of childhood which was essentially romantic and immutable.

The 'welfare' of children in the context here discussed has only a tangential connection to the great issues of universal education and social equity which were addressed in this period. The intended audience of the Olympia Exhibitions was very clearly the middle class, and the aims of many of the exhibitors were primarily commercial. The fact that such an event was discussed under the rubric of 'welfare' at all suggests the ways this category was in the process of being defined, and already polarizing opinion. Nesbit's fiction lent itself to the new language of children's welfare, in its advocacy of the 'softer' approach and particularly in its belief in the necessity of imaginative play. In this early example of author-led marketing, the children's book emerges as commercial object, philosophical treatise, and invitation to respond to an ideology of the freedom of imagination. Looking at Nesbit's work in this particular context suggests just how contingent and shifting these definitions prove to be.[4]

Notes

1. See Briggs, Chapter 13 *passim*. A very small illustration of this decline in Nesbit's public standing can possibly be identified by comparing the information given in the 1912 and 1914 Catalogues for the puppeteer and showman, Clunn Lewis. In 1912, he lists George Bernard Shaw, G. K. Chesterton, and E. Nesbit among the 'warm friends and admirers' of his marionette plays (which are, according to the 1912 Catalogue, ideal family entertainment and 'traditional drama – thrilling in their tragedy, clean and hearty in their humour'). In the 1914 Catalogue, Nesbit's name has been dropped from the list.
2. It is difficult to be absolutely certain as no information about her is given, but it seems likely that the Olympia storyteller is the Elizabeth Clark who went on to publish several collections of fairy tales and advice on reading them aloud in the 1930s. See her *Tales of Jack and Jane* (1935) and *The Elizabeth Clark Collection* (1935).
3. Lectures included 'Women Voters in Finland,' 'What Can Women Do for London?' 'How English Law Treats the Wife,' and 'Women's Place in Local Government.' There were several speakers from the NUWSS: Frances Dickson, the President of the Domestic Workers' Union spoke on 'The Organisation of Domestic Workers on Business Lines' and physician (and eugenicist) Elizabeth Sloan-Chesser gave a number of talks including 'The Necessity for Sex Teaching' and 'The Mistakes Mothers Make in the Nursery.' The public health activist Maud Adeline Cloudsley Brereton lectured on the title 'The Business World and her Babies' and the social reformer Lucy Deane Streatfield spoke on 'The Unmarried Mother and her Child.'
4. I would like to thank Karín Lesnik-Oberstein for discussing some ideas around the essay with me, and particularly Sue Walsh who read and commented on it. I am also grateful to the archive keeper at Earl's Court Exhibition Centre, Brian Browne, for all his assistance.

Works cited

'A Fairyland in London.' *The Daily News and Leader.* 1 January 1913: 1.

Bourne Taylor, Jenny. 'Between Atavism and Altruism: The Child on the Threshold in Victorian Psychology and Edwardian Children's Fiction.' *Children in Culture: New Approaches.* Ed. Karín Lesnik-Oberstein. London: Palgrave, 1998. 89–121.

Briggs, Julia. *A Woman of Passion: The Life of E. Nesbit 1858–1924.* London: Hutchinson, 1987.

——. 'E. Nesbit, the Bastables, and *The Red House*: A Response.' *Children's Literature* 25 (1997): 71–85.

Children's Welfare Exhibition December 31st 1912–January 11th 1913 Catalogue and Programme. Olympia Library (Ref. A12080).

Children's Welfare Exhibition April 11th–30th 1914 Catalogue and Programme. Olympia Library (Ref. A14010).

Douglas, James. 'Grim Games of London Urchins in the Park.' *The Daily News and Leader*, 10 April 1914: 2.

Gubar, Marah. 'Partners in Crime: E. Nesbit and the Art of Thieving.' *Style* 35: 3 (Winter 2001): 20–44.

Hendrick, Harry, *Child Welfare in England 1872–1981*. London: Routledge, 1994.

MacDonald, Greville. 'The Fairy Tale in Education.' *The Contemporary Review* (April 1913): 21–5.

Nesbit, E[dith]. *The Railway Children*. 1906. Puffin, London: 1994.

——. *The Story of the Amulet*. 1906. Penguin, London: 1996.

——. *Harding's Luck*. London, Hodder & Stoughton: 1909.

——. *The Magic City*. 1910. SeaStar, New York: 2000.

——. 'A Magic World.' *The Daily News & Leader*. 6 January 1913: 5.

——. *The Story of the Treasure Seekers: Being the Adventures of the Bastable Children in Search of a Fortune*. 1899. Penguin, London: 1994.

——. *Wings and the Child*. London: Hodder and Stoughton, 1913.

Perham, Hilda. 'Little People.' *The Daily News & Leader* 30 December 1912: 5.

——. 'Grown Ups.' *The Daily News & Leader* 30 December 1912: 5

Piper, Christine. 'Moral Campaigns for Children's Welfare in the Nineteenth Century.' *Moral Agendas for Child Welfare*. Ed. Michael King. London and New York: Routledge, 1999: 33–52.

Rose, Jacqueline, *The Case of Peter Pan or The Impossibility of Children's Fiction*. London: Macmillan, 1984.

Rothwell, Erika. '"You Catch It if You Try to Do Otherwise": The Limitations of E. Nesbit's Cross-Written Vision of the Child.' *Children's Literature* 25 (1997): 60–70.

'Saki' (H. H. Munro). 'The Toys of Peace.' 1913. *The Complete Short Stories*. London: Penguin, 2000. 391–93.

Stainton Rogers, Wendy and Rex. *Stories of Childhood: Shifting Agendas of Child Concern*. Hemel Hempstead: Harvester-Wheatsheaf, 1992.

Steedman, Carolyn. *Childhood, Culture, and Class in Britain: Margaret McMillan, 1860–1931*. London: Virago, 1990.

——. 'Bodies, Figures and Physiology: Margaret McMillan and the Late Nineteenth Century Remaking of Working-Class Childhood.' *In the Name of the Child: Health and Welfare, 1880–1940*. Ed. Roger Cooter. London: Routledge, 1992: 19–44.

Walsh, Sue. 'Effigies of Effie: On Kipling's Biographies.' *Children's Literature: New Approaches*. Ed. Karín Lesnik-Oberstein. Basingstoke and New York: Palgrave Macmillan, 2004: 25–50.

'Women's Work for the Nation: Why it Will Fill a Special Section.' *Daily News* 8 April 1914, 5.

9
'Girls! Girls, Everywhere!': Angela Brazil's Edwardian School Stories

Michelle Smith

> Girls! Girls everywhere! Girls in the passages, girls in the hall, racing upstairs and scurrying downstairs, diving into dormitories and running into classrooms, overflowing on to the landing and hustling along the corridor – everywhere, girls! There were tall and short, and fat and thin, and all degrees from pretty to plain; girls with fair hair and girls with dark hair, blue-eyed, brown-eyed, and grey-eyed girls; demure girls, romping girls, clever girls, stupid girls – but never a silent girl.
>
> (Angela Brazil, *The School by the Sea* [1914] 9)

The preceding quotation is an example of the way in which the Edwardian school novels of Angela Brazil celebrated the contemporary idea of less restricted girlhood, while still providing a sense of restraint in a somewhat segregated feminine world. Brazil's stories are representative of a new style of schoolgirl novel, with a less formal tone and, as Gillian Avery notes, a unique schoolgirl vernacular (207). The novels are also significant when considering childhood and pedagogy because of the way they register transitions in physical education and academic curricula for girls. Written in the early twentieth century, after the late-Victorian social and cultural shifts that placed more girls in schools for a longer duration, creating a literate 'girl' readership and girls' culture, Brazil's stories are a site in which a new vision of juvenile femininity is fully realized. As Sheila Fletcher remarks, Brazil

> gives her readers ... an exciting sense of the changes that were over-taking girls' schools; and team games, along with the gymnasium,

laboratory, and the tentative discussion of careers, appear as emblems of that brave new world which was rising from its Victorian foundations. (78)

This essay examines the changing conditions in girls' education, particularly the developing pedagogy of public secondary schools and also broader social concerns regarding motherhood and national degeneration as they intersect with Empire, and relates these wider developments to girls' schools as represented in Brazil's stories from 1906 to 1914.

Educational reforms, combined with broader societal shifts that brought women into public employments, made appropriate educational content for girls a critical issue in the late nineteenth century. The main expansion of colleges for women and girls' public schools occurred after 1870 (Pederson 13); there was an increase in the number of high schools for girls; an examination system enabling comparison of educational standards was introduced; and women were gradually admitted to university degrees. In her 1907 book on English girls' high schools, the headmistress of Manchester High School, Sara Burstall, quotes from the Schools Inquiry Commission (1867) upon the faults in girls' education prior to eventual reforms such as the Endowed Schools Act (1869): ' "Want of thoroughness and foundation; slovenliness and showy superficiality; inattention to rudiments; undue time given to accomplishment, and these not taught intelligently or in any scientific manner; want of organisation" ' (6).

The Education Act of 1870 was a significant move towards a national public education system, although the burden of tuition costs remained, and it did not extend to secondary schooling. In areas that were covered by a School Board, every child was entitled to attend school, and additionally a process of certification was adopted for head teachers. The subsequent Acts of 1876 and 1880 made school attendance compulsory for all children, with minimum leaving ages established (the minimum age rose from 10 to 11 in 1893, and from 11 to 12 in 1899) (Horn 22). It was not until the Act of 1902 that public secondary education was similarly accessible. Through these reforms, most children received some kind of formal education, and its duration was expanded for many of them, while in the Edwardian period secondary schooling became increasingly common.

In support of the view that girls needed a thorough education, Burstall suggests that education for girls should not differ substantially from that of boys: 'After all a girl is a human being, with a right to complete development, to a share in the spiritual inheritance of the race, to the opportunities of making the best of her faculties, of pursuing more advanced studies if she has the ability' (13). It is of significance that Burstall brings the term 'race' to bear, with the responsibility of motherhood having supreme importance for the cultivation of national strength. An equivalent education could be advocated on national grounds if curricula were explicitly linked with the 'natural' place of women in the private sphere:

> We see clearly now that the normal work of woman is to be the maker of a home, to be a wife, and above all a mother. Does a liberal education fit her for this? The answer is surely yes, if it makes her a better woman, abler and stronger in body, in intellect, and in character. (Burstall 13)

Burstall's support for a 'liberal education' is predicated on such an education preparing the girl for work in the home and for forming the character of her children (although Burstall does concede that some girls may need to work or might never marry). The question was how far what she calls 'technical instruction' should be extended, if the intention behind its inclusion in the curriculum was for improvement in domestic skills.

The Victorian ideology of separate male and female spheres is advanced in John Ruskin's 'Of Queens' Gardens' in *Sesame and Lilies* (1865). He contends that a girl should receive a similar education, with the same degree of seriousness as a boy, but that it must be 'differently directed,' as her command of knowledge need not be progressive but 'general and accomplished for daily and helpful use' (160–1). Ruskin's view of girls learning similar material to boys but for a different purpose is evident more than half a century later in Burstall's approach to the incorporation of scientific subjects into the curriculum for girls, and their usefulness for preparation for domestic duties: 'these life sciences [nature study, botany and zoology] are as important in the woman's characteristic activity for the young of the race as are physics and chemistry for men's industries' (110–1). Yet Burstall also advocates a focus on moral training and a need to ensure that girls do not have free influence on one another within school as do boys: 'The question is not the same for girls, whose work in the world is not to go out and rule, or in ordinary cases to deal in a practical way with large numbers of various kinds of other girls and women' (175). Regulation of girls' schools, therefore, was perceived as needing to differ insofar as girls must be 'contained' by adults, whereas boys were afforded greater freedoms in rehearsal for later life.

Nevertheless, the education of girls is conceived of as just as important to the nation: 'The teaching of cookery and the domestic arts to girls of every class is advocated on national grounds, as is the teaching of military drill and marksmanship to boys' (Burstall 194). Burstall suggests that the differences in curriculum reflect biological difference, and she replicates the views of Ruskin by arguing that the 'natural duty' of men is for national defence in the event of war, whereas it is the duty of women to do housework. As Carol Dyhouse notes, 'around the turn of the century the conservative arguments for confining women to their "traditional role" as housewives and mothers was being rephrased in terms of social Darwinistic assumptions about evolution and racial progress' (47). The intent of practical classes such as sewing, knitting, cookery, and hygiene was to improve standards in the home, in part to combat infant and child mortality, which was a strong thread of concern in rhetoric on national degeneration. Anna Davin notes that from the mid-1870s the birth rate was in decline and a significant number of babies did not survive infancy (10). The height of this anxiety can be seen in the work of the 1904 Inter-Departmental Committee on Physical Deterioration, which was prompted by the large number of men rejected for Army service for not meeting physical criteria. Mothers were regarded as integral to the development of the 'imperial race' and with the perception of a degree of failure in this task, ensuring that the next generation of mothers was adequately educated was of critical importance for the nation's future.

Arguments for the importance of girls' education not only emphasized the way in which schooling could create better mothers through domestic instruction, but also the prospect that increasing intellectual pursuits during girls' education would better equip them as guides for their children and companions to their husbands. Dorothea Beale, head of Cheltenham Ladies' College (1858–1906), and founder of St Hilda's teachers' training college, in *Work and Play in Girls' Schools by Three Headmistresses* (1898), draws less of a distinction between the education of boys and girls than that which Burstall evinces, suggesting that teaching should aim to develop 'to the highest excellence the intellectual powers common to both [sexes]' (7). As Beale argues: 'Surely women trained in good schools and colleges have as wives and mothers shared the labours and entered more fully as companions into the lives of husbands and children' (5). Intended as a manual for Secondary School teachers, *Work and Play* details a course of instruction covering academic disciplines including the humanities, mathematics, science, and 'aesthetics' (music, art), in addition to sections on 'The Moral Side of Education' and 'Cultivation of the Body.' The intellectual instruction of the girl is inseparable from the moral responsibility she will take up in the home, and her ability to propagate physical health in her children.

These and other pedagogical concerns, including domestic instruction and physical education, are translated into Brazil's early school novels in several ways. Beverly Lyon Clark suggests that the school story was transformed in the twentieth century when the canonical story became split into 'elite' and 'non-elite' streams for adults and children: 'British girls' stories were becoming more popular and jocular, acquiring a tone close to that of nineteenth-century canonical boys' stories – with the advent of Angela Brazil and other writers' (229). Brazil's stories are indeed a turning point in the genre, marking the beginning of a new style of language and address within the somewhat established girls' school setting. The formulaic mould Brazil cast enabled her eventually to write 46 school stories. If Brazil was the catalyst for change, then the works of L. T. Meade were the standard by which change could be measured. Beginning with the popular *A World of Girls* (1886), Meade authored girls' school and college-based stories and an astounding number of books about girls, publishing more than 250 works into the twentieth century. Mavis Reimer suggests that *A World of Girls* established the genre's formulae – Meade's schoolgirl heroines are fallible and impulsive, and those who display the qualities of independence and strength in their actions are admired (44). While Meade was a pioneer in popularizing the school story, Brazil's concentration upon girls agedfrom approximately 10 to 15 sees more of a focus on girls considered still malleable by their education, unlike the older girls of many Meade stories.

The plot of Brazil's first book set in a girls' school, *The Fortunes of Philippa: A School Story* (1906), mirrors the biographical background of her own mother. Angelica Brazil (née McKinnel) born to a Scottish father and a Spanish mother, was raised for a decade in Rio de Janeiro and then sent to an English school. The novel begins with the eponymous Philippa Seaton resident in San Carlos, South America, where she has been raised by her father (the British Consul and plantation owner), Juanita ('a mulatto nurse'), and Tasso ('the black bearer') (10). Her father has kept her restricted in the Government house and is fearful that Philippa has not learnt accomplishments that she would have acquired under the influence of a mother: ' "You're ten years old now, growing a tall girl, and not learning half the things you ought to. I feel there's something wrong about you, but I don't know quite how to set it right" ' (7).

Philippa's father detects a problematic difference between his daughter and the way in which English girls ought to behave. She is initially strongly aligned with the local servants, and her first dispute with her uncle's family in England concerns the plan to modify her ways before she attends school. Philippa is emphatic that she will return to San Carlos and continue to speak Spanish as ' "Juanita and Tasso can't speak anything else" ' (29). Yet, despite her resolve, within two years in England she has forgotten how to speak Spanish and has left behind her 'foreign ways,' and is considered by her Aunt as ready to be formally schooled. It is necessary to first eliminate the worst and most obvious markers of Philippa's 'foreignness' before she can be polished in the subtleties of suitable behaviour at the 'The Hollies,' a school accommodating only 40 girls, located in a 'healthy' environment away from London. The school amalgamates contemporary models of femininity (signified by sport, maths, and chemistry) with traditional restrictions and domestic accomplishments:

> We learnt mathematics at The Hollies, but we curtsied to our teachers as we left the room; we had chemistry classes in a well-fitted laboratory, but we were taught the most exquisite darning and the finest of open hem-stitch; we played cricket, hockey, and all modern games, but we used backboards and were made to walk round the schoolroom balancing books upon our heads; we had the best of professors for languages and literature, and we were taught to receive visitors graciously, to dispense afternoon tea, arrange flowers, and to write and answer invitations correctly. (54)

After a year at the school, at the age of 13, Philippa is considered to be 'greatly improved' (142), and her past in San Carlos is a distant memory.

Fears about the affects of intellectual exertion upon developing girls are, however, played out when Philippa begins to sit crookedly because of an aching back, lolling on her desk from exhaustion, fidgeting from nervousness, and eventually fainting. In pedagogical texts of the period, sufficient physical health is coupled with the development of the intellect; and both abilities are presented as being irreversibly damaged if not overseen in childhood, or as detrimental to the body or mind if overexerted. Balance of the intellectual meant restricting academic work periods. *Work and Play* includes a sample daily timetable, which is guided by the principle that girls up until the age of 12 should only study for three hours per day; 14-year olds for up to four hours; and for those aged up to 16 six hours is maximum for any girl lest she become 'anaemic and weak-backed' (Beale 414). In *The Fortunes of Philippa*, the doctor determines that Phillipa's illness is ' "a decided case of nervous breakdown, due to overwork" ' (162) and she travels with her aunt to Brighton to recover. This event is the catalyst for change in The Hollies' timetable, serving as a demonstration of the feared ill consequences of mental and physical overexertion: academic work hours are relaxed and walks on the high-road are replaced by 'daily rambles' over the hills or among the woods (163). The teacher responsible for much of the strenuous regulation leaves the school and is replaced by a new teacher who promises a less regimented curriculum.

The novel closes with Philippa having left school, running the house for her father, who has returned to England permanently, and aspiring to work to improve the local village so as not to be 'aimless' (206). While some contact with the colonial world remains, the transformation of Philippa through her schooling into an acceptably British girl is made clear: 'my father says that the little foreign plant which he sent over so long ago to harden in our gray northern clime has taken root, and changed from a tropical blossom into an English rose' (208). The transformation from an exotic flower into a quintessentially English one, at its simplest level, represents the cultural assimilation of Philippa to a more refined and less 'wild' or uncultivated version of juvenile femininity. Her change from blossom to a more sophisticated rose also marks a maturation process of 'blooming' that Amy King suggests could function as 'a culturally pervasive shorthand for young female subjectivity' (194). Through her transformation from blossom to rose, Philippa has acquired an acceptable *English* subjectivity.

The importance of play to balance academic work for girls is also evident in *The Nicest Girl in the School* (1909), where the students at Morton Priory have twice weekly games of hockey, two organized walks per week, and remaining spare time spent outside. The ideology of a healthy mind in a healthy body, ensuring that the potential negative effects of educating girls are averted, is embedded in the structure of the curricula at the school. *The New Girl at St. Chad's* (1912) similarly presents a school in which work and play are balanced in the schedule.

The principal's motto is *mens sana in corpore sano* (a healthy mind in a healthy body) and this ideal is linked not only with examination success and 'the clean bill of health' of the students but also 'the high moral tone that prevailed throughout' (40). Like the example of Philippa, this novel mirrors historical concerns about mental exertion taking a physical toll upon girls. The school scrutinizes girls' weight, lungs, teeth, and chest measurements; if any girl is found to be unhealthy she is 'turned out to grass' and is only required to participate in half of her usual lessons until she regains physical strength (69).

The frequent plot device of the absent mother in Brazil's school stories enables the staging of education as a problem of social and self-development rather than one of transmission of appropriate values and behaviour from mother to daughter in the home. The lack of a female relative serving as an idealized model of femininity transfers even more significance to the school environment for the development of the girl in all respects, particularly those outside the purely academic. Gwen Gascoyne in *The Youngest Girl in the Fifth* (1913) is 14 years old, often wishes that she were a boy (she is tall for her age and awkward), and does not have a mother. Gwen, however, is not a boarder at her school, unlike most Brazil protagonists, and a greater burden is placed upon her own self-development outside school. Life with her family and friend Dick Chambers is uniquely important to the narrative. Her interactions with him enable contrasts between the 'modern' girl and Victorian femininity, with Gwen envious of the way Dick can run for a bus without skirts hampering his movement, and the way in which she performs a rescue of a boy who fell when climbing.

While Dick remarks that girls are ordinarily afraid of crisis situations, Gwen explains that 'modern girls' are not prone to inaction: ' "They used to do the shrieking business in old fashioned novels. It's gone out of fashion since hockey came in" ' (81). The frightened, passive girl is relegated to the pages of fiction, distanced from the real Edwardian girl, but simultaneously the reader is, of course, presented with fictional modern girls in the story she is reading. Hockey, a game adopted widely in schools for the middle-classes, represents active girlhood and a shift to include such team games in the realm of acceptable physical activity. By the time of Brazil's stories, it had been more than a decade since the game had infiltrated most schools – the symbolic final acceptance of which is evident in 1891 when Dorothea Beale relented and adopted hockey at her school despite her earlier fears of compromising womanliness (Fletcher 34). Organized team sports in girls' school stories are associated with alteration in the ideal girl from one who is weak to one who is strong and capable of physical exertion, indicating a move from Victorian to Edwardian concepts of the female child. Gwen demonstrates the qualities that will later bring success to her and the school on the tennis court when she rescues school teacher Miss Roberts – who breaks her leg in an avalanche – with calm capability as a result of her having taken a St. John's Ambulance course.

With the flawed performance of British troops in the Boer War (1899–1902) imparting several lessons about national degeneration and readiness for battle, nursing became an important and acceptable occupation in the Edwardian era in both domestic and military senses. Girls were able to train for potential nursing work through the Voluntary Aid Detachment (VAD) nursing reserve schemes between 1906 and 1914 and also, to some extent, with the Girl Guides, which was officially founded in 1910. In *A Pair of Schoolgirls: A Story of School Days* (1912), Avondale College conducts a popular scheme based upon the model of the Guides[1]: a Guild of First Aid and Field Ambulance. Like the Guides, the purpose of the Guild is 'character training, as developed through work for others' (156). An article in *The Girl's Realm* from 1909 points to the concerns that parents held about the Guiding scheme making for 'rough-and-ready' girls: 'Some parents...were rather alarmed at the idea of their children running about the country and becoming somewhat gypsy-like in their habits and ideas' (Roberts 340). One student's mother in Brazil's novel replicates these fears about masculine traits being imparted to girls: 'she thought it was something like the Boy Scouts, and she said she couldn't have me careering about the country on Saturday afternoons – she didn't approve of it for girls' (156). The differentiation of Guiding, or in this case, Guild activities, from those intended for boys is predicated upon a caring or altruistic component. The principal, Miss Tempest, emphasizes these aspects of the Guild, coupling them with feminine capacity for 'improving' the working classes: ' "There is nobody who cannot make some little corner of the world better by her presence, and be of use to her poorer neighbours" ' (157). Membership of the Guild involves pledging to sew one item per year to be sent to the Ragged School Mission – a genteel act of benevolence that may have eased the minds of mothers – but the real focus of activity is upon the ambulance classes where legs are placed in hockey stick splints and jaws are bandaged shut. The training culminates in a camp drill and practice in field work with boys from the local orphanage acting as injured soldiers:

> The officers and patrol leaders at once took command, and began to instruct each group of ambulance workers in the particular duties they were expected to perform. One detachment started to build a fire (there is a science in the building of fires in the open), a second ran up the Red Cross flag and arranged a temporary hospital with supplies from the transport wagon, while a third went out to render first aid to the wounded. (162)

The field work practice runs with the precision of a military operation, with patrols of girls assigned to tasks including camp cookery, nursing, and signalling. While there is a comical aspect to the descriptions of the girls' urgent responses to pretended danger, a realistic consideration of such work as a future employment possibility is also delivered[2]: 'Alison, who had helped put up a tent, and given imaginary chloroform under the directions of a supposed army surgeon, was immensely proud of herself, and half-inclined to regard the work of the Red Cross Sisterhood as her vocation in life' (164). The combination of adventure and excitement (Alison calls the training 'ripping') with a traditional caring vocation is an example of the modern girlhood celebrated in Brazil's novels that amalgamates new and old visions of femininity.

The field work drill practice draws upon the concept of encouraging individual capability and skills that can work for the benefit of all. Education in the Edwardian period was understood as a process of developing the individual child to his or her full potential, with the overarching ethos that this process would benefit society as a whole. By comparing the development of each child with representations of the advancement of the nation, education was seen to be of vital significance for the Empire. As Beale writes:

> The most civilised nations are devoting their best energies to the work of education, realising that upon this depends their very existence – that it is not by starving the individual life, and merging it in the general, but by developing each to perfection, that the common good will be secured. (3)

The refinement of educational practice is constructed as vital to ensure that England remains grouped with these 'most civilised' of countries and marks out its superiority in comparison with those countries whose children remain 'undeveloped.' The distinguishing of the self within the constraints of a set of ideals – such as physical and moral strength – that support the imperial project functions to benefit the 'common good' rather than the individual alone. Jane Frances Dove, in her 'Cultivation of the Body' (1898), suggests that games for girls should be encouraged as they have a 'higher function,' which not only encourages self-reliance, determination, and courage, but also 'learning to sink individual preferences in the effort of loyally working with others for the common good' (400). Even the family unit must be subordinated to a concern for the place of that unit within a community and then within the nation: 'To be a good citizen, it is essential that she should have wide interests, a sense of discipline and organisation, *esprit de corps*, a power of corporate action' (Dove 401).

In Brazil's novel *The New Girl at St. Chad's*, Miss Cavendish, the Girton-educated principal, compares her school to an army, with each girl required to preserve its rules for the good of the whole. The heroine, Honor Fitzgerald, a stereotypical 'wild,' 'hot-headed' and 'idle' Irish girl, is thoughtless regarding her sick mother and unable to submit to discipline from a string of governesses. Despite some initial incidents at the school prompted by her selfishness, Honor comes to feel that she is a 'unit' in a larger community, and recognizes the importance of fitting in with 'universal custom' and the notion of *esprit de corps* (58). This thread throughout many of Brazil's pre-war novels foreshadows the emphasis on *'Esprit de corps* and zeal for games' which Avery suggests only became a pervasive concern in the work of other writers of girls' school stories 'between the wars' (207). The school and the individuals within it in this novel are presented as a small scale version of the nation and its citizens:

> A large public school is indeed a vast democracy, and members are estimated only by the value they prove themselves to be to the commonweal: their private possessions and affairs matter little to the general community, but their examination successes, cricket scores, or tennis championships are of vital importance. (186–7)

In one school term, Honor transforms from a selfish and idle girl to one who is concerned for others in her family (particularly her sick mother) and for the 'commonweal' (she now has 'higher ideals and noble aspirations' [287]).

As Edwardian national imperatives were inextricably entwined with imperial aims, schooling and even innocuous domestic tasks could take on importance for the Empire. In her essay 'Home Arts' (1911), Margaret A. Gilliland notes the movement to incorporate domestic education into the school curriculum enables girls to become 'builders of homes and makers of men' (155): 'The old "blue-stocking" type, who prided herself on not knowing how to sew and mend, and who thought cooking menial, and beneath her, no longer appeals to anyone... But at the same time we no longer share the conception of a woman's whole duty held by our grandmothers' (152). The bluestocking figure is invoked to caution against excessive emphasis on education to the neglect of domesticity. A process of negotiation is therefore at work in which mid-Victorian conceptions of women's domestic duty are modified to incorporate ideas of feminine freedom while still upholding the value of domestic work for the nation.

Miss Drummond, the principal in *A Fourth Form Friendship* (1912), views herself as conversant with the latest in pedagogical methods and introduces a specially constructed cottage on the school grounds in which lessons in cookery and cleaning are conducted (46). She poses the possibility that the domestic skills acquired at the cottage may be more useful in 'some emergency' than anything else taught at school: '"I think, also, that a great future for many of our English girls lies in the Colonies, where domestic help is often at a premium, and the most delicately nurtured lady must sometimes set to work, and be her own cook and laundress"' (46). Miss Drummond also demonstrates the fusion of old and new modes of femininity in practical terms:

> We can very well emulate our great-grandmothers in this respect... and thus make a happy combination of ancient and modern. Because you are studying French and algebra is no reason at all why you should not also know how to fry an omelet or boil a potato. A cultivated brain ought surely to be able to grasp domestic economy better than an untrained one. (46)

Contrary to fears that academic study for girls would negatively impact upon the acquisition of domestic skills, she argues that one form of knowledge may complement the other.

Within the confines of the school setting there are sets of regulations and procedures which mimic or have similar functions to those of the nation more widely. Brazil's own school experiences lead her to complain that there was 'no common ground upon which we [girl pupils] could meet, no mutual object to be gained' (*My Own Schooldays* 150). Her vision of a school system incorporating social responsibility is rendered throughout her stories. In *The Leader of the Lower School* (1913), large schools are described as miniature states: 'Quite apart from the rule of the mistresses, it has its own particular institution and its own system of self-government. In their special domain its officers are of quite as much importance as Members of Parliament' (44). The girls' school was a female preserve with almost exclusively female teaching staff, and school stories provided for the girl reader an ongoing enclosed 'world' in which heroines who could be admired or emulated were located. Gill Frith suggests this segregation allowed a display of less restrictive behaviour for girls, outside of the accepted markers of the 'feminine': 'In a world of girls, to be female is *normal*, and not a *problem*. To be assertive, physically active, daring, ambitious, is not a source of tension' (121). Indeed, Brazil's heroines engage in perilous rescues, plot to prevent 'spies' attacking England, ride untamed horses, and explore forbidden locations, but these activities often cause conflict with school headmistresses who construct clear bounds to their institutions.

There is a sense of containment in the physical location of the schools, with unaccompanied straying from school bounds a serious transgression. Reimer argues that like women of the middle classes who worked outside the home, 'schoolgirls threatened the stability of domestic ideology when they moved into the public sphere of school' (47). In Brazil's novels, the extent to which girls are located in the public sphere is controlled by the situation of most schools in the country or in isolated locations. *The Nicest Girl in the School* depicts a school housed in a former Franciscan monastery, and the contrast between the historical and contemporary purposes of the building again emphasizes the cultural significance of the Edwardian schoolgirl figure:

> it now seemed a strange irony of fate that feminine petticoats should reign supreme within the very walls where the grey brothers had lived in such seclusion. The old refectory where they had dined, and the cloister where they had been wont to meditate, were now given up to a lively, laughing crew of girls, whose twentieth-century costumes among the quaint surroundings made a curious blend of ancient and modern. (32)

The schoolgirl comes to represent 'modernity,' with her feminine freedom contrasted with an austere vision of masculinity. The monastery itself is a fitting representation of an enclosed 'world of girls,' described as 'a little self-contained kingdom, shut off from the rest of the world' (33). With tennis courts, playing fields, an art studio, music rooms, a laboratory, gymnasium, home farm, fruit and vegetable garden and sanatorium, there is little reason for the boarders to move outside the school's bounds. Within the school, there is significant regulation of behaviour, including a system of prefects and 'order marks,' and also of evening leisure time with girls conducting useful tasks such as sewing (59).

The School by the Sea (1914) is set in an isolated former convent at the end of a narrow peninsula described as a 'kingdom by the sea' (21). The location also enables the creation of a separate world of girls, but makes for an even stronger contrast between a quiet vision of femininity and the active one which the girls' school creates:

> No pale-faced novices these, with downcast eyes and cheeks sunken with fasting; no timid glances, no soft ethereal footfalls or gliding garments – the old order had changed indeed, and yielded place to a rosy, racy, healthy, hearty, well-grown set of twentieth-century schoolgirls, overflowing with vigorous young life and abounding spirits, mentally and physically fit, and about as different from their medieval forerunners as a hockey stick from a spindle. (10–11)

The hockey stick is a marker of difference of the modern girl and is contrasted with the domestic via the image of a spindle that produces an antiquated vision of laborious women's work. The building in which women were once cloistered and silent dates from the fourteenth century, but the necessity of providing a different education for contemporary girls is foregrounded for reasons of health and individual development: 'Inside the ancient walls everything was strictly modern and hygienic, with the latest patterns of desks, the most sanitary wall-papers, and each up-to-date appliance that educational authorities might suggest or devise' (26). This blending of historical restriction with the celebration of contemporary opportunity for girls provides an apt metaphor for their education more generally, the limits of which are subject to negotiation between old and new visions of femininity in Brazil's Edwardian school stories.

Notes

1. While the scheme is not incorporated with any external organization, the principal, Miss Tempest, frequently delivers quotations from and adopts ideas contained within the first Girl Guide handbook (1912).
2. The end of term exhibition of physical exercises in *The New Girl at St. Chad's* includes military drill and, for the first time, flag signalling. One student believes

it is a skill that might prove important to have attained during catastrophe or even, inexplicably, in normal life: 'It might come in useful if there were a war...and at any rate, it will be very convenient at home' (*New Girl* 277).

Works cited

Avery, Gillian. *Childhood's Pattern: A Study of the Heroes and Heroines of Children's Fiction 1770–1950*. Leicester: Hodder and Stoughton, 1975.

Beale, Dorothea, Lucy H. M. Soulsby, and Jane Francis Dove. *Work and Play in Girls' Schools by Three Headmistresses*. London: Longmans, Green and Co., 1898.

Brazil, Angela. *The Fortunes of Philippa: A School Story*. London: Blackie and Son, 1906.

——. *The Nicest Girl in the School*. London: Blackie and Son, 1909.

——. *A Fourth Form Friendship: A School Story*. London: Blackie and Son, 1912.

——. *A Pair of Schoolgirls: A Story of School Days*. London: Blackie and Son, 1912.

——. *The New Girl at St. Chad's*. London: Blackie and Son, 1912.

——. *The Leader of the Lower School: A Tale of School Life*. London: Blackie and Son, 1913.

——. *The Youngest Girl in the Fifth*. London: Blackie and Son, 1913.

——. *My Own Schooldays*. London: Blackie and Son, 1925.

——. *The School by the Sea*. 1914. London: Blackie and Sons, 1936.

Burstall, Sara A. *English High Schools for Girls: Their Aims, Organisation, and Management*. London: Longmans, Green, and Co., 1907.

Davin, Anna. 'Imperialism and Motherhood.' *History Workshop Journal* 5 (1978): 9–65.

Dove, Jane Francis. 'Cultivation of the Body.' In Beale, Soulsby, and Dove 396–423.

Dyhouse, Carol. 'Social Darwinistic Ideas and the Development of Women's Education in England, 1880–1920.' *History of Education* 5.1 (1976): 41–58.

Fletcher, Sheila. *Women First: The Female Tradition in English Physical Education 1880–1980*. London: Athlone, 1984.

Frith, Gill. ' "The Time of Your Life": The Meaning of the School Story.' *Language, Gender and Childhood*. Ed. Carolyn Steedman et al. London: Routledge, 1985. 113–36.

Gilliland, Margaret A. 'Home Arts.' *Public Schools for Girls: A Series of Papers on Their History, Aims, and Schemes of Study*. Ed. Sara A. Burstall and M. A. Douglas. London: Longmans, Green and Co., 1911. 153–65.

Horn, Pamela. *The Victorian and Edwardian Schoolchild*. Gloucester: Alan Sutton, 1989.

King, Amy M. *Bloom: The Botanical Vernacular in the English Novel*. Oxford: Oxford University Press, 2003.

Lyon Clark, Beverly. *Regendering the School Story: Sassy Sissies and Tattling Tomboys*. New York: Routledge, 1996.

Meade, L. T. *A World of Girls*. London: Cassell and Co., 1886.

Pederson, Joyce Senders. *The Reform of Girls' Secondary and Higher Education in Victorian England: A Study of Elites and Educational Change*. New York: Garland Publishing, 1987.

Reimer, Mavis. '"These Two Irreconcilable Things: Art and Young Girls": The Case of the Girls' School Story.' *Girls, Boys, Books, Toys: Gender in Children's Literature and Culture.* Ed. Beverley Lyon Clark and Margaret R. Higonnet. Baltimore: Johns Hopkins University Press, 1999. 40–52.

Roberts, Walter T. 'Girls as Scouts.' *The Girl's Realm* 12 (1909): 337–40.

Ruskin, John. 'Of Queens' Gardens.' *Sesame and Lilies: Two Lectures Delivered at Manchester in 1864.* London: Smith, Elder and Co., 1865. 119–96.

10
Towards the Modern Man: Edwardian Boyhood in the Juvenile Periodical Press

Stephanie Olsen

Gordon Stables, the flamboyant writer on health matters for the *Boy's Own Paper*, remarked that Edwardian boys faced dangers that were 'very, *very,* real' (558). He advised that:

> The very first stepping-stones to good health and success are the giving up of bad habits, whether school vices or smoking and the declaration made to yourself and before Heaven in your own chambers that *you will not read sensational or impure literature again.* You thus bid fair to purify your minds and bodies also, and remove the most dangerous obstacles to your advancement in life. (558, emphasis added)

The religious and secular press both promoted the same view: a boy's life course was fragile, and the few years before adulthood would make a significant difference in producing either the next generation of responsible citizens and heads of family, or moral and physical degenerates. Disparate groups, which one might otherwise expect to be at odds with one another, agreed that better than encouraging boys to cease the practice of bad habits, was to prevent them from ever starting them. As will be shown, the importance of this project led writers to blur the distinction between fact and fiction.

This essay examines how boys were informally educated, through the fictional stories in popular periodicals, to become responsible men and caring fathers. This moral fiction aimed at correcting the 'immoral' fiction of penny dreadfuls, an undertaking especially important at the turn of the twentieth century when, as Martin Francis and John Tosh (in several works) have outlined, a rapidly changing society provoked questions about the place of men in the family. The legislation of this era is indicative of an augmenting concern for the rising generation's physical and moral health. Several key acts served to bolster the effectiveness of pre-existing education and anti-cruelty acts, most notably the Children's Act of 1908, but also the Education Acts of 1901 and 1902, the 1901 Factory and Workshop Act and Intoxicating Liquors (Sale to Children) Act, and the Prevention of Cruelty to Children Act of 1904. These laws demonstrated a new concern for children in their own right, and not as possessions of their fathers. Since many Edwardian boys were falling short of modern physical, educational and moral standards, organizations (the Boy Scouts being the most influential) were formed to ameliorate these shortcomings. The juvenile periodical press was also an important part of this attempt and collaborated with these groups. Important religious organizations, like the Religious Tract Society, the Church of England Temperance Society, and the Band of Hope Unions, sought to inculcate in boys the morals and attitudes needed for their future roles by publishing juvenile fiction, usually in the form of periodicals. The Religious Tract Society met the challenge of secularized education (after the 1870 Education Act) by producing a series of juvenile periodicals which had an implicitly Christian basis (Hewitt 62). Although echoing earlier Victorian modes, Edwardian periodicals adapted their messages according to an increasingly competitive and expanding juvenile publishing industry, and in response to broader changes in British society and culture. This was exemplified by the introduction of 'secular,' market-driven competitors, such as the *Boy's Herald* and the *Boy's Friend*, published by Lord Northcliffe's Amalgamated Press. The *Boy's Own Paper*, started by the evangelical Religious Tract Society in 1879 and catering to a mostly middle-class audience, dominated the market until it was overtaken by the more working-class focused papers of the Amalgamated Press at the turn of the century (Boyd 70–1).

Many constants remained regarding childhood in the Victorian and Edwardian eras. A preoccupation with boyhood especially dominated the prescriptive and fictional writings of both periods. That the future of Britain depended on the proper upbringing and education of boys was not in doubt. What was in doubt was whether boys were being adequately taught at home and in school. Victorian publishers had begun to fill that gap; Edwardian publishers sought to refine this informal education in a changing market. Periodicals blurred the distinction between fiction and non-fiction by making fiction serve religious and moral ideologies. The details of the short story, drama or serial novel were chosen, informed and made relevant by their service in advancing Christian truths. Thus in a sense it is irrelevant whether the details of a moral tale were imagined or reported. They were made real by the perceived truth which underlay them.

The periodicals Edwardian publishers produced were structured with fiction as the strongest component, while there were usually also illustrations and non-fictional articles, either in the form of biography or of 'true' story-telling in the first person. For the purposes of this study the term fiction is loosely defined, reflecting its fluid uses in the periodicals. The non-fiction and advice columns of periodicals lent weight and precision to the morals hidden in the fictional accounts and in the illustrations. One of the main aims of the non-fictional elements was to make sure that boys read the *right* kind of fiction and that they understood what lessons to draw from their reading. It is only possible clearly to understand these messages when the various narrative forms are juxtaposed. The messages of the pieces were of crucial importance to the writers.

What, therefore, was promoted in the periodicals? In short, it was the message that boys should be trustworthy, honest, hardworking, punctual, polite, unselfish, justly independent and self-reliant and abstain from bad habits (Edwards 'Your Editor's Advice' 400). These habits included drinking, smoking, gambling, sexual gratification (alone or with others) and swearing. That 'the British race would be all the better for it' was agreed by groups as diverse as the Amalgamated Press, the various societies of the Band of Hope, the Church of England Temperance Society, and the Religious Tract Society (Edwards, 'Teetotalism' 416). Boys should prioritize family above all else and obey their parents, even if they felt their advice unreasonable or outdated. 'No matter how keen their desire may be to see the world outside, their first duty is to their parents' (Edwards, 'Editor's Den.' *Boy's Friend* II.94 [1903], 709). Moral messages were clearly contained within the fictional element, but were made manifest by their location next to apparently non-fictional moral guidance.

The Victorian emphasis on strict evangelical messages was certainly becoming unpopular, in favour of more subtle moral messages which would be more palatable to the Edwardian young. Yet, even in so-called secular papers (as Lord Northcliffe's are understood to be), a strong Christian foundation can be uncovered. The values promoted in the texts were Christian in origin, though it would be far too simplistic to dismiss the papers as relics from an evangelical past. They were certainly of their age, competing in a modern publishing industry and with the modern reader in mind. The Edwardian period was a pivotal time when a modern understanding of boyhood emerged. Boys were no longer miniature adults: they were often viewed as naturally good and pure and could be moral beacons for adults, but their good qualities could easily become polluted under the wrong influences. Edwardian boyhood was a distinct and crucial phase of development, one in which boys were trained in the serious matter of character-building for manhood, while also catering to their specific pastimes and fantasy world. This new and growing concern for boys was indicative of an increasing fear that many men were not fit for a modern Britain, with their manliness and their morality in question, as G. R. Searle has shown. Evidence from the major boys' papers shows a strong concern in the Edwardian period for training boys in an informal and indirect way: while there was an abundance of explicit moral instructions in these papers, it was common for the educational value to be implicitly loaded into the morals of particular stories, and into the general tenor of the publications over this entire period. The most discussed example has been the lessons of fair play that were found in the *Boy's Own Paper*'s sporting serial stories (for example, MacDonald 522). Yet many other types of stories contained moral messages, and were made stronger when juxtaposed with more overtly religious non-fictional accounts. For example, on the same page next to two of the stories discussed below, one such non-fictional account was a little question and answer piece by a physician on the dangers of alcohol (*Onward* 26–7). Another is a short biography of Lord Avebury, as a moral man of business and science, whom readers were encouraged to emulate (Sidebotham 33–4). Moral training was therefore not reducible to one or other particular story, but was formed from a general and long-running appreciation, in the reader, of the whole. Boys were also given advice on how to prepare for a modern career and how to provide themselves with a healthy lifestyle. More important than these outward attainments, they were also instructed how to lead a manly life.

The inner qualities of manliness were actively taught. As John Tosh puts it: 'It was the consistent aim of boys' education to internalise these moral qualities – to make them second nature so that they could be expressed in action instinctively and convincingly. Virtue was held to be inseparable from manliness' ('The Old Adam' 232). All of these organizations, both religious and 'secular,' made clear in their informal teachings for boys that the attributes of a 'real' man, of a real gentleman, were open to any class. It was simply that 'the boys who keep on trying have made the world's best men' (Apples 96). Equally, *no* boy should be drinking, smoking, gambling or physically 'impure.' Real success was in becoming a 'real' man, one who took seriously his responsibilities to his family and to his country. The editor of the Amalgamated Press juvenile papers, Hamilton Edwards, clearly expressed this: 'I want them all to remember that success in life, is, after all, not so much about the mere making of money, as the making of one's self a useful, honest citizen of our great empire' (Edwards, 'Editor's Den.' III.115 [1903], 176).

The juvenile publishing industry had long recognized the influence fiction could have on its readers. As early as 1886 Edward Salmon had made the connection clear:

> It is impossible to overrate the importance of the influence of such a supply [of fiction] on the national character and culture. Mind, equally with body, will develop according to what it feeds on; and just as the strength or weakness of a man's muscle depends on whether he leads a healthy or vicious life, so will the strength or weakness of his moral sense largely depend upon whether he reads in his youth that which is pure or that which is foul. (248)

To boys, stories became real; their thoughts, actions and moral sense were shaped by reading as much as by their contact with the world around them (Salmon 248). The juvenile papers recognized that reading could have a decisive impact on boys' development. While they had different motivations, they all recognized the importance of the boy to society, and in the words of one commentator, 'to the character and well-being of the nation and the state' (King 818). Thus, in the Edwardian period, 'frantic educational and religious dashes' were made at boys (King 818).

As one *Boy's Own Paper* writer declared, 'People say, "Boys will be boys"; but they are wrong – boys will be men. And to prepare for their manhood not a day is to be lost' (Williamson 487). There was a new sense of urgency in the Edwardian papers: modern life was fast-paced and the years before adulthood so few that moral guidance, as well as the education required for a modern workforce, needed to be passed on effectively and efficiently. Positive images of masculinity were mixed with warnings against the temptations of modern life. It was feared that the 'ugly thoughts, wicked memories and unclean pictures' of bad books would etch themselves into boys' hearts (Howatt 134). One young reader of the *Band of Hope Review* wrote, 'If a boy reads rubbish he nearly always thinks about it afterwards, and feels inclined to do the same things himself. And it robs him of strength of will, and care for his character' (Blight 50). Gordon Stables, and countless other writers of the period blamed 'penny dreadfuls' for boys' descent into vice and violence, which produced immoral, ungodly and unproductive lives. Lives like this were ruined, with redemption by moral influence or example difficult. It was far better positively to influence the young before they 'ruined' their lives. The fear, however, was that the publishers of penny dreadfuls and even the producers of newer inventions like cinematography understood the boy, and could therefore influence his moral behaviour and his upbringing more than 'the Sunday-school teacher and the Band of Hope lecturer, and better even than the woman who bore him' (King 820). Yet there was hope that with the availability of the right sort of reading material the current generation of boys would know what to choose. Hamilton Edwards believed this to be true regarding his own papers. 'The present-day fellow carries plenty of common-sense in his head, and when he reads a thrilling story, he wants it to be thrilling in a sensible manner, and not a mass of blood-curdling improbabilities' (Edwards, 'The Penny Dreadful' 70). The advice to boys was clear: 'Do not load up your heart then with hateful things you must carry with you to the last; load up rather with thoughts that are beautiful and true and lovely: these will lend you wings to help you mount higher and be happier' (Howatt 134). Morally correct fiction was prescribed, as it was thought that 'good books' could also be inscribed on boys' hearts.

In the *Boy's Own Paper*, as in other periodicals, fictional and non-fictional accounts often merged, and though many of these accounts were probably not genuine, they were lent more credibility by supposedly being the experience of real boys. In an article entitled 'Mother and Home,' a clean-cut Christian young man is reported as having said that he had been one of the worst boys in town, but seeing the example of a boy from a good home who was respectful to his mother, he decided that he would try to be the same to his own mother. Though he is mocked for his new behaviour, his whole life begins to improve and the narrator comments: 'thus one boy's kindness to his mother is still bringing forth good fruit in the life of a man' (16). These stories and numerous similar ones served to instruct readers to be accountable to God, to their families and to themselves.

A regular feature of the *Boy's Own Paper* was 'Talks to Boys: by an Old One.' These were described as 'chats' with readers in a 'manly, straightforward manner, giving sound advice and pointing the road to a pure,

Christian life' (*Annual Report* 126). Their advice was often placed in the broader framework of a moral nation, constituted of pious, domesticated and loyal male subjects. This concept was encapsulated in the notion of the 'Briton,' a trope commonly used to denote the characteristics required of the male citizens of a great Nation. This was more significant, however, in instructing boys in their behaviour at home, within their families, in school and at work, than in invoking some grander idea of the Briton in his great Empire. Scholars such as Patrick Dunae, J. A. Mangan, Robert H. MacDonald, and Kelly Boyd have focused on the *Boy's Own Paper*'s imperial message, yet it emphasized male moral duties, in the home and in the wider world, over and above imperial adventure. A recitation for five boys in the temperance paper *Young Standard Bearer* demonstrates that boys were vitally important to the nation and its fate. The last paragraph, to be recited in unison, summed up the point:

Yes, little Britons are we, are we,
Not very big yet, and not very strong;
Yet we are growing and men shall be,
So we must keep us from all that's wrong;
Fair is our country, her fame is great,
And God has sent us our best to do;
Nor need we until we're grown-up wait,
But even now may be Britons true. (Chiltern 30)

The connection between the individual conduct of boys and imperialism (or even jingoism) was made clear in numerous stories, though this was not necessarily the model of imperial masculinity which scholars have argued dominated this era. It was supposed to have captured the imagination of the Edwardian young, at the expense of male feelings of domesticity. This was, after all, the period when imperialism was at its height and fascinated many Britons, perhaps especially young boys, who were drawn to stories and images depicting imperial adventure. Yet, the evidence from boys' papers suggests that the relationship between imperialism and boyhood training was more complicated than simply preparing readers for their future roles as imperial men. Frequently these imperial stories were employed to entice the reader, who would then be subjected to the papers' weighty messages about morality and duty to family and self.

By generally focusing on categories (such as man, nation, and Empire) with which readers from different backgrounds could agree and identify, and by boiling down the religious, moral and physical precepts to their essences, the papers provided messages that could be universally understood. Diversity of perspective and of opinion in Edwardian life were therefore minimized in order to provide boys with a clear, fairly uniform prescriptive pattern of manhood. Far more important than class, status or social manners were the inner qualities of the boy, which were to be cultivated for manhood. The publications defined a man in similar terms:

> What a man says–is something;
> What a man does–is more;
> What a man is–that is most. (*Young Standard Bearer* 75)

In the Church of England Temperance Society paper, the *Young Crusader*, a short story called 'Uprooting the Passions' shows the inter-twining of the fictional and prescriptive genres. In this story, a young boy who is walking with an old man is asked to pull up increasingly big shrubs. He pulls up the first ones with ease, but the task becomes more difficult, until he can no longer move the roots at all. The old man then makes the connection to the passions clear: when young, it is easy to 'pull out' passions with a little self-denial, 'but if we let them cast their roots deep into our souls, then no human power can uproot them – the Almighty hand of the Creator alone can pluck them up' (52). This fictional boy had a good role model in the wise, older man and consequently, the readers of the *Young Crusader*, who might not have such a role model in their real lives, could access moral instruction through their reading material. The periodical press, with its unique combination of narrative forms and genres, became the Edwardian child's moral guardian.

In the temperance literature for the young, there had been an incomplete shift to using scientific information, rather than moral exhortations, in order to teach temperance principles. The message was unequivocal: 'The greatest modern enemy to health, character and prosperity, is strong drink' (Hicks 19). Also, there was still a persistent desire to educate boys through fiction. In many stories, boys are shown to be more intelligent and responsible than their own intemperate fathers. In 'The Boy who Beat His Father,' Mark Halliday is a widower with one son, who is liked by his fellow workers but not respected by them because he is the 'slave of drink.' Halliday looks to his young son Paul 'as if he were a sort of moral prodigy,' as the youth not only abstains from alcohol but tries to encourage his father to become steadier and to drink less. The roles of the father and son became increasingly reversed as the youth 'leap[s] prematurely into manhood' and begins admonishing his father for his drinking and swearing. As the narrator explains, 'Paul was deliberately taking in hand the moral education of his father,' and told his father on several occasions that he would beat him if he misbehaved (Hannigan 27). At the end of this story, Paul saves his father from a dangerous work-related accident and rejoices that he has 'conquered' his father (Hannigan 28). The significance of this story, and many others like it, is twofold. Lacking moral virtue, the contemporary generation of parents was seen to have failed. Boys required a better moral education in order to be better men and fathers of the future. To rectify this moral void required a mix of fact and fiction, laced with the same moral tone, rendering its real and imagined components equally true. Moralizing fiction was seen to benefit both boys *and* parents. The child could thus act as a moral beacon for his family, encouraging good behaviour in his parents and even disciplining them when they strayed. Stories were also meant to teach boys how proper fathers behaved, with the aim of influencing their later lives. Fiction, therefore, was thought to be a powerful proselytising force.

In the March 1908 issue of the Religious Tract Society's publication for its workers, *Seed Time and Harvest*, for example, a pictorial story appeared entitled 'Which Path Will You Take?' which demonstrated the importance for young boys of taking the right path while they were still young enough to shape. This was a greatly reduced facsimile of a 'striking' story board that had recently been published by the RTS to be purchased by teachers in elementary schools, Sunday schools, mission halls, boys' clubs and similar institutions. In short, it was to be shown anywhere in Britain where groups of boys were gathered for moral instruction or character-building; it was also translated into many different languages for missionary purposes abroad. Images were often used as fictional forms, reinforcing stories. The title, according to the RTS, 'seems to us well calculated to be of service in the training of the rising generation' ('Which Path' 17). The pictures received support from educational and religious leaders. The Bishop of Manchester, Edmund Knox, believed that it would teach boys honesty and industry. The Rev. Canon Denton Thompson wrote that 'It will not only attract the eye and impress the mind, but also be retained by the memory, and as such, I am sure it will prove a potent force in the development of moral character' ('Which Path' 17).

The story is presented in two parts: in one, the boy goes through the life stages appropriate to a young Briton who will take up his rightful place as citizen and head of family. He is attentive at school, practises fair play at cricket, learns a respectable trade, provides for a comfortable home, takes pride in his family, and retires to a quiet life of dignity and refinement. The other one demonstrates what could go wrong if boys are not properly guided: the young boy falls asleep at his lessons; gets into mischief in the street, gambles on horses, neglects his family in favour of drink, and ends up a beggar on the street. The social status of this boy is rather ambiguous, signalling the relevance of the story's weighty message to boys of different social classes. According to this scheme, the building of moral character, in conjunction with a commitment to work and family, allowed boys of merit (regardless of standing) to reach the higher echelons of society; conversely, a poor work ethic, disregard for morality and the authority of the father, drinking and gambling, would lead to poverty and depravity, irrespective of the class into which one was born.

Boys were not expected to find the right path independent of any authority or moral guidance, but it was clear that families, especially fathers, were failing in this regard. Several publications for boys directly took on this fatherly role. The Religious Tract Society established the *Boy's Own Paper* in order to provide a moral paternal voice in a perceived void in the juvenile periodical market. There was cooperation between publications and youth groups, many of which were either started or at least greatly enlarged at this time. The Church of England Temperance Society publications and other temperance papers encouraged participation in the Bands of Hope. The Amalgamated Press papers encouraged participation in its own 'League of Boy Friends,' and also the Boy's Brigade and the Boy Scouts. In these papers, Hamilton Edwards, their editor, took on the paternal role. He claimed that every week he received 500 to 700 letters from readers of the *Boy's Friend* (Edwards, 'My Readers' Letters' 244), which attested to the relevance of the fatherly answers and advice he provided in his papers.

Though many of the stories in the secular Amalgamated Press papers were far more sensationalistic than their religious counterparts, some stories did promote, in exaggerated form, similar moral goals for boys as the other papers. It was in the Editor's replies to letters, however, that this moral message was made most clear. This epistolary form was probably more fictional than Edwards liked readers to believe, but in this kind of literature fancy could also be 'fact' so long as it was based on received moral truths or on youthful experiences. Even if sometimes fictional, the letters and replies printed in Amalgamated Press papers would have been plausible to their young readers. They provide an interesting way of accessing some of the common preoccupations of Edwardian boys, and the advice they engendered. This teaching of expectations was perceived by Edwards and the publishers of the other papers not to be adequately practised at home or at school:

> It seems to me a pity that boys are not taught at school the admirable quality of moral courage; are not taught to admire the lad who can deny himself some foolish pleasure because it is wrong; are not taught the manliness of being able to say 'No' at the right moment. But they are not; and their parents also neglect this side of their teaching, with the result that many a lad finds himself in evil paths simply because he is unable to say 'No.' (Edwards, 'Editor's Den.' *Boy's Friend* VIII.316 [1901], 39)

One of Edwards's main concerns was underage smoking, which he denounced vociferously as detrimental to boys themselves and to society. The passing of the Children's Act of 1908, which banned smoking for those under 16 years of age vindicated Edwards's position. In the temperance periodicals, smoking was linked to drinking as a secondary vice.

It was widely believed that the critical time for boys to resist various temptations was when they left school and started work, often at the age of just 14. Men at work who were 'a disgrace to manhood' were expected to test the principles of boys:

> To drink, smoke, gamble, and swear; to talk mockingly of religion and sneer at those who are guided by Christian principles; to deprecate all that is good and elevating, and to gloat over the letting loose of the passions, is the daily curriculum of these base men. (Knowles, 'A Critical Time for Youth' 159)

What was required was to teach boys, through the reading of periodicals (but also of course by other means, such as in groups like the Band of Hope), which principles were important for them to uphold, and to make these strong enough to withstand future temptations or humiliations. Christian faith was an essential component in teaching and upholding these principles, for both the religious and 'secular' papers.

Many stories had belief in God as their driving force. Owen Kildare's 'My Rise from the Slums to Manhood: A True Story' (1903) is a story of the author's rise from orphaned street urchin to respectable man. He had believed himself to be a real man when he could pick on the smaller boys selling papers in the streets, and had graduated to becoming a boxer and a bouncer in the most disreputable places in town. He had never had anyone to love nor guide him, and thus he found success in morally reprehensible ways. Only after he meets a young woman who not only teaches him to read, but also shows him the error of his ways, does he begin to think about God and about doing good deeds for others. In the end, he becomes a 'real' man: he finds a respectable job, is respectful of others and wants to marry and set up a home with his young teacher. The twist in the plot comes when the woman unexpectedly dies, and the hero is injured in his manual work. Instead of becoming a traditional 'real' man by getting married and establishing a family, he uses his newly found intellectual skills to teach others how to become 'real' men and followers of Jesus. This story was meant to be read by the entire family at home, its Christian message an appealing lesson for parents to share with their sons. As the reader is provided with the hero's life story from his beginnings, it would have been easy for boys to identify with him and therefore perhaps to absorb the message more fully than in more rigidly didactic evangelical tales.

The process of moral enculturation through reading was not, therefore, intended to be accomplished by boys alone. It resulted from subtle negotiations among the publishers, the parents and the boys themselves. The Religious Tract Society publications, in particular, were not bound by rigid distinctions between juvenile and adult reading matter, but rather were intended for family reading. This served to encourage family cohesion and proper moral transferral from parents to son. In contrast, the Amalgamated Press publications were intended for boys' reading alone, yet parental approval was sought and even published to ensure the papers' wholesome content, thus obviating the charge that they were penny dreadfuls. One mother wrote to the *Boy's Herald* in 1904 to say that she approved of its anti-drinking and anti-smoking stance, but believed it should also take a position against boxing ('A Mistaken Idea' 512). Thus the papers were viewed as being equipped to assist parents in raising their boys: 'Let us teach them to be peaceful, law-abiding, God-fearing citizens' ('A Mistaken Idea' 512). The papers sought to entertain, but more importantly, to shape boys in a period of rapid change. Helen MacDowall commented in 1913 that most parents tried

> to hand over our responsibilities to others, not because we shrink from trouble but because we feel painfully unfit for our infinitely difficult fourfold work of turning out healthy, educated, moral and religious children. (MacDowall 402)

Many stories were meant to be read by parents to their children, in the hopes that discussions on morality would ensue.

One such story was Maud Maddick's 'Mr. Boy Next Door' (1911), about Norrie, a rich boy with loving parents. Norrie is cheerful and loving and prays frequently. He gives his dog, his favourite possession, to Tom, the boy next door. Tom is portrayed as an angry and resentful boy who lives in poverty with his granny and has no one to love. Norrie realizes that Tom also needs something to love, after which Tom bursts forth with gratitude:

> I can't thank you–you're the best thing of any sort I've ever met, you funny little chap, with your prayers and your songs. I shall always love you for this, and if you can really put up with a great rough sort of chap like – like I am – oh, do let me be your friend. (Maddick 532)

This type of story, to be read to children, provided an opportunity for parents to discuss with their children the qualities which would make them and those around them happy. Norrie is not content because he is rich, but rather because he is loved by his parents and by God. Consequently he is considerate and polite to all. Tom, by contrast, was mean, not because he was poor or uneducated, but because he had nothing to love. In giving Tom the dog, Norrie actually shows him the path to God by softening his defensiveness with love and consideration.

The first verse of a poem in the 1914 *Band of Hope Review* neatly sums up the preoccupation of authors and publishers of Edwardian boys' periodicals.

> If boys should get discouraged
> At lessons or at work,
> And say, 'There's no use trying';

And all the hard tasks shirk,
And keep on shirking and shirking,
Till the boy become a man,
I wonder what the world would do
To carry out its plan. ('Keep On' 96)

The Edwardian juvenile periodical press, although varied in its methods and motivations, provided a unified message for boys of various classes. It facilitated the transmission of common values and of expected behaviours, in order to educate boys on their future roles as men, husbands, fathers and Britons. It also promoted improvements in their physical health and work-related skills. This education was informal, not too heavy-handed or didactic, and often catered to boys' desire for fun and play. It created a space for boys to be morally instructed outside of the stricter confines of church, chapel, school or even home. The organizations' goals were much broader than simply reforming individual boys: they were to ensure the growth of the next generation of strong and moral men, capable of heading their families, and of becoming good citizens, in peace time and in the build-up to war. The message was uncompromising, even if its medium blurred the boundary between fiction and reality.[1]

Note

1. The author would like to thank Adrienne Gavin and Andrew Humphries for their careful and thoughtful comments on this essay. Michèle Cohen, Brian Lewis, and Elizabeth Elbourne deserve much appreciation for their guidance of my research in this area. Thank you to G.W. and Inge Rumler Olsen who are a source of constant support and sound advice. Finally, this work would not have been possible without the intellectual and emotional input of Rob Boddice.

Works cited

'A Mistaken Idea.' *Boy's Herald* 1. 32 (1904): 512.
Annual Report. London: Religious Tract Society, 1916.
Apples of Gold. 'Keep On.' *Band of Hope Review* (1914): 96.
Blight, Frederick. 'What Boys Say about Reading.' *Band of Hope Review Annual* (1908): 50.
Boyd, Kelly. *Manliness and the Boys' Story Papers in Britain: A Cultural History, 1855–1940*. Houndmills: Palgrave Macmillan, 2003.
Chiltern, Faith. 'Little Britons.' *Young Standard Bearer* XXVIII.4 (March 1908): 30.

Dunae, Patrick. 'Boys' Literature and the Idea of Empire, 1870–1914.' *Victorian Studies* 24 (1980): 105–21.

Edwards, Hamilton. 'Editor's Den.' *Boy's Friend* VIII.316 (1901): 39.

——. 'Editor's Den.' *Boy's Friend* III.115 (1903): 176.

——. 'Editor's Den.' *Boy's Friend* II.94 (1903): 709.

——. 'Editor's Den–My Reader's Letters.' *Boy's Friend* IV.16 (1901): 244.

——. 'The Penny Dreadful.' IX.460 *Boy's Herald* (1912): 70.

——. 'Teetotalism.' *Boy's Herald* 1.26 (1904): 416

——. 'Your Editor's Advice.' *Boy's Herald* I.25 (1904): 400.

Francis, Martin. 'Domestication of the Male? Recent Research on Nineteenth- and Twentieth-Century British Masculinity.' *Historical Journal* 45.3 (2002): 637–52.

Hannigan, D. F. 'The Boy Who Beat His Father.' *Onward* XXXVI (1901): 27–8.

Hewitt, Gordon. *Let the People Read.* London: Lutterworth Press, 1949.

Hicks, Edward Lee. 'For the Children's Sake.' *Onward* XXXXIV (1909): 19.

Howatt, Rev. J Reid. 'For the Young.' *Sunday at Home* (1902–3): 134.

Kildare, Owen. 'My Rise from the Slums to Manhood: A True Story.' *Leisure Hour* (1903): 22–32.

King, W. Scott. 'The Boy: What He Is and What Are We Going to Make of Him.' *Sunday at Home* (1913): 818–20.

Knowles, S. 'A Critical Time for Youth.' *Every Band of Hope Boy's Reciter.* No. 14 (c. 1903): 159.

——. 'The Changed Home.' *Every Band of Hope Boy's Reciter* No. 77 (c. 1901): 73.

MacDonald, Robert H. 'Reproducing the Middle-Class Boy: From Purity to Patriotism in the Boys' Magazines, 1892–1914.' *Journal of Contemporary History* 24.3. (1989): 519–39.

MacDowall, Helen. 'My Boys.' *Sunday at Home* (1913): 401–05.

Maddick, Maud. 'Mr. Boy Next Door: A Story to be Read by, or to, the Children on Sunday Afternoon or at any Time.' *Sunday at Home* (1911): 530–32.

Mangan, J. A. *The Games Ethic and Imperialism: Aspects of the Diffusion of an Ideal.* Harmondsworth: Viking, 1985.

——. 'Noble Specimens of Manhood: Schoolboy Literature and the Creation of a Colonial Chivalric Code.' *Imperialism and Juvenile Literature.* Ed. Jeffery Richards. Manchester: Manchester University Press, 1989. 173–94.

'Mother and Home.' *Boy's Own Paper.* New Series, Part 1 (1911): 16.

Onward. XXXVI (1901): 26–7.

Salmon, Edward. 'What Boys Read.' *Fortnightly Review* XLV (February, 1886): 248–59.

Searle, G. R. *The Quest for National Efficiency: A Study in British Politics and Political Thought, 1899–1914.* Berkeley: University of California Press, 1971.

Sidebotham, William. 'Lord Avebury – the Man and his Work.' *Leisure Hour* (1903): 33–4.

Stables, Gordon. 'Doings for the Month.' *Boy's Own Paper* XXVII.1376 (27 May 1905): 558.

Tosh, John. *A Man's Place: Masculinity and the Middle-Class Home in Victorian England.* New Haven: Yale University Press, 1999.

——. 'The Old Adam and the New Man: Emerging Themes in the History of English Masculinities, 1750–1850.' *English Masculinities 1660–1800.* Eds. Tim Hitchcock and Michèle Cohen, London: Longman, 1999. 217–38.

Tosh, John, ed. 'Manliness, Masculinities and the New Imperialism, 1880–1900.' *Manliness and Masculinities in Nineteenth-Century Britain.* Harlow: Pearson Longman, 2005. 192–214.

'Uprooting the Passions.' *Young Crusader* (March 1908): 52.

'Which Path Will You Take.' *Seed Time and Harvest* (1908): 17.

Williamson, David. 'How to Succeed in Life: Some Finger-posts for Boys.' *Boy's Own Paper* XXXII.1633 (30 April 1910): 487.

Young Standard Bearer XXIX.10 (September 1909): 75.

Part IV
Savagery and the Child

11
Primitive Minds: Anthropology, Children, and Savages in Andrew Lang and Rudyard Kipling

Karen Sands-O'Connor

> Primitives see with eyes like ours, but they do not perceive with the same minds.
>
> (Lucien Lévy-Bruhl, *How Natives Think*, 1910, 31)
>
> What a child may do...a childlike race may do.
>
> (Andrew Lang, *Magic and Religion*, 1901, 48)

Victorians like James Frazer fomented interest in anthropological study, but Edwardians applied ideas of the field to other areas. Artists saw themselves either as 'becoming modern' or consciously choosing to 'go primitive.' Educators and psychoanalysts examined childhood in the same ways that so-called primitive races were being viewed. Edwardian children's authors combined the approaches, creating works that concentrated on contrasts between childhood and savagery on one hand, and adulthood and civilization on the other. The end result was children's literature that consciously privileged white, British children over all others, contributing to one of the field's 'Golden Ages' as well as to imperial understandings of race and childhood. The work of folktale collector Andrew Lang and writer Rudyard Kipling expose the ways in which anthropology could be used to define childhood, adulthood, Britishness, and Otherness.

Anthropology as a field had much to offer the study of childhood in the Edwardian period. Both fields studied the mental and moral development of 'lesser' people, and ways that these people could be guided towards greater development by those more civilized. The 1904 Code for Public Elementary Education in Britain emphasized this connection by suggesting teachers must ' "train the children carefully in the habits of observation and clear reasoning" ' (quoted in Hattersley 257) in order that they might ' "arouse in them a living interest in the ideals and achievements of mankind" ' (quoted in Hattersley 257). This represented a change from the Victorian period, according to G. Winthrop Young, who observed that, 'Originally, almost aboriginally, the early life of the child *was* its education' (165). Child minds, like aboriginal minds, had to be carefully developed. Edwardian authors played a role in this development, through judicious use of both social and physical anthropology.

Ideas from social anthropology led to the primitivist movement by valuing an 'aesthetic idea of a wholeness of life lost in modernization' (Daly 131). Notions of simplicity and naturalism had long been associated with both children and noble savages. However, Andrew Lang specifically applied anthropological ideas about myth and magic to children's literature in editing and compiling his popular 'colour' fairy books. Schooled in the tradition of British social anthropologist Edward Tylor, Lang agreed with Tylor that the development of literary understanding of the mythic/religious moved, 'from mythology (the efforts of primitive men to explain the natural phenomena of the world around them) to the folklore of the modern European peasantry, on up to the nursery tales of civilised children' (Stocking 52). However, Lang also believed in the possibility for a deep and mature connection to the spiritual by 'savages': 'the religious and mythical conception is present, not only (where it has been universally recognized) in the faiths of the ancient civilized people...but also in the ideas of the lowest known savages' (Lang, *Myth, Ritual and Religion* 2: 3). The notion that 'savage' people might be as ardent in their search for religious meaning as those more 'civilized' allowed Lang, as he put it, to avoid 'dubious theories of race. To us, myths appear to be affected (in their origins) much less by the race than by the stage of culture attained by the people who cherish them' (*Myth, Ritual and Religion* 2: 45). The people he labels 'savages' are non-white, but – despite this – their skin colour does not make them less intelligent, only less cultured. Lang valued the contributions of all people to human understanding; however, he also maintained a cultural hierarchy which placed emphasis on attaining the benefits of progress and civilization.

For Lang, proper understanding of the development of myth and belief would 'expedite progress' (*Magic and Religion* 9). Lang felt it necessary to study 'savage tribes' (*Modern Mythology* xix) to learn about 'the mythopoeic state of mind' (*Modern Mythology* xix). However, he does not limit the 'unprogressive' mind to 'savages'; in many instances, he connects his ideas with the developing mind of a child. In a discussion of taboo, for example, Lang uses his own childhood as example: 'All my life I have had...private taboos, though nobody knows better that they are nonsense. But some solitary experience in childhood probably suggested a relation of cause and effect' (*Magic and Religion* 263). He grants to all people – 'savage' and civilized alike – the reliance on unscientific methods, but also the innate ability to question and make up rules and stories about their world; that is, to progress. This idea formed the basis of his anthropological work: 'What a savage child naturally asks about, his yet more savage ancestors may have pondered' (*Magic and Religion* 225). Understanding contemporary 'savage' thought would help civilized people – adults and children – to understand their own methods of reasoning, leading them to a more scientific understanding of the world.

His attitudes towards anthropology shaped the production of Lang's work for children. On one hand, Lang's 12 colour fairy books, published between 1889 and 1910, reveal an internationalism which is unusual for its time: the books, as a set, include tales from all over the world. On the other hand, out of 379 tales given an originating source by Lang, 267 of these are European, and many non-European tales are mediated by white folklorists. Two particular volumes, *The Brown Fairy Book* (1904) and *The Orange Fairy Book* (1906), both published after his anthropological study, *Magic and Religion* (1901), illustrate his desire to convey to children the aesthetic nature of people he labels as 'brown,' 'black,' and 'red' (*Brown Fairy Book* vii). These two books contain a number of stories taken from anthropological journals and academic folktale collections. Lang (and his wife, who did most of the editing – a point he acknowledges several times in prefaces, although never on the title page) felt that the 'outlandish natives' (*Brown Fairy Book* viii) had to be toned down to 'make them suitable for children' (*Orange Fairy Book* vi), by which he meant white children. Comparing the source tales with his own versions produced for children reveals some of Lang's prejudices. In *The Brown Fairy Book*, 'The Bunyip' is an Australian tale collected/ written by W. Dunlop and T. V. Holmes that Lang read in *The Journal of the Anthropological Institute of Britain and Ireland*; 'The Sacred Milk of Koumongoé' is a tale from southern Africa that Lang borrowed from Edouard Jacottet's *Contes Populaires des Bassoutos* (1895). In *The Orange Fairy Book*, Lang took a Native Canadian tale from *The Journal of the Anthropological Institute of Great Britain and Ireland* as the basis for 'The Owl and the Eagle.'

Of all of these tales, 'The Bunyip' is least altered from the academic source. The basic story, in which a group of youths go fishing and one catches the calf of a mythical creature, resulting in a flooding of the village and a transformation of the villagers into black swans, remains the same in both Lang's version and the version told by Dunlop and Holmes. In fact, it is only in small but significant details that the story is altered at all. In the Dunlop and Holmes version, the youth who catches the Bunyip calf is brave enough that he 'raised his spear and brandished it' (23) at the mother Bunyip; this in turn 'infused part of his own courage into the breasts of his companions' (23) and they help him carry the Bunyip 'off in triumph' (23). Their 'triumph was short' (23), according to the text; the Bunyip mother causes the river to rise up after them. Lang, however, has the hero acting alone and with violence: 'flinging his spear at the mother to keep her back, he threw the little Bunyip on to his shoulders and set out for camp' (72). Dunlop and Holmes's hero threatens but does not harm the mother, and his companions share the blame for the action of kidnapping the calf; this makes the ending, in which the entire village is punished and redeemed, more psychologically satisfying. Lang, on the other hand, argues for rugged individualism – a prevalent ideology in the Edwardian era – but also an uncomfortable sort of justice, in which innocent bystanders are punished along with the guilty hero.

The other detail that changes between the two versions of 'The Bunyip' is also small; as the flood waters rise, the Dunlop and Holmes tale remarks:

> Those that were dearest to each other rushed together in the vain hope of yielding mutual assistance. Mothers clasped their children, husbands their wives, and the young betrothed ones, who a few hours before would not even have touched each others' hands, frantically clung together in the hope that they might swim through the water, and save themselves for the happiness they had looked forward to from their earliest years. (24)

The Lang version seriously shortens this, commenting simply that, 'Parents and children clung together, as if by that means they could drive back the advancing flood' (75). This revision achieves two things. First, it takes away the agency of the people and makes them appear unscientific; they cling together in a mystical belief that this will make the flood disappear, rather than in hope of offering aid to each other as in the Dunlop and Holmes version. Second, Lang removes all trace of sexuality by referring only to the parent-child bond, deleting Dunlop's and Holmes's unspoken 'happiness' that lovers anticipate. Primitives, according to Lang, are innocent of scientific thinking. White child readers, a type of advanced primitive in Lang's hierarchy of people, are innocent too – of the nature of sexuality.

These tendencies, to on the one hand sanitize the 'savage' tales and on the other make them more irrational, can be seen in other tales as well. 'The Sacred Milk of Koumongoé,' taken from Jacottet's 'Koumongoé' is a complicated taboo tale from southern Africa. A brother and sister are forbidden to drink the sap of their parents' tree, Koumongoé. The brother forces his sister, Thakané, to obtain some of the sap, which then flows out of control and floods the fields where the parents are working. When the father discovers that Thakané has broken taboo, he takes her to another tribe to be eaten by the chief. The story, in Jacottet's version, details a series of fatherly attempts to sacrifice girl children. Thakané is saved from her punishment by the chief's son, who takes her in concubinage while the cannibal chief eats her father instead. However, when Thakané has a daughter of her own, her new husband informs her of the custom of eating girl babies in their tribe, and Thakané must save her daughter by giving her away to an old woman who lives under the river. Thakané's daughter reaches the age of sexual maturity, and 'la vielle femme la fit passer au fond des eaux par les rites de la nubilité' ['The old woman baptized her in a ritual of maturation' (Sands-O'Connor's translation)] (197). This ritual of maturation results in her safety from her cannibal grandfather, and returning to the tribe. At this time Thakané's husband at last decides to pay the bride-price for Thakané and they journey back to her home. Thakané's father's hard-heartedness has transformed his spirit into a boulder that blocks their way: 'Ce rocher n'était autre que Rahlabakoané; son coeur s'était changé en rocher après sa mort' ['This boulder was none other than Rahlabokoané, whose heart had turned to stone upon his death' (Sands-O'Connor's translation)] (202). He, as boulder, consumes them all – at which point he falls into a canyon and smashes to pieces, leaving the family to continue on to Thakané's home, where the marriage is legitimized.

Lang is clearly uncomfortable with the sexuality in Jacottet's version, and edits it out. Thakané and Masilo get married in his tribe before she becomes pregnant, and Lang's version makes the marriage accord with European custom because, rather than requiring Masilo to pay a bride-price, the text suggests that Masilo's parents, 'willingly accepted Thakané as their daughter-in-law, though she did not bring any marriage portion' (148). But this means that the final return journey to Thakané's home no longer makes sense, and the Lang version ends with Thakané's daughter's return. There is no mention of Thakané's daughter's sexual maturation; in fact, Masilo implores Thakané to give 'the child back to him' (152), a slight but significant shift from the Jacottet version in which Masilo asks for 'son enfant' (199) – his child – to be returned. As in English, a parent might refer to a son or daughter as 'his' or 'her' *child*, even after the age of maturity, but Lang's switch to 'the' child removes this possibility. The shift to European or 'civilized' marital customs removes a great deal of the story's sexual significance. Thakané's father's desire to see her consumed for breaking taboo is overcome by Masilo's ability to accept his daughter's sexual maturity in Jacottet's version. Lang removes Thakané's agency and that of her daughter; both are objects to be traded, and must rely only on luck to be placed with guardians who will not threaten their life or sexuality. In making these changes, Lang adheres to, as Stephen Humphries suggests, 'middle-class theories of adolescence, which prescribed a prolonged, regulated and institutional-ized dependency on adults as essential to normal and healthy sexual development' (135) in order to prevent 'an orgy of depravity, idleness and crime' (135). Children, because they are primitive in their understanding of the world, must be kept innocent as long as possible.

Similar changes are made in the tale from British Columbia, transcribed by Charles Hill Tout, which Lang recast as 'The Owl and the Eagle' in *The Orange Fairy Book*. The story is problematic for Lang in terms of the marriage described. The eponymous birds marry two human sisters; the Tout version takes this cross-species marriage as a matter of course; the birds 'each took one to wife' (49). The Lang version, however, spends considerable time explaining why a human woman would want to marry a bird, despite the fact that the offspring of these marriages (one sister gives birth to a human and one to a frog) suggests a basic narrative disregard for biology. Lang otherwise follows the plotline of the Tout version, but at the end, when the clever sisters kill a witch who has stolen their husbands, Lang's version adds in a surprising sentence found nowhere in the Tout version: 'The sisters were savages who had never seen a missionary' (240). Marrying birds is bad enough, Lang implies, though this can be explained away if the birds exhibit 'kindness and cleverness' (237); but women must be savage if they are willing to kill – even if the victim is a kidnapping witch who has threatened them and their family.

Throughout these tales, Lang's revisions from the source materials indicate a desire to align the tales with 'civilized' European morality, even at the expense of narrative closure or heroic agency. Although Lang clearly wants his readers to value stories from people all over the world, he deliberately alters narratives to suit his ideas of progress, civi-lization and childhood. Further, by labelling the tales as 'savage' and in need of editing, he suggests that they are of lesser value than the European tales he includes – many of which describe similar incidents (Gretel, in Lang's version of 'Hansel and Gretel,' is not called 'savage' for pushing her witch in the oven). Lang's fairy tale books introduce child readers to non-European tales, but in ways that point the child reader away from the 'savage' practices within the stories, and thus keeps both white child and non-white savage firmly in their places.

Lang may or may not have recognized his revisions of source tales as significant; Talal Asad suggests that it was not until the 1960s that Oxford, where Lang was an honorary fellow, became 'self-conscious about its concern with "the translation of culture" ' (142). However, Lang did seem to prefer European versions of folk stories. This can be seen in his use of source tales mediated by white interpreters (Jacottet was a missionary; Tout, Dunlop, and Holmes were, of varying degrees, professional anthropologists and folklorists). Lang's preferences can also be seen in his literary tastes; Jonathan Rose writes, 'As an anthropologist, Andrew Lang was fascinated by literature that appealed to the primal, childlike nature of the reader' (182). Therefore, it is no surprise that he was one of the first British champions of Rudyard Kipling.

Like Lang, Kipling took folk source material and made it his own. However, his methods were different. The second mode of 'anthropological' Edwardian children's literature is one that does not accept the link between 'primitive' and 'child,' focusing instead on the distinction between 'primitive' and 'civilized.' This style of writing is exemplified by Rudyard Kipling. Kipling privileges white European children in his Edwardian fiction, from the *Just So Stories* (1902) to *Puck of Pook's Hill* (1906) and *Rewards and Fairies* (1910), by adapting the tools of physical anthropology for children's fiction.

Lang had used his background in social anthropology to inform his folktale collections for children; Kipling's work is imbued with ideas of physical anthropology, a branch that relies on physical characteristics to draw conclusions about human potential. John McBratney suggests that Kipling follows the arguments of physical anthropologist Paul Broca (150). Kipling's connection to Broca mirrors such ideas as this, from one of the early translations of Broca's ideas into English:

> We speak of aptitudes intellectual, moral and social. There exist races eminently perfectible, who enjoyed the advantage of outstripping all the rest, and engendering high civilisation. There are, again, some who have never taken the initiative in progress, but who have accepted or adopted it by imitation. Others, finally, have resisted all the efforts made to rescue them from a savage life. ('Broca on Anthropology' 45)

Broca's ideas were mirrored, applauded, and expanded upon in Britain by anthropologists such as James Prichard, Frederic Farrar and James Hunt. Hunt, who claimed to advocate for the status of Africans as humans, still added that it was 'the duty of conscientious anatomists carefully to record all deviations from the human standard of organization and analogy with inferior types, which are frequently manifested in the negro race' (4). The dedication of these anthropologists to separating and classifying different races and their 'types' contained and sustained a deep contradiction: that although races could intermix and produce offspring, the races themselves – and by extension their characteristic physical and moral features – remained ultimately fixed and unchanging. These ideas were first propagated in the 1850s and 1860s, but were still being investigated and debated at the turn of the century, most notably by Franz Boas, who despite his critique of some aspects of physical anthropology still maintained a belief in 'the largest divisions of mankind ... Europeans, Africans, and Mongols' (157).

Although many have noted references to physical anthropology in Kipling's Indian works (see Said, *Orientalism* 226–7), some of the strongest evidence of Kipling's attachment to ideas of physical anthropology appears in works he wrote and published specifically for his own children, John and Elsie, during the Edwardian period. Kipling, unlike Lang, did not lump all children and primitives together; rather, white children are born civilized, and therefore have more responsibility for themselves and others. The *Just So Stories* seem to be loosely connected, but when viewed with ideas of physical anthropology in mind, they take on a different light. Set all over the world, most of them still remain within the boundaries of the British Empire. This global-yet-local vision is reinforced by poems at the end of each tale; the poem at the end of 'How the Camel got his Hump' leads the reader away from the 'Howling Desert' (13) of Arabia and to the camel in the zoo, for example. The stories are designed to place Britain and its children in the centre and in control of their world.

This sense of British control is underscored by the agency given to British characters and removed from non-British characters in the tales. The Hibernian in 'How the Whale got his Throat' orders the Whale to 'Take me to my natal-shore' (5) before relieving the Whale of the pain of having the Hibernian inside of him; and the Neolithic family living in what would become Britain rely solely on themselves rather than higher powers. However, characters in the colonial world are at the mercy of the miraculous. The Man in 'How the Camel got his Hump' has to rely on a Djinn to help him (15), the Old-Man Kangaroo must consult small and large gods (63–4), the Ethiopian turns for advice to a Wise Baviaan (38), and the Man and his daughter in 'The Crab that Played with the Sea' must look for relief to the Eldest Magician (134).

Kipling's characters are also given traits which ally them with Broca's theories of intellectual, moral and social order. The Man and his daughter in 'The Crab that Played with the Sea' want the Sea to row their boat for them, so the Eldest Magician tells them, '"You are lazy...So your children shall be lazy. They shall be the laziest people in the world"' (144), and Kipling follows this by pronouncing them the 'Malazy' (144) people (the Malaysians). The Ethiopian is equated with an animal, the Leopard; they hunt together and eat together. If anything, the Ethiopian is *less* valuable than the leopard even by his own estimate. When he praises the leopard's new coat, the leopard asks him why he 'didn't go spotty too' (43); the Ethiopian replies, '"Oh, plain black's best for a nigger"' (43). This hierarchy accords with physical anthropology; John Crawfurd, in, 'On the Classification of the Races of Man' asserts that, 'The negroes of Africa have never attained the civilisation of the Egyptians... [they are] equal in bodily strength to Europeans, but inferior not only to them, but even to most Asiatic nations in mental capacity' (368); additionally, Malays are 'inferior' (356) to the Chinese. Kipling's human characters in these tales are at the low end of the evolutionary scale, races that, according to Broca, resist efforts to civilize them.

In the middle of the evolutionary scale – those who can accept or adopt civilization but not create it – is the Parsee in 'How the Rhinoceros got his Skin.' Although Kipling places the Parsee on the horn of Africa, his Parsee is drawn as, and according to Lisa Lewis (223) named after, an Indian (the Parsee sect of Zoroastrans left Persia in the eighth century). The Parsee is more civilized than either the Ethiopian or the Malaysians; he is not a hunter, but a baker. He also is clothed; he wears a hat. However, he is unable to master his world, and is subject to the ravages of a rhinoceros who eats the cakes he bakes. Historically, Parsees were seen by the British as a superior kind of Indian, with many of the (positive) qualities of European people. They were a result of, as Prichard suggests, an 'advantageous' (147) mix of races, 'of one kindred...with the Indo-European nations' (137). However, while they had some of the good qualities of the European, they also had some of the bad qualities of the Asian. The Parsee is not a permanent dweller in the land; in the end, although he tricks the rhinoceros, he 'went away in the direction of Oratavo, Amygdala, the Upland Meadows of Anantarivo, and the Marshes of Sonaput' (30). Kipling's language here is significant; the Parsee simply 'went away,' and is thus a wanderer, not a colonizer. Lack of permanence is a significant trait of the middle order of humans, according to physical anthropology; Frederic Farrar, for example, suggests that Gypsies are 'tattered and houseless, yet retaining to the last the clearest marks of their Asiatic origin' (398). Kipling's Parsee, like Gypsies, nomads, and others, can learn and adopt some tenets of civilization, but never master them.

Three of the tales in the book relate habits of the 'higher orders' of humans, as suggested by physical anthropology. 'How the First Letter was Written' and 'How the Alphabet was Made' are both set near Merrow Down in Surrey; its characters are 'Neolithic' (91) humans that, according to Kipling, are 'Primitive, and...lived cavily in a Cave' (91). 'The Cat that Walked by Himself,' according to Lisa Lewis, 'suggests an American setting' (234) and others, such as Charles Carrington, have connected the story with Kipling's American wife, Carrie. These characters, all associated with Britain and America, have traits that set them apart from other characters in this book. First, though labelled 'Primitive' they are actually already civilized; they have a permanent home and keep it clean. The Woman, in 'The Cat' story, 'picked out a nice dry Cave...to lie down in, and she strewed clean sand on the floor; and she lit a nice wood fire at the back of the cave' (149–50); Taffy's mother, in the other two stories, would prefer Taffy 'to stay at home and help hang up hides to dry on the big drying-poles outside their Neolithic Cave' (109). Second, they have an interest in language and communication. The 'Alphabet' story was written in 1901, at the time when the origin of the alphabet was being hotly debated; as John P. Peters has discussed, it is significant that the debate was 'racial' in nature. Kipling gives the creation of the alphabet to ancestors of the British. All three stories additionally comment on manners. Even though these stories are set in pre-historical times, Kipling proves that white 'primitives' are actually as civilized as their modern-day counterparts, underscoring the idea that, as Farrar argues, 'the races of man, under all zones, have maintained, wherever we can trace their records, an absolute and unalterable fixity' (394).

The *Just So Stories* were precursors to Kipling's other Edwardian works, also written for his children. The two *Puck* books continue his discussion of racial hierarchies. Una and Dan, in the fictional narratives set around Kipling's home in Sussex, meet historical figures that lead them to understand the superior 'stock' of people that built Britain. The *Puck* books appear, at first glance, to celebrate the multicultural nature of Britain in much the same way his earlier novel *Kim* (1901) 'celebrated' India's ethnic diversity. However, the problem with seeing Kipling as celebratory of multiculturalism is, as Marianna Torgovnick points out in *Gone Primitive*, that 'the interpenetration of third and first world is not just festive. Behind the festivities are social and economic facts we should not forget' (40). In Kipling's case, these social and economic facts are distortions of history used to 'prove' racial hierarchies.

John McBratney discusses Kipling's racial hierarchies and their connection to ideas of anthropology when he writes,

> Kipling held views on racial intermixture that represented a popularized version of Broca's distinction. According to these views, members of races 'distant' from each other produced offspring whose chances of survival were poor – a viewpoint roughly corresponding to Broca's concept of dysgenesic crossing... However, in a reworking of Broca's concept of eugenesic crossing, members of races 'proximate' to each other intermarry to beneficial effect. (150–1)

This is why, according to McBratney, Kim must remain ultimately distanced from Indians, but also why the Romans and the early Britons – being from proximate races – could produce, ultimately, the British Empire. Kipling shows how the people of Britain changed, and yet at the same time remained the same, in two passages in *Puck of Pook's Hill*. In the first, he indicates the different religions that came to Britain:

> The Phoenicians brought some over when they came to buy tin; and the Gauls, and the Jutes, and the Danes, and the Frisians, and the Angles brought more when they landed. They were always landing in those days, or being driven back to their ships, and they always brought their Gods with them. (17)

By separating native inhabitants from invaders, and further separating the invaders from their gods, Kipling can allow for *influence* without implying *confluence* of peoples. He underscores this by Una's confusion between the Hobden that is their gamekeeper and the Hobden that Puck knows: ' "You're quite right," Puck replied, "I meant old Hobden's ninth great-grandfather... I've known the family, father and son, so long that I get confused sometimes" ' (21). The British remain the same throughout time, even as they take what is good from various cultures they encounter.

Ambreen Hai suggests that, 'in Kipling's own parable of imperial nationhood the storyteller engenders not only the tribe, but the future of the tribe in every sense, and shapes its perpetuation' (604). Despite acknowledgement of the different 'tribes' that make up the ancestry of modern Britain, Kipling maintains a nativism that fears 'that the physical and mental qualities embodied in a finite number of human types might be diluted through mixture with other, inferior, racial stocks' (Livingstone 182). He thus keeps certain groups forever divorced from the 'true' British in his stories. Kadmiel, the Jewish money-lender in *Puck of Pook's Hill*, shows Jewish people as living in, but separate from, Britain: 'Israel follows his quest. /In every land a guest,/...As it was ordered to be' (200). The Picts, too, are excluded from Britain's heritage, because they are sub-human: ' "Leave the Picts alone," I said. "Stop the heather-burning at once, and – they are improvident little animals – send them a shipload or two of corn now and then" ' (136). On the other hand, George Washington, in *Rewards and Fairies*, is considered one of the British tribe; Puck comments, ' "I'm sorry we lost him out of Old England" ' (160). Kipling, through his depictions of 'true' British people, makes his mythology of England into history.

Following the publication of *Rewards and Fairies*, Kipling wrote 'an Epilogue to the Puck stories by "collaborating" with C. R. L. Fletcher in *A History of England* for young readers' (Green 215). Although it is not known to what extent Kipling influenced the text of the *History* (the poetry at the end of each chapter is undoubtedly all his), it is certain from his letters that he did not regard the *History* as an 'embarrassment' as David Gilmour sees it in retrospect (177). Indeed, Fletcher's history reaffirms Kipling's own views on racial separation, as seen in this quotation from a letter concerning the *History* in 1910: 'It's curious how the Celt clings to the memory of a wrong! I couldn't conceive say of a Sussex bard singing of the burning of the Quakers, say, at Lewes a couple of hundred years ago...I suppose it's because we English are so composite in blood' (to Alfred Perceval Graves 19 October 1910, *Letters* 456). Here as elsewhere, Kipling confirms and denies the unchanging nature of 'English' character without any seeming irony. 'I remember like yesterday,' Kipling writes in the *History*'s opening poem, 'River Tale,'

> The earliest Cockney who came my way,
> When he pushed through the forest that lined the Strand,
> With paint on his face and a club in his hand. (9)

Or, as Paul Broca wrote in 1868:

> These races are...primordial, or, if you like, as old as the species itself; they are moreover permanent and immutable, that is to say, neither the influence of media, crossing, or selection can durably lead them away from their primitive type. ('Report' 232–3)

Through his literature, Kipling is able to educate the white British child reader into ideas of racial hierarchy and fixity of the races, thereby encouraging British children to see their proper place as civilizer and manager of the world.

In many ways, Edwardian children's literature was a literature of anthropology. Children were seen as primitives who had to be trained into civilized ways. Andrew Lang used the social anthropology of Tylor and others to prove that all humans had valuable contributions to make, as well as subtly to imply that those contributions could best be put to use by white, British children. Kipling's physical anthropology, after the ideas of Broca, underscored the differences between races and assured white privilege and responsibility. Using anthropological language and methodology, Kipling and Lang exemplify how authors of this time period explored the 'primitive minds' of the British Empire – the ones inside and outside of their books.

Works cited

Asad, Talal. 'The Concept of Cultural Translation in British Social Anthropology.' *Writing Culture: The Poetics and Politics of Ethnography*. Ed. James Clifford and George E. Marcus. Berkeley: University of California Press, 1986. 141–64.

Boas, Franz. 'Review of William Z. Ripley, "The Races of Europe."' 1899. *Race, Language and Culture*. New York: The Free Press, 1940: 155–9.

Broca, Paul. 'Broca on Anthropology (Continued).' *Anthropological Review* 6.20 (January 1868): 35–52.

——. 'Report on the Transactions of the Anthropological Society of Paris during 1865–1867.' *Anthropological Review* 6.22 (July 1868): 225–46.

Carrington, Charles. 'If You Can Bring Fresh Eyes to Read These Verses.' *Kipling Journal* 56 (December 1982): 20–7.

Crawfurd, John. 'On the Classification of the Races of Man.' *Transactions of the Ethnological Society of London* 1 (1861): 354–78.

Daly, Nicholas. *Modernism, Romance and the Fin de Siècle: Popular Fiction and British Culture, 1880–1914*. Cambridge: Cambridge University Press, 1999.

Dunlop, W. and T. V. Holmes. 'Australian Folklore Stories.' *The Journal of the Anthropological Institute of Great Britain and Ireland* 28 (1899): 22–34.

Farrar, Frederic W. 'Fixity of Type.' *Transactions of the Ethnological Society of London* 3 (1865): 394–9.

Fletcher, C. R. L. and Rudyard Kipling. *A School History of England*. Oxford: Clarendon, 1941.

Gilmour, David. *The Long Recessional: The Imperial Life of Rudyard Kipling*. New York: Farrar, Straus, and Giroux, 2002.

Green, Roger Lancelyn. *Kipling and the Children*. London: Elek, 1965.

Hai, Ambreen. 'On Truth and Lie in a Colonial Sense: Kipling's Tales of Tale-Telling.' *ELH* 64.2 (1997): 599–625.

Hattersley, Roy. *The Edwardians*. New York: St. Martin's, 2005.

Humphries, Stephen. *Hooligans or Rebels? An Oral History of Working-Class Childhood and Youth 1889–1939*. London: Basil Blackwell, 1981.

Hunt, James. 'Introductory Address on the Study of Anthropology.' *Anthropological Review* 1.1 (May 1863): 1–20.

Jacottet, Edouard. *Contes Populaires des Bassoutos*. Paris: Ernest Leroux, 1895.

Kipling, Rudyard. *Just So Stories*. 1902. Ed. Lisa Lewis. Oxford: Oxford University Press, 1995.

——. *The Letters of Rudyard Kipling, vol. 3: 1900–10*. Ed. Thomas Pinney. London: Macmillan, 1996.

——. *Puck of Pook's Hill*. 1906. Harmondsworth, England: Puffin, 1987.

——. *Rewards and Fairies*. 1910. Harmondsworth, England: Puffin, 1987.

Lang, Andrew. *The Brown Fairy Book*. 1904. New York: Dover, 1965.

——. 'The Bunyip.' *The Brown Fairy Book*. 1904. New York: Dover, 1965. 71–6.

——. *Magic and Religion*. London: Longmans, 1901.

——. *Modern Mythology*. 1897. New York: AMS Press, 1968.

——. *Myth, Ritual and Religion*. 2 vols. Rev. ed. London: Longmans, 1899.

——. *The Orange Fairy Book*. 1906. New York: Dover, 1968.

——. 'The Owl and the Eagle.' *The Orange Fairy Book*. 1906. New York: Dover, 1968. 236–40.

——. 'The Sacred Milk of Koumongoé.' *The Brown Fairy Book*. 1904. New York: Dover, 1965. 143–53.

Lévy-Bruhl, Lucien. *How Natives Think*. 1910. Introd. Ruth L. Bunzel. Trans. Lillian A. Clare. New York: Washington Square, 1966.

Lewis, Lisa. 'Explanatory Notes.' *Just So Stories*. Rudyard Kipling. Oxford: Oxford University Press, 1995: 219–37.

Livingstone, David N. 'Science and Society: Nathaniel S. Shaler and Racial Ideology.' *Transactions of the Institute of British Geographers*. New Series 9.2 (1984): 181–210.

McBratney, John. *Imperial Subjects, Imperial Space: Rudyard Kipling's Fiction of the Native-Born*. Columbus: Ohio State University Press, 2002.

Peters, John P. 'Notes on Recent Theories of the Origin of the Alphabet.' *Journal of the American Oriental Society* 22 (1901): 177–98.

Prichard, James Cowles. 'Anniversary Address for 1848, to the Ethnological Society of London on the Recent Progress of Ethnology.' *Journal of the Ethnological Society of London* 2 (1850): 119–49.

Rose, Jonathan. *The Edwardian Temperament 1895–1919*. Athens, Ohio: Ohio University Press, 1986.

Said, Edward. *Orientalism*. 25th Anniversary Edition. New York: Vintage, 1994.

Stocking, George W. Jr. *After Tylor: British Social Anthropology 1888–1951*. Madison: University of Wisconsin Press, 1995.

Torgovnick, Marianna. *Gone Primitive: Savage Intellects, Modern Lives*. Chicago: University of Chicago Press, 1990.

Tout, Charles Hill. 'Report on the Ethnology of the Siciatl of British Columbia, a Coast Division of the Salish Stock.' *The Journal of the Anthropological Society of Great Britain and Ireland* 34 (1904): 20–91.

Young, G. Winthrop. 'Education.' *Edwardian England 1901–1910*. 1933. Ed. F. J. C. Hearnshaw. Freeport, New York: Books for Libraries, 1968. 160–84.

12
Truth and Claw: The Beastly Children and Childlike Beasts of Saki, Beatrix Potter, and Kenneth Grahame

Elizabeth Hale

This essay explores how three writers active in the Edwardian period represent childish bad behaviour. Despite their obvious differences of genre and approach, Beatrix Potter, Kenneth Grahame, and Saki (Hector Hugh Munro) share an interest in bad or naughty characters, adult and child. These characters are driven by a fierce internal logic that cuts across social convention and the needs or desires of other characters: particularly when they write about children, Potter, Grahame, and Saki characterize bad behaviour as wild, natural, and even honest. They do this by associating wildness with animal behaviour; in doing so, they draw on Romantic ideals of the child's purity and honesty (in the face of corrupt adult society), as well as ideals of animality. The term 'beastly' is thus useful here. Bad behaviour can be termed 'beastly,' in the sense of 'acting in any manner unworthy of a reasonable creature,' but it can also simply mean 'resembling a beast in conduct, or in obeying the animal instincts' (*OED*). Beastly children and childlike beasts live ruthlessly, pay heed only to what they want, are inconsiderate of the wants of those around them, and cause trouble. However troublesome to adults this behaviour might be, it underscores the natural and original qualities of idealized childhood, in stark opposition to the corruption and mixed motives of the adult world.

A word here about the choice of writers. Saki wrote for adults, with a sardonic maliciousness that is absent from the children's books of Potter and Grahame. But their works bear comparison because they show the ruthless child from the perspectives of adult and child readers, and demonstrate that understanding Edwardian ideas about childhood requires one to examine children as they appear in works by adults for adults, as well as those for children. They also demonstrate a peculiarly Edwardian nostalgia for rural England and a distaste for the city and post-industrial society. This nostalgia for pastoral life underscores the affection for animals and children that can be seen in their work, be it satirical and savage (as in Saki), gently nostalgic (as in Grahame), or delicately ironic (as in Potter).

Saki's child characters act with an 'inexorable child logic' ('The Penance,' 426) that shocks, but also silences and awes adult characters. To underscore their wildness, or their kinship with the natural world, Saki shows them using, and associating with, animals in ways that show their purity of ruthlessness and expose the muddled and compromised nature of adult life. The ruthless child protagonists of Saki can best be seen in his two stories 'Sredni Vashtar' (1910) and 'The Penance,' (1910). The boy animals of three of Beatrix Potter's tales: *The Tale of Peter Rabbit* (1902), *The Tale of Tom Kitten* (1907), and *The Tale of Squirrel Nutkin* (1903), act with a similar fierceness of desire and disregard for adult rules, as do the young animals of Kenneth Grahame's *The Wind in the Willows* (1908), in particular, Portly Otter.

These beastly children are notable for a fierce internal logic that makes almost no reference to the adult world and its rules: in other words, they do exactly what they want to do, without consulting others. But what might be represented as selfishness by earlier or later writers, is used here to reveal how disappointing and muddled adult life is; beastly children's 'naughty' actions promise to cut through this mediocrity and provide a truthful, though possibly brutal, new way of doing things. As we shall see, however, though their fictional children symbolize the new and the original, Grahame, Potter and Saki draw on Victorian and Romantic ideas about childhood, and show their radical children at work in nostalgic natural settings. At the same time, this natural setting and the association of children and their unrepentant bad behaviour with animals marks them out as peculiarly Edwardian.

Saki's children are not literally animals (unlike any of Potter's and Grahame's characters). But they are strongly associated with animals, and ally themselves with animals, setting themselves against a set of mediocre late-Victorian adults. The bleak 'Sredni Vashtar' tells of Conradin, a sickly ten-year-old orphan boy, who lives with the despicable Mrs De Ropp:

> Mrs De Ropp was Conradin's cousin and guardian, and in his eyes she represented those three-fifths of the world that are necessary and

disagreeable and real; the other two-fifths, in perpetual antagonism to the foregoing, were summed up in himself and his imagination. (136)

Conradin is hemmed in by his illness and by Mrs De Ropp's 'coddling restrictions and drawn-out dulness' (136). Confined to her house and sad suburban garden, where he cannot play or pick the fruit from the trees, he nevertheless creates a kingdom of his own in a 'disused tool-shed' (137). In it, he keeps two animals, a 'ragged-plumaged Houdan hen, on which [he] lavished an affection that had scarcely another outlet,' and a 'large polecat-ferret, which a friendly butcher-boy had once smuggled, cage and all, into its present quarters,' and which Conradin is 'dreadfully afraid of' (137). He worships the ferret, naming it 'Sredni Vashtar,' giving it votive offerings of 'red flowers' and 'scarlet berries,' and scattering nutmeg before it (137–38). Conradin channels his hatred of Mrs De Ropp into his worship of the ferret, convincing himself that Sredni Vashtar is responsible for her illness from toothache. When Mrs De Ropp begins to notice how much time he is spending in the tool-shed, she investigates, and has the Houdan hen taken away (thus symbolizing the death of Conradin's ability to love). Conradin swallows his rage, but prays to his ferret-god for vengeance. Mrs De Ropp next sets her sights on the ferret:

'What are you keeping in that locked hutch?' she asked. 'I believe it's guinea pigs. I'll have them all cleared away.'
    Conradin shut his lips tight, but the Woman ransacked his bedroom till she found the carefully hidden key, and forthwith marched down to the shed to complete her discovery...And Conradin fervently breathed his prayer for the last time. But he knew as he prayed that he did not believe. He knew that the Woman would come out presently with that pursed smile he loathed so well on her face, and that in an hour or two the gardener would carry away his wonderful god, a god no longer, but a simple brown ferret in a hutch. (139)

For Conradin the ferret symbolizes strength, wellness, and his selfhood, all of which are threatened by his cousin-guardian and the doctor, who insist that he has only five years to live. He therefore prays with redoubled vigour to his 'threatened idol,' successfully so, for Mrs De Ropp does not return from the tool-shed. Out from the door-way comes 'a long, low, yellow-and-brown beast, with eyes a-blink at the waning daylight, and dark wet stains round the fur of jaws and throat' (140). It is left to Mrs De Ropp's maid to make the gruesome discovery while Conrad drops to his knees in homage to the 'great polecat-ferret' (140).

This story is remarkable for its indictment of adult meddling in the lives of children and its endorsement of the imagination over the 'real' world of conformity and social expectation. It is also remarkable for its association of the child's will to love and to power with the animal world. Conrad is explicitly associated with two caged animals: one, a domestic animal, a hen, on which he lavishes love, and whose removal from his life indicates the loss of his ability to love; and the other, a wild beast, the polecat-ferret whom he reveres but also fears, and whose release proves fatal for Mrs De Ropp. Although like him, they are confined, and underscore his powerlessness in the socialized adult world, the animals are also associated with the release of his imaginative inner life. Conradin's prayers never directly state what he wants Sredni Vashtar to do; instead, he communicates without words to the polecat-ferret, and it is that that makes the association of the boy and the beast true and powerful. Indeed, Conradin lives a truer, better life with the hen and the ferret than do the adults surrounding him: this is what makes us sympathize with him, and not with his slaughtered guardian.

This unsettling vision of childhood pervades Saki's stories, as Grahame Greene observes:

> Unhappiness wonderfully aids the memory, and the best stories of Munro are all of childhood, its humour and its anarchy as well as its cruelty and unhappiness...The victims...are sufficiently foolish to awaken no sympathy – they are the middle-aged, the people with power; it is right that they should suffer a temporary humiliation...behind all these stories is an exacting sense of justice. (75)

Indeed, the children in Saki's stories themselves have an exacting sense of justice, as well as of truth. We see this in 'The Penance,' in which the allegiance between children and animals is further underlined. In it, an adult, Octavian Ruttle, who has killed a cat that he wrongly suspects of killing his chickens, is made to pay for his actions by the children next door. Octavian has checked with the 'adults' of the house to whom the cat belongs before killing it; they agree that the 'children will mind, but they need not know' (422). But the children do find out what has happened; they love their little cat, and are enraged at the injustice of his actions; they lay siege to Octavian until he agrees to do penance.

Even before he has killed the cat Octavian is uneasy about the children. Their parents are in India, and they are staying with relatives. In the course of the several months they have been living next door to Octavian, he has not been able to learn their names. They remain a 'puzzle' (422), and 'non-commital' (423) towards him. They gain a strong influence over him; in some ways, they seem to act as an externalized conscience for Octavian, who, as an amiable fellow 'depended in large measure on the unstinted approval of his fellows' (422). He is already uneasy about killing the cat; the children's outrage shakes him further.

> And as he passed beneath the shadow of the high blank wall he glanced up and became aware that his hunting had had undesired witnesses. Three white set faces were looking down at him.
> 'I'm sorry, but it had to be done,' said Octavian with genuine apology in his voice.
> 'Beast!'
> The answer came from three throats with startling intensity.
> Octavian felt that the blank wall would not be more impervious to his explanations than the bunch of human hostility that peered over its coping. (423)

It is as if nature itself is speaking through the 'throats' of the children. Like the cat, they are not named; they remain 'as non-committal as the long blank wall that shut them off from the meadow' (423). Their allegiance to the little cat is as fierce in its intensity as Conradin's for the hen and ferret. And the way they exact penance from Octavian has a similar ruthlessness. At first, Octavian makes feeble attempts at appeasement, giving them sweets, which they scornfully scatter on the ground of the wood. Then, noting their interest in his baby daughter, Olivia, who is playing in the meadow, he attempts to lure them into friendship by encouraging them to play with her. He assumes their interest in her is affectionate. It is far more calculating and predatory. They distract Octavian and take Olivia to the piggery roof:

> 'What are you going to do with her?' he panted. There was no mistaking the grim trend of mischief in those flushed but sternly composed young faces.
> 'Frow her down and the pigs will d'vour her, every bit 'cept the palms of their hands,' said the other boy.

This...proposal...alarmed Octavian, since it might be carried into effect at a moment's notice; there had been cases, he remembered, of pigs eating babies.

'You surely wouldn't treat my poor little Olivia in that way?' he pleaded.

'You killed our little cat,' came in stern reminder from three throats. (426)

The children's love for their cat equals Octavian's for his daughter. And their ruthlessness, their 'inexorable child logic,' parodies Octavian's weaker version of ruthlessness. He believes he has been just in killing the little cat: 'It had been a distasteful and seemingly ruthless deed, but circumstances had demanded the doing of it' (422). But he is driven by his weak desire to be liked by others, to use his baby daughter as a lure. So the children turn the tables on him, by threatening an unpleasant death for Olivia in the pigsty. Olivia falls 'with a soft, unctuous splash into a morass of muck and decaying straw' (426); Octavian clambers in, and, realising he will not be able to rescue his daughter, who is sinking into the mire and will soon be choked, agrees to do penance in exchange for the children's help in saving his infant. In penance he stands vigil in the dusk at the deceased cat's grave, holding a candle and repeating 'I'm a miserable Beast,' until the children show their satisfaction and proclaim him to be 'un-Beast' (427).

It is unclear which party is more 'beastly' in this story. Certainly both parties are cruel. But the children's actions are beastly in the sense of 'resembling a beast in conduct, or in obeying the animal instincts,' unlike Octavian who is guilty of 'acting in any manner unworthy of a reasonable creature.' In their fierce love of the cat, and in their pitiless pursuit of Octavian's conscience, they seem to him like the distilled voice of nature, protesting the unfair death of the cat; they are not a kindly nature, but one in Tennysonian terms 'red in tooth and claw,' ('In Memoriam A. H. H.' Canto 56, 15). They thus invoke a pure and honest ferocity lacked by adult humans.

A similar fierce purity can be seen in the child heroes of Beatrix Potter's *The Tale of Peter Rabbit* (1902), *The Tale of Tom Kitten* (1907), and *The Tale of Squirrel Nutkin* (1903), who are driven by greed, wildness, and rudeness. They are not calculating or manipulative to the same extent as Saki's children, nor do they avoid punishment. But they share a strength of will and a directness of purpose, and as child animals they invoke beastly nature perhaps even more strongly. For example, the 'very naughty' Peter Rabbit is driven by greed (2). Greed leads him to ignore his mother's warnings, and go to Mr McGregor's garden, where he eats too many lettuces, French beans, and radishes. Feeling sick, he looks for some parsley to settle his stomach, whereupon he is chased by Mr McGregor. He flees home and collapses, whereupon his mother doses him with camomile tea, and sends him to bed without supper. As in Saki's stories, Peter is distinguished from the other characters in the tale by his 'naughty' behaviour. The way he follows his desire, in this case his greed, shows that he is not as socialized as his sisters, who obediently fold up their pink cloaks and pick blackberries for supper, delaying gratification until such time as their mother awards it them.

The story follows a trajectory from greed, to satisfaction of greed, then peril, followed by punishment. One might feel that Peter ends the tale in a rather abject way, stripped of his clothes, denied supper, and put to bed. However, as Alison Lurie points out, there is a 'concealed moral...that disobedience and exploration are more fun than good behaviour, and not really all that dangerous, whatever Mother may say' (5). Readers identify with Peter, and assume that his spirit is not quenched, even by camomile tea, or by his transformation from bold rascal, to frightened boy, to baby rabbit.

One way that the story marks Peter out visually for hero-status is his clothes: his smart blue jacket with brass buttons, and his little shoes. He is wearing those clothes when he enters the forbidden garden; as he flees, he sheds them, first his shoes, and then his jacket:

> He lost one of his shoes among the cabbages, and the other shoes among the potatoes. After losing them, he ran on four legs and went faster, so that I think he might have got away altogether if he had not unfortunately run into a gooseberry net, and got caught by the large buttons on his jacket. (13)

Losing his clothes enables Peter to go faster, to run on all fours, like a rabbit, not a little boy. As he sheds his clothes, Peter also sheds his bravado. Certainly, the longer he is chased, the more frightened and tired he becomes, and the less we see him standing upright. Out of the last six illustrations of Peter, five show him in horizontal mode. The penultimate picture of Peter shows him stretched at full length on the floor of the rabbit hole; the last one shows him tucked in bed in the distance (though his ears are up again). The story seems to return Peter to infancy, but also to an animal state: one might debate whether he sheds his naughtiness along with his clothes, or whether Potter represents the essential, animal creature lurking beneath the socializing clothes imposed upon him by his mother.

Beatrix Potter wrote *The Tale of Peter Rabbit* to entertain the son of a friend, Noel Moore, who was recuperating from scarlet fever. Peter ends the story like the little boy, tucked up in bed, ministered to by his caring mother. Peter's journey, then, offers a fantasy of a child acting boldly, but also being restored to the maternal embrace. This transformation is remarkable for its completeness. Peter Rabbit does not do things by halves. Like other fictional Edwardian children, he is utterly committed to whatever course of action he is involved in: whether he is being a bold, naughty little boy, or frightened rabbit, or sick infant. In this, Peter is similar to Portly Otter, who, as we shall see, is driven by desire for adventure or for return to the family bosom.

We see a similar absoluteness of character in Tom Kitten and his sisters, Moppet and Mittens, in *The Tale of Tom Kitten* (1907), and their resistance to forced socialization by their mother. The story opens with them in their natural state: unclothed, and grubby: 'They had dear little fur coats of their own; and they tumbled about the doorstep and played in the dust' (149). But the adult social world intervenes, in the form of visitors for afternoon tea; their mother, Mrs Tabitha Twitchett, scrubs their faces, brushes their fur, and combs their tails and whiskers, then forces Moppet and Mittens into 'clean pinafores and tuckers,' and Tom into 'all sorts of elegant uncomfortable clothes' (151).

Tom soon undermines this socialized image. His body has already resisted being made tidy and elegant: as the narrative tells us, 'Tom Kitten was very fat, and he had grown; several buttons burst off. His mother sewed them on again' (151). Next, Mrs Twitchett sends the kittens into the garden, telling them to keep clean, and walk on their hind legs (another reference to socialization). This proves almost impossible for Moppet and Mittens, who 'trod upon their pinafores and fell on their noses. When they stood up there were several green smears!' (152). Tom's clothes are even more constricting, and he virtually erupts from them: 'Tom Kitten was quite unable to jump when walking upon his hind legs in trousers. He came up the rockery by degrees, breaking the ferns and shedding buttons right and left. He was all in pieces when he reached the top of the wall' (153). Although the children disobey their mother, getting very dirty and losing their clothes, the narrative does not blame them. Instead, it is Mrs Twitchett who is at fault: it is she who 'unwisely turned them out into the garden' (151). Like Saki's adults, she ignores at her peril the nature of her children. Expecting them to behave like socialized adults is foolish: this message is reinforced when on discovering them clothes-free and grubby she smacks them and packs them off to bed:

> She sent them upstairs: and I am sorry to say she told her friends that they were in bed with the measles; which was not true. Quite the contrary; they were not in bed; *not* in the least. Somehow there were very extraordinary noises over-head, which disturbed the dignity and repose of the tea-party. (157)

It does not do to ask children to deny their nature: in this case, the child-animal exuberance of Tom, Mittens, and Moppet bursts through the layers of social expectations placed on them by their mother. By unconsciously returning to their desired natural state, they 'disturb the dignity and repose' of the pompous adults in their world. One can almost hear Saki cheering them on.

Peter Rabbit and Tom Kitten are in large part formed from the nineteenth-century concept of the 'good bad boy.' The idea makes its most famous appearance in the form of Tom Sawyer, a scape-grace with a good heart who, even if he is later reformed, is a better, more interesting person, than the milksop who has never had the spirit to get into trouble (Lurie 6). This may be why, although Peter is infantilized, we do not feel that he has been erased of spirit. Indeed, his initial high spirits are reflective of an Edwardian interest in childish ingenuity and independence (see, for comparison, Edith Nesbit's Bastable children in *The Wouldbegoods*, whose independence is contrasted favourably with the milksop Alfred-next-door), and therefore mitigate the tame ending of the story.

If Peter Rabbit and Tom Kitten are good bad boys, then what are we to make of Squirrel Nutkin's behaviour in *The Tale of Squirrel Nutkin* (1903), which is closer in spirit to the disrespectful, cynical behaviour of Saki's stern children? The tale runs thus: a group of squirrels go to a small island to gather nuts. With the exception of Squirrel Nutkin, they pay their respects to the owl, Old Brown, the elder statesman of the island. While the other squirrels bring him offerings of food, Squirrel Nutkin dances up and down, chanting riddles, and being 'excessively impertinent in his manners' (25). Each day he adds to his impertinence: he pokes Old Brown with a nettle, he sings silly songs; instead of gathering nuts, he plays at skittles. Old Brown remains impassive in the face of such rudeness, until the sixth day when

> Nutkin...took a running jump right onto the head of Old Brown!...Then all at once there was a flutterment and a scufflement and a loud 'Squeak!'
> The other squirrels scuttered away into the bushes.
> When they came back very cautiously, peeping round the tree – there was Old Brown sitting on his door-step, quite still, with his eyes closed, as if nothing had happened.
> But Nutkin was in his waist-coat pocket! (34)

Old Brown holds the squirrel by the tail, intending to skin and eat him, but Nutkin 'pulled so very hard that his tail broke in two,' and escapes (35).

The moral of this story is ambiguous. Nutkin is punished by the loss of his tail, but it is not clear if he is reformed, though his ego is wounded: 'And to this day, if you meet Nutkin up a tree and ask him a riddle, he will throw sticks at you, and stamp his feet and scold, and shout – "cuck-cuck-cuck-cur-r-r-cuck-k-k!"' (36). There is no sense, however, that Nutkin has grown or learned a lesson. He is as rude and defiant at the end of the story as he is at the beginning. Unlike Peter Rabbit, who grows and learns, or Tom Kitten, whose naughtiness comes from innocent mischief, Squirrel Nutkin is fixed as a bad boy. He is also fixed in his animal state, unlike Peter Rabbit and the Twitchett Kittens who fluctuate between animal nudity and socialized clothes-wearing. It is too simple to say that Beatrix Potter consistently equates childish 'naughtiness' with animal behaviour, but notably, *The Tale of Squirrel Nutkin* is the least anthropomorphized of the stories: no one wears any clothes (even Old Brown, raising the question of how he could put Nutkin in his waistcoat pocket). The tale is also set in an uncharacteristically undomesticated landscape, whose island savagery might be compared with Conradin's pagan worship of Sredni Vashtar.

Beatrix Potter's tales are generally set in pre-industrial village life, with action placed in various versions of outdoor nature in various stages of domestication (such as Mr McGregor's market garden, and the meadow of 'The Penance'). Occasionally, wilder versions of nature can be seen, as in *Squirrel Nutkin*, but generally, her vision is in nature, a vision that is shared by Kenneth Grahame in *The Wind in the Willows* (1908).

For the most part, *The Wind in the Willows* focuses on the adventures of the four adult animals, Mole, Ratty, Toad, and Badger. But Chapter 7 of the novel centres on the actions of a disruptive child animal, Portly Otter, the son of Ratty and Mole's friend, Otter. Portly has gone missing. He is known to be '"adventurous"' and '"self-possessed,"' but Otter worries that his son, who '"hasn't learnt to swim very well yet,"' may have gone down to the weir, which has a '"fascination"' for him, and which is very full of water (127). Ratty and Mole therefore join the search party. They go out on the river at night, lit by the full moon. Coming to an island, they find 'sleeping soundly in entire peace and contentment, the little, round, podgy, childish form of the baby otter,' curled up between the hooves of the god, Pan, who is 'disposed in majestic ease' (136). Given that *The Wind in the Willows* invokes so many themes of Arcadian existence (comfortable rural and domestic life, far from the corrupt concerns of urban and political life) it is appropriate to find in the Arcadian nature god, Pan, the *genius loci* of this pastoral idyll. Pan is the 'shepherd god and protector of shepherds...also a hunting god, concerned with small animals such as hares, partridges, and small birds' (Roberts 530). As such, he guards Portly Otter, and by extension all the small animals that live along the river. This explicit association of childhood and the spirit of nature is as strong as in 'Sredni Vashtar' and 'The Penance,' in which the children symbolize implacable nature with their 'inexorable child logic,' and by extension can be considered disciples of Pan. It is also much more direct than in *The Tale of Squirrel Nutkin*, in which Old Brown functions as the *genius loci* of the island, standing in for nature, red in tooth and claw or for Pan's cruel streak.

Jean Perrot suggests persuasively that Grahame is strongly influenced by ideas linking Pan and childhood put forward by Robert Louis Stevenson in *Virginibus Puerisque*. For Stevenson, according to Perrot,

> Pan was...the representative of a genuine natural energy...[an] authentic force which characterized the child as a true modern hero, embodying both the complexities of human experience and those extreme moods which are governed by two specific laws: "Sometimes it comes by the spirit of delight and sometimes by the spirit of terror" (Perrot 156).

Stevenson's 'Pan's Pipes' (1878), 'depicts the child as harbouring the pagan energy of the forest deity' (Perrot 157). This is an idea that takes hold strongly in Edwardian fiction, and that it is associated with the pastoral should not be surprising. As John Moore points out,

> children and childhood have been endemic to pastoral from the beginning; children's literature merely aligns it with elements that had been there from the start. The fourth of Virgil's *Eclogues* announces the arrival of an Arcadian age, its commencement marked by the birth of a child. Arcadia or the Golden Age is the mytho-historical childhood of the race. (47)

The pastoral child-animals of Grahame, Potter, and Saki, then, embody the pagan impulse. This may account for the fierceness of their desires. Portly Otter, for instance, is depicted as a creature driven almost entirely by instinct. He wants to go to the river, though he has been told not to: he goes to the river. Once there, he is scared, and wants to go home. He pays no attention to the rules that bind the adult creatures of the novel. Portly's directness of purpose could make him a rather limited character – indeed, he lacks the complexity of Mole, Ratty, and other adult characters. But the novel suggests that it be seen rather as showing the innocence, and indeed blessedness, of childhood, in contrast to the fallenness of adulthood. And Portly's association with Pan underscores the nostalgia that runs through *The Wind in the Willows*, a nostalgia for the Golden Age.

Indeed, childhood in all three authors can be associated with the classical concept of the Ages of Man. In this formulation childhood is akin to the Golden Age, where humans and gods lived together, while adulthood is like the Iron Age, where humans are separated from the gods, and must struggle to stay alive. Grahame explicitly spells out this concept in *The Golden Age* (1895), a book of childhood reminiscences, in which adults are 'Olympians,' and the children are named for Greek heroes. In *The Wind in the Willows*, he reverses this concept somewhat, associating children more closely with gods than adults. Edwardian writers are taken with the idea of the blessedness of childhood, as can be seen most starkly in J. M. Barrie's idea of Peter Pan, the boy who never grows up, and who remains separated from adulthood. Edith Nesbit, too, brings her child characters into contact with the Olympian pantheon in *The Enchanted Castle* (1907), where the statues in a large estate come to life at night, and can be seen by humans once a year. Adults think they are mad or dreaming, but the children in the tale accept the magic of the gods with little hesitation.

A side-effect of their innocence is that the children have little idea of the significance of meeting the gods, accepting as natural what awes, silences, or shocks adults. Portly Otter blithely accepts that he is protected by Pan, the god of nature, in contrast to the struggle that his adult counterparts carry out to assure his safety. His return home shows how unaware of, indeed, how innocent he is of the trouble he has caused, and how close he may have come to danger.

> As they drew near the familiar ford, the mole took the boat in to the bank, and they lifted Portly out and set him on his legs on the tow-path, gave him his marching orders and a friendly farewell pat on the back, and shoved out into midstream. They watched the little animal as he waddled along the path contentedly and with importance; watched him till they saw his muzzle suddenly lift and his waddle break into a clumsy amble as he quickened his pace with shrill whines and wriggles of recognition. (138–9)

Given that, in previous passages, Ratty has commented on Portly's self-possession and adventurous spirit, it may be surprising to see Portly depicted as so very animal-like and infantile. Portly does not possess speech, or at least, his speech is not reported. His return home is described in terms of pure instinct, but that equates to his natural response on waking on the island, and finding that Pan has gone:

> His face grew blank, and he fell to hunting round in a circle with pleading whines. As a child that has fallen happily asleep in its nurse's arms, and wakes to find itself alone and laid in a strange place, and searches corners and cupboards, and runs from room to room, despair growing silently in its heart, even so Portly searched the island and searched, dogged and unwearying, till at last the black moment came for giving it up, and sitting down and crying bitterly. (137)

Ratty, Mole, and Portly have all witnessed Pan on this island. Portly does so with a sense of security that allies him closely with this kind but cruel god. Ratty and Mole, as adults, have a stronger sense of awe, or even terror:

> Then suddenly the Mole felt a great Awe fall upon him, an awe that turned his muscles to water, bowed his head, and rooted his feet to the ground...With difficulty he turned to look for his friend, and saw him at his side cowed, stricken, and trembling violently. (135)

204 Childhood in Edwardian Fiction

On waking, the older animals forget what they have seen, though they remember that they have been in the presence of something great and magical, 'as one wakened suddenly from a beautiful dream, who struggles to recall it, and can recapture nothing but a dim sense of the beauty of it, the beauty!' (137). This contrasts strongly with Portly's 'dogged and unwearying' searching, and bitter tears, which represents both a greater sense of loss and Portly's relationship with Pan (and nature) which is closer even than that of Ratty and Mole.

Kenneth Grahame's wife Elspeth recalls him making the following statement about the honesty of animals and their closeness to nature:

> Every animal, by instinct, lives according to his nature ... No animal is ever tempted to belie his nature. No animal, in other words, knows how to tell a lie. Every animal is honest. Every animal is straight-forward. Every animal is true – and is therefore, according to his nature, both beautiful and good. (Grahame and Grahame 28)

The adult characters of *The Wind in the Willows* are attuned to their instincts (defined by the *Oxford English Dictionary as* 'an innate, typically fixed pattern of behavior in animals in response to certain stimuli,' such as birds having a fixed instinct to build nests, or beavers to build dams.) Ratty hears the call to adventure in the Wide World; Mole, to the Wild Wood, and later to his underground home. Toad's instinct is to all things mechanical. But they struggle with those instincts, Mole and Ratty more successfully than Toad, and to a large measure they deny them. This makes them adults, and to a certain extent it makes them less honest, less true to their nature than the animals that Kenneth Grahame so admires. Portly, however, being a child, is driven by his instincts, is true to his nature (his instinct, as an Otter, draws him to the river at large). Like the children of Saki's stories, or Beatrix Potter's Tales, his instincts cause trouble in the socialized, Iron Age world of the adults. And yet, because the older animals recognize the honesty of his ruthlessness, the way he innocently follows his instincts, he is swiftly forgiven.

At this point one might reasonably ask what makes this so Edwardian. Have children not always been idealized and portrayed as single-minded, innocent and close to nature? Certainly the Romantic vision of the child, with its emphasis on natural innocence and the importance of the countryside as a place for raising children is not so different. But the emphasis on the child as part of nature, as ruthlessly truthful regardless of whether he is good or bad, on the importance of desires, drives and instincts, as opposed to the compromised nature of socialized adult existence, is what distinguishes the Edwardian vision of childhood in these texts.

Additionally, in these texts we find little sense of how a child might become an adult. In none of these stories do we sense that the children grow or mature. This is quite different from most Victorian children's stories, in which the development of the child's moral sense, logic, and identity is paramount: Victorian children are important because they are going to become adults. Victorian writers look for the seeds of adulthood in their child characters. For example, the final chapter of *Alice in Wonderland* (1865) explicitly draws attention to Alice's future womanhood, and the end of *Tom Brown's Schooldays* (1857) shows Tom's character development reaching fruition when he returns to Rugby chapel as a man. They emphasize that the incidents and challenges of child life are valuable in training them for adulthood, rather than being contained in a separate unit of experience as in Edwardian writers' works. Edwardian children are important because they are children, not because they are going to become adults: indeed, Edwardian writers represent childhood as a timeless space entirely separate from adulthood.

Perhaps this comes from the feelings of nostalgia for the protected time of childhood; however, such protection may also be a fantasy, especially for these three writers, none of whom had comfortable upbringings. After the death of their mother, Hector Hugh Munro and his brother and sister were sent to live with aunts; the flat detachment of Saki's child characters from the concerns of the people around them may very well be inspired by a childhood spent as a guest in other people's houses. Beatrix Potter's odd childhood, detached from, or suppressed by, her parents (depending on which biography we read), causes many to see her tales as fantasies of escape, or of behaving badly. And Kenneth Grahame was orphaned at an early age then reared by his grandmother. His books of childhood reminiscences, *The Golden Age* (1895) and *Dream Days* (1898) show how conscious he was of the difference between adult and child concerns, and represent each group as operating on a different plane of existence. Each of these writers must surely have developed a strong inward imagination to respond to their life situations.

Whether the idea of a protected childhood is a fantasy or a recollection, there is a strong sense of nostalgia among these writers, expressed not only in the idea of the innocent detachment of childhood but also in the representation of rural nature. The representation of an Arcadian, even Tennysonian nature, red in tooth and claw, but not seriously so, is associated, in the case of Beatrix Potter's work, with pre-industrial British village life. The clothing of her animals in eighteenth-century mob-caps, jackets, and waistcoats, points to a more genteel age and social order. Saki's children are detached and isolated, but they live a comfortable rural existence, on, or near, working farms, piggeries, horses, and other livestock. And *The Wind in the Willows*, particularly the chapters involving Ratty and Mole, is resolutely pastoral in tone. Childhood, then, is associated in these works with rural idyll, though it is an idyll in which ruthlessness and badness can exist.

Other Edwardian writers also revel in the 'badness' or directness of child characters: in Edith Nesbit's *The Wouldbegoods* (1901), the Bastable children do a number of things that might be considered 'bad' by adults, but these actions are performed with the best intentions, and according to the rules of child logic. P. G. Wodehouse's Arcadian comedies (Edwardian and otherwise) show a range of inexorable children, more than willing to discomfit foolish adults and young-old boys, such as Bertie Wooster. Rudyard Kipling's *Stalky and Co.* (1899), set on the coast of Devon, close to nature, shows the fierce logic of his boy heroes, and revels in the way they use their bad behaviour to expose the sanctimoniousness, laziness, or foolishness of adults.

If childhood is Arcadian, or belongs to a golden age, then by extension adulthood is inevitably decayed, of the 'iron age.' Natural childhood contrasts with the 'civilized,' fallen world of adults. Its expression in these works as a kind of feral brutality is what distinguishes this natural childhood from its Romantic and Victorian predecessors. In applying Tennyson's idea of 'nature, red in tooth and claw' to children, then, Edwardian writers embrace the brutal honesty of their beastly children.

Works cited

Grahame, Kenneth. *The Wind in the Willows*. 1908. London: Methuen Children's Books, 1979.

Grahame, Kenneth and Elspeth Grahame. *First Whispers of The Wind in the Willows*. Philadelphia. J. B. Lippincott Company, 1945.

Greene, Graham. 'The Burden of Childhood.' *The Lost Childhood and Other Essays*. London, Eyre & Spottiswoode, 1951. 74–6.

Lurie, Alison. 'The Good Bad Boy.' *The New York Review of Books* 51.11 (24 June 2004): 1–6.

Moore, John David. 'Pottering about in the Garden: Kenneth Grahame's Version of Pastoral in "The Wind in the Willows."' *The Journal of the Midwest Modern Language Association* 23.1. (Spring 1990): 45–60.

Perrot, Jean. 'Pan and *Puer Aeternus*: Aestheticism and the Spirit of the Age.' *Poetics Today* 13.1 (Spring 1992): 155–67.

Potter, Beatrix. *Beatrix Potter: The Complete Tales*. London: Frederick Warne, 2002.

——. The Tale of Peter Rabbit. 1902. *Beatrix Potter: The Complete Tales*. 6–20.

——. The Tale of Squirrel Nutkin. 1903. *Beatrix Potter: The Complete Tales*. 21–36.

——. The Tale of Tom Kitten. 1907. *Beatrix Potter: The Complete Tales*. 147–58.

Roberts, John, ed. *The Oxford Dictionary of the Classical World*. Oxford: Oxford University Press, 2005.

Saki [Hector Hugh Munro]. 'The Penance.' 1910. *The Penguin Complete Saki*. Harmondsworth: Penguin, 1976. 422–27.

——. 'Sredni Vashtar.' 1910. *The Penguin Complete Saki*, Harmondsworth: Penguin, 1976. 136–40.

Tennyson, Alfred Lord: 'In Memoriam, A. H. H.' *The Works of Alfred Lord Tennyson*. Ware: Wordsworth, 1994. 309–92.

13
Murdering Adulthood: From Child Killers to Boy Soldiers in Saki's Fiction

Brian Gibson

'Reginald's Choir Treat' (1902) is to turn the church singers into a Bacchanalian procession, leading the undressed children into town and shocking its piously decent folk. In 'Gabriel-Ernest' (1909), Van Cheele finds the wild nude lad he had met the day before in his woods reclining cheekily on his couch. The fiction of Saki (H. H. Munro, 1870–1916) is known for its dandy pranks and drawing-room embarrassments, and his Edwardian stories of youth rebelling against adults are still widely read today. Around 1993, when Martin Stephen asked *Daily Telegraph* readers for their favourite Saki stories, four of the top ten tales focused on children (xvi–xvii); in the spring of 2007, BBC4 aired a documentary on Saki followed by adaptations of three stories, all involving children (Johns). Yet Saki's tricksters are usually post-Wildean dandies such as the young men Reginald and Clovis or 'self-possessed' adolescent girls ('The Open Window' 259), New Women-in-training, such as Vera or Matilda ('The Boar-Pig').

Although some of Saki's first fictions to appear in newspapers (1900–03) were political satires based on recent children's classics – Lewis Carroll's Alice books and Rudyard Kipling's *The Jungle Book* (1894) and *Just So Stories* (1902) – Saki's stories feature few children. In those stories, the distinctive voice of Saki the author-narrator, though often sympathetically aligned with the children as underdogs, remains an erudite, dryly witty, adult voice. Yet most of these child-centred stories – in part, fictionally refracted treatments of Munro's late-Victorian childhood – are some of the most intense and defiant of Saki's works. Although flecked with fantastic, pagan elements common to the era, these tales are much more darkly oppressive and psychologically realistic than most Edwardian children-centred literature. Far more than Hilaire Belloc, Saki's writing refutes 'Victorian sentiment...[with] a comic ruthlessness' (Briggs 170).

Childhood in Saki's fiction is language-based and does not begin until a boy or girl can become the satirist writ small, using his or her imagination to unwrite adult authority, for, as Susan Honeyman notes, 'literary children are frequently idealized as sites of resistance to the inflexible, systematizing logic of adult discourse' (116). The children in Saki's stories – perhaps channelling Munro's resentment of his tyrannical aunts – deny any close biological ties and often ally their wild natures with non-speaking animals for revenge against the unthinking, uncompassionate adults who stifle them. Childhood is murderously inimical to adulthood and in 'Sredni Vashtar' (1910), 'The Penance' (1910), and 'The Lumber-Room' (1913), in particular, children battle their indoctrinating guardians by building an inner story frame, becoming authors of their own re-ordering fictions. These story spaces they create, and ritually return to, grant enough speculative and surveillance power to thwart, even kill, those adults who have run Edwardian society into a rut of boredom and complacency. As this routine threatens to be broken by war, however, the looming military threat replaces and recreates Saki's rebellious children. Saki, co-opted by the increasingly militaristic attitudes of Munro – in a zealous return to his public-school childhood and the legacy of his imperial police officer father – begins to constrict children in a conformist, jingoistic frame. The only good child is the boy who will grow up to be a soldier. After murdering adult authority, the children's rebellion and violence is channelled into unacceptable murderous adulthood (suffragettes), acceptable murderous adulthood (soldiers defending King and country), or slowly self-murdering adult authority (apathetic, useless middle- and upper-class existence).

Munro never knew his mother – two winters after bringing him into the world, Mary Frances Munro, pregnant with her fourth child, was charged by a cow in the Devon countryside and died – and he would not spend time with his father until he was 16. Munro's childhood home, outside Barnstaple, was run by two head-butting, battle-axe aunts, Aunt Tom and Aunt Augusta; the latter, claimed Munro's sister Ethel in her 'Biography of Saki' (1924), was the 'autocrat...a woman of ungovernable temper, of fierce likes and dislikes, imperious, a moral coward, possessing no brains worth speaking of, and a primitive disposition' (640). Aunts are frequent targets in Saki's fiction, where they are associated with promoting marriage and social conformity. By the 1880s, Dieter Petzold notes, the mid-Victorian view of 'the child as a moral being' was being replaced by an interest in the child's 'freedom from obligations and his amoral status' (33). It is this 'amorality of youth,' Jonathan Rose notes, that makes children so important in Saki's fiction (189). Late Victorian books show children leading more independent lives (Petzold 33), but Saki shows childhood and adulthood as antithetical forces; children's independence is necessary because children and adults are so irreconcilable that they are usually not even blood-related and adulthood must often be slain. In 'Sredni Vashtar,' 'The Penance,' and 'The Lumber-Room,' the adult is a guardian or neighbour, not a mother, so their interfering adult authority seems all the less natural and more imposed.

In 'Sredni Vashtar,' Mrs De Ropp, Conradin's 'cousin and guardian,' so suffocates the boy with her bourgeois concern for 'respectability' (138) and 'thwarting him "for his good"' that if not for 'his imagination... rampant under the spur of loneliness, he would have succumbed long ago' (136). Conradin is ten but 'the doctor' has declared that 'the boy would not live another five years' (136), so the guardian must die for the child to survive and his creativity thrive. Ethel Munro notes that Munro was a 'delicate child' and the 'family doctor at Barnstaple... declared that the three of us would never live to grow up' (637).

'The Penance' builds a simple metonym for the insurmountable barrier between the adult and children, 'as non-committal as the long blank wall that shut them off from the meadow, a wall over which their three heads sometimes appeared at odd moments' (423). The three children, furious with their neighbour for killing their cat because he thought (wrongly) it was eating his chickens, remain 'a standing puzzle' to the adult, baffled in his non-child-ness (422), for 'the blank wall would not be more impervious to his explanations than the bunch of human hostility that peered over its coping' (423). Here are children as a nameless, unfathomable opposing force to adults, who are so concerned, as Octavian is, with 'the unstinted approval of his fellows' (422) that they no longer recall the sense of deep injustice that came naturally to them when they were young. The 'startling intensity' with which the trio call Octavian '"Beast!"' (423) has long ago been snuffed out by adult conventions.

In 'The Lumber-Room,' where Nicholas is kept at home by his cousins' aunt, the greatest offence is the guardian's misuse of imagination so that she can improvise punishments and forbearances: 'His cousins' aunt... insisted, by an unwarranted stretch of imagination, in styling herself his aunt also' and she 'had hastily invented the Jagborough [beach] expedition in order to impress on Nicholas the delights that he had justly forfeited by his disgraceful conduct at the breakfast-table' (372).

Saki's stories about children are anti-Victorian, amoral tales which savage the sentiment and teaching of good behaviour common to didactic children's tales; they are flavoured with two of Petzold's five ingredients for the 'new, anti-Victorian picture of the child:...his separateness from adults; his self-centeredness and lack of compassion' (33). Judging by critics' frequent concerns over Saki's 'cruelty' (for example, Greene vii–xi; Waugh xii; Maxey 58), Saki's stories continue to challenge bourgeois readers' moral sensibilities as much as the bachelor's tale upsets the aunt in 'The Story-Teller' (1913). The man tells three children, bored by their aunt's '*un*enterprising and deplorably *un*interesting' (350, emphasis added) story, a tale about a ' "horribly good" ' (351) girl. Her goodness is her undoing: she is initially rewarded with entry to a prince's park, but when a wolf comes to eat the pigs there, he hunts the girl, whose hiding-spot in some myrtle bushes is revealed by the clinking of her large medals for ' "obedience... punctuality, and... good behaviour" ' (351). The girl's markers of goodness give her away and the wolf restores savage, natural order by devouring her. The education (or disciplining, in Foucault's terms) of obedience, punctuality, and good behaviour for children is more unnatural than any sort of badness, and needs to be unlearnt and untold: the aunt declares the bachelor's story ' "A most improper story to tell young children! You have undermined the effect of years of careful teaching" ' (354). In Saki's child-centred stories, the young become authors of their own transgressive stories, turning them against the adult authorities who restrict them for their own 'good' – ' "boys are Nature's raw material" ' that teachers ' "are supposed to be moulding" ' (*The Unbearable Bassington* 579) – and moving into a space beyond words, discovering their own ' "unspeakable ferocity" ' ('The Story-Teller' 353) as they lead ' "improper" ' lives. Such ferocity keeps at bay the nostalgia of much child-centred Edwardian fiction, such as J. M. Barrie's Peter Pan tales and Kenneth Grahame's *The Wind in the Willows* (1908), although Grahame's earlier works, including *The Golden Age* (1895), offer 'morally casual and self-absorbed' children too (Grylls 109). Nature 'is divine' in Saki's fiction only because it is threatening, not magical or protective, as in most Edwardian children's fiction (Lurie 183). Saki's natural world is resolutely savage and unknowable (wild animals do not talk in his tales), while child and adult are so at odds that the nostalgic adult reader is shut out of the narrative. The un-adult-ness of rebellious children, full of unrest and unorthodoxy, enables them to undo the goodness, obedience, and decorum that adults force on them. Children imitate in miniature, slyly pervert, and unmake from within the religious and social rituals of a bourgeois Edwardian society which attempts to inflict true ' "cruelty" ' by bringing children to ' "what we call civilisation," ' as noted in Henry de Vere Stacpoole's 1908 novel *The Blue Lagoon* (113). Children can be as 'resolute and audible' and full of 'immense conviction' ('The Story-Teller' 350) and 'decision' (353) as adults, but, not yet fully indoctrinated by society, they are closer to a natural wildness that subverts the pretences of so-called civilization. They also do not try to convert others: 'children are content to convince themselves, and do not vulgarize their beliefs by trying to convince other people' ('The She-Wolf' 235).

The dull religiosity that bolstered adults' need to convert children likely became clear to Munro every Sunday, which Aunt Tom and Aunt Augusta bookended with their churchgoing. Tom 'took us regularly to Pilton Church on Sunday mornings' but attended mostly for appearance's sake and to gather gossip, Ethel Munro recalls, while 'Aunt Augusta's religion was not elastic; it was definite and High Church and took her into Barnstaple on Sunday evenings' (639, 641). Auberon Waugh argues that Munro's probable homosexuality explains his anger with Christianity (ix), but Saki's anger may be more of a fictional backlash against aunts who associated religion with conformity: 'Except ye be converted, and become as little children, ye shall not enter into the Kingdom of Heaven' (Matt. 18:3). Saki's boys and girls reject conversion to the compliant child-figures that adults want them to be in order to enter their lifeless world. 'The Quest' (*c.* 1910) pits a nature-aligned sense of childness against an unimaginative adult Christianity, which was largely responsible for the two attitudes towards children in the nineteenth century: that children were innately depraved, 'nourished by the Wesleyan and Evangelical movements, believ[ing] devoutly in original sin and the need to break the child's will,' and the Romantic notion of the primal innocence and 'natural goodness of children' (Grylls 39), an idea 'embryonic in Christianity' (38). In 'The Quest,' the missing Erik leads Clovis to imagine the headline ' " "Infant son of a prominent Nonconformist devoured by spotted Hyæna.' Your husband isn't a prominent Nonconformist, but his mother came of Wesleyan stock, and you must allow the newspapers some latitude" ' (148). Any religion, even the ironic 'Nonconformism,' suggests the social conformity Clovis and others always rebel against. Saki also suggests that the non-angelicness of children makes them no different from animals but threatening to status-conscious, hidebound adults.

In 'Sredni Vashtar,' 'The Penance,' and 'The Lumber-Room,' the children triumph over adult authority and surveillance within secret, sacred spaces that are physical manifestations of their imagination.

They become the true authority-figures as their wild imaginations break free of adult restrictions and even distance themselves from the author-narrator. Saki defers to his child protagonists' interior spaces by offering exterior spaces which are only partially described or, in 'The Penance,' walled off. There is no secret Eden in Saki's stories. Although 'childhood is often associated with a beautiful enclosed garden in Victorian and Edwardian art' (Wullschläger 148), the garden in Saki's fiction is associated with nature controlled, cultivated, tamed, and watched by adults. Saki's 'antipastoral' stories, with their roots in Carroll and Edward Lear, concern 'children severed from the world of adults... landscape[s] of isolation ... [are] approached indirectly ... [through] humour and irony' (Natov 159). Saki also starkly illustrates how 'the domestic space of the home... is constituted for the child through relations of power and control' (James et al. 54). The sense of claustrophobia, of being trapped by a guardian's watchful eye, which is more in keeping with Victorian than Edwardian settings for child-centred fiction (Wullschläger 145), suggests that these tales tap into the adult Munro's remembrance of his 1870s childhood: 'The house was too dark, verandas kept much of the sunlight out, the flower and vegetable gardens were surrounded by high walls and a hedge, and on rainy days we were kept indoors... we slept in rooms with windows shut and shuttered' (Ethel Munro 637–38). The guardian is a guard, and this dungeon-like world is transformed by Saki into Foucault's camp as 'diagram of a power that acts by means of general visibility ... the spatial "nesting" of hierarchized surveillance' (Foucault 171). Home and garden in Saki's stories are usually places of enclosure and surveillance that 'permit an internal, articulated and detailed control – to render visible those who are inside it... to act on those it shelters, to provide a hold on their conduct, to carry the effects of power right to them' (Foucault 172), yet Saki's wild children ultimately undo adults' taming by imitating, upturning, and parodying adult religiosity, ritual, and lessons within the domestic space as the child becomes successful reviser and new author of rituals, stories, and plots.

For Conradin in 'Sredni Vashtar,' a tool-shed is both 'a playroom and a cathedral' he has populated with a 'legion of phantoms, evoked partly from fragments of history' (137), revising adult lessons even as he keeps his animal talismans – Houdan hen (which Munro himself had as a boy) and polecat-ferret – secret from his guardian in this 'disused' building. The shed is the repository for Conradin's imagination and as tucked away in a 'forgotten corner' as Conradin's hate for Mrs De Ropp, 'which he was perfectly able to mask' (137). It is Conradin's refuge because 'the dull, cheerless garden [was] overlooked by so many windows that were ready to open with a message not to do this or that, or a reminder that medicines were due' (137). Mrs De Ropp's ability for surveillance is limited, however, for she is 'short-sighted' (138), unable to see through Conradin's mask or apprehend the threat of the polecat-ferret. In infernal opposition to his cousin, the 'Woman,' associated by capitalization with 'Heaven,' he turns the animal into 'a god and a religion' that requires worship 'with mystic and elaborate ceremonial' every Thursday (137). Conradin's animist, pseudo-Eastern religion involves offerings and festivals (one to prolong a toothache for Mrs De Ropp), and the creature is aligned with the 'fierce impatient side of things, as opposed to the Woman's religion' (138). After Mrs De Ropp removes the hen, Conradin requests her death in a vague refrain: ' "Do one thing for me, Sredni Vashtar" ' (138, 139). In the long moments when Mrs De Ropp is in the tool-shed again, looking for the other pet, Conradin stops inwardly believing but expresses his imagination aloud, chanting 'loudly and defiantly the hymn of his threatened idol':

Sredni Vashtar went forth,
His thoughts were red thoughts and his teeth were white.
His enemies called for peace, but he brought them death.
Sredni Vashtar the Beautiful. (139)

The boy becomes the idol on whom he transferred his wish for revenge, as he does not offer a hymn *to* his idol but the hymn *of* his idol. Conradin makes manifest his pagan imagination, willing it to strike his civilizing guardian. Conradin's wild foresight has transformed the tool-shed into a powerful retreat for his divine imagination, and as Mrs De Ropp enters the shed, surveillance is reversed: 'From the furthest window of the dining-room the door of the shed could just be seen beyond the corner of the shrubbery, and there Conrad stationed himself... he drew closer to the window-pane... still Conradin stood and waited and watched' (140). Whereas Mrs De Ropp once 'counted for nearly every-thing' (136), now only Conradin matters, the child-surveillant looking down impassively and reflecting, in his counting of birds flitting across the lawn, a child-like perception of time dragging and winding on, not the appointment-making, measuring minutes or 'temporal elaboration[s] of [an] act' (Foucault 151) in the adult work world, whereby 'Time penetrates the body... with... all the meticulous controls of power' (152). After Conradin's 'eyes were rewarded' by wild nature, not a taming human, emerging from 'that doorway... with eyes a-blink at the waning daylight, and dark wet stains around the fur of jaws and throat' (140), the secret new master calmly tells the maid that her former mistress '"went down to the shed some time ago"' (140). Then Conradin takes over the rare toast ritual that his cousin tried to placate him with after she had got rid of his hen. The child's relish in becoming the new authority is drawn out in a child-like sense of amorphous, unquantifiable, 'felt' time:

> Conradin fished a toasting-fork out of the sideboard drawer and proceeded to toast himself a piece of bread. And during the toasting of it and the buttering of it with much butter and the slow enjoyment of eating it, Conradin listened to the noises and silences which fell in quick spasms beyond the dining-room door.
> 'Whoever will break it to the poor child? I couldn't for the life of me!' exclaimed a shrill voice. And while they debated the matter among themselves, Conradin made himself another piece of toast. (140)

The three children in 'The Penance' are vengeful, disciplining judges on behalf of their cat that their neighbour has murdered; their verbal and written judgments of Octavian as '"Beast"' (423, 424) throws back at the adult a word usually reserved for bad children, reducing him to less than animal or child in their mind. When they kidnap Octavian's daughter Olivia, the two boy revisionaries' threats to Octavian are adapted from English and Biblical history: hanging her in chains over a fire or letting pigs devour her (425). The act of remorse they extract from Octavian in exchange for the baby who is the equivalent to their pet (though both are still superior to the adult) is a ritual, involving Octavian standing in a white sheet by the cat's grave, holding a candle while repeating his child-authorized identity: '" "I'm a miserable Beast' "' (426). The children control time and space here, with the time childishly uncertain – their demand that Octavian stands by the grave for a '"long, long time"' is satisfied by his reply of '"half an hour"' (427). While Octavian had colluded with the children's guardian in killing their tabby cat, deciding '"that they need not know"' (422), the children know all from their spot atop the barrier that Octavian can never surmount:

> as he passed beneath the shadow of the high blank wall he glanced up and became aware that his hunting had had undesired witnesses. Three white set faces were looking down at him, and if ever an artist

wanted a threefold study of cold human hate, impotent yet unyielding, raging yet masked in stillness, he would have found it in the triple gaze that met Octavian's eye. (423)

The authority of the imperious-sounding 'Octavian' is undone by this triumvirate, which adopts that sense of stillness and self-masking that so sustained Conradin, a cold look that returns the sense of adult detachment that children usually feel: 'their range of sight did not seem to concern itself with Octavian's presence...he became depressingly aware of the aloofness of their gaze' (424). The man feels like a scolded child and hopes 'for an opportunity for sloughing off the disgrace that enwrapped him, and earning some happier nickname from his three unsparing judges' (424). When the children threaten to drop Olivia into the piggery, their 'inexorable child-logic rose like an unyielding rampart before Octavian's scared pleadings' (426); the child's world is an enclosed fortress at war with the adult world's pretences and conventions. Even after the children let down a ladder – its rungs cannot enable Octavian to ascend the blank wall between him and childhood but only move across them over the mud to extricate his powerless infant – and Octavian begins his penance, he feels watched: 'The house loomed inscrutable in the middle distance, but' Octavian 'felt certain that three pairs of solemn eyes were watching his moth-shared vigil' (427). Here 'the inmate...never know[s] whether he is being looked at any one moment; but he must be sure that he may always be so' (Foucault 201). 'Visibility is a trap' (Foucault 200) that imprisons the adult in constant awareness of his inferior adultness. After Octavian fulfills his penance, the three cleanse his conscience with a last act of revision – 'a sheet of copy-book paper lying beside the blank wall, on which was written the message "Un-Beast"' (427). The nameless children utterly co-opt, revise, reinvent, and so *un*do school-taught histories, surveillance, and writing – all typical methods of adult authority over children.

In 'The Lumber-Room,' Nicholas must stay at home after his *'soi-disant'* (372) aunt has deemed him in 'disgrace' (371), calling Nicholas' placing of a frog in his ritual serving of bread-and-milk a 'sin' (372). His seemingly 'forbidden paradise' is a 'gooseberry garden' (373) yet Nicholas is uninterested, allowing the aunt to 'keep a watchful eye on the two doors that led' to the garden (373). The watcher is trapped by her useless vigil: 'it was a belief that would keep her on self-imposed sentry-duty for the greater part of the afternoon' (373). Nicholas is then free to visit the library, not to gain knowledge but a key that grants him access to the mysterious lumber-room. The adult-ordained usefulness of objects and lessons, for indoctrination and discipline, is rejected as Nicholas imagines stories for the objects in a room that offers an outpost for the true higher authority now: 'one high window opening on to the forbidden garden being its only source of illumination' (374). When the 'aunt-by-assertion' (374) cries into the garden, '"It's no *use* trying to hide there; I can see you all the time"' (375, emphasis added), the irony of who watches whom is clear to Nicholas – 'It was probably the first time for twenty years that any one had smiled in that lumber-room' (375) – who is making true use of his imagination in a room containing so many objects his guardian thinks would 'spoil by use' (374). When he comes to his trapped aunt after she has cried for help, the child deftly turns the adult's language of sin back on her:

'I was told I wasn't to go into the gooseberry garden,' said Nicholas promptly.

'I told you not to, and now I tell you that you may,' came the voice from the rain-water tank, rather impatiently.

'Your voice doesn't sound like aunt's,' objected Nicholas; 'you may be the Evil One tempting me to be disobedient. Aunt often tells me that the Evil One tempts me and that I always yield. This time I'm not going to yield.'

'Don't talk nonsense,' said the prisoner in the tank; 'go and fetch the ladder.'

'Will there be strawberry jam for tea?' asked Nicholas innocently.

'Certainly there will be,' said the aunt, privately resolving that Nicholas should have none of it.

'Now I know that you are the Evil One and not aunt,' shouted Nicholas gleefully; 'when we asked aunt for strawberry jam yesterday she said there wasn't any. I know there are four jars of it in the store cupboard, because I looked, and of course you know it's there, but *she* doesn't, because she said there wasn't any. Oh, Devil, you *have* sold yourself!' (376)

The adult's authority over Nicholas's body (where to go and not go) is dismissed, she calls her own pious language '"nonsense,"' and she becomes the '"Evil One."' This adult preacher of honesty is caught by her lie about a sweetened addition to their afternoon routine. Nicholas has returned the key, so the sacred lumber-room is still his, offering not only books that show birds beyond England's limited avian reality, but a piece of 'framed tapestry that... [t]o Nicholas was a living, breathing story' (374). The tapestry shows a hunter who has just shot a stag and the hunter's two dogs, but Nicholas also sees 'four galloping wolves... coming in his direction' (374). Nicholas adds his own imaginative threads to the tapestry. The boy-author was so enraptured by his revision that he fell into that childish sense of time (in contrast to his guardian's sense of her entrapment), sitting 'for many golden minutes revolving the possibilities of the scene' (375) and now, as the usual ritual of tea is 'partaken of in a fearsome silence' with the aunt feeling she has 'suffered *un*dignified and *un*merited detention in a rain-water tank for thirty-five minutes' (376), Nicholas returns to his story: 'it was just possible, he considered, that the huntsman would escape with his hounds while the wolves feasted on the stricken stag' (377). The larger story, where disgraced, hunted boy and controlling, hunting guardian are reversed, is eclipsed by Nicholas' secret world woven from a tapestry where the hero can slip away from his pursuers.

Saki – in his respectful distance from the children's point of view and sacred spaces, and with the children's inward resolutions of adult-posed problems – refuses the adult guardian, the adult reader, and even himself, as author-narrator, full access to the children's private spaces, reminding us 'of the inaccessibility of that inner identity we call childhood' (Honeyman 51). The adult reader cannot enjoy 'an adult's refuge – escape from the "artifice of civilization" that includes routine, responsibility, public activity, and abstraction' (Honeyman 52), for that is precisely the world that Saki's children and stories attack. The author-narrator's usual omniscient detachment from the narrative (for example, he knows Nicholas's guardian was 'privately resolving that Nicholas should have none of it') fades by the end, overtaken by Conradin's relished revision of the toast ritual, the children's panoptical surveillance of and final note to Octavian, and Nicholas' rumination on the tapestry. The children have made the narrative their own, asserting the fierce, unconquerable spirit of their wild natures and imaginations. They instinctively unwrite and revise adults' authority and authorship, in large part because, like *Peter Pan*, as Munro noted in a 17 June 1908 *Morning Post* review of the play, they do not have the '"besetting sin of the modern child, self-consciousness"' (quoted in Langguth 156).

Saki's rebellious, revisionist boys can become Reginald, Saki's first dandy figure, or Gabriel-Ernest. Those tricksters slyly challenge the adult reader's moral assumptions about child nakedness, sexuality, and same-sex desire, even 100 years later, when Ruth Maxey, misinterpreting the author-narrator's point of view and satirical aims, erroneously feels that 'Reginald's Choir Treat' and 'Gabriel-Ernest' edge into 'sexual perversion' and a 'paedophiliac' tale (58). The former is only concerned with the pagan implosion of uptight, religious authority, thus remaking 'the spirit of the thing' ('Reginald's Choir Treat' 18), while the latter, in Saki's uniquely macabre-camp style, takes a doubly satirical bite out of the aunt figure and religion. Maxey falsely asks which side – children's or adults' – Saki is on, but Saki is always on the side of a jarring disruption, much as Munro enjoyed pranks and hoaxes on his trip to Europe with his sister (Langguth 36–8). The stories are concerned with the reversal of power, as Stephen notes (xvii), and with wildness, such 'anarchy and danger' often 'associated with boyhood' (Carey vii). The flip side of such boyhood at the time, however, as suggested in J. M. Barrie's *Peter and Wendy* (1911), was a staunch jingoism.

As Europe's desire for war grew, Saki's stories set in female-disciplined, domestic confines give way to Munro's desire to connect with a public-school education and his father's imperial career outside the home. By 1913, a (con)fused Munro-Saki anticipated and promoted war as a conformist disruption, the great chance to bring Edwardian society out of its rut; murderers of adulthood become murdering adults. Children grow down from heretic disciples – mimicking and imitating adult ways and the adult world only in order to supplant and subvert it – to disciplined inheritors of the Edwardian status quo. Once children seize power, they can only defend it, as is clear in two later stories.

In 'Hyacinth,' a story that echoes plot points of Saki's other stories, particularly 'The Penance,' the supposed 'angel-child' (523) Hyacinth (his floral name the only gesture to an unorthodox masculinity) reveals himself to be a devious trickster but acts out of deference to adult convention, not in defiance of it. Hyacinth, whose rebelliousness is only recognized, in a sharp departure from Sakian tradition, by his aunt, threatens to kill the three Jutterly children because their father is running against his in the local election. While the story affords Saki an opportunity for satirizing political hopefuls' infantilism and mendacity, Hyacinth is a conformist dressed up in child rebel's clothing. He is intent on ensuring his father's authority and power, talks of being ' "on the job" ' (523), and, most tellingly, Mr Jutterly calls him, ' "my little man" ' (521). Hyacinth is a politician-in-training who happens to be working outside the rules because he is too young to be fully constrained by the system.

In 'The Toys of Peace' (1914), bourgeois children pervert the purpose and identity of those toys in order to oppose a placid, complacent adult world but only by wishing for a European war to shake Edwardian

England out of its lethargy. This world is represented by the very newspapers that Munro wrote for as a reporter. Eleanor Bope shows her brother, a footnote to the story declares, 'An actual extract from a London paper of March 1914' that reports on the suggestion by the '"National Peace Council"' to have boys play with '"'peace toys'"' (393). Eleanor and Harvey believe that '"influence and upbringing"' (393) can overcome a child's '"primitive instinct...and hereditary tendencies"' even though nine-year-old Bertie and ten-year-old Eric are descended from military patriarchs, as Munro himself was (394). Yet the children cannot be shaped as if they are the adults' toys but they instead shape the toys – of John Stuart Mill, 'Mrs. Hemans...the poetess,' astronomer Sir John Herschel, Sunday-school founder Robert Raikes, and local politicians (395–6) – into participants in the battles they have studied. To deny war is to deny a fundamental part of social history, Saki suggests, but to deny boys' militancy is to deny their nature, and even the National Peace Council at the time '"admits [boys] naturally love fighting...[it is in] their primitive instincts"' (393). The children are eager for a European war, even if it is a small, faraway Balkan war such as the Siege of Adrianople that they wish to re-enact; the grindings and workings of civil democracy and political economy are uninteresting and ineffective, and when the boys turn Mill and the other toys into military figures and forts, Harvey concludes that their '"experiment... [h]as failed. We have begun too late"' (398). Yet Saki suggests that the experiment cannot begin early enough, for boys' natural Darwinian instincts are for the excitement of war.

Rebellious boys are to become militant defenders of Empire, the barrier is no longer between childhood and adulthood but between England and the enemy (usually Germany), and attacks on female guardians are replaced by anti-suffragettism (as males alone can take up arms) and the all-important realization of patrilineal responsibility to one's fighting 'forefathers.' While Saki's stories of children had recognized 'the individual's independence from, rather than obligation to, God and society' (Petzold 33) such delinquency, where the child is 'author of his acts' (Foucault 253), becomes, to Munro-Saki, a nation-threatening delinquency of 'failure in or neglect of duty' (*OED*) to father and empire. Saki was typically Edwardian in his 'worshipp[ing of] little boys' (Wullschläger 109) but the inwardness, flippancy, and apathy of a Reginald or Clovis unsettled Munro as he anticipated a great conflict only a decade after England's manly mettle was sorely tested by the Boer War. 'Wildean aestheticism' was displaced, then, into that English 'ideal of youth ... asceticism: duty, team spirit, male fellowship, the outdoor life, sacrifice not to art and grace but to patriotism' (Wullschläger 116). By 1915, Munro was issuing a call to arms, declaring in 'An Old Love' (1915) that boys' first and oldest love was for war. And so Munro-Saki slipped into the didactic tendency of Victorian literature that Saki's stories so often countered, revealing, as Jacqueline Rose puts it, 'what it is that [the adult], through literature, want[s] or demand[s] of the child' (137).

Saki's darkest childhood stories may have tapped into Munro's resentment of his aunts (often bleeding into misogyny), but a Saki enlisted by Munro into offering more militant attitudes (re)turned to his adolescence in the shadow of his colonial policeman father. After attending the imperial training-ground of Bedford Grammar School for a short time, Munro travelled with his father in Europe in 1887, 1888, and 1889, studied at home with him in Heanton from 1889 to 1891, and wintered in Davos with him in 1892–3. In 1893, the son went off to become, like his father, an imperial police officer in Burma until he returned home after too many bouts with malaria. While Saki's child-centred stories show the young battling 'the police functions of surveillance ... [and] the religious functions of encouraging obedience and work' (Foucault 173), Munro briefly became a police officer and ended his life as a guardian of empire, working obediently in the trenches to defend King and country. At the end of *When William Came* (1913), in a world where England has been conquered by the Germans, only Baden-Powell's stout, virile Boy Scouts can refuse to march for the occupiers, and so as a young man waits for

> the writing of yet another chapter in the history of his country's submission ... a dull flush crept into his grey face; a look that was partly new-born hope and resurrected pride, partly remorse and shame, burned in his eyes ... He had given up the fight ... [but] in thousands of English homes throughout the land there were young hearts that had not forgotten ... would not yield. (813)

In the wake of the Boer War, Baden-Powell wished to ensure the next generation would avoid becoming 'wishy washy slackers without any go or patriotism in them' (281), and Munro-Saki looks to the youth organization Baden-Powell founded to usher in hope and a new century: ' "to every period of history there corresponded a privileged age and a particular division of human life: ... childhood of the nineteenth, adolescence of the twentieth" ' (Philippe Ariès, quoted in Wullschläger 7). When Munro enlisted in late 1914 to avoid such 'shame' and self-reproach, he put his rebelliously anti-female authority, late-Victorian childhood behind him and slipped into the mould of his father's manly imperial model he had found in his adolescence. A friend of Munro recalled that, as a soldier, 'he did his utmost to conform himself to [military discipline] and to force others to do the same' (Reynolds xxv). And two years later, with the single sniper's bullet that rang out on the front on a November day in 1916, Munro's ' "awfully great adventure" ' (*Peter and Wendy* 150) ended as so many other Edwardians' did.

Works cited

Baden-Powell, Robert. *Scouting for Boys: A Handbook for Instruction in Good Citizenship*. 1908. London: Pearson, 1926.

Barrie, J. M. *Peter Pan in Kensington Gardens* [1906] and *Peter and Wendy* [1911]. Ed. Peter Hollindale. Oxford: Oxford University Press, 1999.

Briggs, Julia. 'Transitions (1890–1914).' *Children's Literature: An Illustrated History*. Ed. Peter Hunt. New York: Oxford University Press, 1995. 167–91.

Carey, John. 'Introduction.' *Short Stories and The Unbearable Bassington*. By Saki. New York: Oxford University Press, 1994. vii–xxiv.

Foucault, Michel. *Discipline and Punish: The Birth of the Prison*. 1975. Trans. Alan Sheridan. New York: Pantheon, 1977.

Greene, Graham. 'Introduction.' *The Best of Saki (H. H. Munro)*. 1950. Harmondsworth: Penguin, 1983. vii–xi.

Grylls, David. *Guardians and Angels: Parents and Children in Nineteenth-Century Literature*. London: Faber and Faber, 1978.

Honeyman, Susan. *Elusive Childhood: Impossible Representations in Modern Fiction*. Columbus, OH: Ohio State University Press, 2005.

James, Allison, Chris Jenks, and Alan Prout. *Theorizing Childhood*. Cambridge: Polity, 1998.

Johns, Ian. 'A walk on the Wilde Side.' *The Times* 30 April 2007. 26 May 2007, http://infoweb.newsbank.com/iw-search/we/InfoWeb?p_product=UKNB&p_theme=aggregated5&p_action=doc&p_docid=118D6BA9BB97D818&d_place=LTIB&f_subsection=sFEATURES&f_issue=2007-04-30&f_publisher=

Langguth, A. J. *Saki: A Life of Hector Hugh Munro, With Six Short Stories Never Before Collected*. New York: Simon and Schuster, 1981.

Lurie, Alison. *Boys and Girls Forever: Children's Classics from Cinderella to Harry Potter*. New York: Penguin, 2003.

Maxey, Ruth. ' "Children are given us to discourage our better instincts": The Paradoxical Treatment of Children in Saki's Short Fiction.' *Journal of the Short Story in English* 45 (Autumn 2005): 47–62.

Munro, Ethel M. 'Biography of Saki.' 1924. *The Short Stories of Saki (H. H. Munro)*. 2nd ed. New York: The Modern Library [Random House], 1958. 635–715.

Natov, Roni. *The Poetics of Childhood*. Milton Park: Routledge, 2006.

Petzold, Dieter. 'A Race Apart: Children in Late Victorian and Edwardian Children's Books.' *Children's Literature Association Quarterly* 17.3 (Fall 1992): 33–6.

Reynolds, Rothay. 'Hector Hugh Munro.' *The Toys of Peace*. 1919. By Saki. New York: Viking, 1928. xv–xxvii.

Rose, Jacqueline. *The Case of Peter Pan or The Impossibility of Children's Fiction*. London: Macmillan, 1984.

Rose, Jonathan. *The Edwardian Temperament, 1895–1919*. London: Ohio University Press, 1986.

Saki [H(ector). H(ugh) Munro]. 'Hyacinth.' *The Penguin Complete Saki*. 518–23.

——. 'The Lumber-Room.' 1913. *The Penguin Complete Saki*. 371–7.

——. 'An Old Love.' 1915. *Short Stories 2*. By Saki. Ed. Peter Haining. London: Dent, 1983. 206–08.

——. 'The Open Window.' 1911. *The Penguin Complete Saki*. 259–62.

——. 'The Penance.' 1910. *The Penguin Complete Saki*. 422–27.

——. *The Penguin Complete Saki*. 1976. London: Penguin, 1982.

——. 'The Quest' [c. 1910]. *The Penguin Complete Saki*. 147–51.

——. 'Reginald's Choir-Treat.' 1902. *The Penguin Complete Saki*. 16–18.

——. 'The She-Wolf.' *The Penguin Complete Saki*. 235–41.

——. 'Sredni Vashtar.' 1910. *The Penguin Complete Saki*. 136–40.

——. 'The Story-Teller.' 1913. *The Penguin Complete Saki*. 349–54.

——. 'The Toys of Peace.' 1914. *The Penguin Complete Saki*. 393–98.

——. 'The Unbearable Bassington.' 1912. *The Penguin Complete Saki*. 567–687.

——. 'When William Came.' 1913. *The Penguin Complete Saki*. 689–814.

Stacpoole, H. de Vere. *The Blue Lagoon: A Romance*. 1908. Project Gutenberg e-text. 1 June 2007, <http://www.netlibrary.com>.

Stephen, Martin. 'Introduction.' *The Best of Saki*. London: J. M. Dent, 1993. xi–xviii.

Waugh, Auberon. 'Introduction.' *The Chronicles of Clovis*. Harmondsworth: Penguin, 1986. vii–xii.

Wullschläger, Jackie. *Inventing Wonderland: The Lives and Fantasies of Lewis Carroll, Edward Lear, J. M. Barrie, Kenneth Grahame and A. A. Milne*. Toronto: Free Press, 1995.

Notes on Contributors

Jenny Bavidge is a Lecturer in the Department of English at the University of Greenwich, UK. She has edited (with Robert Bond) a special edition of the *Literary London* Journal on the work of Iain Sinclair and the collection of essays *City Visions: The Work of Iain Sinclair* (Cambridge Scholars Press, 2007). Her book *Theorists of the City* in the Routledge Critical Thinkers Series was published in 2006. Published articles include an essay on E. Nesbit's London (in *The Swarming Streets: Twentieth Century Literary Representations of London*. Ed. Lawrence Phillips, 2004) and 'Stories in Space: The Geographies of Children's Literature' in the Journal *Children's Geographies* (December 2006). She currently holds a Promising Researcher Fellowship (in conjunction with the University of Reading) and is working towards a book on children's literature and the city.

Michelle Beissel Heath has just finished her graduate study at The George Washington University in Washington, DC, USA, completing a PhD dissertation on the cultural work of games, sports and play in British literature from 1860–1920. Her research interests include children's literature, juvenilia, domesticity and the effects of empire at home.

Jane Darcy is a Senior Lecturer in English Literature at the University of Central Lancashire, Preston, UK. She is a late Victorian and Edwardian Literature specialist with a PhD on Thomas Hardy and many years teaching experience at undergraduate and postgraduate level in the literature of that period. Her current research is in late Victorian and Edwardian writing for children. She has also designed and taught modules on literature for children and the fairy tale. She has previously written on *The Secret Garden* for *The Lion and the Unicorn* (Dec 1995) and has more recently had published a book chapter on Louisa Molesworth in *Popular Victorian Women Writers* (eds Boardman and Jones, 2002) and a chapter on 'Disney and the European Fairy Tale' in *Issues in Americanisation and Culture* (eds Campbell et al, 2002).

Adrienne E. Gavin is a Reader in English at Canterbury Christ Church University, UK whose research interests lie in Victorian and Edwardian Literature, Children's Literature, Women's Writing, Crime Fiction,

224

Biography, and the Short Story. She is author of *Dark Horse: A Life of Anna Sewell* (Sutton, 2004), the proposal for which won the Biographers' Club Prize 2000 and is co-editor (with Christopher Routledge) of *Mystery in Children's Literature: From the Rational to the Supernatural* (Palgrave, 2001) and (with Suzanne Bray and Peter Merchant) of *Re-Embroidering the Robe: Faith, Myth and Literature Creation Since 1850* (2008). Editor of a critical edition of Caroline Clive's *Paul Ferroll* (forthcoming), she is engaged in research on Stacpoole's *The Blue Lagoon* and continues her research on Anna Sewell and *Black Beauty*.

Brian Gibson received his PhD in English at the University of Alberta in Edmonton, Canada after completing his dissertation, *Beastly Humans: Ambivalence, Dependent Dissidence, and Metamorphosis in the Fiction of Saki*. He teaches at the University of Alberta. He has presented and published numerous papers on Saki's work, including 'Saki's Dependent Dissidence: Exploring 'The East Wing'' (*English Language Notes*, March 2005). He is also a film critic for *Vue Weekly*; his first novel, *Bleeding Daylight*, was published in 2004.

Elizabeth Hale is a lecturer in English literature and writing in the School of English, Communication and Theatre, University of New England, in Australia. She received her MA and PhD from the Department of English and American Literature at Brandeis University, Massachusetts, and BA Hons in English and Latin from the University of Otago, New Zealand. Her research interests focus around the areas of children's literature, Victorian literature, and the Classical Tradition in both. Her PhD explored the representation of classical scholars in Victorian fiction for adults and children. She is currently revising parts of that thesis into a book on intellectual or gifted children in Victorian and Edwardian literature. In 2005, her co-edited collection of critical essays (with Sarah Winters), *Marvellous Codes: The Fiction of Margaret Mahy*, was published by Victoria University Press. Her article on *Agnes Grey* and *The Nanny Diaries*, 'Long-Suffering Professional Females: The Case of Nanny-Lit' was published in *Chick Lit: The New Woman's Fiction* (Mallory Young and Suzanne Ferriss, eds. Routledge: New York, 2005). She is currently co-editing *The Three Worlds of Maurice Gee* with Lawrence Jones. 'Underworlds Down Under,' her article on concepts of the underworld in *The Navigator* and *Under the Mountain* is forthcoming from Otago University Press in *NZ Gothic: The Darker Side of Kiwi Culture* (eds. Jenny Lawn, Misha Kavka, Mary Paul).

Andrew F. Humphries is a Senior Lecturer in English and Drama Education at Canterbury Christ Church University where he is a programme leader for PGCE English Secondary on which he teaches Shakespeare, Drama and Literature. He also teaches PGCE Primary English and lectures on twentieth-century literature in the Department of English. He has an MA from Cambridge University and is currently working on a PhD in English entitled *Motion Human Inhuman: Transport, Travel, and Technological Mobility in the Novels of in D. H. Lawrence*. He has recently presented conference papers on the Edwardian fiction of D. H. Lawrence and Rudyard Kipling. He has also worked as a Head of English and Head of Drama in several secondary schools.

Paul March-Russell is Honorary Lecturer and Director of Part-Time Studies in the School of Comparative Literature at the University of Kent, UK. He has edited May Sinclair's *Uncanny Stories* (Wordsworth, 2006) and he is co-editor, with Carmen Casaliggi, of *Ruskin in Perspective* (Cambridge Scholars Publishing, 2007). His other publications on Edwardian writers include articles on Joseph Conrad, E.M. Forster, Rudyard Kipling, and most recently, Mina Loy (as part of *On Joanna Russ*, edited by Farah Mendlesohn, Wesleyan University Press, forthcoming). He is currently completing an introduction to the short story to be published by Edinburgh University Press.

Karen L. McGavock gained a Master of Arts degree in English and Educational Studies at the University of Dundee and her Doctor of Philosophy degree in English Literature at the University of Glasgow. Karen's topic was 'Children's Literature and the Deconstruction of Childhood' and explored the works of Lewis Carroll, J. M. Barrie, C. S. Lewis, and J. K. Rowling. She has taught and researched at the Open University, been active in the development of wider access activities at the University of Stirling and now works in the School of Education at the University of Dundee, Scotland, UK, where her research focuses on peer learning in primary schools throughout Fife. She was recently elected a Fellow of the Royal Society for the Arts.

Stephanie Olsen is currently completing her doctoral dissertation entitled *Raising Fathers, Raising Boys: Education and Enculturation in Britain, 1880–1914* at the Department of History, McGill University. She was awarded scholarships by the Social Sciences and Humanities Research Council of Canada (Canada Graduate Scholarship) and by the *Fondation Ricard*. She has presented her work at numerous international conferences, is the founder of the annual McGill-Queen's Graduate Conference in History and the author of a recent article in the journal *Fathering*. She has been awarded a two-year SSHRC post-doctoral fellowship to be held at Princeton University.

Karen Sands-O'Connor is Associate Professor of English at Buffalo State College in New York, USA. She has been a tutor for Roehampton University's Children's Literature International Summer School (CLISS) in London, and she has written extensively on race in children's literature, most significantly in her book from Routledge Press, *Soon Come Home to this Island: West Indians in British Children's Literature* (2007).

Michelle Smith completed her PhD in the School of Culture and Communication at the University of Melbourne, Australia in 2007. She is currently revising her thesis, entitled *Learning to Mother for the Empire: Girlhood, Print Culture and Pedagogy, 1880–1914*, for publication as a monograph. She also holds an MA from Melbourne and graduated with First Class Honours in her Bachelors degree from the University of Queensland. She has presented conference papers on the *Girl's Own Paper* and Edith Nesbit and has published on the origins of the Girl Guide movement and Bessie Marchant's adventure fiction. She teaches literature at the University of Melbourne and is the editor of the interdisciplinary postgraduate journal *Traffic*.

Index

adolescence, 182, 211–12, 216, 221–2
adult convention, 106, 108, 210, 219
adult-in-child, 45–6
adventures, 6, 7, 9, 12, 15, 35, 39, 59, 64, 76, 95, 98, 101, 112, 116, 120, 140, 152, 165, 198, 201, 203–4, 222
affection, 45, 57, 59, 81, 92, 110, 117, 128, 192–3, 195
agency, 11, 13, 16, 65, 180, 182, 184
alcohol, 26, 82, 118, 137, 161–3, 166–9, 181
alphabet, 186
ambivalence, 17, 107, 115, 119, 121
amorality, 18, 108, 112, 208–22
animals, 10–11, 17, 18, 47, 86–7, 99, 107–8, 185, 188, 193–5, 200, 201, 211–15
  see also birds; childlike beasts; *and individual animals*
Anna of the Five Towns, 14, 24
anthropology, 9, 10, 11, 12, 18, 25, 114, 177–89
anti-Victorianism, 9, 12, 25, 211
anxiety, 19, 23, 42, 45, 120, 127, 146
Arcadia, 4, 19, 23, 25, 31, 201–2, 205–6
Asquith, Lady Cynthia, 49, 105
aunts, 12, 14, 80, 83–4, 105, 116, 138, 148–9, 205, 209–12, 216–18, 219, 221
author-narrators, 208, 213, 218
authority, 12, 14, 99, 126, 156, 168, 209, 210, 211–13, 215–19, 222
autonomy, 11, 13, 16, 65, 107
Avery, Gillian, 24, 143, 153

Babylon, 99–101
bachelors, 16, 53–70, 211
Baden-Powell, Agnes, 16
Baden-Powell, Robert, 15, 54, 90, 221
Band of Hope, 128, 160, 161, 164, 168–9

Review, 163, 171–2
Bannerman, Helen, 15
Barrie, J.M., 6, 7, 13–14, 16, 17, 23, 37–51, 53–70, 85, 90, 95, 101, 103, 109, 111, 202, 211, 219
Bastables, 12, 54, 138, 140, 199, 206
Beale, Dorothea, 146, 149–50, 152
beastly children, 10, 18, 191–206
  see also animals
Belloc, Hilaire, 15, 209
Bennett, Arnold, 14, 24, 121
Bill the Minder, 15
billiards, 92–4
birds, 17, 32, 55–7, 62–3, 71, 71 n.3, 76, 86–7, 109, 120, 182, 201, 204, 214, 217
Birkin, Andrew, 41, 46–7, 55, 57, 70
Blackwood, Algernon, 5, 14–15, 54, 61, 71 n.4
blindness, 27, 64–5, 68, 69
Blue Bird, The (L'Oiseau Bleu), 16
Blue Lagoon, The, 14, 54, 112, 212
Bluebell in Fairyland, 16
boarding schools, 3, 81, 143–56
Boer War, 8, 151, 220–1
boundaries, 2, 6, 9–10, 42, 44, 48, 87, 135, 172, 184
Bourne Taylor, Jenny, 10, 126, 135, 139
Boy Scouts, 9, 16, 54, 90, 128, 151, 160, 168, 221
Boy who Beat His Father, The, 166
Boy's Brigade, 168
Boy's Friend, 160–1, 168–9
Boy's Herald, 160, 170
Brazil, Angela, 14, 17, 143–56
Briggs, Julia, 4, 128, 132–3, 135, 140, 141 n.1, 209
Broca, Paul, 183–5, 187–9
brothers, 26, 35, 39, 45, 57, 107, 108, 128, 135–6, 155, 181, 205, 220
Brown Fairy Book, The, 18, 179
Bulley, Eleanor, 31

Bunyip, The, 179–80
Burnett, Frances Hodgson, 5, 7, 13–14, 16–17, 24, 32–5, 63, 75–87, 90, 111, 126, 135
Burnett, Lionel, 75–6, 78, 84–5
Burstall, Sara A., 144–6
Butler, Samuel, 14, 121

Carpenter, Humphrey, 23–4, 37, 41
Carroll, Lewis, 208, 213
cats, 186, 194–6, 210, 215
Cautionary Tales for Children, 15
caves, 136, 186
'Celestial Omnibus, The', 5, 14
chemistry, 145, 148
Chesterton, G.K., 125, 129, 141 n.1
child development, 9, 126, 133, 135
child logic, 192, 196, 201, 206, 216
child, lost *see* lost children
Child of the Jago, A, 13
child readers, 10, 18, 24, 34, 42, 80, 181, 183, 189, 191
child welfare, 8–9, 17, 23, 125–41
'Child-Who-Was-Tired, The', 15
childcare, 129–30, 138
childhood *see specific subject entries*
  otherness of, 6, 65, 103–21, 177
  sentimental construction of, 37–8, 40
childlike beasts, 18, 191–206, 209
Children of the Nation, 8
Children's Act of 1908, 8, 37, 45, 160, 169
Children's Encyclopedia, The, 15
Children's Welfare Exhibitions, 17, 125–41
Christian Science, 76–8, 82
Christina's Fairy Book, 15
Church of England Temperance Society, 160–1, 166, 168
'Clairvoyance', 71
Clark, Elizabeth, 132, 141 n. 2
Clayhanger trilogy, 14
colonies *see* Empire
commercial influences, 17, 25, 38, 40–52, 125–41
commodification, 5, 16, 37, 41–2, 49
Condition of England, The, 8

conformity, 18, 33, 107, 194, 209, 212, 219
conscience, 111, 195–6, 216
continuity, between childhood and adulthood, 17, 103, 115
conventions, 5, 18, 44, 48, 81, 106, 191, 216
  adult convention, 106, 108, 210, 219
Cooper, E.H., 3, 6, 54
Corke, Helen, 110
country houses, 5, 12, 64, 77, 82
cousins, 90, 192–3, 210, 214–15
Coveney, Peter, 11, 15, 103
Crawfurd, John, 185
cruelty, 194, 211–12
cult of childhood, 1, 3, 12, 15, 31, 37–51, 53
Cunningham, Hugh, 4, 8, 23
cycling, 89–90

Daily News and Leader, 125, 127–31, 133–4, 136, 139
darkness, 113, 119–20
deconstruction of childhood, 49–50
Deep England, 16, 29–30, 32–3, 35
demythologization, 5, 16, 40, 43
desperation, 11, 18, 57–8, 66, 70, 90, 116
Dickens, Charles, 5, 129
directness, 196, 202, 206
disobedience, 106, 197, 217
disrupted childhoods, 103–21
disruption, 7, 16–17, 23–35, 45, 100, 103, 110, 201, 219
doctors, 13, 149, 193, 210
domesticity, 7, 17, 89–101, 154, 165
'Door in the Wall, The', 14
double-voicedness, 140
dream children, 16, 53–70
Dream Days, 12, 205
dreams, 27, 30, 38, 79, 83, 111–12
  see also dream children
Dunlop, W., 179–80, 183
Dusinberre, J., 105, 111–12, 114
duty, 19, 145–6, 152, 154, 161, 165, 184, 220

Editor's Den, 161, 163, 169
education *see* girls' education; school
   stories; schools
Education of Uncle Paul, The, 54, 61
Edwards, Hamilton, 161, 163–4,
   168–9
Elizabeth and Her German Garden, 13
Empire, 9, 12, 17–18, 25–6,
   144, 152, 154, 165, 184, 187,
   189, 220
Enchanted Castle, The, 202
enchantments, 32–3, 133
English identity, 16, 29–31
Englishness, 6, 29, 32, 36
Escape, 4, 6–7, 9, 11, 18, 100, 103, 105,
   112–14, 138, 205, 218
eugenics, 9, 125, 127
excitement, 9, 113, 115, 117, 119,
   152, 220
exhibitions *see* Children's Welfare
   Exhibitions

fairy tales, 98, 109, 112–13, 125–6,
   129, 132–3, 135, 141 n.2,
   183, 224
Fairyland, 31, 128, 131
   see also *Prisoner in Fairyland, A*
Farrar, Frederic, 184, 186
Father and Son, 15
fathers, 11, 15, 33, 47, 80–1, 83, 86,
   92, 95, 99, 147–9, 181–2, 187
   and child rebellion, 209, 219–22
   and juvenile periodicals, 160,
      166–8, 172
   and Lawrence, D.H., 113–15, 117,
      119–20
   and longing for children, 57, 59,
      61–2, 65
femininity, 148, 150, 152, 154, 156
ferocity, 196, 211
ferrets, 193–5
fetishism, 5, 16, 37–8, 40–2
First World War *see* World War I
Five Children and It, 34–5
flirtation, 7, 95–7
Flowers, 32, 45, 48, 76, 83–4, 109,
   148–9, 193, 213
Food of the Gods, The, 14
Ford, Ford Madox, 15

forever children, 56, 61, 63, 70
Forster, E.M., 5, 14, 30–1, 121, 226
Fortunes of Philippa, The, 147–50
Fourth Form Friendship, A, 154
Frazer, James, 106, 177
freedom, 4, 6–7, 48, 64, 76, 106–7,
   109, 111, 118, 130, 138, 141, 146,
   154–5, 210
Freud, Sigmund, 9, 14, 33, 40, 60, 111
fun, 7, 31, 44, 94, 97–8, 105, 172, 197

'Gabriel-Ernest', 208, 218–19
games, 6–7, 9, 17, 19, 31, 48, 55, 59,
   66, 85, 89–101, 106, 112, 120,
   136–7, 143, 148–50, 153,
   173, 187
Garden God, The, 15
gardens, 5–8, 11, 17, 32–3, 45, 56,
   64–5, 75–87, 90, 119, 198–9, 206,
   213, 216–17
Gerzina, Gretchen, 77, 85
ghost children, 27, 54, 63–4,
   67–9, 71
Girl Guides, 6, 9, 16, 90, 128, 151, 227
girls' education, 17, 143–57
   see also school stories
God, 77, 164–5, 170–1, 220
gods, 10, 14, 185, 187, 202–3
   see also Pan
Golden Age, The, 3, 12, 14, 23, 177,
   202, 205–6, 211
good behaviour, 167, 197, 211
Gorst, F. E., 8
Gospel
   of Fun, 7, 31
   of Work, 7
Gosse, Edmund, 15
Gothic romance, 28, 34
Grahame, Kenneth, 10, 12, 14, 18, 23,
   30–1, 34, 85, 191–206, 211
grandmothers, 154, 205
Greene, Graham, 60, 194, 206, 211,
   222
Greenwood Hat, The, 43
grief, 6, 16, 27–8, 54–6, 58–9, 64,
   68–70, 81, 84, 119
guardians, 24, 57, 70, 182, 192, 194,
   209–10, 213–15, 217–18, 221–2
Guides *see* Girl Guides

hair, 113, 117–18
Handbook for Girl Guides, The, 16, 156 n.1
Harding's Luck, 136, 138
Hardy, Thomas, 13, 80
health, 8–9, 15, 78, 126, 128, 132, 147–8, 156, 159, 166, 172
Hicks, Seymour, 16
history, 23–35
hockey, 148–50, 156
Hole in the Wall, The, 15
'Holiday Books', 60
Hollindale, Peter, 39, 42, 45, 49
Holmes, T.V., 179–80, 183
home, 5–8, 16–17, 28, 64, 76, 85–6, 89–90, 92, 94–6, 112, 114, 117–19, 131–2, 145–7, 150, 154–5, 164–5, 169–70, 172, 181, 186, 202, 210, 213, 216, 219, 221
'Home Arts', 154, 157
honesty, 108, 191, 204, 206, 217
Houdan hen, 193, 213
House with the Green Shutters, The, 15
house-within-the-house, 100
houses, 96, 99
    see also domesticity; home
'How Pearl Button was Kidnapped', 15
'How the Alphabet was Made', 186
'How the Camel got his Hump', 184
'How the First Letter was Written', 186
'How the Rhinoceros got his Skin', 185–6
'How the Whale got his Throat', 184
Howkins, Alun, 25, 29
'Howling Desert', 184
Hudson, W.H., 15, 69, 71
humour, 118, 141, 194, 213
husbands, 81, 93–4, 117–18, 146, 172, 180–2, 212
Hynes, Samuel, 19, 106

idyllic worlds, 17–18, 64, 85, 103, 109
imagination, 4–5, 9, 12, 30–1, 79, 84, 115, 120, 132–3, 141, 165, 193–4, 205, 209–10, 212–14, 217–18
Imperialism, 10, 165, 173
    see also Empire

In the Closed Room, 17, 63, 75, 82, 87
independence, 12, 25, 147, 199, 210, 220
    see also autonomy
India/Indians, 33, 77, 81, 87, 90, 184–5, 187, 195
inexorable child logic, 192, 196, 201, 206, 216
injustice, 194, 210
innocence, 9, 11, 13, 40, 106, 112, 114, 202–4, 212
instinctive knowledge, 84, 86–7
instincts, 7, 10, 18, 26, 106, 202–5
intangible children *see* dream children
integrity, 11
intellectual pursuit, 17, 146
'Intercessor', 16, 25, 27–9, 33
Iron Age, 202, 204, 206
irony, 37, 49, 110, 188, 192, 212–13, 217
islands, 6, 8, 11, 14, 56, 61, 112, 199–201, 203
Isle of Wight, 109, 112
isolation, 14, 120, 213

Jacottet, E., 181–3
Jane Eyre (char.), 33
Jenks, Chris, 37, 38, 40
Jewish people, 130, 188
Jim Davis, 15
Jimbo: A Fantasy, 15
jingoism, 165, 209, 219
Jolly Roger, 96, 98
journeys, 26–7, 181, 198
Joyce, James, 120
Jude the Obscure, 13, 80
'Judge and Jury', 95
Jungle Books, 13, 35, 54, 139, 208
Just So Stories, 18, 54, 183–4, 186, 208
justice, 180, 194

Keating, Peter, 1, 5, 11–12, 24–5, 78
Kensington Gardens, 39, 41, 43, 50, 55–6, 58, 62, 64
Key, Ellen, 4, 40, 51, 105
killing, 43, 49, 58, 63, 116, 194–6, 210, 215
Kim, 54, 186–7

Kincaid, James, 60, 98
Kipling, Rudyard, 5, 13–14, 16, 18, 25–9, 31–5, 53–70, 139, 177–89, 206, 208
kisses, 27, 64, 67, 69, 113
knowledge, 10, 32, 43, 84, 86–7, 93, 135, 145, 154, 216

Lady Chatterley's Lover, 104
Lang, Andrew, 14, 18, 177–9, 189–90
laughter, 118–19
Lawrence, D.H., 6–7, 14, 29–30, 103–24
League of Boy Friends, 168
Lear, Edward, 213
Little Black Sambo, 15
Little Boy Lost, A, 15, 69, 71
Little Lord Fauntleroy, 24, 75–7, 87
Little Princess, A, 75, 78, 81, 84–7
Little White Bird, The, 16, 39, 50–1, 53–70
Llewelyn Davies boys, 39, 43, 57, 70
logic, 120, 191–2, 205–6, 209
longing, 5–6, 16, 38, 47, 53–70
loss, 6, 15, 16, 27, 47, 53–70, 76, 78, 85, 108, 194, 200, 204
lost children, 5–6, 21, 27, 47, 65, 95
love, 14–15, 60, 68–9, 77, 109, 114, 133, 170–1, 193–4, 196, 221
'Lumber-Room, The', 18, 209–10, 212, 216–18, 223
Lurie, Alison, 197, 199

MacDonald, Greville, 129, 132–3
Maeterlinck, Maurice, 16
magic, 4, 10, 31–5, 51, 78–80, 133–6, 177–9, 202
Magic and Religion, 177–9
Magic City, The, 125–7, 132–5, 139
'Magic World, A', 130, 133, 142
male narrators, 64, 69, 71
manhood, 162–3, 166–7, 169–70, 173
manliness, 89, 162, 169, 172, 174, 222
Mansfield, Katherine, 15
marriage, 92, 108–9, 181–2, 209
Marvell, Andrew, 4
masculinity, 9, 12, 54, 151, 155, 163, 165, 219
Masefield, John, 15

Masterman, C.F.G., 8
maturity, 8, 104, 115–16, 182
Maytham, 75–6, 86
Meade, L.T., 147
medicine, 44–5, 214
Mee, Arthur, 15
memory, 27, 63, 68, 76, 167, 188, 194
metaphor, 27, 45, 84, 107, 135, 156
microcosms, 16, 24, 135
military drill, 146, 156
Mill, J.S., 26, 137, 220
mimicry of adult behaviours, 95–6, 107
miners, 117, 119–20
Minima Moralia, 30
mischief, 11, 27, 168, 195, 200
Misselthwaite Manor, 33, 79, 85
Modernism, 14, 30
Moore, Dorothea, 6
moors, 27, 87
moral character, 18, 167–8
moral messages, 9, 161–2, 168
Morrison, Arthur, 15
mothers, 9, 28, 42, 45–7, 78, 80, 83, 85, 92–5, 97–8, 139, 144–8, 150–1, 164, 170, 180, 197–9, 205, 209–10, 212
  and Lawrence, D.H., 105, 107, 113–14, 116–18
  and longing for children, 56–9, 61–2, 65, 69–70
'Mr Boy Next Door', 171
Munro, Ethel, 212–13
Munro, H.H. *see* Saki
mute code, 27–8, 32, 67
My Robin, 86
mysteries, 27, 32–3, 135, 216
mysticism, 6, 10, 16, 23–35, 80, 83–4, 180, 214
mythologies, 16, 23–35, 43, 112, 178, 188

narrators, 27, 29, 34, 54–5, 57, 63–70, 79–80, 82, 85–7, 167
Nash, Andrew, 60, 63, 71 n.2
national degeneration/decadence, 9, 19, 144, 146, 151
national identity *see* English identity
naughtiness, 140, 191–2, 197–8, 200

234   *Index*

neglect, 7, 27, 67, 77, 79, 81, 107–8, 154, 168–9
Nesbit, Edith, 9, 12–14, 17, 23–4, 34–5, 54, 90, 99, 101, 125–41, 199, 202, 206
  see also Bastables
Neverland, 24, 41, 44, 47, 49, 95–6, 98–9, 101, 109, 112
New Girl at St. Chad's, The, 149, 153, 156
New Treasure Seekers, The, 12, 139
Nicest Girl in School, The, 149, 155, 157
Nicolson, Juliet, 24
Nonconformism, 212
Nostalgia, 49, 76, 78, 106–7, 192, 202, 205, 211

offerings, 193, 199, 214
'Old Love, An', 221
Oliver Twist, 85
Olympians, 12, 202
'Open Window, The', 208
Orange Fairy Book, The, 18, 179, 182, 190
Orwell, George, 3, 30, 35
Other House, The, 13
otherness of childhood, 6, 65, 103–21, 177
outsiders, 29, 81, 84
'Owl and the Eagle, The', 179, 182

paedophilia, 59–60, 219
paganism, 5, 10, 23–35, 201–2, 208, 214, 219
Pair of Schoolgirls, A, 151–2, 156
Pan (god), 30–1, 33–4, 39, 46, 87, 201–4
  see also Peter Pan (char.)
parents, 1, 8–9, 11, 13, 24, 28, 33, 81–4, 92, 151, 161, 167, 169–71, 180–2, 195, 205
  and Lawrence, D.H., 105, 113, 116
  and longing for children, 54, 57–8, 63, 66, 70
  see also fathers; mothers
pathos, 5, 61
peace toys, 25, 136–7, 220

'Penance, The', 18, 192, 194–6, 200–1, 209–10, 212–13, 215–16, 218–19
'Penny Dreadful, The', 164
penny dreadfuls, 159, 164, 170
Perfect Summer, The, 24
periodicals, 9, 14, 18, 159–72
Peter and Wendy, 7, 16–17, 37–51, 54, 78, 90, 95–9, 101, 109, 111, 219, 222
Peter Pan (play), 7, 13, 16, 37–51, 53–4, 85, 98
Peter Pan (char.), 5, 7, 13, 16, 19, 37–51, 97–8, 101, 112, 121, 128, 134, 202, 218, 222
  in *The Little White Bird*, 55–7, 63, 67, 70
Petzold, Dieter, 4, 209–11, 220
Phoenix and the Carpet, The, 34, 35
physical anthropology, 18, 178, 183–6, 189
physical health, 9, 15, 147–8, 172
piggeries, 195, 206, 216
pigs, 58, 195–6, 211, 215
pirates, 43–4, 96, 98–9
play, 8, 17, 89–101
plot, 79, 81, 147, 170, 213
polecat-ferret, 193–4, 213–14
  see also 'Sredni Vashtar'
Potter, Beatrix, 10, 14, 18, 191–206
prayers, 171, 193–4
pretences, 47, 94, 212, 216
Prichard, James, 184–5
Priestley, J.B., 3
primitive, 10
primitives, 10, 18, 26, 106, 108, 177–89
primitivism, 7, 106–7, 178
Prisoner in Fairyland, A, 5, 15, 31, 54, 61, 128, 131
progress, 16, 30, 127, 131, 136, 178–9, 182–3
psychological realism, 34, 85, 114
Puck of Pook's Hill, 16, 18, 26, 31–2, 35, 54, 183, 186–8
punishment, 80, 97, 181, 196–7
purity, 60, 136, 173, 191–2, 196

'Quest, The', 212

rabbits, 34, 197–8
  see also Tale of Peter Rabbit, The
racial hierarchy concepts, 10, 18, 186–7, 189
racial separation, 188
Rackham, Arthur, 39, 41, 55
Railway Children, The, 13, 25, 138–9, 142
Rainbow, The, 114–15, 121
realism, 2, 5, 14, 24, 34, 57, 85, 109–10, 114, 140
rebellion and adult warfare, 18, 208–22
rebirth, 17, 84
reflexivity, 45
regeneration, 6, 13, 17, 76, 121
'Reginald's Choir Treat', 208, 218–20
Reid, Forrest, 15
relationships, 16, 40, 53–5, 57–9, 69–70, 80, 86, 115–17, 119–20, 204
religion, 11, 14, 169, 187, 212, 219
Religious Tract Society, 160–1, 167–8
resistance, 18, 95, 99, 107, 116, 198, 209
responsibilities, 10, 17–18, 47, 103, 131, 145, 147, 154, 163, 171, 184, 189, 218, 220
  adult responsibilities, 105, 108, 110
revenge, 62, 209, 214
Rewards and Fairies, 16, 18, 26, 31, 54, 183, 188
rhetoric, 29, 125–7, 129, 135–6, 139–40, 146
rights, 1, 8–9, 57, 66, 68–9
ritual, 213, 215–16, 218
'River Tale', 188
rivers, 180–1, 201–2, 204
robins, 86
Robinson, W. Heath, 15
romance, Gothic, 28, 33–4
Romanticism, 1, 5, 9, 11–12, 18, 22, 23, 40, 83, 86–7, 140, 191–2, 204, 206, 212
Romantick Lady, The, 78
Rose, Jacqueline, 40, 41, 42, 43, 45, 49, 50, 57, 60, 63, 85, 134, 140, 221
Rose, Jonathan, 1, 5, 7, 11, 19 n.1, 31, 183, 210

routine, 30–1, 119, 209, 217–18
rural England, 25, 29, 192
Ruskin, John, 145–6
ruthlessness, 10, 191–2, 195–6, 204, 206

Sacred Milk of Koumongoé, The, 179, 181–2, 190
Saki, 10, 14, 16, 18, 25–6, 28–9, 103, 105, 111, 136–8, 191–206, 208–22
savagery, 5, 9–10, 25–6, 106, 112, 175, 177
savages, 10, 18, 121, 177–9, 182–3, 192, 211
School by the Sea, The, 143, 156
school stories, 9, 17, 143–57
schools, 3, 81, 119, 150, 156, 160, 165, 168–9, 172, 225, 227
  see also school stories
Scouting for Boys, 16, 54
Scouts *see* Boy Scouts
Scribner's Magazine, 55, 63
sea, 112–13, 143, 156, 185
Secret Garden, The, 5, 7, 13, 16–17, 23–4, 32–5, 57–8, 61–3, 67, 69, 75–87, 90, 111, 224
selfishness, 44, 81, 153, 192
sentimental construction of childhood, 37–8, 40
Sentimental Tommy, 13, 39–40, 53
sentimentality, 1, 5, 12–13, 16, 23, 29–30, 37–8, 40–4, 48–9, 60, 77, 110, 114, 138
sentimentalization, 5, 13, 23, 29, 38, 41–2
separated lives, 17, 103–21
separateness, 4, 104, 120–1, 211
sexuality, 14, 29, 40, 97–8, 112–13, 161, 180–2, 218–19
Shaw, George Bernard, 41, 141
Shelley: An Essay, 1
'She-Wolf, The', 212
Shuttle, The, 17, 75, 77–8, 80–2, 84
Sigmund Freud, 9, 14, 19, 33, 40, 51, 60, 111, 121
sisters, 81–2, 136, 181–2, 197–8, 205, 219
smoking, 159, 161, 163, 169

social anthropology, 18, 114, 178, 183, 189
sons, 33, 47, 57, 59, 64, 70, 75–6, 85, 98, 117, 129, 136, 166–7, 170, 182, 187, 198, 201, 221
Sons and Lovers, 7, 17, 70, 103, 105, 115–21
Soul of London, The, 31
South African War *see* Boer War
sports, 17, 89–101
   see also games
'Sredni Vashtar', 14, 18, 105, 192–5, 200–1, 209–10, 212–16, 218
Stacpoole, H. de Vere, 14, 54, 112, 212
Stalky & Co., 13, 54
Stevenson, Robert Louis, 201
'Story of a Panic, The', 14
Story of the Amulet, The, 17, 90, 99–100, 138
Story of the Treasure Seekers, The, 12, 24, 139
'Story-Teller, The', 211–12
subversion, 43, 48–9, 212, 219
suffrage movement, 129, 131–2
surveillance, 212–14, 216, 221

Tale of Peter Rabbit, The, 18, 192, 196–200
Tale of Squirrel Nutkin, The, 18, 192, 196, 199–201
Tale of Tom Kitten, The, 18, 192, 196, 198–200
teachers, 11, 24, 148–9, 164, 167, 178, 211
territorial tensions, 7
Terry the Girl Guide, 6
'They', 5, 16, 25–7, 32, 53–5, 63–70
Thompson, Francis, 1
Thwaite, Ann, 81, 82, 84, 85

'To His Coy Mistress', 4
Tom Brown's Schooldays, 205
Tom Sawyer (char.), 199
toys, 7, 26, 55, 58, 64, 66–7, 85, 136–7, 158, 219–20, 223
'Toys of Peace, The', 16, 25, 136, 219, 223
trees, 32–3, 43, 47, 49, 61, 99, 181, 193, 200
Trespasser, The, 17, 103, 105, 109–15, 112
Turn of the Screw, The, 13, 63, 114

underground home, 47, 96, 204

Victorian attitudes, 1, 7, 11, 13, 24, 29, 61, 87, 89–90, 114, 161, 177, 205, 213, 221
Von Arnim, Elizabeth, 13

War, 14, 18, 208–22
   see also Boer War; World War I
Waugh, Auberon, 212
Way of All Flesh, The, 14
Wells, H.G., 14, 29, 121
What Maisie Knew, 7, 13, 17, 90–9, 99
When William Came, 221
White Peacock, The, 17, 103, 105–9, 115
Wind in the Willows, The, 18, 23, 34, 78, 85–6, 192, 198, 200–4, 206, 211
'world apart', 13, 65, 70
World of Girls, A, 147
World War I, 1, 3, 14, 16–19, 24, 35, 77
Wouldbegoods, The, 12, 199, 206

Youngest Girl in the Fifth, The, 150–1